GRIP

Clifford Johnson

ISBN: 9798283648132

Cover Artwork: Original oil paintings by Clifford Johnson

Clifford Johnson was born in Woolwich, South East London in 1960. He left school at 16, got a job in a factory and left home at 17. During his career he has had many jobs, which provided the wonderful opportunity to meet some unforgettable characters, facets of which you will meet in his books. Clifford has been... an IT training manager, stable boy, riding instructor, labourer, tea boy, mainframe computer operator, office worker, sales assistant, IT help desk operator, furniture mover, driver's mate (delivering explosives), security guard and dustman. Temporary jobs included roofer (three weeks), barman (one night), banksman (one day), council worker (one week), soft drinks delivery driver (two weeks), plumbing call centre operative (3 months) and bouncer (one night only).

Clifford has had a lifelong passion for creativity and as an artist has worked in metal, wood, glass and oils, successfully selling his work. Clifford's literary journey began as a result of his dyslexia; a teacher laughed and informed him that dyslexic people can't write books. As a result of this challenge he wrote his first book, *Bolt from the Blue*. The encouraging reviews, combined with a wish to revisit his characters with whom he felt a genuine affection, resulted in this second adventure. Both books feature his own oil paintings on the covers.

He now lives in rural Herefordshire with his wife Sally Boehme, a jewellery artist.

Also by Clifford Johnson:

Bolt From The Blue

Elements of drama, humour, love and loss combine to tell this exciting tale. The story begins with two deaths in Italy, which spark the fuse that streaks across Europe, burning a path to London and the door of Ronny Moon and Vicky Blaine. The lives of this happy couple and their friends then collide with the glamorous but deadly world of organised crime. People they've never met want them dead and when an organisation with almost limitless money wants something, it gets it.

Acknowledgements

Please note: in fairness to all the wonderful people who helped me with my research, bear in mind this is a work of fiction and for the sake of the plot I have occasionally woven fiction around some of the facts supplied to me. Any technical inaccuracies are my doing and deliberate and not a mistake by the professionals from whom I took advice and inspiration.

In alphabetical order:

Alec Stanley, ex-Royal Engineers, for his professional advice on firearms.

Adrian, manager at Skopes Menswear, for his assistance.

Coastguard Station, Watchet, Somerset.

Dr Dave Frederick BSc, PhD, retired teacher, for proofing this book in conjunction with

Dr Graham Baker PhD, MA, MSc, PGCE BA (Hons), retired lecturer.

Dennis Davis, private pilot, for giving me so much of his time and explaining something about his fascinating experiences.

Death on Demand, a murder mystery enactment company for their kind permission in allowing me to use the wonderful quote 'Any woman who…..'

Dawn Manning, Facility Co-ordinator at Shobdon Airfield, for her time and effort in finding a pilot with the right experience.

Emma Price, professional Make-up and Special Effects Artist, for her patience in helping me understand something of this amazing world.

Kirstie Wright MCO ptom, Optometrist, for sparing me her valuable time to explain how strong emotions, like rage, affect pupil dilation.

Matt, the HGV driver who answered all my questions and allowed me to leap onto his car transporter.

Mr Robert Hughes FRCS MA MB B.Chir retired Vascular Surgeon, for his medical and maritime advice.

Tony Scarlet, ex-helicopter engineer, for advice on various aspects, including Radar.

The '57 Chevrolet Owners' Club for help on technical points about the car.

You, the reader. I would very much like to thank you, a kindred spirit and fellow armchair adventurer.

For Sally Boehme,

without whose help my dream of writing this book would have remained just that. I'm dyslexic and I hand-wrote the manuscript phonetically with pen and pad. Sally spent many hours tirelessly deciphering my unique spelling and typed all 106,000 words for me. Sally, you make dreams come true in this and so many other ways.

CONTENTS

Part One:

CHAPTER 1
AUTUMN 1993
SOUTH EAST LONDON
SUNDAY MORNING

'Do you know how long it's been since these hands killed anyone?' Ronny Moon sat dejectedly on one of the large sofas which faced each other in the comfortable living room. He continued to look gloomily at his hands resting in his lap. After further thought, he added, 'I haven't stabbed, shot, poisoned or bludgeoned anybody for ages. I can't even bring myself to steal anything! I just don't feel like robbing banks or planning a diamond heist'. He gave a great sigh and looked mournfully at Vicky, who sat on the opposite sofa. She tipped her small head slightly to one side and compressed her thin lips in a sympathetic attitude.

'I'm sorry Ron, have you no ideas at all?'

He frowned in consternation, wanting to be completely honest before answering.

She sat quietly, watching him. Ron was almost thirty years old, five feet eight and stocky, with broad sloping shoulders. His light brown hair was roughly parted in the centre and swept back. It was doubtful if he had ever owned a comb. If he had, its whereabouts was long forgotten. He was dressed in his usual style, although the term style when referring to Ron's mode of dress was stretching the word until the cracks showed. In Ron's case, it referred to a baggy sweatshirt, original colour unknown and jeans faded by time rather than design. A slightly overweight, scruffy package, but *her* scruffy package and Vicky loved him. As she continued to watch, Ron's face collapsed into a sad, hopeless expression.

'No, nothing, I don't have any ideas, at least none I can get excited about. Let's face it, I just don't feel like killing anyone.' He became slightly more animated, adding, 'This is partly your fault.'

'Oh yes?' Vicky folded her arms, leaned back smiling and waited to hear how she was responsible for his writer's block.

'Well, I'm so happy.' He said miserably.

'Could have fooled me.'

'You know what I mean, you and me, it's wonderful'.

She doubted anyone had ever said "wonderful" in a less enthusiastic fashion.

He continued to explain his reasoning. 'Before you came along I was lonely, sad, moody. I think I've lost my edge.'

She glanced at the fake coal fire, which although gas, was furnished with all the correct accoutrements. 'I could hit you with that poker and make you unhappy if you think it would help?'

Ron made a noise between a snort and a laugh. Vicky always cheered him up; he was so lucky and happy, damn it! Like a bolt from the blue[1], Vicky had entered his life quickly and with no small amount of drama. To the world she appeared plain, which had even been Ron's impression when he first encountered her. However, in the days and weeks that followed, his opinion had changed dramatically. It was difficult to quantify. The way she smiled, the way she frowned, how she spoke, her dry sense of humour. The longer a person spent in her company, somehow aspects of her character wove together and stole your heart. He looked at her now, smiling at him. She *was* beautiful. Vicky was small in size, very trim, measuring only four feet eleven and a half, but large in character. She was sensitive and kind, with a mischievous sense of humour. Like Ron, easygoing in nature and, not entirely like Ron, extremely clever. If they stood together, the top of her head came to just above Ron's shoulder. Her blonde hair was short, neat, layered and cut in a pixie style. She had a pale complexion and brown eyes. In reality Vicky was a little plain, however, when she smiled, she lit up the room, compelling any recipient to smile in return. Her voice was quiet, her speech clear, each word sharp and precise. The impression was of an educated woman from a well-to-do-background. This was only half true. Vicky was well educated and although the aunt who had raised Vicky and her sister was comfortably off, she was by no means rich.

----

[1] See the first book *Bolt from the Blue.*

Vicky was also clad in faded jeans, although hers were new. She wore a thin cashmere sweater in a pastel yellow. Unlike Ron's baggy sweatshirt, Vicky's clothes were well-fitted and showed off her figure.

Ron rested his elbow on the arm of the sofa and palmed his forehead, now serious. 'Joking aside, I am worried, Vicky. The publisher needs one for this Christmas; I should be well into it by now, it's Autumn. What if I simply don't have any more stories left? Art doesn't come with guarantees. Just because you had something good yesterday, doesn't mean you can create something good today. I love writing but…'

Vicky stood up and crossed to the tall bookcase to her left. 'Look Ron, eight best sellers!' She plucked one at random, held it up and turned it over to read the back. Ron glimpsed the title on the cover; *The Italian Way* with a close-up picture of a revolver.

'"Ronny Moon does it again! Yet another extravaganza of murder and mayhem that will have you on the edge of your seat. *The New York Times.*"' She replaced the book, turned to face him and waved at the line of them. 'They're all the same, each one a bestseller; I just know you have more.' Pep talk over, she sat down, leaned forward, hugging her knees and thought hard: she did not like to see him worried. 'What about a hitman; you know, a contract killer?' Ron wrinkled his nose. She tried again, 'Okay… erm… a good murder for love, money or power?'

'They're not really plot lines but motives. Look, thanks for trying to help, but…' He shrugged, 'I'm just not getting any sparks.'

Vicky wasn't willing to give up so easily. She chewed her lower lip and concentrated. 'I know, a Mafia story! That one I picked up just now was Mafia-based.'

Ron nodded. '*The Italian Way*, yes, it sold thousands.'

'Well, what about another mafia storyline? Someone double-crosses them, someone has a score to settle and sets them up to get even… a power struggle from within the organisation, lots of action.'

'I'll give it some thought. All good ideas.' He knew she was doing her best: he wouldn't dim her bright enthusiastic little face for all the world.

She sat back. 'Come on, it's Sunday. Let's relax and read the papers. Put it out of your head for now and hit it fresh on Monday. Perhaps you can have a chat with Shades. You said yourself you've had some of your best ideas talking to him.'

Ron nodded and smiled at the thought of Shades. He was quite a character. With his brother Tony, he ran a club called *The Blue Parrot*. The club was a magnet for the best, or worst, that London had to offer, depending on your point of view. Shades and Tony loved the club's edgy reputation. Shades was not his real name: he had acquired it because in the past he was never seen in public without his dark suits and even darker sunglasses. Although the suits remained, he had stopped wearing the sunglasses. The name had stuck and Shades thought it gave him a mysterious air, so to the world, Shades it was and Shades it would stay.

'It's funny the way it works, we just chat. Ideas seem to drop into line and before I know it, I have the framework of a storyline. Sometimes, I go off in a direction that has very little to do with what he's said. I don't really know how it works.'

'Why haven't you spoken to him yet? You've been stuck for a while.'

Ron shrugged, 'He's spending all his free time with Jane when she's not working with you. I don't want to get in the way, you know, young love and all that.'

'It's the other way around, Jane is spending all her free time with Shades. It's not the same thing.'

'No?'

'No. Jane is very keen on Shades, but I'm not sure what Shades feels. Perhaps you could ask him. I think Jane's getting mixed signals.'

'Ooo, I'm not getting involved. I know you and Jane talk about everything, but a guy doesn't just ask another guy what his feelings are about a woman.'

'No?'

'No! He'd tell me to mind my own business.'

Vicky reflected for a quiet minute, then offered, 'I'll tell you what, Jane isn't needed until tomorrow afternoon, so I won't be either. We both have the morning off. Why don't we go to the club and see Shades? If Jane is there I'll chat to her and give you a chance to talk to him. See if he can get you started on an idea. Leave it for today, it's Sunday morning. Let's enjoy the day and relax.'

'Okay, let's do that.' Ron got up and fetched a bundle of newspapers from the doormat. He was on excellent terms with the local newsagent and it was Ron and Vicky's Sunday treat to lounge about and work their way through the newspapers together. The gas fire with its mock coals glowed warmly. Ron's cat Finbar dozed on his rug in front of the flames. Ron made more coffee and collected his pet particular favourite chocolate biscuits from the kitchen. They swung their legs up onto their respective sofas, and began to leaf through the Sunday papers and colour supplements; in companionable silence.

Vicky held a large paper, which effectively obscured her view of Ron and his of her. From behind the paper wall she suddenly spoke sharply, making him jump. 'Stop frowning at the computer! We agreed you would give it a rest until Monday.'

Surprised, Ron switched his attention to her direction. Still the paper wall blocked his view. Uncertain how she knew he had been looking at his PC didn't deter him from making a childish face at her.

From behind her paper Vicky sternly tacked on, 'And don't pull faces, you're not a child.'

Ron's mouth opened in surprise, he quickly closed it. There was a sharp rustle as he straightened and lifted his paper. *How the hell did she do stuff like that?*

'That's better.' Vicky grinned. Even from behind the newspaper, she enjoyed a clear view of him reflected in the glass of a nearby photograph.

Finbar dozed, biscuits were nibbled and the Sunday papers slid gently to the floor like Autumn leaves. Vicky and Ron's peaceful Sunday drifted pleasantly into evening.

They lived in a light industrial part of South East London, conveniently not far from bars, clubs and shops, but unusually quiet. The street consisted of Victorian warehouses and buildings. When first built they were considered utilitarian, but now in 1993, against the glass and steel backdrop of the city, they took on a nostalgic elegance, clad as they were in warm brick. Some were enhanced further with graceful curves and thin iron frame windows. All were solid and low rise. As yet, Ron and Vicky's was the only residential dwelling, high up on the second floor.

As daylight faded, streetlights flickered on. A chilly Autumn breeze tumbled some dry leaves dropped by the London Planes lining the street. It was an odd name for the majestic trees found all over the city. The London Plane is a hybrid of the Oriental Plane and American Plane, not a native tree at all. Whatever the origin, the trees made Ron's street, like many others, more beautiful with their presence, enriching the characterful street, which, apart from tarmac and modern streetlights, had remained remarkably unchanged by the passing years.

In the flat, Vicky and Ron had gone to bed. Ron slept peacefully next to Vicky, his arm resting on her waist. She fidgeted and made soft muttering noises, almost but not quite words.

She stood alone on an endless beach, it was dark and cold. The black sea moved slowly, rising and falling like the breath of a monstrous living thing. From far out in the deep water, came a voice, '*Help me Vicky! Help me!*' It was unmistakably her dead sister, Sara. Without hesitation, Vicky plunged into the dark ocean, '*I'm coming!*' Quickly out of her depth, she began to swim. Her waterlogged clothes felt heavy and cold. The voice frantically cried out again, '*Help me!*' Fighting for breath, Vicky called back, '*I'm coming.*' As she swam desperately towards the voice, the water became thicker, like swimming through oil. She toiled onward, her arms became heavy as her strength was sucked away by the ever increasing density of the viscous black water. Moments later, as she struggled desperately to reach her sister, the sea around her took on the consistency of thick mud. A heavy, oozing black bottomless mire. She was making no headway at all. Out in the darkness, Sara's voice seemed to be fading, '*I can't find my way back. I'm lost. Help me!*'

In a slamming moment of crystal clear thought, Vicky knew Sara was no longer out there. She was totally alone. A tiny speck in a world without light, a world of unimaginable vastness, completely and totally alone. Nothing living anywhere except perhaps the black, sucking void that enveloped her. An endless sea that stretched forever both below and around her. She no longer had the strength to move. The cold black sludge closed around her body. It slid over her arms, then shoulders, it crawled up her neck. She felt it cover her mouth, her nose.

'Aaaaaaaah!' Vicky cried out, woke up and sucked a deep lungful of air. Someone was holding her. Her heart slammed blood through her veins and roared in her ears. She gasped for breath. Gradually, the nightmare which had seemed so real moments ago, retreated. She knew she was safe in the dark but familiar bedroom.

Ron was holding her, 'I've got you.'

'I'm alright…. I'm alright.'

'Yes.'

'I'll be alright,' she swallowed, 'Oh, Ron'.

'I know. Was it the same one?'

She nodded, the nod sending a tear rolling down her cheek. 'I don't know what happened to her after she died.'

'I know.' Ron put so much sympathy into those two words, Vicky hugged him for it.

After a few minutes her breathing returned to normal. They sat up in bed, holding hands, both aware that sleep would not come easily after such a terrifying nightmare.

Half an hour later, Vicky's thoughts gradually strayed to happier subjects. 'You know Ron, I'm so pleased to be working with Jane.'

'Mm, I think it's good for you, a new challenge.' He smiled as he remembered the first time he had seen Vicky's work. It had come as a shock.

They were unable to see each other clearly. There was the night glow from the window, because London skies were seldom completely dark, and also a faint glimmer from the bedside clock.

Vicky broke the contemplative silence, 'I couldn't go back to secretarial work after what we went through last year. Losing Sara and everything, I needed a challenge, something to focus on. Jane is so talented as a special effects make-up artist and her friend Magic.... well, she is a *genius*.'

'You mentioned her before. Her name's not really Magic, is it? She's not some hippy?'

Vicky gave a short laugh. 'No, her real name is Margaret Moorcroft. Jane calls her Maggie but everyone at work just calls her Magic.'

'Is she that good?'

'Oh yes.'

'Jane's not jealous, is she?'

'No, no! Maggie taught Jane the craft when Jane was starting out. They've been friends for years. Maggie seems to have taken a shine to me. She's ever so helpful, I'm learning heaps. I'm really lucky to be working with them both. TV and film people clamour to get them, 'specially Maggie. She's the best make-up and special effects advisor working in the industry.'

'I still can't believe you're working in the movie industry, and on a big film too!'

'Well... They are. I'm just an assistant, a gofer really but they talk to me all the time, explaining what they're doing. It's brilliant.'

'And you've got the morning off tomorrow?' Ron glanced at the glowing clock. 'Well, today, it's twenty past four.'

'I don't have to be on set till two tomorrow afternoon, but if we *are* going to the *Blue Parrot* to see Shades in the morning we'd better try and get some more sleep.'

They slid down together, Vicky turned away from Ron but wriggled closer. Ron moved his left arm under her pillow and put his right arm around her shoulders.

After losing her sister the year before, Vicky had been plagued by nightmares. They were becoming less frequent but when she did have one, it took a long while to get back to sleep. She and Ron usually talked for some time. During those three and four o'clock conversations Vicky felt particularly close to him. He could be childish, silly, funny, eccentric, but there for you in times of trouble. Whilst some people clung to the warmth and safety of their beds, Ron would be with you, out in the storm at the solid end of the rope and hold you tight when you needed it most. She knew it and loved him for it.

Ron had once told her it was she who had saved him. After losing his first love in something as senseless and stupid as a road accident, Vicky had been the hands that reached into his dark world and pulled him back into the light. As Tony and Shades had observed, the truth of the matter was they were good for each other and were meant to be together. The balance of the relationship was odd. As a writer, Ron was a genius. The way in which he wove words into wonderful images in the minds of his readers was truly magical. Unfortunately, the brilliance faded dramatically outside this relatively small arena. So Ron relied heavily on Vicky's practical common sense and intelligence.

They were both very tired.

'Thank you.' She whispered quietly.

Ron didn't answer, he merely squeezed her shoulder. Eventually, they fell asleep.

PART ONE

CHAPTER 2
MILAN, ITALY
MONDAY MORNING

Monday began like any other day, on the International Date Line in the middle of the Pacific Ocean, the opposite side of the globe from Ron and Vicky. Monday crept westward across the face of the Earth, touching each country in turn. As usual, thousands of people would die and thousands of people would be born.

Monday would reach Milan a full hour before London. People Ron and Vicky had never met and did not know, were going to die. The deaths would set in motion an unstoppable chain of events that would streak like a fast-burning fuse across the eight hundred miles that separated them, and end at Ron's door with disastrous results.

For the moment, everything seemed normal. It was a little after seven and the good people of Milan were beginning their day... also, one or two bad people.

Salvatore Conelli looked approvingly at his reflection in the bathroom mirror. His dark hair was full and thick but impeccably tidy. He sported a beard; this was also trimmed and neat, as he took pride and care in his appearance. His brown eyes scanned the reflection. Satisfied, he would finish by adding his favourite cologne, *Acqua di Parma*. If style and sophistication had a scent, this was undoubtedly it. Salvatore smiled as he picked up the familiar bright yellow box. He carefully lifted out the slightly tapered glass bottle and unscrewed its black lid. He applied a tiny amount to his wrists. Then, as it was a day off, a day for the family, he also touched his neck. His smile widened as suddenly, he was transported to a sun-drenched orange grove with refreshing notes of lemon, the golden fruits blending with subtle traces of lavender and warm, slightly woody elements. After one final glance in the glass, he walked out of the bathroom, across the expanse of carpet in the equally immaculate and tasteful bedroom, threw open the balcony doors and stood in his bathrobe enjoying, the fresh, early morning air. Humming quietly to himself, he returned to the bedroom to dress.

A few minutes later he entered the luxurious kitchen, dressed in an exquisitely tailored Naples yellow suit, white shirt, dark red and gold paisley silk tie and gold cufflinks. The soles of his glove-soft, handmade leather shoes sounded crisp as he walked across the Carrara marble floor.

The large double doors leading to the patio were open and the long white voiles stirred gently in the morning air. Although it was Autumn, the morning was very pleasant and the sky clear. He passed through the doors and found Anna sitting with a coffee at the table on the pale yellow stone patio. The house was elevated and the view of the well-stocked and maintained garden was beautiful. She heard the movement behind her but did not get up. Salvatore leaned down and kissed the top of her head. 'Good morning.'

She smiled as she caught the familiar scent of fresh soap and the subtle but pleasant fragrance of his cologne; the beautifully light, notes of orange groves and lemons had settled. It seemed entirely appropriate for this wonderful morning.

'Good morning, Sal. Do you want a coffee?'

'I'll get one in a moment'. He placed another chair close to the table and they sat quietly, enjoying the view.

Anna sipped her coffee, cradling her cup. 'Isn't it a beautiful morning?'

He nodded. 'Is Lucia still asleep?'

'Yes, she was so excited about going to her friend's Birthday party, it took forever to get her settled last night.'

Salvatore laughed. 'Oh, to be five years old.' He turned to look at his wife. Anna was wearing a thick white towelling robe and slippers. Even without makeup she was a beauty, her dark brown hair had a shimmer of copper that caught the morning light: it was full, thick and wavy. She wasn't overweight, but curvy and strong in body. She always spoke softly, giving the false impression of being forever calm, which she was not. 'Don't get cold out here in only a robe.'

'I'm fine, it's nice to sit. It won't be quiet once Lucia's awake.'

They both smiled at the thought of their excitable little girl. Salvatore pointed to an open letter on the table; he'd noticed the airmail markings. 'Your sister?'

'Yes, it came yesterday. I was re-reading it while it's peaceful.'

'Is she alright?'

'Yes, she wants us to visit. It's been a while.'

Salvatore was silent for a moment, then said wearily, 'I'm too busy for a trip to London. I couldn't even get away for Nico's sister's wedding. It would have been wonderful to catch up. They're two of my favourite cousins.'

Anna matched her husband's sad expression. 'Yes, the party's tonight. It would have been fun to dance,' she observed gently.

Salvatore felt a surge of guilt. His work often impacted upon their lives. 'I know we can't make the party but you could have a trip to London, visit your sister.'

Anna nodded without comment. She knew he had a lot of responsibilities and Milan was especially busy with the fashion launches and the media attention they brought.

He sensed her disappointment. 'Although I can't take the time to visit Nico for a few days, we can have a family day today, it looks like a beauty.'

Anna raised her eyes to the clear blue of the sky. 'It is.'

'We can take the car and…'

Suddenly, the peace was broken by the ringing of a phone. With a frown Salvatore quickly rose and moved indoors snatching up the receiver, 'Hello?'

'It's Bruno.'

'It's early.'

'Sorry Sal, we've got a problem.'

Salvatore sighed. It was a lovely morning, he was not in the mood for problems. He was in the mood to zip off in his vintage Ferrari with Anna and Lucia and have lunch somewhere out of the city. Far away from crowds, fashion week and problems.

Bruno continued, 'I've looked at the numbers. There's no doubt, Renzo's skimming.'

'Okay, okay, let's meet.'

'I can be with you in twenty minutes.'

Salvatore answered quickly, 'No, not here. Get a street table in the plaza, you know, the cafe I like, *Alfonso's*. We'll talk it over.'

Salvatore had been growing steadily more uncomfortable with work-related meetings at his home. He wanted as much as possible to keep Anna and Lucia very separate from his job. They were two different worlds and he was anxious to keep it that way. 'I'll phone for the car now.' He hung up and scowled at the phone, *Renzo was a pain in the arse!*

Anna came in from the garden, 'Do you want some coffee now?'

'No, I've got to go out. I'll get coffee and breakfast in the town. I'm sorry.'

'Don't worry, be safe.' Anna knew not to ask questions. She was as keen as Salvatore that she and Lucia kept a safe distance from his business. She worried when Salvatore was working: most of his business was just that; business. But occasionally, it could be darker, unpredictable. It was always in the background. She felt a little better if he carried his phone but unfortunately, he seldom did. Salvatore was not vain but he took pride in his appearance. He always felt it spoilt the lines of his suits. Also, he was never that far from either a public phone or an office phone. He was also slightly wary how secure a mobile phone was. Still, she gave it a try. 'Did you want to take your phone?'

'No. Hopefully, I can deal with this quickly and be home lunchtime. Perhaps we can do something this afternoon. I'm having a quick meeting, that's all. Don't worry, Anna.'

Picking up the phone once more, he dialled the familiar number. 'It's Salvatore.'

The short and expected response was prompt, 'On my way, Mr Conelli.'

Eight hundred miles away, Vicky picked up the phone and dialled. 'Hello Shades, it's me.'

'Hiya Toots, what's cookin'?'

Vicky shook her head and grinned. It was obvious he'd been recently watching an old movie in his private cinema he called "The Roxy". 'Don't tell me. Bogart.'

'No, James Cagney. I've been introducing Jane to some culture.'

'Lucky girl. You've sorted out the problems with your home cinema then? The last time we spoke you couldn't use it.'

'Yes, all good now. Cost me some to fix, mind. You 'n' Ron okay?'

'I'm alright, but Ron's hit a wall with his writing. Are you free this morning? Jane and I are working on set this afternoon and I could come over with Ron and keep Jane company if she's there.'

'She's always here.' He said it neutrally and Vicky didn't know if he was pleased or not.

'Is it okay then?'

'Yeah, sure. Me and Tony haven't seen you for a while.'

'Is Tony there?'

'No, he's messing about on the river with the *Grey Lady*. At least that's what he *says*.'

The Grey Lady was Tony's boat, moored on the Thames.

'What do you mean, "that's what he says"?'

'Think he might have a girlfriend.'

'Oh, that's good!'

'I don't *know* he has, you know what he's like.'

She did know what Tony was like. Serious, thoughtful and private. His brother Shades was very different, not only in looks but in character too. However, on the whole they worked together surprisingly well and the club they co-owned was extremely profitable under their dual control.

'Right, I'll see you later this morning. Are you sure we aren't intruding between you and Jane?'

'Is that why you and Ron haven't been around much?'

'Well… yes, partly.' Vicky couldn't resist asking. 'Is it serious with Jane?'

Ron, who had been sipping coffee and listening to the conversation, put a hand across his eyes in shame. *How could she just come out with it?*

Shades didn't sound offended, nor was he giving anything away, 'I'll see you both later.' The line went dead.

Bewildered, she turned to Ron. 'He hung up!'

'Not surprised.' Ron shook his head. 'You've got a cheek.'

'I'm really worried about Jane. I don't want to see her hurt.'

'It's between them, stay out.'

'Okay.'

Ron didn't believe for a moment she would. 'Are we going?'

'Yes, he said he'd be pleased to see us.'

In Milan, Salvatore Conelli sat comfortably in the rear seat of the limousine, his driver smoothly negotiating the busy streets. Of course, he could have used his own car, but disliked driving it in the city, and parking in the centre of Milan was a pain. The organisation supplied a chauffeur and limousine for all of its top operatives and Salvatore used his frequently, especially for business. The driver gently delivered his boss near the piazza and his favourite cafe. Salvatore climbed out. 'Don't wait, I'll phone when I need you.'

'Yes, Mr Conelli.'

With barely a murmur from the powerful engine the limousine slid away. Salvatore walked toward the cafe.

Bruno sat beneath the cheerful yellow and white striped awning outside the cafe. He was smoking, and watched Salvatore approach. Bruno was shorter than Salvatore, only in his thirties but had lost all the hair from the top of his head. He retained a little on the sides and this was cut very short. He was thickset with broad shoulders. He too was dressed in a suit, but somehow lacked the style of Salvatore. The Italians have a word for this; s*prezzatura*, which simply means an easy, natural flair for being stylish, without apparent effort. Whoever had coined the word must have had Salvatore Conelli in mind. Bruno spared no expense and his suits were tailored especially for him but somehow lacked his boss's flair.

As Salvatore approached the table Bruno nodded. 'Sal.'

'Good morning.' Salvatore sat down and in a well practised, smooth movement removed his sunglasses from his jacket pocket. He snapped them open with a flick of his hand, slipped them on and watched the tourists strolling by on the piazza. It was a cool

23

morning, clear, bright and fresh. The expanse of clean, soft light yellow stone was dazzling to the eye.

'Look, you really don't need to be here, I can deal with him.'

Salvatore held up his hand. 'I haven't eaten or had coffee yet.'

Bruno hid his irritation behind a smile. He glanced round and caught the hovering waiter's eye. The man hastily moved closer and looked to Bruno, who nodded toward Salvatore. The waiter turned his attention to his new customer, 'Mr Conelli?'

'Coffee, croissant, thank you.' The waiter glanced at Bruno, who shook his head. The man quickly withdrew.

Bruno knew Salvatore moved at his own pace. It was infuriating that he, Bruno, was made to wait. It was simple: Renzo had been skimming off the profits and he needed to be slapped into line... hard. The organisation had changed a lot over the years and in many ways was like any other large corporation with its rules and protocols. Bruno preferred the old ways, quick, decisive and sometimes painful. This was part of his problem, the organisation preferred a low key, no fuss, out of the limelight approach. The steady accumulation of vast wealth and influence. The old ways, of course, could be employed but not as a first resort. Bruno was extremely high on the corporate ladder but there were those who felt he should rise no further. One reason for this was his temper. It was felt he would sometimes act in the heat of the moment, anger being a barrier to good judgement. Others felt he was excellent material, the perfect leader, and should be at the very top echelon of the organisation. Admittedly, this was an opinion held mainly by Bruno himself.

Milan shone very brightly in the corporation's multi-faceted universe. A great deal of money and power flowed through the city, and Salvatore oversaw the whole operation. One of the reasons the organisation was content with his style of leadership was simply that the money rolled in and the organisation stayed in the shadows. If you dug deep enough, you would find very few, if any, profitable businesses the organisation was not involved in at some level. They did not own all of them; some just paid insurance money. Insurance was a very lucrative aspect and collected monthly to ensure the continued health of the business owners. Salvatore monitored the profits of each of the multiple revenue streams and became involved only if something went wrong, as it seemed to have done with The String, a set of bars near some of the most fashionable shops and design houses on the planet. Four streets, known as the golden rectangle of fashion. The bars, in fact, were entirely owned by the organisation, although it would take a team of very clever legal minds to dig deep enough to prove this. The String was usually a very reliable source of revenue, especially during Milan's Autumn fashion season.

Bruno opened his briefcase and laid some papers carefully on the table. 'When you've finished your coffee…'

Salvatore put down his cup and reluctantly picked up the sheets. He began to scan the rows of numbers and dates with a practised eye. He was very good at his job but today he had been looking forward to spending time with Anna and Lucia. Within two or three minutes it did not look good, in less than five it was suspicious. Salvatore was methodical. In spite of Bruno's mounting irritation, he worked his way steadily through the documents. Long before he reached the end there was no doubt but he read them all anyway. When he'd received Bruno's phone call he believed Renzo to be a pain in the arse. He had modified his earlier opinion, *Renzo was a stupid pain in the arse*. Salvatore handed back the papers to Bruno, who returned them to his case.

Salvatore continued to watch the fashionable multitude scurry about their business. Across the wide open space a crowd was forming as a fashion shoot appeared to be under way. Cameras clicked, impossibly perfect models struck poses, onlookers smiled and pointed. Salvatore did not smile. The shortfall in profits for The String was obvious and not insignificant. Renzo was helping himself to a very considerable slice of the company's money.

Bruno interrupted Salvatore's thoughts. 'Look Sal, you don't need to get involved. I'll sort Renzo. You just needed to know, is all. I'm perfectly able to deal with him.'

Salvatore was more than tempted to let Bruno handle it and go home. The decision whether to become involved himself would seem but a small thing. However, there would be nothing trivial about the consequences of his choice. It was Bruno himself who tipped the scales. Salvatore was on the brink of leaving Renzo to Bruno's unique brand of tact and sensitivity, when Bruno rendered it impossible with his next observation.

'You're more suited to the office side, especially these days.'

Salvatore stopped looking at the piazza and quickly turned his attention to Bruno. 'What is that supposed to mean?'

Bruno shrugged, 'You know.'

'No, I don't know. Suppose you spell it out for me?'

Bruno shifted uncomfortably. Whether he liked it or not, Salvatore was senior. 'Well… you've been concentrating more on the legitimate side of the business for some time now. Buying and renting out property, looking into safe investments… not involved in any tough hard stuff. Renzo needs firm handling, I just thought it was more my area. You know he will listen to me.'

Salvatore was quick to answer. He kept his voice low, but the message was loud and clear. 'Now you listen to me, Bruno; when I tell someone junior to me to do something, they listen and they do it.'

Bruno rolled his bottom lip, shrugged his shoulders and spread his hands palm up in capitulation. 'Sure, I'll leave him to you.'

Salvatore gave Bruno a long, unblinking glare to ensure he got the message.

Now uncomfortable, Bruno glanced down at his case and pulled it onto his lap. 'You want to take the paperwork?'

Satisfied, Salvatore picked up his coffee and turned his attention back to the piazza. 'No, I don't think when I've finished with him he'll be in the mood to concentrate. He's volatile. I was against him running The String when his name came up.' There was a thoughtful pause. 'Leave it to me, I'll call you later.'

Taking his cue, Bruno drained his cup, stubbed out his cigarette and got to his feet. 'I'll be at home tonight.'

Salvatore nodded without taking his eyes off the piazza. Bruno placed some money under his empty cup. He was glad Salvatore was not looking at him: he could relax his face, stop smiling, stop pretending. Bruno walked away quickly. He would not go far, no, he was curious to know how this confrontation with Renzo would play out.

Salvatore stared at the piazza without seeing it; he was thinking about Renzo. This was going to be ugly. The sums involved would mean speaking to other senior members of the organisation. Renzo's future, if indeed he had one, didn't look good. Salvatore hated this aspect of his work. If Renzo was dealt with he wouldn't be involved in the actual event but he would *know* about it. Hope of a pleasant day with the family, along with his good humour, was gone.

In South East London, the mood was considerably brighter. Ron and Vicky, having had breakfast, climbed into Ron's pride and joy, a 1957 Chevrolet *Bel Air*, and in good spirits were advancing on the club to meet Shades. As the Chevy rounded a bend, there it was, *The Blue Parrot*. It was good to see it again. Shades was right, it had been too long.

The Autumn sun gave its rich brickwork a warm glow. The building was extremely large and had wide steps; like a cinema; sweeping up to the entrance. Although beautiful, the steps weren't strictly necessary and a visitor walked up them merely to have the pleasure of walking down similar ones inside. It must be remembered that the original building had been constructed in a time when the huge expense and trouble was felt totally justified, simply because it looked better to the eye. Symmetry and beauty were a great deal more valued two hundred years ago than the pared down, eye-on-the-balance-sheet, contemporary world now. There was an air of comforting solidity to the building. It gave the impression it would stand for ever, a feeling that time not only stretched into its colourful past but forward and no matter how the world around it changed, *The Blue Parrot* would remain. Within its thick walls, glasses had been raised to celebrate both new life and absent friends and of course, all the special days in between that made up a life, like weddings, anniversaries and birthdays. The club had silently witnessed the cycle of life many times. Somehow, the joy and the tears had permeated into the very fabric of the building; it had a presence and depth a modern structure lacks.

Ron drove past the entrance and around behind to a small private yard, entering through one open half of double wooden gates. The tall gates bore the legend, *Private, Deliveries Only* emblazoned in large letters. Apart from Shades and his brother Tony; only Ron, Vicky and Jane were permitted to use it. The yard contained a lock-up garage within its walls. Shades' car was there but there was no sign of Tony's. A fire escape rose two floors to the private flat above the club. Apart from some empty beer barrels stacked neatly against the wall, the yard was bare. Two double fire doors were cut into the wall of the club. It was still early and *The Blue Parrot* would not open its doors to the public for some time.

Ron locked the car and walked with Vicky to one of the fire doors. There was a bell push, marked *Deliveries.* Ron pressed it. After a few moments there was a sound of bolts being drawn back, the door opened, a smiling face appeared and looked at Vicky.

'Of all the gin joints in all…'

She finished his sentence, misquoting the last part for fun. '…the towns in all the world, she walks up to my fire door…, *Casablanca,* that's too easy.'

Shades kissed Vicky on the cheek, she kissed him back and passed through the door. Ron grinned at Shades; it was really good to see him. Ron squeezed Shades' arm as he followed Vicky, Shades patted Ron's back as he passed.

They had entered through one the of emergency exits in the corner of the club. To the right was a substantial stage used for discos at the weekends. The floor in front was clear, ready for dancing. Beyond was a vast space full of round tables, each surrounded by chairs. Between the tables were massive pots containing giant metallic palm trees, which soared towards the ceiling. Lights in the pots shone upwards, illuminating the palms and glinting on the metalwork. To the right and left of the stage were the main bars, set against the walls on raised floors two steps up, with more tables in front of them. A waist-high brass rail swept around the elevated areas. Across the cavernous room, although only a few steps high, was the grand marble staircase which led up to the main entrance doors, currently locked. The ceiling was so high there was easily enough room for the upstairs bar that ran above the entrance and was reached via a set of splendid Victorian metal stairs.

From the upstairs bar, someone was leaning over the rail and waving at them. 'Hi Vicky, hi Ron!'

They looked up and Ron called back, 'Hello Jane!'

Shades led them across the club to the stairs and moments later the four of them were seated around one of the tables in the upstairs bar.

Jane was her normal, breathless, bubbly self. 'Ron, haven't see you for ages, you okay?'

'Well…'

Before he could answer, Jane galloped on. 'Shades said you were having problems with your next book.'

Ron nodded. 'Yes, er… mmm…' He got no further.

'Shades is full of ideas, I bet he'll help.'

'That's what I'm hoping, I usually get some inspiration when we chat.'

Jane nodded enthusiastically. Vicky watched Jane: she was usually chatty but seemed more so than usual, Vicky had the impression she was nervous. As Ron explained his current problem in detail, the ideas he had had and subsequently rejected, Vicky studied Jane and Shades. They were an unlikely couple: Jane was painfully thin and pale but crackled with energy, as if so full of life it overflowed. Her complexion was accentuated by her vibrant copper and uncontrollably curly hair. She looked quickly from Ron to Shades as each spoke, causing her large round spectacles to slide down her nose. They were pushed briskly back with the poke of a forefinger. Occasionally, Jane threw a bright smile at Vicky. It was clear Jane revelled at being in *The Blue Parrot* or rather, in *The Blue Parrot, with Shades.*

Shades was telling Ron about some new customers at the club. He never named names but talked about the characters. The club was a magnet for South East London's more colourful types, although the local police did not share Shades' appreciation of colourful types.

Vicky was a keen observer of people. She thought a great deal of Jane and Shades and really hoped it would work out for them. Focussing her attention on Shades, she wondered if it was possible to glean anything from an unguarded look. Shades was about the same height as Jane and like Jane, thin, but also wiry and amazingly strong for his size. His hair was neat, short and as black as his suit. His brown eyes were quick, missing little. He and his brother Tony were half Italian on their mother's side. Although, raised in Italy, they had spoken both English and Italian at home since birth and had no perceivable Italian accent. They were now very settled in London, running *The Blue Parrot*. Shades loved old movies, always quoting lines and took a schoolboy delight if people guessed the film. He had created his own cinema in the basement, *The Roxy*. It had been a red-letter day for Jane when he had screened a film for her. Admittedly, the police sirens and machine guns had not been exactly romantic but it was Shades' passion and he had shared it with her. Jane had been so happy. Vicky watched Shades talk about customers, films and ideas. It was how Ron worked when he needed storylines. He absorbed it all. From the scrapbook of information, usually a picture would form. Ron listened, waiting for the magic to happen.

When they got together for one of these brainstorming marathons, they often lost track of time.

Vicky had seen the process before but it was new to Jane and it fascinated her. It was an aspect of Shades she knew nothing about.

Suddenly, Shades was conscious he had been talking for some time. He glanced across at Vicky and Jane, 'This must be really boring for you two.' Focussing on Vicky, he added. 'Jane says you're both working this afternoon and perhaps into the evening. Why don't you nip up to the flat? There's food in the kitchen.' He turned to Ron. 'You hungry?'

'No, you keep talking, nothing yet.'

Vicky sensed the audience was not helping. 'Come on, Jane, I'll make some sandwiches.'

Jane looked disappointed but followed Vicky to the bar, behind which was a door marked *Private*. Another set of stairs led up to the front door of the luxury flat Shades and Tony sometimes used if they worked late. Vicky was familiar with the flat, having stayed there with Ron. A dangerous situation the year before had forced them into hiding. Shades and his brother Tony had given them shelter. It was relatively new to Jane and while Vicky was in the small kitchen making sandwiches, she wandered around the neat, spacious living room. It had a luxury hotel feel about it, lacking a little in character, but immaculately clean and tidy with bright neutral tones. Shades' brother Tony was very particular about things around him being clean and tidy, everything having its place. Shades viewed this as a source of amusement and took pleasure in teasing him about it. Tony didn't care and regarded

Shades' digs as juvenile and not worthy of either consideration or comment. There were two bedrooms, a large bathroom and the compact kitchen. The only external door opened onto a balcony, from which the fire escape dropped to the private yard behind the club, where Ron's Chevy was parked. The fire escape also led up to the roof, which was flat, with a waist-high wall surrounding it.

Having made lunch, Vicky joined Jane in the living room. 'I found some cheese and tomatoes.'

'Thanks Vicky.'

They sat and ate. Jane had lost some of her usual fizz, Vicky knew she would prefer to be with Shades. 'I think they wanted us to leave them to it.'

Jane nodded. 'Yes, I hope Shades helps Ron.'

Vicky frowned. 'He's worried, I know he is. He thinks he's lost the creative spark, he's doubting himself.'

Jane was surprised. 'That's silly, Ron's very creative, you know he is. Look at all the books he's written.'

'Mmm.'

Jane suddenly brightened. 'I forgot to tell you. Mags thinks you're ready to make up some of the extras and so do I.'

Vicky was delighted, 'Really?'

'Yes, you've picked up so much helping us.'

'Well, I owe it all to you and Magic. By the way, what should I call her? Everyone on set calls her Magic, but you call her Mags or Maggie.'

Jane laughed. 'Mags and I go back a long way, long before she became such an FX[2] legend. People in the industry call her Magic, I call her Mags, but we've known each other forever. Since you're working together, I'm sure she would be happy if you call her Maggie, she's taken a real shine to you.'

'I know, she's been so helpful, telling me things, showing me tricks.' Not wanting to offend Jane, Vicky added hastily, 'you *both* have.'

'Look Vicky, I'm under no illusions, I'm a very good FX and make-up artist but Mags is in a different league. You spend as much time with her as you can. She really likes you.'

'I wonder why?'

'You're very likeable.'

Vicky shook her head, 'No. Sometimes, she looks at me... I don't know, I feel she's going to say something, then... she doesn't.'

Jane's expression grew serious. 'I think you remind her of somebody.'

'Who?'

Jane felt awkward. 'Erm... I don't want to be all mysterious or anything, but it isn't my story to tell. Can we leave it? I know Mags will tell you in her own time.'

Vicky didn't understand but sensed it would be wrong to press. Jane was not naturally secretive, so

---

[2] FX is the industry term for Special Effects, also SFX.

she must have her reasons. Vicky changed the subject. 'It's fantastic I'll be working on the extras.'

Jane's smile returned, 'It's going to be flat out this afternoon. It's the big explosion scene and there'll be lots of walking wounded staggering about. Mags 'n' me will work on the principal actors for the close shots, but you'll have your hands full giving all the extras nice runny cuts and slashes from broken glass.'

Vicky laughed. 'Sounds funny when you put it like that.'

Jane leaned forward and looked carefully at Vicky, 'Are you okay for this afternoon? You look tired.'

Vicky was quick. 'Absolutely! Wouldn't miss it for the world. I didn't sleep too well, had one of my nightmares.'

'You're still having them?'

'Yes. Don't worry, I'm fine. We'd better wash up and collect Ron. We've got to be on set soon.'

When Vicky and Jane returned to the bar, they found the staff had arrived and were making ready for the lunch trade. Ron was hunched over the table, holding a pen in one hand and his head in the other. Shades was tipping back his chair, balancing on its two back legs, with his hands behind his head, looking thoughtfully at the ceiling. Their approach appeared well-timed, as they heard Shades say, 'I can't think of anything else.' He let the chair fall forward back on to all four legs.

Ron put away his pad and pen. 'Thank you, I'm sure something here will spark an idea. I need to think on it.' He looked enquiringly at Vicky. 'You two ready?'

'Yes, if you drop us at Jane's flat you can go home and we'll drive to the shoot in Jane's car.'

Ron glanced at Jane. 'Don't worry, Ron, I'll drop Vicky off after work.'

So it was agreed. Jane and Vicky kissed Shades good bye on the cheek.

Ron shook hands and said, 'Say "Hi" to Big Tony, tell him sorry we missed him.'

'Sure.' Shades looked sheepishly at Jane and added, 'I, er, thought I'd help with The Quest.' He held up a carrier bag that had been propped unnoticed by the table leg.

Although the reference to The Quest meant nothing to Ron and Vicky, Jane's face lit up, she leapt forward to hug Shades, exclaiming delightedly, 'Thank you.'

Shades extracted himself from her arms. He glanced about to see if any of the staff at the bars were watching but they were busy. 'You're welcome, it's nothing, don't fuss.'

Jane's eyes sparkled. If Vicky didn't know better she would have said that Shades looked slightly embarrassed.

Ron drove to Jane's flat, Vicky in the front, Jane in the back, still clutching the bag Shades had given her. Vicky glanced at Ron, who seemed preoccupied. 'Did you get any ideas?'

'Mm, don't know. Nothing jumps out. He told me about some new customers, some old films. I'll think about it.'

Ron noticed Jane smiling as he looked in the rearview mirror. 'You look happy,' he observed.

Jane snapped out of her daydream and beamed at him. 'Wasn't that sweet of him?'

Vicky turned, 'What did he mean, "help you with The Quest"?'

Jane laughed and pulled a large box of chocolates from the carrier bag, holding it up for them to see. 'I told Shades about my quest for the mystery chocolate.'

Vicky smiled. 'This sounds interesting.'

'When I was a little girl I was given a small box of chocolates and I ate one that was so delicious you can't imagine. It was round, with zig zags and dots. But when I looked at the card of contents it wasn't there! I've been searching ever since. It's called "Jane's Quest for the Lost Chocolate of Her Youth."'

Ron and Vicky laughed, Ron was suspicious. 'You made it up just so people would buy you boxes of chocolates.'

'Oh no, my quest is real.' She sighed. 'The search goes on.'

Ron shook his head, not convinced.

Vicky was not too sure herself but happy to help. 'Don't worry, Jane, ignore Ron, I'll help you.'

Ron laughed. 'I bet you will.'

He deposited the girls outside Jane's flat, they climbed into Jane's car and headed off. Ron went home to face the computer and the blank sheets of lined paper that were becoming more terrifying as the days went by.

PART ONE

CHAPTER 3
MILAN, ITALY
MONDAY LUNCHTIME

Bruno added another cigarette to the full ashtray. He had followed Salvatore at a safe distance and watched him enter the largest of the string of bars under Renzo's control. He had taken a seat to the rear of the cafe opposite. From there, he had a clear view of the entrance. Bruno didn't know what he expected to see. He felt Salvatore was somehow invading his area. Why couldn't he stick to his investment portfolios and his meetings and leave this sort of work to him? Tourists wandered in and out of the busy bar, everything appeared normal and tranquil outside but inside was a different matter.

Renzo's open hand slammed down hard on the desk. 'You come in to my place and call me a thief like I'm some shit criminal! I'm Renzo Fabrini!'

Salvatore didn't raise his voice but he was irritated. 'Firstly, it's not your place, it belongs to the organisation, they all do. Secondly, there is a shortfall and it's very obvious. It's also obvious you have tried to hide it. Your signature is all over the paperwork...'

Renzo didn't let him finish. 'So you been spying on me, you don't trust me.' His hot little eyes glared at Salvatore across the desk.

41

Salvatore took it all in: an angry little man; Renzo had always been angry. He was very short and overweight. At school, because of his size, he had picked fights to prove he was tough. A mean little man who grew more so as the years rolled by. He was accustomed to having things his own way and his opinion of himself was considerably higher than that of those who knew him. It was obvious to Salvatore that he and Bruno had left Renzo with too much power for too long and not kept close tabs on how he ran the bars. So now, evidently Renzo looked upon them as his.

'Look Renzo, you stand a chance of losing a lot more than your job. Remember who you work for. The organisation will want it back and if that is the end of it you will be very, very lucky.'

Beneath Renzo's bluster and apparent outrage, he was frightened. He certainly hadn't forgotten who he worked for, he wished he could. Renzo had seen at first hand what the organisation could do to those who crossed them. There were many facets to the man's character: he was a bully, a thief and a fool, with a big mouth and a small mind. Renzo clung to the vague notion that if he protested loud enough and long enough, just perhaps, suspicion might fall on someone else. His attitude would have been significantly different if he had been confronted by Bruno, but in his eyes, Salvatore was a businessman, an office worker.

'Arrrr! I got bars to run, I don't have to listen to this.' Renzo lurched to his feet and crossed to the office door before Salvatore could stop him.

Bruno sat up attentively as he saw Renzo leave the bar and walk quickly up the street. Salvatore tore after him. Bruno walked to the cafe entrance to keep them in sight. He saw Salvatore attempt to seize Renzo's arm. Bruno smiled, things evidently were not going well. A tall man carrying camera equipment crossed his view. The streets were full of press photographers in Milan for Autumn Fashion Week.

'Hey!'

The man paused, suspicious as to what this stranger wanted. Bruno pointed across the street, where Renzo was shouting at Salvatore. 'I think there's gonna be a fight, you may get some good pictures.'

The press man nodded and hurried towards the two angry men. Probably nothing, but you never knew; wonderful if one pulled a knife. It didn't look likely, since they were both dressed in business suits.

Bruno retreated into the doorway and watched, enjoying the show. That jumped-up little creep plainly had no respect for Salvatore. Bruno wondered how his boss would handle it.

Renzo turned and faced Salvatore, shaking off his hand, 'Let go of me, keep your hands off me!'

Salvatore spoke through gritted teeth. 'Get back in the office, I haven't finished.'

'Well I've finished with you... bean counter, bean counter with your meetings, 'look at me big man', with your meetings. Go back to your office and count your beans. I got a proper business to run.'

'*Nobody* speaks to me like that.'

Renzo turned and started to walk away.

Salvatore lost his temper, Salvatore *really* lost his temper and any self control, truly and completely. The all-consuming rage he felt in those seconds reduced rationality to ashes. His left arm lashed out and gripped Renzo's upper arm fiercely with bruising force. He spun the man round, slamming him against the wall.

Salvatore shouted, 'You *will* listen! Don't you *ever* turn your back on me!'

Renzo could not escape: Salvatore still held his arm with one hand and the other he waved in Renzo's face, forefinger extended, emphasising his words by stabbing the air underneath Renzo's nose. Renzo turned his head away and would not look at him.

'*Look at me when I'm speaking!*'

Renzo snorted as if Salvatore were not worthy of his attention. Salvatore's right arm thrust forward and grasped Renzo's throat. This man *would* look at him! Renzo's head was bent back. Salvatore's fingers clamped around Renzo's neck, Salvatore's face now white with rage, was inches from Renzo's. Salvatore's eyes blazed as he repeated. '*Nobody* speaks to me like that; d'you hear? Nobody!' He shook the now lolling head, Renzo didn't answer. 'Answer me!'

Renzo shut his eyes, Salvatore felt him go limp as he crumpled heavily to the ground.

Salvatore bent down. 'Renzo, Renzo!' He tapped the man's cheek with the palm of his hand. 'Renzo!' He fumbled for Renzo's wrist and squeezed his thumb on the artery... and felt nothing. Shocked, Salvatore slowly straightened, staring down in disbelief. Moments ago, a living, breathing human being had stood before him, but now it was replaced by a lifeless pile of flesh and bone. Salvatore's hands shook, his breath was short and a roaring noise filled his ears. The very fabric of reality seemed to swirl about him as his mind struggled to accept what he'd done. This couldn't be real.

There was a muffled babbling noise like people's voices heard under water, incoherent. He breathed deeply. How long he stood there he didn't know. He had killed Renzo! Salvatore became aware of people's voices, there were cries and shouts for help and... something else. Something strange. *Whizz click, whizz click.* He turned and stared directly into the dark barrel of a professional camera lens capturing the grisly scene in perfect clarity, again and again, with him standing over the body. The motor advanced the film in the bulk loader over and over again. Salvatore lurched toward the cameraman, who lowered his camera and after a second's hesitation, turned and ran into the crowd.

Bruno had seen enough. A lot of people were crowding around Renzo's body, waving and calling for a doctor to be fetched. Salvatore and the cameraman had disappeared from view. Bruno hurried in the opposite direction. In a relatively quiet part of the busy street, he stopped at a public bench and sat for a moment. This would need some thought. Could Renzo actually be dead? It certainly didn't look good.

And Salvatore, the main man! Mr Milan, the organisation's golden boy, killing Renzo in the street. Bruno smiled, and right in front of the *press!* He rubbed his hands together. And the whole thing captured on *film!* They would surely ask him to take over: finally he would have his chance to show what he, Bruno, could do. Bruno's smile faded. Wait, things had been hushed up before. People threatened or paid off. The organisation had an uncomplicated relationship with the media. You bury the story or we bury the reporter. Maybe he could take advantage of the situation, maybe he couldn't. For the moment, the best thing to do was go home and stay near the phone and see how it panned out. One thing for sure, Q would not be happy.

The photographer had ducked into a tourist souvenir shop and watched Salvatore from behind a tall revolving rack of postcards. Salvatore was across the busy street, standing motionless, scanning faces as Milan's many visitors and natives swirled around him like a fast-flowing river. After a few moments, he moved on. The photographer waited until he was out of sight and nipped out of the shop, heading in the opposite direction to double back to the man on the ground. Perhaps he could learn more for his story? He was sure he had some great pictures. Now he needed a great back story. Disappointing if the man had just fainted. He needn't have worried: Renzo would sleep forever.

Salvatore caught sight of a public phone. Searching was useless, the photographer could be anywhere. It was essential to kill the story before it broke. He needed the organisation to help. He must get home, get to his office and see what could be done. Salvatore snatched up the receiver and called his driver.

It wasn't long before the driver delivered him smoothly to his front door. As Salvatore put his key in the lock, he glanced at the car port. His own beautiful red Ferrari was parked as usual but Anna's nippy little yellow sports car was gone. She was out with his daughter. They would not be far; he remembered he'd said he hoped to be home for lunch. Under normal circumstances, he would have been a little sorry he'd missed them but these weren't normal circumstances. He went quickly to his office, shut the door and dropped heavily into the comfortable leather chair. Phone Uncle, it was the thing to do. It was the *only* thing to do. He reached for the phone.

Uncle Q was semi-retired, but, there was nothing semi about his power. Always present at all of the important organisation meetings, his view carried unquestionable weight. The respect he commanded was without equal. He was known to everyone as Q or Uncle. In Salvatore's case it was actually true. Uncle Q was one of Salvatore's mother's brothers. Q had a lot of time for Salvatore, having known him all his life and he adored Salvatore's daughter, Lucia. If this thing could be straightened out, undoubtedly it was Uncle who could make it happen. Salvatore always spoke to and greeted Uncle Q warmly, but in truth he never felt comfortable in his company. The stories of his exploits as a young man and his rise through the organisation were, if only half true, nightmarish.

He dialled. The help answered. 'It's Salvatore, is he in?'

After the obligatory, 'I'll enquire Mr Conelli,' and some clicks on the line, a rich, confident voice spoke in Salvatore's ear.

'Sal! It's good to hear you. I thought you had forgotten your Uncle. How's Anna and your beautiful daughter?'

'Hello Uncle, they're fine.'

'Anna I can understand, but how could an ugly guy like you make such a beautiful little girl?' He laughed at his own joke. Uncle Q was in a very good mood; a pity it wasn't going to last.

'Q, we've got a problem.'

'You 'n' Anna?'

'No. We, the organisation.'

Uncle was instantly serious, 'Tell me.'

'Renzo's been helping himself to the profits. Bruno ran all the figures and brought it to me. There was no doubt, he had tried to hide it but he's done a sloppy job. The shortfall is obvious and big.'

'Stupid, stupid. We'll have to bring him in. Have you spoken to Renzo himself yet?'

There was a pause, 'I saw him this morning. He denied it, got angry, walked out of the office, I followed. We had it out in the street.'

'Sal, for God's sake, we don't do business in the street.'

'It gets worse.'

'Tell me everything.'

'There was a scuffle, I grabbed him, he talked to me as if I was an office boy, I shook him… I had him by the throat…'

Uncle was silent, Salvatore gripped the phone tightly. 'He's dead.'

He heard a long sigh at the other end of the line. Without waiting for a response, Salvatore decided to break all the bad news and get it over with. 'A press photographer caught it on film.'

'Jesus!'

'I know, I know. Can we get the story buried? Can we stop it?'

'Okay, okay, slow down. Do you know which news service? Was it a local paper?'

'I don't know.'

'Did anyone else recognise you?'

'No, don't think so, it all happened so fast.'

'Okay, get the hell off this line, I'll see what I can find out. And stay by the phone.'

'Alright… I'm sorry.'

'Yeah.'

The line went dead, Salvatore hung up slowly. He stared at the phone. Could Uncle sort out this mess? He had considerable influence, but this? Salvatore shifted his attention to the silver-framed photograph of Anna and Lucia. Had he thrown away his own life at

49

the same time he took Renzo's? It still didn't seem real. One moment Renzo was alive and the next... if only he could go back. If he had let Bruno handle it, he would be with Anna and Lucia now. He leaned forward, rested his elbows on the desk, held his head with both hands and stared down at the desk.

The afternoon wore on, still he sat at his desk. In his younger days he had given and received his share of cuts and bruises. He had even broken a man's nose. But this, this was new. Deeply disturbed, he tried to bring order to his thoughts. Salvatore knew Bruno had killed people in the past. He suspected that Bruno saw it merely as part of the job. Should he phone Bruno? No, no, wait for Uncle. Don't talk to anyone, best keep the line free.

He picked up the framed photograph and gazed at Lucia. He gently stroked her hair with his thumb. Would he be there to see her grown? For some time he sat looking sadly at the happy little girl who smiled back at him.

Suddenly, the little girl in the photograph spoke to him. 'Oh Daddy, it's on the ground, someone killed it!'

Salvatore jumped visibly and looked up quickly.

The real Lucia had burst into the office, closely followed by Anna: his little girl was seriously distressed. 'Momma said it was alright but it's NOT! Horrible nasty people, so pretty! NOW it's squished flat! It came down to say hello, now it's flat! It should have stayed up in the blue. Some... some, nasty, nasty, FLATTED IT!' A flood of tears quickly followed. She ran to him, and he turned in his chair to gather her into his arms. Still seated, he was able to see over her head, which was buried in his chest. He looked at Anna for an explanation. Anna was smiling, so he assumed that the situation was perhaps not as grave as Lucia thought.

Keeping her voice suitably serious, Anna explained, 'The gardener's been watering. There's a film of oil in one of the puddles and Lucia thinks someone's run over a rainbow.'

Despite his worries, Salvatore smiled. Lucia often did or said things that made him smile, as her five-and-a-half-year-old mind struggled to make sense of the world. He held Lucia away so he could talk to the red, tear-stained face. 'Now listen, Lucia, the sky is very big. Rainbows stretch right across them. Rainbows are really, really big. You only saw a tiny, weeny bit of a rainbow in the puddle. The big rainbow won't even miss it. In fact, I bet the pretty rainbow gave it to the muddy old puddle to cheer it up, so don't worry, okay?'

There was much wiping of eyes and sniffing. Finally, the drama seemed to be over. 'Okay, I'm going to talk to the puddle.'

'Alright, see you later.'

Lucia ran out of the office with renewed energy. Anna studied Salvatore: he'd watched Lucia leave with such sadness she was prompted to ask, 'Is everything alright, Sal?'

He took a deep breath, 'No. Come in and close the door.'

While Lucia played happily in the garden, Salvatore poured out the whole story to Anna. She sat gravely, taking it all in. When he had finished, they sat in silence. He and Anna were close; though it hadn't always been so, but now, their relationship was solid. Even so, he didn't know how she would take the news. Anna knew who Salvatore worked for, she also realised that his particular role in the organisation was almost that of a businessman. But the organisation was always there in the background, casting a shadow over her life. Occasionally, he was involved in things they both wished he was not; the string of clubs was a good example, as ultimately, he was supposed to oversee the operation.

'How long did you hold him?'

'It all happened so quickly, I don't know, not long. I wanted him to look at me, I didn't mean to strangle the man.'

'I don't think you did.'

Salvatore frowned, 'But… he's dead.'

Anna nodded, 'I know, I know. You remember I was training to be a nurse before we were married?'

'Yes.'

Anna explained her reasoning. 'It can happen more easily than you would think. Any pressure on a structure called the carotid bulb that controls the heart rate and blood pressure can be extremely dangerous. It's situated where the common carotid artery splits into the internal and external carotid arteries.'

Salvatore looked blank.

Anna simplified her explanation, 'Roughly where you see doctors checking for a pulse in the neck. If you press on both sides it can cause cardiac arrest, which results in death. Perhaps you could explain it was a tussle that went tragically wrong.' She decided not to mention that if he had pumped Renzo's chest he might have been resuscitated.

Salvatore didn't think anyone would listen to explanations, so his response was swift. 'No, no, the authorities are aware of who I am and who I work for. This is a golden opportunity for them to take out someone senior in the organisation. They won't pass it up.' He paused then added, 'I feel a little better that you believe I didn't mean for it to happen.'

Anna squeezed his hand.

Suddenly, the phone rang, Salvatore switched it to the desk speaker and put his finger to his lips, indicating he did not want the caller to know she was in the room.

'Hello.'

'It's Uncle.'

'Any news?'

'The *Courier Della Sera* (Milan's evening newspaper) will be running a story that a prominent bar manager, a local man, was killed on the street and the assailant ran into the crowd. There are lots of descriptions of you, but they contradict each other and the paper doesn't have pictures. Are you sure it was a press photographer?'

'All I know is it wasn't a tourist, the equipment was too professional.'

'Okay. Stay home, don't talk to anyone but me. I'll keep digging. If we can get the film we may be able to keep a lid on the situation.'

'Thank you.'

'You *should* thank me, I've been on the phone constantly since I spoke to you. I'll call you when I know more.'

'Okay.'

There was a click and Uncle rang off.

'I think Uncle is pretty pissed.'

'He'll do all he can, he has a soft spot for you and you know he adores Lucia. I'd better go check on her. I'm sure he realises it was an accident; no-one wants death and drama.'

PART ONE

CHAPTER 4
FILM LOCATION, SOUTH EAST LONDON
MONDAY, LATE AFTERNOON

'Okay, I want lots of death and drama.' The Director scanned the crowd of bleeding, slashed and lacerated extras. Bringing the megaphone to his lips, he spoke again, 'Beautiful job Magic, lovely gruesome stuff.'

Magic Marge, aka Maggie waved a hand at some of the extras and called back, 'That's Vicky's work.'

The Director glanced at Vicky, who stood next to Maggie and boomed, 'Good job, Vicky!

Directors all have their own style. This young man, like a good many of his time, was enchanted with the space race and particularly enjoyed the checklist at Mission Control before the launch using a similar method in his work. 'Right, this is just after the explosion.' He consulted his clipboard. 'Scene thirty-two. Quiet on set. Lights. Sound. Roll film.'

The clapper board was held in front of a running camera. *Explosion Scene 32.*

The Director addressed the actors. 'In your own time... ACTION.' The statement was punctuated with a sweeping arm and a pointing finger.

Vicky and Maggie crept away from the bright lights of the scene and slipped quietly into one of the huge trailers. They had been working for some hours. Jane was still busy in another make-up trailer, completing the make up on one of the lead actors for the next scene. Maggie had overseen Vicky's work on the big crowd scene now in progress.

Outside the trailer, they could hear muffled screams of anguish, cries for help and the occasional small explosion. All good signs that things were going beautifully. The Director would be happy, he had a soft spot for a good bloodbath. His absolute favourite SFX was setting people alight. From the sounds of horror and carnage, he was having a particularly pleasant time.

The trailer had the familiar scent of hairspray and a faint aroma of acetone. To Vicky, the sights and smells felt exciting: she loved it all; the bright lights, the brushes and the makeup. Vicky felt truly in her element.

In the relative quiet and calm of the trailer, Maggie collapsed into a vacant make-up chair. 'Ooo, I am pooped. Give me a minute and I'll make some tea.'

'I'll do it.' Vicky moved to the kettle. 'I can't thank you enough, Maggie, I've learnt so much. Honestly, today has been wonderful.'

Maggie waved her hand dismissively, 'It's a pleasure, treasure. You've picked it up like a pro.'

Vicky made the tea and joined her. Maggie was in her mid-forties, tall, slim, smartly dressed in black trousers, a neat green roll neck sweater and a make-up belt full of brushes and items she used the most. She had an air of quiet confidence about her. Unlike Vicky, she wore make-up but, as you would expect, it was expertly applied. Maggie looked considerably younger than she was. She had known Jane a number of years and was fully aware of Jane's chocolate quest.

'Let's help Jane with her Quest.' So saying, she took a chocolate from the now open box Jane had left out to share.

Vicky asked, 'She's not really serious, is she?'

Maggie smiled. 'I wouldn't like to say, you're never quite sure with Jane.'

Vicky was sure…, well, almost sure, they were pulling her leg.

It was their first break; it had been a marathon to get the crown scene extras made up. While they sipped tea, Maggie peered at Vicky, 'You alright, love? You look tired.'

'I'm fine, didn't sleep too well.'

Maggie was concerned, 'You weren't worrying about the shoot, were you?'

'No! I was looking forward to it. Anyway, Jane only told me I was going to work on the extras today.'

Vicky considered Maggie. Should she tell her about the nightmare? Maggie projected the calm, confident manner of someone at the top of their game. Responsibility rested easily with her. Vicky felt safe in her company, as if nothing could happen that Maggie couldn't cope with. Vicky had only ever met one other person in her life whose calm, intelligent nature made her feel a childlike safety. Strangely, it was Shades' brother, Big Tony. She loved Tony like a brother of her own.   She decided to take the plunge.   'I have nightmares… there's a recurring one about my sister.' She had Maggie's full attention.   There was a pause. Maggie waited. 'Last year was a stressful time for me. My sister became involved with someone who proved to be a very dangerous man. I really don't want to go into the details. I know my sister is dead, but I can never visit her grave, it's… lost.' She swallowed and her eyes shone with tears.

Maggie put down her cup with an audible clatter and the colour drained from her face.

Vicky realised she had upset her and, she leaned forward. 'I'm sorry, I shouldn't have said anything, it's my problem.'

'It's alright, you weren't to know.'

Vicky didn't understand but was somehow sure she shouldn't ask.

Maggie took a moment, then, 'I don't want to go into details either, but I understand, I really do. Jane hasn't told you anything about me, has she?'

'She told me you were a special effects genius and all the studios line up to get you to work for them.'

Maggie gave a sad smile.   'Yes, they do.'   She hesitated, then added quickly, 'I was married, you know?'

Vicky shook her head slightly.

'Well I was. We were happy. After our daughter was born we couldn't have been more happy.' Maggie spoke very quietly, 'My husband was called Mark and my little girl….' Maggie trailed off, then tried again,

58

'My little girl was called Susan. Mark loved to sail but I get seasick so it was only the two of them out together.' There was a long pause. 'They found the boat capsized and drifting, but they never found them. So I have no grave to visit either.'

Vicky rose quickly to her feet and swept across the room. Linked by their shared grief, the two women hugged each other tightly.

Vicky's voice was full of compassion as she whispered in Maggie's ear. 'I'm *so* sorry, Maggie.'

Maggie pulled back, rested both arms on Vicky's shoulders and looked at her face. 'She would have been about your age now, all grown up.'

Vicky felt a wave of emotion. In that instant, she understood Maggie's warmth and closeness. She, Vicky, had in a small way partly filled the terrible, sad, lonely space in Maggie's heart. She could find no words that seemed adequate.

Suddenly, the door burst open and Jane bounced in. 'I'm *so* tired! I'm gasping for a cup of tea.'

Maggie let go of Vicky and turned her back to Jane as she moved to the kettle, 'I'll make you one.'

'Oh thanks, lovely.' Jane threw herself dramatically into a chair and smiled at Vicky. The smile quickly faded. 'You alright? You look a bit upset.'

'Yes, yes, I'm a little tired, that's all.'

Satisfied, Jane changed the subject, 'I've finished making up the principal actors for the next scene. Hey Vicky, how about what the Director said about your cuts and slashes on the walking wounded? You've really done well, hasn't she, Maggie?'

Maggie turned from the kettle, now composed and in control, 'She's come on wonderfully, taken to it like a duck to water.'

Vicky shook her head. 'It's because of you two; I really am *so* grateful.'

Jane would have none of it. 'We can teach but not everyone gets it.' She turned to Maggie. 'The Director asked if you can go and see him. He's talking about shooting the star in the head and not the chest. He wants to talk to you, he said about ten minutes.'

'No rest for the wicked. I'll wander over now.' She handed the tea to a grateful Jane, smiled at Vicky and left the trailer.

Jane kicked off her shoes and wriggled her toes, 'My poor feet! Maggie is so much older than us but she never stops. Don't know how she does it. Have you had a nice chat with her? She really likes you.'

Vicky spoke quietly, 'She told me.'

'What, that she likes you?'

'No. About the accident.'

'Ah. It's a compliment, you know. She would normally never mention it.'

Vicky nodded.

Jane watched Vicky over her cup; she looked very tired and very serious. Jane put down her cup and pulled her shoes on, 'Come on, let's got and watch how Maggie shoots someone in the head. It's beautiful to watch, real art.'

Vicky loved Jane for putting shoes back on her tired feet, she realised, Jane was trying to lift the mood. They left the trailer to go and watch Maggie's art in action.

As they hurried across the lot toward the bright lights where the scene was being shot, Vicky smiled to herself. The idea of accompanying a friend to watch someone get their brains blown out was a curious way to cheer a person up. Although special effects was a strange line of work, Vicky was fast growing to love both that world and the people who inhabited it.

After standing around for some time, Maggie finally appeared from the second make-up special effects unit with the principal actor. The actor was in costume but looked normal.

Maggie joined Jane and Vicky, who was about to ask Maggie if the Director had changed his mind, when the man himself suddenly spoke in a loud voice. 'Okay folks, quiet on set. Everyone in first positions.' He glanced at the star, who gave a slight nod to show he was ready. 'Lights, sound, roll film.'

The clapperboard man stepped into the frame. 'Scene 42, star dies.'

The Director raised his arm. 'In your own time, ACTION.' The arm came down.

The star spoke with confidence and passion. 'I've got you and there isn't a damn thing you can do about it.'

The second actor took a step closer. 'Come on Jim, we've known each other for years; you can't do this!

61

Not to me. I'll disappear, you'll never see me again. Just let me go.'

'No! I made a promise, you'll get away with it over my dead body.'

'If that's what it takes.' The second actor swiftly pulled out a gun and fired. There was an explosion of noise. Instantly, the star's forehead had a red bullet hole, which ran with blood. The star fell forward out of shot and landed face down on a thick, air-filled cushion.

'And CUT!'

Vicky, who had visibly jumped at the gunshot, had her mouth open and a splayed hand covering her heart. She was relieved to see the star stand up and smile, accepting the congratulations from the crew.

Vicky turned to Maggie with admiration. 'I didn't see *anything*! How did you disguise the blood pack and detonator on his forehead... his forehead!' She repeated incredulously.

Jane spoke in Vicky's ear loud enough for Maggie to hear. 'Magic.'

Later, as the shoot wrapped for the day, Vicky said goodbye and received another hug from Maggie. As arranged, Jane dropped Vicky at the flat she shared with Ron. It was now almost seven, dark and turning very cold.

Vicky entered the flat, hoping she would see Ron scribbling on his big writing pad, or sitting at his PC, chewing his pen and murmuring quietly to himself. Sometimes, he spoke lines aloud or made gestures with his hands and pulled faces. He liked to test out lines and body language for real to be sure it was believable and natural. However, the room was empty, the writing pad lying on the desk. Copious lines had been written but all were crossed out. At the bottom of the page was a very good doodle of the left front light from a 1957 Chevrolet.

'Ron?'

The answer was muffled by the kitchen door. 'I'm in here.'

Vicky entered the kitchen, but stopped abruptly in the doorway.

Ron was standing close to the fridge: he wasn't looking at her and seemed preoccupied with the fridge, squinting at the crack in the partly open door. He had one eye closed and was concentrating hard. 'Hi, you okay?' He seemed distracted with the door and spoke as if his mind was elsewhere.

Vicky answered slowly. 'I'm okay, not too sure about you though.' She narrowed her eyes. 'What on earth are you doing?'

Ron continued to peer into the fridge as he slowly closed and reopened the door, 'Do you know, I don't think the little light's going off in there, when I shut the door.'

Vicky stared at him for a moment then, refusing to be drawn into Ron's evidently shrinking world, asked briskly, 'Still no ideas, then?'

He ceased his white goods experimentations, shut the door and sat down heavily at the kitchen table. 'No.' He sighed and his shoulders dropped.

'Do you want a drink?' She asked, in an effort to cheer him up.

He looked up. 'Are you having one?'

'Yes, come on.' Vicky returned to the comfortable living room, Ron following her.

With drinks in hand they stretched out on a sofa. Vicky raised her brandy. 'Cheers.' They touched glasses.

They sat quietly together enjoying their drinks, then Ron asked, 'Do you want some tea?[3] I've had a sandwich, myself.'

Vicky shook her head. 'I'm fine, we grabbed a bite from the catering truck.'

Ron rallied a little. 'So come on, tell me about your day.'

Vicky was tired, but the success of her work and the new closeness she felt with Maggie warmed her and lifted her spirits, giving her a burst of energy. 'Maggie and Jane are brilliant, I'm learning so much. We have fun too; Jane and I arrived at the shoot a little early and had time for a quick cup of tea with Maggie in the trailer. I made some comment to Maggie about the film industry being male-dominated and that I hoped I would fit in. Do you know what she said?'

---

[3] In the UK, the word tea can also refer to an evening meal.

Ron smiled because Vicky was smiling at the recollection. 'No, what?'

'"Oh, don't worry about that, be yourself. I always say, any woman who strives to be like a man, clearly lacks ambition". I laughed, poor Jane had a mouthful of tea and nearly drowned.'

Ron laughed. 'That *is* a good line, I may steal that for one of my characters.'

Vicky went on to tell him about the rest of her eventful afternoon, the compliments from the director and the heart-to-heart with Maggie. Ron listened, nodding and smiling, happy that she was happy.

Having reached the end of her news, Vicky was suddenly aware how much happier Ron appeared. His own creativity was stalled and she knew he was worried. But there he sat, looking pleased. She knew he was happy for her and she loved him for it. Vicky also felt just a little guilty that her art was blooming while he was unable to find even a seed of an idea. She wanted them both to be content. 'Still no luck with a plot line then?'

Ron's face fell. 'No. Nothing Shades told me sparked anything.' He stood, wandered restlessly to his line of best sellers and eyed them thoughtfully. He turned to Vicky, 'Just any story won't do. I have to feel...' He balled his fists and pressed them to his chest. 'I have to feel it here. People work hard for their money, sometimes doing jobs they hate. They deserve value, I owe it to them to create something I'm proud of.' He shook his head. 'I mean, not everyone will like it, no book can do that. But if most people do, I've got it right. I love writing but…' He gave a great sigh. 'Nothing seems right. I can't find a ticket.'

'Ticket?'

'Oh!' Ron hadn't meant to use the word and now it was out he knew Vicky would expect an explanation. He sat down, feeling a little embarrassed. 'Yes, erm, I've never really told you about that, have I?'

She smiled, now intrigued. 'Come on then, what's the dark secret?'

'Well, it's not dark.' He glanced at the kitchen door. 'But you already think I'm nuts.'

'So you've nothing to worry about, have you?'

He shrugged. 'Well, when I write a book, I imagine they're tickets. If a reader buys the book, they've really bought a ticket. They expect to go on a journey, an adventure. Not as themselves but as a heroine or hero. It's my job to give them an adventure, to experience things they've never felt, go to places they've never been and at the end, feel glad they chose this book, this ticket, this adventure.'

Ron felt a little shy about sharing his feelings and ideas on writing. 'You probably think I'm cracked, obsessing about tickets.'

'In the kitchen, yes, I thought you were. "Does the little light go off when I shut the door?" Who cares?'

Mellowed by the brandy, Ron grinned. 'You're right, of course.'

'I know you'll find your next story; perhaps you're trying too hard. Something will click.'

He was thoughtful. 'It's a strange thing, you know.'

'What?'

'I get ideas driving, or in the shower, sometimes just when I'm drifting off to sleep. But, hardly ever when I'm sitting at my desk. Why do you think that is? It's odd, isn't it?'

'You're odd!'

The reference to the shower had reminded her of the time he had been struck with inspiration while in the bathroom, with no paper and only a particularly juicy felt tip pen and a toilet roll to hand. It had soaked through multiple layers, the result of which was for a few days they had the unique experience of using toilet tissue with the legend, *Get the gardener to strangle the neighbour on Saturday.*

'Just do me a favour and take a notepad into the bathroom.'

He knew what she was referring to and laughed. His eyes wandered back to his desk and the scribbled notes he had made with Shades. 'I don't think there's anything there.'

Vicky was determined to be upbeat, she could see that behind the smiles he was really worried. 'Shades said he would phone if he had any more suggestions. Maybe he'll come up with something.'

'Yes, perhaps.'

Then unexpectedly, she made a suggestion. 'Come on Ron, let's go to bed.'

He looked at his watch. 'It's a bit early.'

She grinned. 'I didn't mean to sleep.'

'Oh? Oh.' The penny dropped.

It was a little after nine when the light went out in the bedroom of their flat in South East London.

In Milan, Anna Conelli had also gone to bed early. In her case, it was because her tension headache had deteriorated into a splitter. She rested her throbbing head on the cool pillow and lay awake. It was difficult to think clearly with the pain. She was running some scenarios through her mind, the possible implications to her family. Would Sal go to prison? Would the organisation support her? She loved Salvatore. It hadn't always been that way and the beginning of their relationship had been unorthodox. But against the odds, it had worked. They had a daughter they both adored. As time passed, her love for Salvatore had deepened.

Salvatore sat in his office; he had attempted to work, but was unable to stay focused. Recently, on behalf of the organisation, he had purchased some very exclusive property in Milan's prestigious fashion quarter. It was currently generating huge retail fees. These came from some of the design houses currently involved with Milan's Autumn launch and also from top-flight buyers who represented the retail elite. These buyers had the power to order staggering quantities at equally phenomenal and eye-watering expense.

Both the fashion houses and buyers didn't even flinch when presented with the huge cost of renting accommodation in the heart of the city. The domestic services to maintain these new properties took some setting up. Salvatore was supposed to be overseeing it but he simply couldn't concentrate. Reasoning that he might not be at liberty to continue with his workload, he had compiled a rough list of pressing decisions, also a list of other projects and their progress, ready to hand over to Uncle. It was possible Uncle could distribute the work to other key people in the organisation.

He felt he really should phone Bruno to appraise him of the situation, but he was delaying the call for two reasons: He didn't want the line busy, in case Uncle called with news, also he simply didn't like Bruno. Reluctantly, Salvatore picked up his phone; he would make it a quick call. Somebody should keep an eye on The String. The city was vibrating with energy and excitement; The String was running at full capacity with bars and restaurants fully loaded with people from all over the world, drawn by the fashion magnet.

'Bruno, it's me.'

Bruno feigned ignorance. 'Hello Sal. Did you have the meeting with Renzo?'

'Yes.'

'I hope you came down hard on him.'

'He's dead.'

'That's *too* hard.' Bruno smiled at his own joke.

'I'm not joking, Bruno, Renzo's dead.'

'What happened?' Still smiling, Bruno made his voice sound shocked and innocent, no mean feat.

'Can't go into it now. But I think you should inform the managers there's been an accident. Any problems, they must contact you.'

This was the beginning of Bruno's new responsibility and power. If things went badly for Salvatore, (and Bruno hoped sincerely they would) he Bruno, would be asked to step in and effectively take over the running of Milan. Sure, Uncle and a few of the old school were always in the background, but eventually, the city would be his.

'Okay, leave it to me.'

'I'll call tomorrow, don't know when. I'm talking to Uncle. I'll let you know what's happening when I know myself. I'd better get off the line.'

'Okay, ciao.' Bruno hung up. He sat with his hand on the receiver, thinking. It was no surprise Salvatore was talking to Uncle. He was hoping Uncle could get him out of the mess. Bruno took his hand from the receiver and lit a cigarette. He inhaled deeply, then slowly allowed the smoke to drift out and laughed.

Salvatore sat in his padded leather chair and stared vacantly at the phone. What a mess. He closed his tired eyes and shook his head slightly. What was going to happen?

PART ONE

CHAPTER 5
ITALY
MONDAY, LATE EVENING

Two hundred miles from Milan, far down near the edge of the Adriatic Sea, the lights of a small Italian village glowed. A little inland from the village, his cousin Nico was in contrast to Salvatore, enjoying one of the best days of his life. He breathed deeply the fresh country air of Italy and sighed with contentment. It had been a truly beautiful day. This was especially fortuitous for Nico because by the following morning he would be dead.

Nico's sister's wedding had been perfection personified and the party, which showed no sign of ending, would be the talk of the village for weeks. No, for years.

Nico smiled to himself. Like all the guests, he had danced, eaten and drunk. He was feeling pleasantly tired, full and mellow.

The Autumn weather had also been perfect; cool, clear and windstill. The party had spilled out of the beautifully decorated barn, which was festooned with flowers and hundreds of little white lights. The music played, over two hundred guests danced, laughed and chatted happily. Over the course of the afternoon, the shadows had stretched across the ground, then as the sun dipped below the horizon, the blue sky had darkened and now the stars shone cold and bright in the moonlit sky. The happy couple moved through the crowd, waving, nodding and laughing as they made their way to the wedding car. The partygoers walked with them toward the road to wave them off, everyone chatting and laughing.

Nico snatched up his camera. He believed he'd already captured some excellent shots. He was proud of his new camera, the best that money could buy. The family would be eager for many copies; he just needed some final pictures of the happy couple driving away. The darkness would be no match for his state of the art flashgun.

Nico joined the throng, who were cheering and waving as the wedding car roared away. The bride flung the wedding bouquet over her shoulder: it soared into the air and down again in a graceful arc and was caught by a very elderly aunt; who smiled and blushed, as the crowd burst with laughter.

Anxious to return to the dancing, the guests drifted back to the party and music once again filled the air.

Nico lingered. Perhaps, just perhaps, as the vanishing car touched the top of the far away hill, if he adjusted his camera settings carefully, he might get a shot of it silhouetted against the deep inky blue, star-filled sky. The moonshine silvered the grey road which snaked into the distance. It was a long shot, but you never knew. He had plenty of film and the wine gave him bravado. He crossed the road, setting his camera to manual as he walked.

For the sleepy driver there was a twilight moment. Thoughts and memories from the past fused with the present. That often-remembered holiday became real once again. Relaxing on the warm sun bed, the mesmerising gentle swish of tyres melted into the whisper of breaking waves, sliding up and falling back gently on a warm, golden beach.

Shhhhhhhh, thump. The false reality abruptly vanished, replaced by the very real road, lit by the truck's headlights. Its powerful beams bored a tunnel of white light into the darkness. The driver yawned, turned up the volume on the murmuring radio and cracked open the window, totally unaware of what lay behind on the hard tarmac. The red taillights of the truck shrank and were lost in the darkness.

Nico's camera lay broken by the roadside. Droplets of blood covered the smashed lens.

It was a night of extreme contrasts for the people whose lives were about to converge.

In South East London, Ronnie Moon lay fast asleep with his arm resting gently around Vicky's waist, who slept deeply and peacefully beside him.

In Italy, Anna Conelli slept badly, occasionally waking to find herself alone, then slipping in and out of a light, troubled sleep.

Salvatore Conelli, exhausted and worried, dozed intermittently through the night, still sitting in his office chair, waiting for news.

Their daughter Lucia Conelli, smiled in her sleep and dreamed of slides made of rainbows she could play on for hours. Sliding down in the sunshine and riding through clouds, then running up them and sliding down again and again.

Salvatore's cousin Nico would neither dream nor wake again. In the dark fields surrounding the village, for some time the only sound to be heard was music and laughter. The sounds were softened by distance as they drifted across the countryside. All at once, a piercing scream tore the serene atmosphere to shreds as it reverberated around the dark hills. A short time later an ambulance streaked along the roads in a blaze of blue light. It shattered the peaceful countryside with its loud, pulsing bell.

PART ONE

CHAPTER 6
MILAN
TUESDAY MORNING, VERY EARLY

The urgent ringing of the bell awoke Salvatore with a jolt. For several confused seconds he knew neither where he was or what the noise signified. The thin veil of sleep which briefly held back his troubles was destroyed, abruptly, they poured back into his mind. Realising he had fallen asleep in his office chair, he stretched out and picked up the ringing phone.

'Yes?'

'It's Uncle.'

'What news?' Now fully awake, he sat up and held the phone more tightly than was necessary.

'Not good, Salvatore, not good at all.'

'You couldn't stop the story?'

'It *was* a reporter, but he wasn't from one of our newspapers. He was French, here for Fashion Week. The story broke in France, the papers are having a field day, "*Killer Fashion Week*", "*Clothes to die for.*"'

Salvatore closed his eyes and rested his free hand across his forehead. It was the worst possible outcome.

Uncle was still talking in his ear. 'We may be able to make the news travel slower here in Italy, exert pressure. But we are only talking about a few hours at best. Once ANSA pick it up there is little we can do.'

ANSA stood for *Agenzia Nazionale Stampa Associata*, Italy's leading news service, a co-operative owned by several newspapers and supported by public funds. Too many people involved to control a big story, even for Uncle Q's unquestionable influence. Salvatore was painfully aware of the problem.

'The police will be knocking on your door soon, they'll have no choice. The photograph of you with your hand on Renzo's neck is front page. What do you want to do? We can get you out of town.'

'No. I won't leave Anna and Lucia to face this and they can't go on the run. I will not have this touch them, it's my mess.'

'Call me if you want anything.'

'Thank you, Uncle.'

Salvatore carefully replaced the receiver and sat motionless.

He didn't remember going to the kitchen and making coffee or getting his coat. He sat in the garden at the table, watching the steam rise slowly and vanish in the cool morning air. It wouldn't be light for hours. Salvatore sat very still. The patio area was lit by moonglow and a soft light from the under-counter strips in the kitchen behind him in the house. It was still and quiet, hard to believe he would be in a police cell before the end of the day. There would be a trial, a foregone conclusion. How long would he get? He knew some very well placed people in the Italian legal system who had connections with the organisation, but by no means all. There were some even now, who fought hard to stamp out the organisation. Everyone knew who he worked for. The Italian Government and the country itself couldn't be seen to be lenient in the eyes of the world on so obvious a murder on the streets of Milan. Salvatore could see no way out. He would have to be sure Anna and Lucia were taken care of.

He was thinking of her and there she was, watching him from the door. No lounging in a robe, sipping coffee today. Anna was wearing a floral dress, a beige leather belt at her waist. An ankle length loose cardigan with cape sleeves protected her from the cool Autumn morning. She looked tired and troubled. He stood up. Silently, she moved to him. They held each other in a brief but emotional embrace. Today, their lives would change forever.

They sat at the table. There was a feeling of other-worldliness; the beautifully manicured garden was transformed by moon and star-shine into a shadowy, surreal landscape. For all its shadows and darkness, somehow, there was sanctuary and calm in sitting somewhere without walls, beneath a ceiling of stars which stretched into infinity.

Anna held his hand across the table. She focussed her attention on him, eager for news, desperate for good news.

'I heard the phone.'

'It was Uncle.'

Anna couldn't bring herself to ask. Salvatore hesitated. She would be distressed but he couldn't delay telling her, there simply wasn't time.

'It's not good.'

She squeezed his hand. He held hers tightly and relayed Uncle's depressing news.

They sat without speaking, still holding hands. After thinking hard for a few moments, Anna gave up and shook her head.

'I can't think. I didn't sleep well.' She glanced at his coffee. 'I'll get a coffee.'

Anna left him in the garden. As she stepped into the kitchen, the phone rang again. She picked it up. Salvatore turned in his chair: he could see Anna through the open door. He saw the shocked expression on her face and heard the little gasp, then, 'Oh, I'm so sorry! Oh my goodness! Of course, yes. I'll tell him… such a shock. I'll come if I can, we've got some problems here. I won't burden you with them. Yes, yes. Thank you for letting us know. I'm so, so sorry. Good bye.'

Stunned, Anna walked slowly outside and sat down. Salvatore stared at her, concerned.

'What is it?'

Anna had been staring blankly at the table, trying to take in the news. 'It's your cousin, Nico.'

'Yes?'

'He's dead.'

'No! Oh NO!'

'You know his sister got married yesterday; we were invited, but you had too much work on.'

'Mm.'

'Well, after the wedding, he was taking some photographs. It seems he was involved in a hit and run. They think he was standing in the road taking a last picture of the wedding car as it drove away. They're not sure, he was alone.'

Salvatore shook his head slowly. 'It's unbelievable, he was only my age.'

'You grew up together.'

'Yes, we were very close.'

Salvatore rose and moved quickly into the living room. He returned holding a small framed photograph of himself and Nico. He sat and gazed at it. Anna stood behind him and placed her hands on his shoulders, looking over his head at the photograph.

He whispered. 'I can't believe it.'

'You look like brothers, apart from the scar on his chin and his poor ear.'

'Yes, people thought we *were* brothers. He got the scar on his face, the missing tooth and the scarred ear from a scooter accident. I was there. He was showing off. He spent a week in hospital, broke his arm too.' Salvatore smiled sadly. 'All us children were jealous because they made a fuss of him and he didn't have to go to school. Poor Nico! The family must be devastated.'

Anna had heard the story many times. She knew how close to Nico Salvatore had been. News like that to come on this day of all days.

Salvatore continued to stare at the picture. 'What a terrible day.' Abruptly, he straightened then stood up. The change was obvious.

Anna asked, 'What? What is it?'

'Don't know! Don't know... Maybe... Don't know. Could be too late. I've got to phone Uncle.'

He rushed into the house and disappeared into his office, shutting the door quickly, leaving Anna confused as to her husband's sudden change of mood.

Forty-five minutes later, Anna's confusion had company; Bruno was also at a loss to explain a mysterious call from Salvatore which, given the circumstances, didn't make much sense. Salvatore had sounded almost happy. What the hell was there to be happy about? The police would soon be hammering on his door. Bruno pondered on the brief, hurried conversation. All Salvatore had said, was, 'No time to explain. Pack a bag for two or three weeks. Get over here fast, we're going on a trip.'

What trip? Bruno didn't want to go on any trip. Bruno wanted to stay right here and assume his rightful place running Milan. However, what choice did he have?

He'd packed his case, made the short journey over to Salvatore's house and found it buzzing with activity.

Anna was packing Lucia's clothes, Salvatore was on the phone and Lucia was running in and out shouting, 'Holiday, holiday, holiday!' She was very excited to be woken when it was still dark. Anna had told her she was going on a surprise adventure to Grandmama's. It was to be a holiday for her, full of fun and surprises, which was true, as Grandmama and Grandpapa always spoilt her. Anna had helped her dress quickly. Lucia's expensive clothes were also practical for play but Lucia's own choice in jewellery was less practical. She wore fifteen necklaces and countless bracelets which, along with the necklaces, rattled as she dashed about. Her copious adornments prompted Anna to ask a question, 'Are you sure you need *all* your jewellery, Lucia?'

Lucia stopped short, tipped her head to one side and considered the question. Grown-up people could be so funny. They were very clever and knew so much but sometimes, she still needed to explain things to them. Mamma was looking at her but Papa seemed to be busy. She had better explain to both of them. 'Papa?'

Salvatore finished his call, although preoccupied and somewhat harassed, he bent down to bring his face level with hers. 'Yes?'

As Lucia patiently explained her reasoning to Salvatore and Anna, her bright little face shone a welcome light into their dark day. They thanked her with a hug and hastily continued with their urgent preparations. Her logic was faultless: if one necklace and bracelet looked pretty on her then obviously, all of them together would layer up the effect. She had patiently explained it all to her parents, who thought the idea charming. Bruno thought the child looked ridiculous. Lucia knew for certain that she looked magnificent.

Salvatore turned his attention to a bewildered Bruno who stood in the kitchen as the bejewelled comet in the shape of a child circled him.

'You packed your case?'

Bruno nodded, 'In the car.'

'Great. Throw mine in, will you? He pointed at the two large cases sitting near the front door.

Bruno shrugged, 'Sure. What's going on? Where are we going?' This is what he said. But what he thought was, *What? I'm a bellboy now? Put your own stinking case in the car. I should be giving* you *orders.* It was a habit Bruno had adopted of late, to help him deal with his mounting frustration with Salvatore.

Salvatore shook his head, 'No time,' then to Anna, 'All set?'

Anna clipped Lucia's case shut, 'Yes, she's packed, mine's in the bedroom.'

'Right, let's go.'

Salvatore collected Anna's case from the bedroom, picked up Lucia's and hurried out of the house. Bruno had finished stowing Salvatore's two cases and stood by his car, watching them. Salvatore placed Anna's case in the small boot of his beautiful Ferrari, he put Lucia's case in the passenger footwell and knelt down to hug his daughter. 'You have a lovely holiday, tell me all about it won't you?'

'Oh yes! We are going to do lots and lots and lots.'

Salvatore hugged her tight again.

Bruno glanced at his watch. W*hat was keeping the police?*

Salvatore stood up and lifted Lucia into the child seat fitted to the rear seat. He embraced his wife and pulled a brown envelope from his jacket pocket. 'It can't be helped.' Anna took the envelope and held it to her chest. She seemed very emotional and worried.

Bruno frowned, w*hat's happening?*

'Good bye Sal, you have the number, don't forget to call.'

'I won't, don't worry.'

She slid into his Ferrari, leaned back and clipped the seatbelt around Lucia, who waved madly at him. The peace of the garden was broken by the familiar snarl as the Ferrari's engine roared into life. Anna lost no time and quickly pulled away, moving smartly down the drive with Lucia still waving. The car turned onto the road and disappeared from view.

Salvatore stared at the empty drive for a moment, then turned to Bruno. 'Okay, let's go.'

'Are you going to tell me where?'

'We need to get out of here, Uncle says the police will be here this afternoon, perhaps earlier.'

Salvatore got quickly into Bruno's car. Bruno hesitated, the last thing in the world he wanted to do was help Salvatore escape but what choice did he have? He climbed behind the wheel.

It was still dark as they pulled out of the drive, Salvatore gave Bruno an address. 'First, we pick up Rifsky.'

Bruno glanced sharply at Salvatore, his solemn expression made more so by the shadows cast by the dashboard light. Bruno knew Rifsky, a Russian, who headed up the closest thing to a security force the organisation had. He was intelligent, followed orders well and was totally without conscience, excellent traits which the organisation fully utilised. He was usually found with his small team around the casinos, dealing efficiently with whatever came up. Bruno hadn't been aware he was in town. *Had he been brought in? And if so, why?*

It was an unlikely and unusual alliance. The organisation as a rule *never* employed Russians. Indeed, there had been considerable resistance to Rifsky's appointment. Surprisingly, it was Uncle whose voice had carried the day and as often happened, the vote. Uncle Q crossed paths with many of the rich and powerful. It seemed Rifsky had needed to escape Russia fast. He had a reputation for getting results and had used his many skills as a freelance operative. Those he had worked for in the past had mentioned to Q that Rifsky was a valuable asset and if the organisation didn't secure his services, someone else would. The organisation had money, the organisation was accustomed to the best. As far as surveillance and security were concerned, Rifsky *was* the best, so it followed that they should employ him.

Q had met Rifsky personally and after an interview, offered him the job. As often happened, Q's judgement had been proved sound. Rifsky, given free rein, had hand-picked a security force. Within a month, it had earned its keep and saved the organisation considerable expense rooting out corruption within the organisation and two schemes in the casinos. The con had gone undetected until Rifsky and his team put a glass over that particular casino and found it wanting. Some of the tables were rigged with the management taking a cut from a regular punter whose engineered good luck soon ran out.

In a quiet area a little out of the city, they found him sitting on a bench outside a small apartment. Picking up his case and a small bag which he slung over his shoulder, he moved toward the car. Rifsky was a compact, solid-looking character in his mid-thirties with short, fair hair. He had the disquieting habit of not blinking as much as was considered normal, often disconcerting those in his presence. Rifsky was a man who went with the flow of life. He was, nevertheless, careful what he said and everything he did was considered. Unlike Bruno, he was very aware of cause and effect.

Rifsky wasn't his real name: his surname was long and unpronounceable for anyone outside Russia. 'Rifsky' was close enough to his Christian name and easy to say. He was more than happy not to have his true identity made public knowledge because unsurprisingly, he'd made enemies. Acknowledging Bruno and Salvatore with a brief nod, he climbed into the back seat. He didn't know where they were going and didn't much care. He was well paid and money was all the explanation he needed.

Salvatore gave Bruno further directions but as far as Bruno could make out, the destination was in the middle of nowhere. Fields! He didn't want Rifsky to think Salvatore hadn't confided in him, he wanted to appear part of the upper management so asked no questions.

It was an hour or so later, when they turned into a track leading to a farm. Salvatore had been directing Bruno with the aid of a small map. The sky was brightening and a crack of gold light stretched across the horizon, although, as yet, the sun itself wasn't high enough to be visible. They got out, stretching stiff limbs and surveyed the fields of smooth grass surrounding them, with some scattered sheep grazing. In the distance a farmhouse could be seen. Beyond the fields, the land rose gently.

Rifsky and Bruno looked about; apart from the sheep they were alone.

Salvatore checked his watch, 'We made good time'.

Exasperated beyond endurance, Bruno raised both arms and let them drop to his sides. Rifsky carefully studied the fields; there appeared to be nothing to worry about. To be sure, he pulled a pair of compact but powerful binoculars from his shoulder bag, turned very, very slowly on his heels and conducted two further sweeps. The farmhouse was the only sign of human presence and that was at least half a mile away. A fire was burning close to the farmhouse and a column of blue grey smoke rose gently into the cloudless sky which grew brighter with every passing moment. It had all the promise of a beautiful, clear Autumn day.

Satisfied with his search, Rifsky got back into the car and leaning his head back on the headrest, closed his eyes.

Salvatore stretched his legs and wandered around the field. Bruno watched him, the tension rising. Finally, he could stand it no longer and went after him. 'Sal, are you going to tell me what the hell I am doing, standing in the middle of nowhere, in a field of *sheep*?'

Salvatore opened his mouth to explain but abruptly turned and looked up at the sky. The faint sound of an engine could be heard. The sun had risen over the horizon and out of the pale blue a tiny dot quickly transformed into a small aeroplane. As they watched, its wings gave two tilts before levelling and its lights flashed.

'He's seen us. Let's get the cases.'

'What about my car?'

'You see the farmhouse? They've been told to collect it and store it in the barn. They've been paid enough not to ask questions. Leave the keys in the ignition.'

Bruno hurried after Salvatore, who was walking briskly back to the car. Rifsky had heard the plane, seen the wing dip and was already standing next to the car with the cases at his feet. He watched the machine circle then line up for the descent into the field. It dropped neatly onto the grass. With a landing speed of around eighty knots it had been chosen for that very purpose, requiring a landing strip of less than two thousand feet. It taxied to the car, then turned slightly away before coming to rest; the pilot kept the engine ticking over as the cases were stowed. His three passengers strapped in for the take off, the pilot pointed to some headsets and they all slipped them on. Rifsky sat in the front with the pilot, Salvatore and Bruno to the rear. The pilot lost no time, the engine note rose and the aircraft began to move. It soon accelerated across the grass, the rumble of its wheels ceased and Bruno felt his stomach lurch as the plane lifted.

Bruno looked out of the window as the plane banked. Already, two people from the farmhouse were making for his car, having seen the plane.

Salvatore spoke to the pilot. 'How low can you fly?'

'Low enough,' came the answer. Salvatore smiled, Rifsky looked over but didn't ask any questions. The pilot continued, 'If we hug the contours of the land and on a clear day it shouldn't be a problem, we'll be below radar. To follow the nap of the land will mean a less than smooth flight, I'm afraid.'

Rifsky nodded and smiled. He knew more about getting in and out of countries undetected than anyone. He was aware that as long as the plane could fly below a hundred feet or through valleys and stayed away from military airspace, they should remain invisible. From time to time, he leaned forward to eye the altimeter, but left the flying to the pilot. Rifsky enjoyed flying.

Bruno *hated* flying. The prospect of dipping and diving over hills and valleys filled him with dread. Not only did he suffer from motion sickness, he was frightened of flying and avoided even commercial flights. This *was* a nightmare! He hated Salvatore even more for putting him through it.

Rifsky was considering the security aspects. He didn't know the full story but Salvatore and Bruno were clearly on a covert trip. He reasoned it prudent to ask some questions, if they were trying to avoid radar detection, the aircraft identification transponder must be switched off.

'Transponder is off?' He asked.

'Yes.' The pilot tapped the switch.

Rifsky studied the pilot, who appeared relaxed, even happy, as he cleared some trees and flew low over a field and small river.

'Ex-military?'

Without looking at Rifsky, he nodded then addressed everyone. 'Thank you for the fire, the smoke made it easy to judge the wind direction. It wasn't really necessary, we are very fortunate with the weather. The Alps shouldn't pose a problem.'

Bruno's tone was aggressive, with a hint of panic. 'Alps?'

'Yes, no need to go around, we can fly through.'

Rifsky anticipated an interesting experience. Salvatore was pleased they would save time. Bruno was horrified. 'Is that possible in this small plane?'

'Oh yes, but only if the weather is perfect; I've done it a number of times. We can certainly fly through the mountains, following roads and crossing lakes. It's very beautiful. Weaving through the mountains takes longer than a commercial, high altitude flight, of course.'

The plane cruised at approximately 174 knots, tracking the contours of the land, often flying between the towering peaks.

The pilot spoke again. 'I've had a good breakfast but you'll find some sandwiches and rolls in a bag behind you if you're hungry.'

Salvatore looked around and picked up a brown paper carrier bag containing egg salad rolls and a flask of coffee. Rifsky turned in his seat, 'I'm hungry.' He reached out and took his food.

While Rifsky munched happily, Salvatore offered Bruno a roll. 'No!' Even Bruno realised he'd responded more sharply than he'd meant to. He added curtly, 'Thank you,' turned away and looked grimly out of the window as the smell of egg swirled nauseatingly around him.

Unfortunately the crossing, although spectacular, was lost on Bruno, who stared wide-eyed at the razor-sharp ridges as the plane swooped over and through the freezing landscape. Salvatore was preoccupied with his own worries about the days to follow. Only Rifsky and the pilot took pleasure in the experience.

PART ONE

CHAPTER 7
SOUTH EAST LONDON
TUESDAY, 7.10AM

Vicky opened her eyes and looked at Ron sleeping beside her. She stretched, then reached across and gently tousled his untidy hair. He breathed slowly and evenly. She had hoped the early night would help him to relax. She certainly felt good: Ron was a considerate lover. She yawned and stretched again, this time holding the stretch for two or three seconds before relaxing. Her movement stirred him; one eye opened, then shut, then opened again. Then the other. Her blurred face slid into focus.

'Morning.' It was a croak. He sat up, took a sip of water and tried again. 'Good morning.' Remembering the night before, he grinned and kissed her.

She knew what he was thinking and smiled back. 'We'd better get some breakfast.' After a moment, she added impishly, 'To build your strength up.'

He laughed then yawned and shut his eyes, just for a moment. Vicky watched him. Ron was hopeless in the morning and drifted back to sleep very easily. It amused her that, unlike most people who woke only once, Ron would wake up, drift off, wake up and drift off. Sometimes, if his eyes were shut, he would fall asleep while still talking to her. This morning was no different. As she watched, he managed to get one foot out of bed to explore the floor for his slippers. He didn't find them, stopped searching and fell asleep.

Somehow, he found himself standing by the fridge. The door was open and a cold draught played on his leg. 'Why's the fridge door open?'

'What?' She laughed at him.

He opened his eyes, the fridge vanished and he found himself looking at the bedroom wall with one cold leg out of bed and his head on the pillow. 'I said... em... where's my slippers?' He swung the other leg out of bed and sat on the edge.

She grinned at his back. 'No you didn't, you were dreaming about the fridge.'

'Fridge?' His eyes wandered around the bedroom. 'What fridge?'

Vicky got up. No point trying to have a conversation with him before he had his coffee. She loved him so much. He did make her laugh.

After showering they sat with coffee and toast in the living room. Vicky held a coffee in one hand and stroked their cat, Finbar, with the other. Ron asked what her plans were for the day.

'We aren't needed today. The Director is working with the set people and planning camera angles. No make-up. Jane and I are going horse riding this afternoon. What are you up to?'

'Em, I've got that talk at the library coming up. I don't mind supporting them, but I only really agreed because I don't have a storyline to work on.'

'Yes, I was surprised when you said you were giving a talk. I thought you hated talking in public.'

'I do. The publishing house is always asking me to give talks and book signings. I've usually made excuses.'

'Why did you agree to this one?'

'One of those Women's Institute gang leaders cornered me in the library. She didn't give me much choice.'

Vicky laughed. 'I don't think WI groups have gang leaders, exactly.'

'You didn't meet her! She was quite intimidating. I think I would have given her my wallet too if she'd told me to. So I'd better work on what I'm going to say. I wonder what the audience will be like.'

'It will do you good to work on something else.'

'Yes.' He shrugged. 'Might be fun, not done anything like this before. You will come, won't you?'

'Of course I will. I'll be at the back, cheering.'

'Good. To be honest, I'm a bit nervous.'

'You'll be fine.'

'Mmm.' He chewed his toast thoughtfully. 'So that's our plan for today settled, anyway.'

PART ONE

CHAPTER 8
LIGHT AIRCRAFT
TUESDAY, 8AM

Bruno was relieved to leave the Alps behind him. Eventually, the plane flew towards France, skirting Geneva, keeping south of Paris and its busy airspace. Finally, they circled a similar field - minus the sheep - outside a small town. As the plane began the second circuit, Bruno, anxious to be on the ground, became impatient. 'Are we going down or not?'

The pilot answered calmly. 'I'm judging the wind direction.'

Still irritated, Bruno was abrupt. 'How? By flying in circles?'

The pilot ignored Bruno's rudeness. 'Well, you can do it watching cloud shadows but of course, there are none today. Or swirls of crops like wheat.' He laughed. 'That doesn't help us in Autumn.' Before Bruno could erupt, he continued, enjoying his subject. 'The tops of that line of evergreen trees are motionless. This weather window has been excellent for this time of year. No rain lately either so the grass won't be a problem.'

'Is landing on grass a problem?' Bruno couldn't keep the note of alarm from his voice. This amused Rifsky.

'No, as long as it's free of holes and animals. Rain would have been a worry but we're fine.' As he spoke, the pilot had lined up for his final approach, he throttled back and dropped smoothly into the field without incident.

They were met by a private car, driven to the coast and delivered to a small private jetty. The bags and their owners were efficiently transferred to a sizeable inflatable, which lost no time in powering out to a super yacht.

The famous Italian ship-builder Fincantieri had constructed a yacht called the *Destriero*, built to break records, which it did due to its phenomenal sixty-six knot top speed. This had not gone unnoticed by the organisation, which enjoyed the best the world had to offer. It had interests in other ship builders and commissioned a fast super-yacht of its own which shared much of the *Destriero*'s technology. Its top speed was significantly reduced, owing to the additional weight of the luxury fit-out, but for its size it was *very* fast. It was powered by combined diesel, electric and gas turbine engines, CODAG for short. The massive engines were capable of thrusting the yacht through the water at surprising velocity but they where thirsty and extra fuel had been loaded for the trip.

As soon as the passengers were safely aboard and the inflatable secured astern by electric winches, the anchor was raised. The engines fired and the note changed as the Captain opened the throttle. Holding the ship at half speed, the engine temperature climbed, all the gauges looked good. He increased to full power, they would be running at maximum for hours, sacrificing a smooth passage and a comforting hum to a bumpy, choppy ride and a monotonous deep growl. The Captain maintained a careful watch on the dials, aware that the ship was at its limit. He wasn't anticipating any problems as the machine was maintained and tuned to a level that only almost limitless funds could achieve.

Trouble was heading to England fast: it was doing it in style, but it was coming all the same.

The cruiser was called *The Leonardo,* so named because of the genius of its engineering and the artistic splendour of the fit out. Italy knows a thing or two about beautiful lines. The ship was a joy to behold, inviting the eye to glide along its hull, which could slice through the water like a scalpel.

Below deck, the ship was elegant and immaculate, smelling of furniture polish and new carpet. Bruno was feeling uncomfortable, a feeling which quickly escalated as he pealed off his jacket and threw it on a sofa, he felt hot and sick. He knew Salvatore had been aboard *The Leonardo* before, a party six months ago and although Bruno had been invited, he had made an excuse; he hated the water more than flying, 'This ship has bedrooms, doesn't it?' Bruno's tone was borderline aggressive.

Salvatore pointed to a door. 'Down that corridor there are several, help yourself.'

Aware he had been abrupt, Bruno tried to sound casual, 'I may as well lie down.'

Salvatore nodded. Rifsky grinned, 'I think you should.'

Bruno turned on him and snapped, 'I'm tired, it was an early start.'

'You're also green.'

Bruno glared at him but said no more.

Salvatore wasn't smiling but neither did he look unhappy. Bruno didn't feel well, but to admit seasickness was somehow an admission of weakness. He turned and left the cabin, closing the beautifully crafted hardwood door with considerably more force than it required. Rifsky grinned at Salvatore.

Bruno opened the first door he came to and saw a bed, he quickly entered the cabin. Not only did Bruno hate the sea, he hated Rifsky and he *really* hated Salvatore. The ships engines pulsed relentlessly, the drone thundering on. Bruno felt truly ill. He stood swaying with one hand gripping the door handle for support. There was a decision to make, lay down or run to the bathroom and throw up. His stomach decided the matter and he moved as fast as he could to the bathroom. The exact details of what went on behind the bathroom door are not a subject to dwell on: suffice to say the experience was volcanic. After several gut-wrenching minutes, the door slowly opened and an almost transparent version of the man who had entered, emerged, looking white and sweaty. Feeling light-headed, he managed to climb onto the bed, too ill to undress. He lay staring at the ceiling with glassy eyes as waves of dizzy nausea swept over him. In an attempt to ease the sickness and the spinning room, he tried to focus his mind. Bruno began to picture various scenarios, where both Rifsky and Salvatore suffered and got what they deserved. But it was no good, he needed all his strength to simply exist. It was impossible to think, every panting breath a tiny victory. It was a triumph he hadn't passed out or thrown up again. It was unbelievable that something as simple and apparently harmless as the movement of a boat on water could produce such incapacity in a strong young man. Bruno could not have risen from the bed if his life depended on it. The magnitude of the sickness was so great that the fear of death itself was diminished, and possibly preferable to this. Far too ill to think, all that remained was to cling to the bed as it swayed, rose and fell. Each time it sank, he felt he simply couldn't stand it. Then, it did it again, and again, and again. His head swam. Bruno would have given all he possessed if only he could be still. The ship pounded on mercilessly. With each queasy stomach-churning clench he *hated* Salvatore more. Killing him would not be enough, he needed to truly suffer.

Out in the main cabin, Salvatore gestured to Rifsky to sit with him at the far end, well away from the door leading to Bruno's cabin. Salvatore spoke quietly, although the drone of the engines wouldn't have allowed his words to carry far.

'Rifsky, you are head of security, I know you'll be vigilant.' Salvatore hesitated, then added, 'Threats sometimes come from unexpected directions.' His eyes moved to the door then back to Rifsky.

Rifsky glanced at the door, 'I'll be watching out for you.'

It wasn't healthy to openly accuse key members of the organisation. Salvatore didn't trust Rifsky totally. The man's past was what could charitably be called chequered. A very apt description. Light and dark. The light parts were general knowledge. Rifsky was a Russian, who had, on occasion, worked for the KGB. Exactly what he did for them was dark. The full story of why he couldn't return to Russia was also shadowy. There was some speculation he had murdered his superior, who hadn't treated Rifsky with the respect he felt was his due. No one knew where this rumour had started or if it was true. It was known that Rifsky knew a great deal about surveillance; he was an expert on the technical hardware. He was also very good at spotting trouble. He knew instinctively which people needed watching: even before Salvatore had spoken, Rifsky had concerns regarding Bruno. The jealousy and anger Bruno felt for Salvatore was something he was well aware of. Rifsky was unsure if Bruno would have the courage to act and he was surprised Salvatore had picked up on it. But, he agreed that Bruno was… what was the term they had used in Russia? Oh yes, *someone of interest*.

He had been turning this over in his mind when suddenly, he became aware that Salvatore was still watching him, probably wondering why he was grinning.

'Poor Bruno, he's not a natural sailor.'

Salvatore almost smiled, then looked out of the porthole at the rocking horizon. *The Leonardo* ploughed on, leaving a foaming V in its wake.

Rifsky reflected on the security aspects of the voyage, there seemed to be little to be concerned about. By the look of him, Bruno was no threat to anyone at present, not unless he fainted and landed on someone. Rifsky smiled at his private joke. He had looked carefully at the Captain, an elderly man with hair greying at the temples. When they'd boarded, the Captain had welcomed them and outlined the vessel's course. His handling of the ship showed he was clearly experienced. The organisation, no doubt, would not have allowed anyone but the best to pilot their eye-wateringly expensive new toy. Rifsky had placed him firmly in the 'no threat' column. He had considered the young man who had transferred them to the ship in the inflatable but found nothing there to worry him. The youth had appeared eager to please and Rifsky had the impression he lacked confidence. The young man frequently looked to the Captain for instructions. However, Rifsky noted that he seemed adept at handling and securing the inflatable and seemed familiar with the ship. No, Rifsky instinctively felt no danger there, either. He could relax on this voyage, nothing to do, nothing to worry about. His worry would begin as they approached land.

Salvatore climbed the steps to the bridge, treading carefully as the ship rode the huge swells. He found the young man looking at charts and the Captain sitting at the controls.

'How's progress, Captain?'

'We're doing well, considering the conditions. Very big swells, apologies for the rough trip. Are you all well? This kind of sea can cause a lot of sea sickness, you know?'

'I didn't know, but one of my colleagues does.'

The Captain laid his hand on the throttle. 'Do you want a slower, smoother crossing?'

'No, I want to get over as fast as possible. The less time we spend out here, the better.'

'Are you sure? We *will* be on radar, you understand? Travelling fast won't help us be less conspicuous.'

'I know. I'm merely anxious to be across fast and have it done. I feel vulnerable out here. How exactly will we get ashore?'

'We'll keep the ship moving and use the inflatable; it's not without risk but it's worked before.'

Salvatore nodded.

The Captain lifted his hand, his trained eye scanning the gauges: oil pressure good, fuel good; running a little hot but acceptable, revs high, just below the maximum. *The Leonardo* thundered on. The Captain checked the heading: all correct.

Content, Salvatore raised a hand, 'I'll leave you to it, Captain.' He turned and went below.

Rifsky was leafing happily through some magazines he'd found. Salvatore watched the sea and thought of Anna and Lucia. He removed his phone from his jacket and held it. Should he phone her? Anna was expecting a call, but when he had arrived safely, not *en route*. Startled, Salvatore looked up. Rifsky was standing very close, 'I wouldn't advise making calls.'

'No?'

'I thought you had both left your phones in Milan. Is Bruno carrying his?'

Salvatore glanced at Bruno's disregarded jacket on the sofa. 'I don't know, probably.'

Rifsky shook his head, 'If you're trying to hide, using phones is a *very* bad idea. Mobiles aren't secure; anyone with a scanner can listen in, or find you.'

Salvatore used technology but didn't understand it. He looked at the phone in his hand. 'How can someone find me?'

Rifsky smiled. 'It's very simple, they take a bearing on the direction of the signal, then move to a new location, take another bearing and where they cross is where the phone is operating.'

Salvatore put down the phone. 'And anyone can get one of those scanners and eavesdrop?'

'Yes, police, radio hams, school kids.'

The idea of Bruno having a phone that could give away their location didn't sit well. He could pretend it was an accident. 'Can you fix a phone so it can't give away a location?'

Rifsky nodded.

'Without tools? Here on the ship?'

'Easy.'

Salvatore got to his feet and crossed to the sofa. A quick search produced Bruno's mobile, which he handed to Rifsky. 'Fix it so Bruno can't make any calls or switch it on.'

'No problem.' Rifsky examined the phone, smiled at Salvatore, opened a window and dropped the phone overboard. 'It's neutralised.'

Salvatore laughed, which was unexpected, he'd believed it would be a long time before he would laugh again. He picked up his own phone. Rifsky opened the window again and this time, Salvatore threw it over the side. It was stupid even to think about making a call on his own phone, he could see that. He was glad to have his security chief along for the trip.

By lunchtime, *The Leonardo* was powering along off the coast of Cornwall. The Captain explained that the ship had charted a gentle arc, gradually reducing speed. It was risky but the inflatable, close to the shoreline might not be detected in the heavy swell and if *The Leonardo* didn't stop in the water, it wouldn't attract too much interest. The electric winches were once again put to work and the inflatable was lowered carefully into the sea. The young mariner once again piloted the dinghy.   It was a fast, bumpy trip. Salvatore, Bruno and Rifsky held tight to the rope encircling the edge of the inflatable as it bounced toward the deserted stretch of beach. At the clifftop, a man watched the approach. Quickly, he turned and made his way down the cliff path and crunched over the shingle to the water's edge to meet the boat.

Salvatore had been relieved to reach England, but as he watched Rifsky, he began to sense a slowly rising anxiety. Rifsky had been scanning the horizon and sky constantly for some time. There didn't appear to be anything to worry about but nevertheless, Rifsky appeared to be on full alert. Bruno hadn't noticed as Bruno was concerned only about Bruno. He was longing to plant his feet on something solid. However, even reaching the much-anticipated shore would not go well for him. It appeared as if Bruno's hatred of the sea was reciprocated. There was much swearing as Bruno got his beautiful Italian leather shoes wet.

The party was soon standing on the shingle with their luggage. The young man rowed to deeper water and once more started the outboard motor; he would need to run at full throttle to catch up with *The Leonardo*. The man on the beach collected Salvatore's bags and led the group up the slope toward a waiting car, a Mercedes, complete with tinted windows. As they walked, Salvatore dropped back, leaving Bruno and the driver in the lead. He walked alongside Rifsky, who still glanced constantly around him, as if expecting attackers to leap from behind the scrubby bushes which flanked the steep track.

'Is everything okay?'

Rifsky didn't look at him, keeping his attention fixed on their surroundings. Occasionally, he glanced up at the sky. 'Seems to be. We've been very lucky so far.'

Salvatore waited for more.

Rifsky risked a quick glance at him and gave a flash of a smile. 'They're looking for me more than you.'

Salvatore wasn't sure how to react. Rifsky continued, 'There will be air patrols watching the coast, and submarine patrols. It's standard. They're interested in what the Russians are up to. It seems we have slipped through, we have been very lucky.'

'You didn't say anything before.'

They were close to the car now. Rifsky smiled. 'You pay *me* to worry about security.'

Rifsky sat with the driver, Bruno and Salvatore in the rear. They set off quickly: destination, London.

Along the A30 through Cornwall and into Devon, as they skirted the edge of Dartmoor, its bleak rugged beauty went unnoticed. The car motored on and joined the A303. Stonehenge earned a 'Hm' from Bruno, who expected it to be larger. The driver kept strictly to the speed limits, but once they joined the M3, the speedometer rarely dropped below seventy miles an hour. The M25 London ring road was predictably slow-going. Finally, the car threaded its way through the congested streets of South East London.

Just before they reached their destination, they passed *The Blue Parrot*. Salvatore glanced up at the building and admired the elegant proportions and grandeur. Two streets later they had arrived. The driver handed Salvatore the key to the house and helped them in with their bags. He also handed Salvatore an additional bag. 'I was told to give you this.' He held a large, expensive-looking leather bag, then reached into his jacket. Rifsky tensed and watched him very carefully. The driver produced a fat envelope and handed it over, blissfully unaware of how dangerous, possibly suicidal, it was for a stranger to execute such a movement so quickly in the company of Rifsky. The envelope was simply addressed, *S from Q.* Salvatore took both envelope and bag.

The driver returned to the car and it smoothly surged away out of the quiet square to rejoin London's busy traffic.

The house was a three storey Georgian terrace; an elegant building capable of stirring the hearts of both architects and interior designers, with its proportion and opulent decoration. After closing the original heavy front door, which was topped with a beautiful period glass fanlight, the three found themselves in a spacious hall with a black and white marble chequerboard floor. Overhead, a crystal chandelier glittered with tiny rainbows of light.

The organisation had the enviable problem of what to do with a vast income. People like Salvatore bought property worldwide and the rents generated even more cash. This particular house had recently been fully renovated and was already worth considerably more than the organisation had paid for it.

PART ONE

CHAPTER 9
A RIDING SCHOOL IN KENT
TUESDAY, LATE AFTERNOON

While Salvatore, Bruno and Rifsky unpacked after their long journey, a few miles away Vicky and Jane were enjoying a far more relaxed day.

From South East London, it's a short drive to the Kent countryside. The girls had motored to a riding school Jane knew well. She had suggested the trip after discovering Vicky had ridden as a child in Devon. They had shared a lovely afternoon. A small group of riders had ambled from the yard and enjoyed themselves in the wooded area close to the school, trotting and cantering along the bridle paths that weaved through the trees. The season had used every colour in its rich palette to paint the trees in variations of gold, crimson and deep orange, the sunlight causing them to glow as if lit from within.

Although it had been a while, Vicky was pleased to find she felt comfortable back in the saddle. Her horse was called Kalifa and Vicky had found her responsive and easy to handle. They had even sailed over a few fallen logs. The highlight had been a fast gallop through the trees where fallen leaves had deadened the beat of Kalifa's hooves. Vicky had looked over the nodding head at the trees as they hurtled silently towards her. There was almost no sound except the rush of cold air which gave her the impression that she was flying. Strangely enough, this was partly true. At full gallop, there is a moment called the moment of suspension when all four feet leave the ground.

The hour had passed quickly. The girls returned to the school and the horses were handed back to the waiting staff. In no rush to leave, Jane and Vicky wandered to a quiet spot to watch the sunset.

The girls sat in companionable silence on straw bales and enjoyed the scene. Khan, a strong, steady old fellow, dropped his head over the half door to take a good look at Jane and Vicky. Sensing the movement, Jane turned and smiled at him. 'Hello Khan.' He leaned close, his soft lips nuzzling her hair. She reached up and stroked his cheek. Jane could see tiny images of both herself and Vicky reflected in the shining, dark brown eye turned to her.

'No sugar, I'm afraid. Oh, that reminds me.' She turned away from the horse, who moved back to his feed bin to make certain he hadn't missed any. Jane leaned sideways to allow better access to the dark depths of her quilted jacket. 'Ah, thought so. Want some choccie?'

Vicky answered enthusiastically. 'Ooo, please.'

Jane snapped the bar in half and they sat quietly, watching the regular staff down in the yard beginning the early evening routine. The water buckets were being filled for the last time that day. Jane and Vicky looked over the low roofs of the boxes at the sky. It was indeed a wondrous light show. Minute by minute it changed. Currently, the light was a golden orange, it caught the edges of the clouds, which ranged from blue grey to bright orange. Some clouds were almost blinding on their torn paper-white edges. There was a comfortable feeling about a riding school in the mellow, late afternoon sun.

'It's lovely here.' Vicky whispered.

Jane breathed in deeply then exhaled slowly, dropping her shoulders at the same time. 'I do love it here, it's so… uncomplicated.'

A riding school in the Autumn has many fragrances, far more subtle than most people would imagine. The day was unusually varied in temperature. Among the dips and hollows of the shadowy woods, pockets of cold air clung to the damp earth. The school was elevated slightly and in full sun it was surprisingly warm, especially out of the wind. An English Autumn is one of the most changeable of seasons; in one week it can be frosty, foggy, clear and bright or cold and wet. The warmth had heated the silver-grey wood on the doors and walls of the old stables. There was a smell of sweet chaff. Occasionally, a light whisper of air would bring the scent from the sugar beet shed, where the staff soaked the bags of sugar beet in an enormous old bath. This was added to the evening feed. Some saddles and bridles hung over the low wooden wall, which separated the line of boxes from the indoor menage, the tack smelt faintly of warm leather and saddle soap. All these things mingled with the scents from the nearby woods, a cool, earthy note of fallen leaves.

Jane turned her face to the enormous sky. The golden hue was beginning to change to a rosy blush as the Autumn sun touched the horizon. Each moment was like a small gift of light.

Vicky broke the silence. 'I think Ron's growing more odd as the days go by, I found him in the kitchen worrying that the light in the fridge isn't going off.'

Jane laughed. 'He's not odd, he's artistic. He's supposed to be like that. Talking of artistic, you're doing brilliantly with cuts and bruises.'

'Thank you for helping me, Jane.'

'You don't have to keep thanking me, Vicky.'

'I know, but I'm so grateful. After losing my sister, I couldn't go back to an office. I needed a new start, a challenge.'

'You're doing really well. Maggie is impressed.'

Vicky had never explained exactly how she had lost her sister and Jane, being a very close friend, had never asked. In the same way, Vicky didn't like to ask direct questions about Jane's feelings for Shades. But she was worried, for beneath the bubbly veneer, Jane was a sensitive soul. Vicky was concerned Jane would be hurt. She thought it might be safe to approach the subject and see if Jane took it further. With this in mind, while looking at the sky, she observed casually, 'You're spending a lot of time at *The Blue Parrot* lately.'

Talk of the club brought Shades to mind. Jane looked down at the dusty ground.

Vicky glanced sideways. 'Are you alright?'

'No, no I'm not. It's Shades. Do you know, I really love him.'

Vicky smiled, but it faded quickly as she caught the troubled expression on Jane's face.

'I think we're becoming close, then he makes some silly joke and seems to pull back. Of course, I don't help, I tease him sometimes. I get frustrated, I just want a reaction.'

Vicky squeezed Jane's hand but remained silent and let her talk.

'He makes me laugh, I love it when he quotes lines from old films and drops them into the conversation, then I guess which film. But sometimes, I catch him looking so sad. I'm sure there's something on his mind, but he won't let me in. I wish we could be like you and Ron. He loves you to bits and doesn't care who knows.' She stopped and gazed at the changing light show. The horizon was now peachy orange, the few scattered clouds lit from beneath, creating a palette of colour from pink to pale mauve, the top edges shifting to smokey blue and slate grey.

Vicky hesitated for a moment, then took the plunge. 'Look Jane, I wonder if it may be an idea to ask him straight, "is this going anywhere?" I'll be honest, I'm worried about you.'

'I know that's what I should do, but I'm a coward. What if I don't get the answer I want?'

Vicky moved closer and put her arm around Jane's shoulder. Jane moved her head toward Vicky and rested it against hers. The sky began to lose colour, as the sun was now below the horizon. The warm hues cooled quickly. Moments later, the clouds were merely a dull grey against the pale blue of the sky. Jane shivered.

Vicky pulled away slightly and turned to look at her. 'Are you cold?'

Jane didn't answer, her face was now partly in shadow and Vicky couldn't read her expression clearly. She was beginning to wonder if for some reason Jane hadn't heard and was on the brink of repeating the question, when Jane spoke. Her voice was quiet and lacked the usual energy. 'You're not the only one who has disturbing dreams. I think mine may be more like…' She didn't want to say the word, so she decided to simply tell the story and let Vicky make up her own mind.

'When I was a little girl, a small school bus ran through a few of the villages and collected us. I would stand at the bus stop, holding my mum's hand.'

'How old were you?' Vicky asked.

'Only about seven. One morning, I didn't want to get on the bus, I'd had a nightmare. I dreamt all my friends on the bus were screaming and it was dark. The dream was so real I woke up crying and shaking. I put one foot on the step of the bus that morning and stopped. I told my mum I didn't feel well. She knew I loved school. I must have looked pale because she took me home.' Jane was silent then very quietly, she continued with the story, 'There was an accident, the bus crashed. They didn't tell me the details, but one little girl was killed.'

Vicky opened her mouth. 'Wow,' she breathed.

'Nothing like that's ever happened again and I look back on it as a coincidence that was lucky for me.' Jane bit her lip. Vicky knew there was more to come and waited.

'A couple of days ago, I woke up crying. I dreamt Shades was dead. I was standing looking down at him and he was covered in blood.' She swallowed, reliving the moment as she told the story. 'Even after I woke up, it, sort of… followed me. It seemed so real.'

Vicky was at a loss for what to say. She moved close again, put her arm around Jane and hugged her tight. Jane patted Vicky's leg. 'Don't take any notice of me. I'm not myself.' She attempted a smile; Vicky's heart went out to her. Jane was clearly troubled, her feelings for Shades ran deep. Vicky wasn't sure she believed in premonitions. Perhaps seeing Shades dead was a subconscious way of representing loss. Not the loss of a life, but of a relationship that she feared would die. She wasn't sure, but one thing was certain, her friend was very unhappy. Why couldn't Shades let her get close? Jane was a wonderful young woman; kind, clever and funny. What the hell was wrong with him? Vicky found herself wanting to give Shades a shake and a good talking to. The sensible thing was to leave it to them.

That's what Ron would say, but... perhaps... she needed to give this further thought.

Jane drove Vicky home to the flat and headed home herself. She felt a little better having confided in Vicky, who felt worse now her fears had been confirmed. Could she do anything? Should she do anything?

Ron was in the living room, sitting on a sofa with a jam sandwich.

Vicky called from the hall. 'Home!'

'Hello, did you have a good time?'

She walked into the living room. 'It was lovely. Seriously worried about Jane and Shades, though...' She stopped short and asked. 'What are you doing with that sandwich?'

While Vicky had been talking, Ron had taken one slice of bread and jam and was dropping it vertically onto his plate, then writing something on his pad. He looked up.

'It's science.'

'Is it?' She didn't sound convinced.

'Yes. I'm wondering if success with my writing is a matter of luck. It could be I'm having an unlucky streak. You remember before I became a writer, I made a living designing boardgames? I know a thing or two about chance and probability. This shouldn't happen, it proves I'm unlucky, watch!' He dropped his bread and jam, which flopped onto the plate. 'Do you know it's landed jam side down seventeen times out of twenty? What does that tell you?'

'…'

Finally, she found her voice. 'It lands jam side down because the jam and butter are heavier on that side. Your experiment proves beyond doubt that one, you have to find a project, two, you have to get out more and three, you're cracked in the head.'

'Mmm, well, it's a theory. I think I can only fully agree with number one.' He gave up the experiment, reconstructed his sandwich and took a big bite.

Vicky raised the riding crop she was holding. He laughed. She shook her head and walked off to the bathroom, calling over her shoulder, 'I'm off to have a shower and change.'

As Ron stood up, he called out, 'I'll get you a sandwich and put the kettle on, unless you fancy a glass of wine. We've got a very nice Italian red.'

At the same moment, not far away, Bruno put down the bottle of red wine he was holding. 'No wonder we export this crap, it's only good enough for the English.'

Rifsky was channel-hopping; he turned down the TV volume. 'What?'

'Nothing, this wine's crap.'

Rifsky lifted his glass. 'This is good.'

Bruno scowled. 'I feel like wine.'

Rifsky shrugged and sipped his vodka, his eyes wandering back to the TV.

Bruno glanced up at the ceiling. 'What's he doing up there?'

Shrugging again, Rifsky suspended his channel-hopping. Somebody threw a man through a window and two policemen were shot. He smiled, put down the remote control and settled back to watch, putting his hands behind his head and kicking his chair into a reclined position.

Bruno was irritated by Rifsky's easygoing, relaxed attitude. He was especially annoyed that Salvatore hadn't told him what was going on. He should be kept informed! Who did the desk-bound little shit think he was? He glanced at Rifsky, who was smiling at the TV. He looked happy. Bruno scowled thoughtfully once again at the ceiling. Sal had seemed almost happy. Bruno's frown deepened. Why? Sal should be worried, but he wasn't. Sal should be behind bars, but he wasn't. He, Bruno, should be behind Salvatore's desk, running things. But HE WASN'T! He stood up, unable to sit quietly, and moved restlessly around the room. Misery loves company and Rifsky was no company. Bruno wanted to shout at someone. A thought struck him; he spun round, 'You're supposed to be the security man. Someone's stolen my phone.'

Without taking his eyes from the TV, Rifsky answered calmly. 'It's not stolen, it's neutralised for security reasons.'

'Well, I want it back!'

'Can't. Dropped it in the ocean.'

Bruno took a step towards him. 'You destroyed my phone without my permission!'

'You weren't in any condition for discussions. We threw Salvatore's overboard too.' Rifsky stopped watching his film and looked Bruno in the eye. 'We don't want anyone switching on a phone and giving our location away accidentally, do we?'

Bruno was angry but didn't know how to respond, so he turned away quickly and stood by the glass door, glaring into the garden. If he had the chance, Rifsky would get his comeuppance, along with Salvatore.

Meanwhile, upstairs in the bedroom, the man himself was deep in conversation with Anna. 'We're safe in London. How did it go at your end?'

'I arrived no problem, Uncle was already here. The family are very upset, he's talking to them, I think they will help. He said to tell you to sit tight. He's having some trouble contacting Dr Linsky, but he said not to worry, it's only a matter of time.'

'Did you hand over the car and the envelope?'

'Yes, it's a shame.'

Salvatore was philosophical. 'Can't be helped. Lucia's at your Mumma's?'

'Yes, being spoilt. I think they were making cakes today. She's probably asleep by now.'

'I'll phone tomorrow morning, Anna. Give Uncle my thanks, and tell the family I'm *so* sorry to intrude with our problems.'

'I will. Love you.'

'Love you too.'

That evening, Vicky and Ron sat in their living room. Vicky had showered but decided not to dress and snuggled in a thick bathrobe on a sofa. She ate a sandwich and sipped tea while Ron sat on the sofa opposite, dunking chocolate biscuits. Outside, the night had turned chilly and a mist had settled on the London streets. Inside, the flat was warm and bright. The gas fire flickered and gently hissed as the flames danced and drifted up from the coals.

She told Ron about her heart-to-heart with Jane at the riding school.

Ron considered the situation. 'Look Vicky, I love Jane as much as you and I agree it would be wonderful if she and Shades were a couple, but I really think they have to work it out for themselves.'

'Yes, but could you just have a chat with Shades? You know, see if Jane is wasting her time. She's getting mixed signals. She's not sure if the relationship could go anywhere and she's frightened to ask. I really worry she'll get hurt.'

Ron fidgeted uncomfortably. 'I'll see, maybe. Normal guys don't really ask that sort of stuff. I know women talk about *everything*, but…. You know,' he ended hopefully.

She didn't know and wasn't the kind of woman to give up easily. 'You and Shades are close. Anyway, neither of you is normal.'

'Oh thanks a lot.'

'You know, I mean that as a compliment.'

They both watched Finbar, who was sitting on the rug in front of the fire. He had stretched his forepaws out in front of him and was arching his back. Evidently, lying on the rug all day was exhausting.

Vicky pointed. 'That's a d*ownward dog.*'

Ron stared at the cat. 'No, I think you'll find it's a dopey cat.'

Vicky shook her head. 'No, that's a yoga position.'

He laughed. 'Ha, yoga! You're hanging about with Jane too much. I love her but her battiness is rubbing off.'

Vicky snorted. 'So Jane's batty, is she? And this coming from a man who tries to quantify luck with jam sandwich experiments.'

'That's science!'

Vicky peered at him. They were very close but occasionally, Ron's dry sense of humour stealthily slipped by.

Ron only half-believed his luck experiments. The truth was he was both bored and worried that he had r*eally* lost his ability to write best-sellers. Or even moderately good sellers. He'd only played with his food as a distraction. Ron's smile dissolved and his face became solemn.

She knew he was worrying, so she dropped the banter and spoke seriously. 'You'll get there.'

He knew she'd guessed he was fretting. He raised a sad smile. 'It sounds easy: collect the ingredients; guns, knives, fast cars, exotic locations; good people, bad people, dangerous people; love, hate, envy. Mix

121

thoroughly, slowly bring to the boil.' In attempting to make her laugh, he had begun to smile himself.

Vicky joined in and finished the analogy. 'Best served with tea, coffee or wine. Best enjoyed on a cold, rainy night in bed, eating chocolate.'

'Yeah! So that's that sorted out. I'll pop it down on paper tomorrow and send it to my publisher.'

Vicky nodded and dusted her hands in a gesture that indicated job done.

Ron was weary talking and thinking about writing. He changed the subject. 'What are we doing? Do you want to go out?'

Vicky wrinkled her nose. 'Too tired, I'm up and out early tomorrow. The Director wants us all on set first thing. Think I'll read, then get an early night.'

'Fine, I'll slip the cans on and listen to some music.'

Vicky fetched her book, a thriller; Ron slipped on his earphones, Finbar completed his yoga and fell asleep.

At the house, Salvatore opened the envelope the driver had given him. It contained several wads of English banknotes. The leather bag held sneakers, jeans, baseball cap and glasses. The glasses had thick, black frames. The glass was merely that, glass. Not lenses. There was also a pair of electric clippers. He disappeared into the *en suite* bathroom and shut the door.

In the living room, Rifsky smiled to himself as the credits rolled on the screen. 'Was good!'

Bruno was looking through the front windows at the lights of other houses across the small, private park. They were veiled in a light, chilly mist. 'What?'

Rifsky pointed at the TV as he switched it off with the remote. 'Good film.'

Bruno compressed his lips and turned back to the window.

Suddenly, the living room door opened and Salvatore walked into the room, or someone who resembled him. Using the clippers, he had lost his full, thick hair, which was now neatly cropped. The stylish beard was also absent. He wore the thick framed glasses. The immaculate suit had been replaced with a simple blue sweater, dark jeans and trainers. As they looked on, he topped off the disguise with his navy blue baseball cap.

Rifsky grinned and clapped twice. 'Very good!'

Indeed it was. Losing the beard had changed the shape of his face. The glasses obscured his eyebrows and drew the eye. The haircut and baseball cap did an excellent job of masking his usual appearance. The clothes were clean and smart but instantly forgettable. He would blend nicely into London's multi-facetted populace.

Bruno tried hard, very hard, to sound happy. 'Yes, no one will recognise you, especially here.' He could stand it no longer, and added, 'Why are we here?'

Salvatore smiled. 'I'll explain everything. Look, it's been a long day, but I'm not tired. I need to wind

123

down. Before we arrived, I noticed we passed a bar…
The Blue Parrot, I think it was.'

Rifsky looked happy, Bruno indifferent.

Salvatore addressed his security man. 'You feel it's safe?'

Rifsky weighed the situation. 'I know we weren't followed in the car. I've been out in the street, there's no-one watching the place. The driver of our car is part of the organisation?'

'Yes, Uncle arranged all that. There are people in London he says he can trust.'

Rifsky had been in the organisation long enough to know if Uncle said a thing it was true. He shrugged. 'And you look fine, no problem. I would suggest we all speak English from now on. No need to draw attention to ourselves.' In addition to his native Russian, Rifsky spoke Italian and English fluently.

Salvatore nodded. He trusted Rifsky's opinion in security matters, knowing that behind the relaxed persona Rifsky was sharp and missed nothing.

A short time later the three men stood on the wide entrance steps of *The Blue Parrot*. Rifsky glanced up and down the street more out of habit than because he expected trouble. Risky and Bruno wondered why Salvatore hesitated. Unlike them, Salvatore wasn't immune to the club's quiet magic; it was clearly very old. The rich, warm colour of the brickwork visible only around the illuminated doors, over which the electric blue neon sign *The Blue Parrot* glowed. Its brightness dissolved the building above into the darkness of the night as it towered over them.

Salvatore pushed hard on one of the sweepingly graceful bronze door handles so many other hands had touched over the decades.   He entered the club, followed by the others.   They stood on the raised entrance steps and surveyed the titanic room.   There were two bars, one to the right and one to the left, each with raised seating areas in front of them.   Between the bars lay the colossal main floor, constructed of hardwood in a herringbone pattern.   Upon this main floor were more round tables and chairs arranged in small groups.   Between the tables, substantial plant pots contained fake metallic palm trees of gigantic proportions, which soared up to the monumental ceiling, a playground for Victorian metal girders.   The gunmetal grey surface glinted here and there as the lights set in the plant pots far below illuminated the metallic forest and caught the rivets in the ironwork.

Opposite the entrance steps where they stood and beyond the tables and palms was a clear stretch of floor.   This was used for dancing, mainly on Saturday nights.   Running along the back wall of the club between a pair of fire exits was a raised stage, used for live music or the DJ.   There was, in fact, a DJ setting-up on the stage, checking connections and rigging his own lights to the club's state-of-the-art system.   High up on the wall above the disco another great neon sign glowed in cerulean blue, *The Blue Parrot.*   The rust-red brick of the walls gave texture and warmth to the colossal space, the thick walls completely deadening the sounds of London outside. The club smelt of floor polish and warmth; the vintage, beautifully cast radiators worked well.

Rifsky was uncomfortable standing so obviously at the door. The club was busy but the people who sat talking, drinking and laughing were spread out. A vacant table was easy to spot, situated some distance from its nearest neighbour.

Rifsky pointed. 'That one?'

Salvatore also became aware they had been standing too long in the open and threw Rifsky a curt nod. They moved to the table, which was ahead and to the right, between the stage and the right hand bar but situated on the edge of the floorspace near the wall. They all sat, Salvatore with his back to the main floor. Even given his disguise, he felt more comfortable not facing people. Rifsky sat with his back to the wall. He would never dream of sitting in a position where he couldn't watch people approach. He took note of the fire doors not too far away and comforted himself with the knowledge that a sprint and a quick slam down of the opening bar would have him outside in seconds. He smiled. 'This is good.'

Bruno sat between Salvatore and Rifsky. Salvatore glanced behind him: no one was nearby, or watching. 'You two take this, the organisation has been extremely generous. We have more back at the house.' He slid an envelope containing a substantial chunk of cash to each of them. Both men pocketed the money. Rifsky cast a trained eye around the club. People were engrossed in their own conversations and nobody was looking their way, so there was *no possibility* of being overheard. He scanned the upstairs bar, which wasn't visible from the front door as it ran above it and was noticeable only once a person walked out onto the main floor. The bar had a low wall and a heavy brass rail. It was possible to sit at the tables or stand by the rail and look down on the whole club. The bar was accessed via a metal staircase from the ground. Risky took a moment to watch the upstairs bar and staircase. Salvatore watched him, aware he was looking the place over. Any moment, Rifsky would pass judgement. He turned his attention back to his comrades.

'I'll spend some of this money on a round.' Rifsky grinned and stood up.

Salvatore was content if Rifsky was happy.

Rifsky looked to Bruno. 'Bruno?'

'A glass of…' the word *red* was on his lips when he remembered the imported red that had passed his lips earlier, 'beer, lager.'

Rifsky turned to Salvatore.

'Same. Thank you, Rifsky.'

He smiled and moved confidently to the nearest bar.

Bruno took the opportunity to ask, 'Why is Rifsky here?'

'He is the best all-round security man we've got. I feel safer having him along, it was Uncle's idea.'

Bruno snorted. 'He's having a holiday, he was looking at sight-seeing guides back at the house.'

'I know. I also know he did a sweep of the house for cameras and bugs just to be sure the police don't have the house under surveillance. He also checked all the doors and windows and spent a long time watching the street. If Rifsky feels it's okay to relax, so do I.'

Bruno conceded reluctantly. 'Okay, security, I get that; the police are looking for you and there could be an alert out across Europe.'

'I don't think they are or if they are it won't be for long.'

Bruno leaned forward. 'What's happened? Why not?'

Salvatore held up his hand. 'Wait. I'll explain it to you both.'

Bruno sat back and watched Rifsky at the bar.

Shades descended the stairs from the flat high up on the second floor. He pushed open the door marked *Private,* situated behind the upstairs bar, acknowledged the barman and quickly made his way down the metal steps to the ground floor.

Bruno noticed the sudden movement on the stairs; there was something vaguely familiar about the man walking down. Shades reached the bottom and crossed the floor. Salvatore noticed nothing, sitting as he was with his back to the busy club.

Bruno thought hard; where did he know this man from? Suddenly, like a slot machine in one of the clubs in The String, it clicked into line, *the when, the where, the who.* Bruno was pleased with himself for remembering. Could it be useful? Could he use it in some way to hurt Salvatore? Maybe he had something; perhaps, just perhaps, this was a wonderful opportunity. Bruno couldn't put his finger on it, but he felt somehow excited; he had a strong feeling he could use this to his advantage. The idea hadn't formed fully, but he had the distinct impression this was somehow good. He felt more optimistic without really knowing why. Then, a shadow of doubt crossed his mind: this could be simply what he wanted to believe, it might be an opportunity or perhaps it was….

'Nuts?'

Bruno had been watching Shades cross the floor and disappear through another door on the far side of the club behind one of the ground floor bars. He hadn't noticed Rifsky's return with the drinks tray, which he had placed on the table and was now holding out a packet of peanuts. Bruno shook his head, irritated. Something in the exchange made Salvatore smile. They were so opposite in character. Bruno, unhappy and ever hungry to move up the ladder. Rifsky, head of security, a team under him, happy to take orders and bright enough to know that advancements in the organisation carried their own risks. Too much power created envy which in turn, spelt danger.

Rifsky palmed a handful of peanuts and chomped happily, immune to Bruno's black look. Rifsky was indeed an unusual character. Unless someone disliked him enough to become an actual danger, Rifsky truly and completely *didn't care* what anyone thought of him. This simply philosophy removed many burdens suffered by most people. He lived in the present. People often dwell on missed opportunities and mistakes of the past or wish for things their future might hold but as far as Rifsky was concerned, if *now* was good, he was satisfied. Of course, he kept an eye on political manoeuvrings within the organisation but if they posed no threat to him personally, he wasn't interested.

Salvatore risked a glance behind him. He carefully scrutinised the bars and tables. There were other people in the club, some standing at the bars, some seated. No-one was paying them any attention. Absolutely nobody was close enough to possibly hear what they discussed. Salvatore was completely satisfied. He turned back and faced Rifsky and Bruno. 'If anyone comes near us you tell me.'

They both glanced about and nodded.

Satisfied, Salvatore began to explain his plan. 'Okay, I couldn't be sure, but it seems my idea could work. I had to get out of Italy. Even the organisation, with all its power, can't stop a police investigation when a killing is caught on film and splashed across the newspapers.'

Bruno hid his amusement for Salvatore's predicament and projected what he believed to be a suitably concerned and sympathetic attitude. Frowning slightly, he compressed his lips and shook his head sadly. 'That photographer catching it all on film was *really* bad luck.' He thoughtfully sipped his lager.

'Are you planning to go into hiding here? Start a new life?' he asked hopefully.

'No, no I'm not.'

At that moment, the DJ started to test his equipment. It wouldn't be needed until Saturday night but he had no bookings between now and Saturday, so Tony had allowed him to set up and conduct sound checks on the relatively quiet Tuesday night.

'One two, one two, one two, testing.'

Salvatore continued and the others leaned forward to be sure of hearing him. 'You're aware Anna took the Ferrari?'

Bruno acknowledged with a grunt, Rifsky grinned at the thought of the beautiful vintage car.

'She dropped Lucia at Grandmama's and drove the two hundred miles along to coast to the countryside, where my cousin lives. My cousin Nico was killed in a hit and run late on Monday night. It was after a big family wedding, Nico wasn't discovered until very late, the guests had gone, there was only a handful of close family left and the party was all but over.

The ambulance took Nico to a small hospital nearby, in a town not much bigger than a village. Uncle Q is down there, he's spoken to the ambulance crew and the doctor involved that night. There is now, no record of the incident.

People always said my cousin and I looked like brothers.' Salvatore hesitated; he truly had been fond of Nico, but this wasn't the time and his audience wouldn't understand.

Bruno pointed to his own ear, 'Was he the one with the, the…?' He moved his hand in a sweep to his nose and mouth.

Salvatore suddenly became the businessman once more, 'Yes, he had a deformed ear, a misshapen nose and a gold tooth. Messing around on a scooter when we were kids. The plan is to crash the Ferrari and pretend Nico's body is mine.'

Bruno stared at Salvatore. 'How can you expect to get away with that?'

'Because Uncle can spend enough cash to get death certificates and eyewitnesses to say they saw the accident. If the Ferrari is burned out, and a doctor says there weren't enough remains to identify. But the driver was driving *my* car to visit *my* cousin and wearing *my* rings.'

Bruno and Rifsky glanced at Salvatore's hands. Bruno looked up. 'The bag you handed Anna?'

'Yes. Wallet, jewellery, etc. They will say they were all found in or near the crash. Only the doctor and the family will know the truth. The doctor will be well paid and it'll be made clear it would be a very bad idea to ever speak of it.'

People often saw things Q's way after he spoke to them, the method was simple but effective. He would stand in front of them, offering a wad of money, while two large, unsmiling men loomed ominously behind them. Maybe not everyone took the money, but it would take a spade to find one.

Bruno and Rifsky had no doubt about Uncle's formidable powers of persuasion but Bruno wasn't convinced. 'Surely, the family won't let you put your cousin's body in your car and torch it?'

Salvatore shook his head. 'No and I wouldn't ask them to. It's enough to say the body was in the wreck and is now at the mortuary with the effects found in the wreckage. Remember, Nico lives in the country, it's an hour or more to the nearest Police station. By the time the crash is reported, Uncle will have everything in place.'

Bruno was still hopeful. 'Okay, so now you're dead. You can never go home, return to Italy, to Milan.'

'You think not?'

'No.' Bruno answered slowly, not so sure of himself.

'You asked why we are here in London.'

Bruno waited. Rifsky ate more peanuts and sipped his drink, enjoying the story.

'Dr Linsky is in London.'

Bruno frowned in deep thought, 'Linsky, Linsky?' It meant nothing.

Salvatore enlightened him. 'We, the organisation, set him up. It was thought he could be useful. Knife wounds, scars, gunshot wounds could be taken care of, no questions asked. Very convenient for us.'

Bruno thought he knew the answer to the next question, but asked it anyway. 'You're going to see him?'

'If all goes as I hope in Italy and Nico is officially accepted as me, I'll become him. We're the same age and build, we look similar. Some cosmetic surgery on the ear and nose, a gold tooth and I am him. Then it's simple: as Nico, I visit Anna to console her, help out with things and take over from Salvatore.'

Bruno sank back in his chair. This was a disaster; the plan would work. With Uncle pulling the strings, the muscle and money of the organisation backing him, Salvatore could literally get away with murder. He would come back like nothing had happened and continue doing the job that should have been his. The three emotions racing in Bruno's head were bitter disappointment, frustration and anger. They all crossed the finish line together.

Rifsky on the other hand, was an appreciative audience; he clapped quietly three times and beamed. 'Very smart. When do we go to the doctor?'

Salvatore looked glum, giving Bruno a glimmer of hope. 'Problem, Sal?'

'Problem is, we can't locate Dr Linsky. His private work is going very well, too well. Uncle contacted his London clinic, they don't know where he is. All they know is he's somewhere in Devon or Cornwall. He's looking at properties, he intends buying something down there as a convalescent facility. It seems the London practice is more for consultation and minor procedures. He's recently purchased a larger facility in Devon for more complex surgery, but he wants to provide luxury recuperation options for his high-end patients. So he's looking at more property down there. The problem is he's out of contact as he's combining the search with a holiday. The office told Uncle he's had a particularly busy workload of late and is using a gap to take some R and R with his family. They think he may check in at the end of the week, but they can't be certain. So, for now we wait.'

The DJ had begun experimenting with music, checking the sound-to-light equipment.

Salvatore took a deep drink then set down his glass decisively. 'This noise is getting on my nerves, I'm going back to the house.' He rose to his feet.

Bruno remained seated; he had a lot to think about.

Rifsky stood up. 'You want me to come?'

Salvatore patted the air with splayed fingers in a calming motion. 'Sit, enjoy your drink, I'm fine.'

Rifsky slowly sat down.

Salvatore turned and left. It was annoying not being able to contact the doctor and the blasts of noise from the DJ weren't improving his mood.

Rifsky gestured toward Salvatore as he walked to the door. 'He's a very smart man.'

Bruno watched Salvatore disappear through the main door. 'Smart guy.' He said the words so gravely it caused Rifsky to glance at his face. Rifsky didn't miss much, *jealous as hell*. Bruno's unhappiness was a cause of amusement for him and he grinned.

Bruno noticed, it angered him. 'If Salvatore really was dead, you'd be taking orders from me.'

Rifsky remained happy. 'But he's not, is he?' Rifsky was impressed with Salvatore, how he had found a way out after being caught and even photographed.

This admiration added further fuel to Bruno's already burning anger. 'Well, he has enemies, even here in London. He's not safe yet, anything could happen.'

The smile on Rifsky's face snapped off and Bruno saw plainly the tough character beneath the mild veneer. He looked hard at Bruno and spoke slowly and deliberately. 'I'm here to make sure *nothing* happens.'

They stared at each other. Bruno looked away and sipped his drink. Rifsky watched him for a moment longer. Satisfied, he stood up. 'See you at the house.'

Bruno nodded but didn't look at him. Rifsky left him to brood and made his way to the door. Bruno continued to stare at his drink, his mind working. He knew he had a good memory for faces, he had recognised Shades, but he very much doubted Shades would remember him. There was a brother too… Tony, yes that was it. So, was Tony here? And what connection did the brothers have with the club?

A waitress was clearing tables nearby, Bruno beckoned her over. Still balancing a tray of glasses, she hurried closer.

'I can see you're busy, I've a quick question. I was thinking of hiring somewhere like this for a private function. Could you give me the name of the owner?'

'Certainly, you need to speak to Tony Manning or his brother.' She looked about her, 'Did you want me to find one of them for you?'

'No, no, that's fine. I'm considering other venues, too. Thank you anyway.'

The waitress nodded and smiled, relieved to get on with her work and not have to search the club.

Out on the street, Rifsky decided to stroll past the house and check the square for any parked cars and unwelcome observers. There was nothing and nobody about. He stood for a while and methodically checked all the windows on the surrounding buildings. No-one seemed to be near the windows, though it was difficult to be sure in the bad light. But he felt nothing. In Russia, you knew when you were watched. All of Rifsky's senses told him there was nothing; he should feel better than he did. He knew the problem, it was Bruno. Salvatore was indeed smart, he was right to have concerns. He reflected on the conversation they'd had on the ship. Yes, he would keep an eye on Bruno; he was angry and envious, possibly dangerous. While he was thinking, Rifsky had slowly walked around the outside of the private park in the centre of the square. Finally, certain that all was secure, he picked up pace and hurried back to the house. He found Bruno on the doorstep. 'I thought you were staying.'

Bruno grunted, 'The DJ was irritating, I couldn't think.'

'What are you thinking?'

Without answering, Bruno pushed past and opened the door. Rifsky watched him thoughtfully. He'd been right, he was sure now. The danger wasn't in the street, it was in the house.

A few miles away across London, Jane Flutter put down the book she had been reading. She had read the same paragraph twice and still it made no sense. Who was she kidding? She wasn't reading the book, she was merely holding it.

Jane was sitting up in bed, lit by a pool of warm light from the reading lamp above her head. The cosy bedroom with its chintzy fabrics reflected her usually cheerful character. Tonight it felt at odds with her mood. Jane made the happy room vanish by clicking off the light. She lay back on her pillow and sighed. Her anxiety and depression was totally out of character. Usually, even on the darkest of days, Jane could find a smile when most people would have given up the search. She lay in the dark and pondered the situation. Perhaps it would have been better if she'd never met Shades. But you don't choose who you fall in love with, it just happens. She couldn't quantify exactly what it was about him, it was everything; silly quotes from films, his cool tough guy act she enjoyed making fun of, for she knew it *was* an act. Jane felt that beneath the facade dwelt a sensitive soul but something held him back. He seemed reluctant to let her get too close, it was as if he had a wall around him. Was it because he simply didn't love her? Or was something

138

else going on? In the darkness, with no one to see, she could stop pretending she was okay. She wasn't okay, she was deeply sad. Tears rolled off her cheek and made gentle tapping sounds as they fell upon the sheets.

The conversation with Vicky came to her; she pushed it away and shook her head, not wanting to think about it, but the terrible truth wouldn't stay buried. She couldn't go on like this for much longer, because at some point she would have to ask questions, somehow force Shades to be honest with her. But... What if he said he liked her very much, but as a friend? That would be the end, it would be too painful to keep seeing him. Then again, if she said nothing and gave it more time, maybe he would grow to love her the way she loved him.

'Oh! Why, why is it complicated? It shouldn't be!'

Jane was open and loving: if she liked a person they knew it; If she thought something nice, she said it. She found it hard to understand those who were cautious and guarded. But then Jane had been extremely lucky. So far, in relationships she'd had her feelings bruised but, until now, hadn't had her heart broken.

As she lay in the darkness, it was easy to believe the whole world was asleep but her. How she wished for the morning. No matter how bad things appeared at night, they never seemed quite as bad in the light of day.

Jane believed she didn't sleep at all but she did drift in and out of consciousness, although it couldn't be called restful sleep.

CHAPTER 10
RON AND VICKY'S FLAT
WEDNESDAY MORNING

Vicky had woken very early; it was still dark outside. Ron slept peacefully beside her. The bed was gloriously warm and soft and she hovered in the wonderful twilight between sleep and wakefulness. Her drifting mind settled on Jane and Maggie, then to Jane and Shades. These were recent events. Her thoughts melted into memories as sleep claimed her once again. Vicky's mind gently slid back to events long ago. When awake, the years were like a fence, separating her from the past. Now they appeared to dissolve. Happy memories morphed into a perceived present and became real once more. She was once again a little girl, playing on the beach with her sister. The soft, warm bed beneath her body faded into sand, heated by the Summer sun. She stretched, both in the dream and reality. The rustle of the sheets against her bare legs triggered the memory of distant waves breaking on the sea-smoothed rocks.

Vicky lay on her side and gazed at the sea. It was a ribbon of dark blue, edged with white foam breakers. Above, an endless blue sky stretched for ever. Impossibly white gulls circled and swooped. From her low angle, she could see heat ripple the graceful contours of the sand. The air held a mix of fragrances: the sea, warm seaweed baking on rocks and the pleasant scent of sunscreen.

Her sister was running towards her, laughing. Breathless, Sara dropped to her knees on the sand, close to where Vicky lay. Vicky held one hand to her forehead to shield her eyes from the brightness of the clear sky. She smiled broadly at her sister. Sara reached out to touch Vicky's shoulder. Just before her fingers reached her, abruptly, there was a sound. It didn't belong. Sara turned away slightly to look for the cause. The scene dissolved, the sand became cotton sheets once again. Vicky lowered her outstretched arm and silenced the alarm clock. She took a moment to shut her eyes tight. She could still see Sara's face, but now only in memory. The sense of reality had vanished with the dream. She sighed, then felt Ron shift position behind her. The alarm had woken him too. She heard him yawn, then groan. She wondered if the cursed clock had also intruded on some relived happy experience. Vicky still felt the loss of her sister very deeply. If only she had stayed asleep a minute longer, she could have held her again. Lost in introspection, she stared at the blank wall.

Ron's croaking groan snapped her out of her sad thoughts and even made her smile. 'Cooofffeee.'

She rolled over, faced him and said brightly. 'Yes, I'll have one too. And put on the heating while you're getting it, it's freezing in here.'

There were more growls and grunts. The bed rocked as Ron threw one leg out. He paused to gather his strength, then managed to plant both feet on the carpet. He scratched his head, which seemed anchored to the pillow, then hauled himself upright, swaying only slightly. Finally, he stood and opened his eyes just wide enough to navigate to the door without colliding with the frame. He shuffled from the room, as if auditioning for a part in a zombie movie.

Vicky was on the brink of drifting back to her beach when the dull thud of Ron's foot kicking the bedroom door brought her back. He carried a tray with two coffees and half a packet of chocolate biscuits, which he felt he rightly deserved after the effort of going *all* the way to the kitchen and back.

They sat up in bed, listening to the creaking and ticking of the radiators, as the flat began to warm up. The room now held the glorious scent of early morning coffee.

Ron stared vacantly ahead, nibbling his biscuit and sipping coffee. Vicky had learned it was useless trying to talk to him until he was at least halfway down the cup.

When she judged the moment was right, she asked as brightly as she could. 'So, are you going to try writing today?'

'Mmm, probably.' He munched thoughtfully, staring vacantly at some mid-air point between what was left of the biscuit in his hand and the end of the bed. 'Might have an idea.'

Vicky pounced. 'Really? That's good. D'you want to talk about it?'

'Mmm.'

This was unprecedented. Normally, Ron liked to work up an idea and only showed Vicky an almost-finished draft; the fact he wanted to talk to her about a new concept was another sign of how desperate he was.

'Okay, tell me.' She twisted around in the bed, lying on her side, then propped herself up on one elbow cradling her head in her palm, and gave him her full attention. Her expectant face caused him to revise his original statement.

'Well, erm, when I said "idea", it's very rough, just drifted into my head while I was stirring the coffee.'

'I'm pleased you have *any* ideas.'

'Okay, so, what if there is a forensic expert, who works for the police. Every day he's surrounded by death and violence. Now, this guy hates a police inspector he works with, don't know why yet, perhaps he stole his girlfriend or something, I don't know.'

Vicky was hopeful. 'Go on, I like it so far.'

Ron was becoming more animated, as he approached what he viewed as the good bit. (It must be explained that a thriller writer's idea of "the good bit" is usually when something very bad happens.) 'The inspector's body is discovered dead at a crime scene they are investigating. He's been strangled with…' (dramatic pause) 'large amounts of yellow and black crime scene tape, wrapped tightly around his

144

neck.' Ron smiled both at Vicky and the grisly image in his mind. Vicky was disappointed, but desperate not to show it. Ron wasn't fooled. 'You don't like it.'

'No, yes, no, well..., it's very imaginative. I've never heard of a victim strangled using police crime scene tape; but, I just wondered, whether the dark humour doesn't rob the crime of the gravitas a murder requires. I *do* love the idea of a forensic expert being the murderer though. I mean, who knows more about covering his tracks and getting away with it, than a forensic expert?'

Ron was cooling quickly on the whole concept. He popped the remains of his biscuit into his mouth and resumed staring into space, before concluding sadly, 'mm, I don't think I like it, now I've said it aloud, I think you're right, it's too silly.'

Outside, even the misty morning was brighter than Ron. It had rained overnight, the morning was cold and a thick mist blanketed the River Thames and drifted into nearby streets. It wouldn't last, already the tops of the buildings were in clear air. The morning sunshine glinted and sparkled on the glass and steel of the city.

They finished their coffee, then washed and dressed. They were both up because Vicky had a fairly early start and Ron liked to see her off. They sat together in the living room as it was warmer. Vicky placed the empty cereal bowl on the coffee table. She had breakfasted on muesli and watched with disapproval as Ron continued dipping chocolate biscuits in his second

145

coffee. His ability to make biscuits disappear was legendary. No one who knew him would ever contemplate leaving him unsupervised near a biscuit tin.

He was aware she was watching him. 'Not everyone can time it just right, you know; maximum absorption, moments before the loss of structural integrity and disaster.' (Disaster being a cupful of biscuit and coffee or a lap covered in post biscuit mush.) 'The secret is to keep it vertical, less stress…'

Vicky interrupted. 'I should be back a little after lunch, I *really* hope you can get some work done.'

Her comment and emphasis on "really" prompted him to glance up at her, causing disaster. 'Damn! Look at that! All in my coffee!'

She laughed. 'Come on, you've had enough anyway. I've got to go.'

Ron got to his feet and fetched the car keys. Vicky slipped on her long puffy coat and picked up her shoulder bag. Standing together in the living room, Vicky reached up and put her arms round his neck. He leaned down and she kissed him. 'I'll see you later.'

'I'll walk down with you.' He snatched up a thick cardigan that was draped across a sofa.

Moments later, they walked down the entrance steps and round the corner to the car. Vicky unlocked and climbed into Ron's Chevy. Childishly, it always amused him when she slid the seat forward so she could reach the pedals. Vicky was only four feet eleven and a half inches and the huge car made her appear even smaller. By rights, the car should have had its original bench seat but early in its life during the nineteen sixties, a young man had swapped it for bucket seats, which he felt were more cool.

Ron glanced around at the misty street. 'You drive safely, okay?'

'I'll be fine.' She started the engine and the deep burble of the V8 broke the silence. Ron bent down and kissed her again. Vicky hauled the door shut, gave Ron a smile, a wave and moved off. Ron watched the taillights fade, then turned quickly and hurried back to the warmth of the flat to continue perfecting his biscuit dunking technique which obviously needed work.

Vicky drove to the shoot without incident, the mist had almost gone by the time she arrived. Jane greeted her with a brave smile and a coffee.

Vicky noted the dark patches and slight puffiness. 'Are you okay? You look tired.'

'I'm fine, didn't sleep well, don't know why. It's going to be a busy morning.' She handed Vicky a clipboard. 'I'll get set up, you go and round up some of the actors. The list's in order, get the first three. Maggie is already in the make-up trailer.'

Vicky drank some coffee, put the plastic lid back on and hurried off with the clipboard to the catering unit. She loved her work.

Bruno put down the coffee jug and joined Salvatore and Rifsky in the living room. He sat and looked grimly at Salvatore. This one man was the only thing between him climbing one more step up the ladder and running Milan. Bruno sipped his coffee. He was tired, having lain awake in the dark, thinking. There might be a way, but it was dangerous. The organisation may have adopted a business approach, but he was under no illusions. It would act with ruthless violence towards anyone who attacked it or its top people. 'I heard you talking on the phone; what's happening in Italy?'

Thoughtfully, Salvatore rubbed his smooth cheek. It still seemed strange not to feel his beard. 'Progress, the Ferrari has been found. Reports are that it came off the road and crashed. A body was recovered. Anna says Uncle believes there won't be any problems, the family are coming together. Uncle has convinced them it would be Nico's wish to help and if his tragic, untimely death would do a little good for the family in the world he left behind, he would approve.' Although it was how Uncle had pitched the idea to the family, Salvatore knew it was basically true. He felt Nico's loss deeply but didn't have the luxury of time to grieve, especially in the presence of Bruno and Rifsky. He continued quickly, 'People have been paid and now it seems very likely that the investigating officer will be....' he hesitated, 'a friend of the organisation.'

Italy has two main police forces, the *Carabinieri* and the *Polizia*. The organisation had little influence but they did have some. One or two officers, known as 'friends', enjoyed a regular income from the organisation. Many cases involving the organisation's various dark dealings failed to make it to trial for lack of evidence. This evidence was occasionally mislaid or corrupted. Actual facts were sometimes substituted for the organisation's preferred version of events. Salvatore's death in a car crash would be viewed as an open and shut case, for to find evidence to the contrary would be neither wise nor healthy. Bruno had no doubt the investigation would find whatever Uncle decided was appropriate, in this case that Salvatore Conelli had died at the wheel of his Ferrari while driving fast to visit family and evade capture.

'Mmm.' Bruno was barely able to hide his disappointment.

'The only real problem is Dr Linsky.'

Bruno shrugged. 'He's not the only doctor.'

'No, he's not, but travel is dangerous and as Rifsky said, we've been lucky to get here. I'm not going to blow it, we have to be patient, we may be here a while. Rifsky, would you mind picking up some food?'

Rifsky shook his head. 'No problem.'

Salvatore glanced at the sightseeing guides still strewn on the table. 'There's no hurry, you may as well check out some of these.' He looked up at Rifsky. 'We can't sit here looking at each other for days.'

'Are you sure?' His eyes flicked to Bruno and back to Salvatore, who understood the question. Did he feel comfortable alone with Bruno? Bruno noticed nothing, disgusted that Rifsky appeared to be off sightseeing. He'd leaned forward and picked up his coffee, then proceeded to blow on it. Salvatore glanced at him and back to Rifsky.

'Yes, I'm sure. See you this afternoon.'

Rifsky nodded and fetched his coat. If anything happened to Salvatore, there wouldn't be any doubt who was responsible. Bruno wouldn't be so stupid as to try anything in the house.

Bruno scowled at Salvatore over his cup then asked, 'And what are you going to do?'

'I think I'll stay near the phone, in case there's any news. I'll read.' He tilted his head toward the bookcase. 'And you?'

Bruno shrugged. 'I don't know, go for a walk I suppose.' He wanted to think. There must be some way he could use the situation to his advantage.

Rifsky had collected some money from his room and put on his coat. He stood at the living room door. 'I'm going.'

Bruno swung his jacket onto his shoulder and walked past Rifsky, who watched him leave. He turned a serious face to Salvatore. 'Sure?'

'I'm fine. Go.'

Salvatore rose, selected a book and sat down. Rifsky wasn't totally happy, but he'd been told to go so he did.

PART ONE

CHAPTER 11
WEDNESDAY LUNCHTIME

Things had not gone well at the film shoot; the atmosphere was oppressive and tense. A camera had jammed in the middle of what would have been a good take. After that, nothing seemed to go right. One of the actors called another actor by the wrong character name on three successive takes. The shooting schedule was now behind. The director expected to be watching film and cutting in the afternoon but shooting was still in progress and tempers were frayed.

The part of the deranged, murdering psychopath had been given to a huge, bearded man with strikingly piercing eyes, who in reality, was a sensitive, well regarded actor called Jim.

The director was his opposite in every way. He was a small, clean shaven, bespectacled man, whose insensitivity made him disliked by acquaintances and hated by those who knew him well. His explosive temper was no secret in the industry but no-one guessed his tempestuous moods were fast becoming unstable and veering towards dangerous. In an attempt to really get into the head of a murdering psychopath, he had visited prisons and institutions, spending hours with the mentally ill and engaging in long, whispered conversations. This practice had done little to improve his own stability.

The film unit had finally wrapped for the day; much later than expected and now the normally busy set was silent and deserted. Only the FX unit showed a light. As the youngest member of the team, she was tidying up before leaving the set. The director hadn't been pleased with the make-up or the SFX, not pleased at all. As she busied herself replacing bottles and brushes in their correct spaces, the director moved slightly closer. In his hand he gripped a steel tube, part of the stock of heavy tubes and clips used by the riggers, who set up the lighting. This particular tube was two feet long and thick.

The director stood watching her, partly hidden by rails of costumes. There she was, all his frustration focussed on her: *she* had made the mistakes on purpose. She didn't think he had noticed; *she wanted* his film to fail. Someone was paying her to *make* his film fail; *she thought him a fool.* He was a great director and some stupid little girl was trying to sabotage *his* film, *his* masterpiece! Some insignificant child. He raised the heavy bar over his right shoulder, both hands clamped around one end, and advanced. A lifetime of anger was condensed into a single burst of savage power as he swung at her head. She caught the movement in the corner of her eye and turned slightly, in time for the steel pipe to strike her temple with shattering force.

Ron stopped reading, lowered his writing pad and looked across at Vicky, who was sitting on the sofa opposite, listening intently.

'So, what do you think?   I was going to call it *Murder at the Movies*.'

She knew he was struggling to find a plot, and wanted more than anything to be supportive, but she had to be honest. 'So it's about a film director, who descends into madness?'

'Yes, starts to act in reality what the characters do in the film.'   Ron waited for her verdict.   She looked uncomfortable. 'You don't like it, do you?'   He asked slowly.

Vicky shifted in her seat and answered reluctantly. 'I think you can do better.'

He thought so too.   'You're right, it's crap!'   With that, he tore out the sheet, balled it up and gently tossed it in a long arc across the room.   It landed close to Finbar, who had been dozing on his rug.   He sprang into action and pounced on the crumpled ball.

'The cat likes it,' Vicky offered, to try and lift Ron's obvious gloom.

He smiled sadly. 'As long as someone does.'

'Look Ron, you'll think of something, I know you will.' She got up and joined him on his sofa.   As she sat down she moved her head to touch his.   Ron slid his arm around her shoulders.   They sat leaning against each other.   Ron was worried, Vicky was worried that Ron was worried.   Finbar wasn't worried and continued to paw the ball of paper around the rug.

Vicky frowned as a thought struck her, she moved her head away and turned to look at him accusingly. 'Oi!' She said sharply, making him jump.

'What?'

'Film unit, mad director kills the young FX make-up girl!'

'Yes?'

'*I'm* a young FX make-up girl and *you* killed me off.'

He laughed. 'It's not personal, I'm just scratching around for ideas.'

Pretending to be annoyed, to cheer him up she added, 'Hum! Not personal! It's subconscious. This is about biscuits, isn't it? It's because I've rationed your chocolate biscuits you've killed me off.' She dug him in the ribs, knowing how ticklish he was, then did it again. They had a mock struggle on the sofa, her sitting on him and rendering him powerless with multiple ticklish digs in his ribs. This resulted in Ron collapsing into an embarrassingly girlish fit of giggles. It was some time before normality was restored.

He felt better and sounded slightly more optimistic as he shared his news, 'I've got some good news, well, possibly good news.'

'Oh yes?'

'But first, have you had lunch?'

'Yes, I had something from the caterers on the shoot with Jane and Mags.'

'Good.'

'Why? Where are we going?'

'Shades phoned, he sounded excited, wants me to go over. He's had an idea. Tony's there too. I thought you'd want to come.'

Vicky was close to both brothers, but she and Tony were especially close. 'I haven't seen Tony for ages and if Shades really has come up with something for you, that would be great!'

'He wouldn't tell me over the phone, so it may be nothing but he did seem very excited. It's got to be worth talking to him, I'm getting nowhere here.' He glanced sadly at the ball of paper on the floor. Finbar had begun to chew the edges.

When they arrived at *The Blue Parrot,* Shades was in high spirits. He greeted Vicky with, '*Of all the gin joints in all the towns in all the world, she walks into mine.*' He often greeted Vicky with his favourite line and Vicky felt obliged to answer with her usual response.

'*Casablanca.* Where's Tony?'

Shades pointed at the ceiling. '*Top of the World.*'

Ron got this quote. 'James Cagney, *White Heat.*'

Shades grinned; he loved it when friends guessed the film. He truly was in excellent spirits. Ron began to feel optimistic; perhaps he really had something.

'So, come on, what's the story idea?'

With a theatrical flourish, Shades turned his hand palm up and swept his arm in the direction of a nearby table. 'Sit down, I'll tell you all about it, it's dynamite!'

Vicky jumped in quickly. 'Before you two get started, is it okay to go up?'

'Sure, Tony was pleased when he heard you were coming over. He's with his friends.' Shades winked.

Vicky smiled. 'I'll leave you both to it.'

Shades and Ron sat down. Vicky walked up the metal staircase to the upstairs bar. She and Ron were known to the staff and when Vicky told the barman, 'Shades said to go up,' he lifted the counter flap to allow her through. She thanked him and opened the small door marked *Private*, then made her way up the stairs to the front door of the private flat, high up on the second floor above the club. She knocked, but there was no reply. Vicky pushed open the door and entered. 'Tony?'

As usual, the flat was tidy and immaculate. She smiled to herself. She often had a fanciful thought when entering the flat: she imagined that any speck of dust which decided to rest somewhere would soon catch the look of disapproval in Tony's eye and drift smartly out of the nearest window.

She crossed to the balcony door which opened onto the fire escape. The metal steps led down to the yard behind the club, which the brothers used as a car park. The fire escape also rose up to the roof. Very few people were aware of the existence of the roof terrace, and only Shades, Ron and Vicky knew what Tony kept up there.

Vicky climbed the metal steps and walked onto the roof. It was huge and flat with a wall skirting the edge.

Vicky could see over it, but at her height, the wall was relatively high. She called again, 'Tony?'

A deep baritone voice answered, 'Hello, Vicky.'

She moved towards it. As she walked around one of the cooling vents for the club below, there, standing by his dove coop, was Tony. Vicky hurried over. 'Tony, it's so good to see you.'

'It's been too long.'

As Vicky tilted her head up to kiss him on the cheek, at six feet four he was required to bend down so she could reach. He straightened and beamed down at her. Tony was a huge man, not only tall but wide, with powerful shoulders and a barrel chest. When Vicky had first encountered him, she had been intimidated by his size and serious nature. That was over a year ago, now things were very different. Vicky loved Shades like a brother, but she and Tony had a special bond. He was very different to Shades. They were both deep but where Shades' dry sense of humour was always just below the surface, Tony was more serious; quieter. Tony was an interesting character; he possessed a rare gift. Most of the time he knew what people around him were thinking. It wasn't that he could read minds, it was an uncanny ability to pick up nuances in speech and body language and he always knew when people were lying.

Vicky's small pale face, beautiful to Ron, plain to the world, looked up into Tony's strong features.

'I can't believe how the time has gone, it must be three months.' She turned to look at Tony's dove coop. 'How're the birds?'

'Yes, fine.' He held out a huge hand and a dove flapped from the coop to land on it. The contrast of the little bird and Tony's size always charmed her. Tony was uncharacteristically shy about the doves, as he had once explained the problem to her. The doves didn't fit his public image down in the club and he had sworn her to secrecy when she'd discovered them.

'Is Ron talking to Shades?'

'Yes, thank goodness. I really hope Shades has some good ideas to get him started.'

Tony held the dove near the coop and it hopped off his hand. 'It's chilly up here, come down to the flat and I'll make you a coffee.'

In the flat a few minutes later, Vicky sat hugging a coffee cup and chatting to Tony. The flat was warm, she'd removed her coat and sat with him on a leather sofa. She'd made Tony laugh when she recounted some of the strange things Ron had been up to, such as worrying about the fridge light and the jam sandwich luck experiments. Vicky had attempted to make light of the situation but Tony sensed she was really worried. 'I can see why you hope he can get started on a new book, but he'll be alright, look at all the awards he's won. Don't be concerned about odd behaviour. He's creative; so odd is normal, at least for him.'

She nodded thoughtfully but clearly remained troubled, so to make her smile, he added. 'Password?'

Vicky brightened: Ron's computer password was a source of amusement between them. Everyone knew Ron was forgetful and forever mislaying things such as car keys, watch and wallet. He once mislaid his car, forgetting which car park he'd left it in. So when one of his computer programmes had demanded a password, Vicky feared the worst. Ron's creativity and dry sense of humour conspired to come up with a unique solution: *Invalid.* He'd proudly explained his dubious logic to Tony and Vicky. If he forgot it, his own machine would remind him with the helpful prompt *Your password is invalid.* Vicky was still at a loss to decide if the solution was brilliant or bonkers.

Tony was pleased to see her smile. 'I'm sure he'll think of something soon. You *know* he's a very talented writer.'

'I know you're right; but it's *never* been this long between stories, and he's losing confidence. What's Shades' idea?'

Tony shook his head. 'Don't know. He said a little bird told him, then laughed. I can't talk to him when he's in one of his stupid, playful moods. He seems really sure it's a good idea though. How're you getting on?'

'At work, you mean?'

'Mm.'

'Oh Tony, I love it.'

'Really?'

'Yes. Not only am I working with Jane but Maggie Moorcroft, aka Magic.'

'Magic?'

'They call her Magic Marge or mostly just Magic. She's a make-up artist and special effects genius. Totally at the top of her game. All the studios want her. I'm so lucky to be working with her.' Vicky became self conscious. 'The thing is, she seems to have taken a real shine to me.'

Tony responded without hesitation. 'You're an easy person to like.'

She shook her head, slightly embarrassed. 'Anyway, I'm learning so much.' Vicky enthusiastically launched into all the things she'd learned and spoke at some length about Maggie. Tony was fascinated as Vicky explained some of Maggie's techniques and innovations. There was a lull in the conversation. Tony had the impression Vicky wanted to say something but seemed hesitant.

'Come on, what is it?'

Vicky shook her head; Tony was so quick. 'Okay, it's about Shades and Jane.'

Tony nodded, knowing what was coming. 'You're worried about Jane.'

'Mm.'

'Shades seems to be keeping Jane at a distance.'

She nodded. 'Exactly it. Ron says to stay out of it, but I don't want to see Jane hurt.'

Tony took a moment before answering. He'd been worried for some time about his brother's reluctance to form close relationships, perhaps Vicky could give him a nudge. She was sensitive enough to do it right. 'The

160

thing is Vicky, as we tumble through life, we are shaped by what it throws at us. I can understand Shades' caution.'

'He's… been hurt before?' Tony nodded and Vicky had the strong impression he didn't want to go into details. She answered thoughtfully, 'I don't believe Jane would hurt him.'

Tony smiled. 'Neither do I, but it's not about what *we* think, is it? Look, talk to him, explain you're worried. I know he jokes and messes about but he's no fool. He'll understand your concern.'

'Do you think I'm interfering?'

'You're worried about your friend, he'll see that.' Tony noticed that although her bright little face was full of enthusiasm when she talked of her work, now she looked more serious, she appeared tired. 'Are you really okay?'

She frowned and tilted her head slightly, unsure what he meant. Tony focussed the question. 'The nightmares?'

She understood and looked even more serious. 'I still get them, Tony. Not as often, but yes.' She brightened. 'When I wake up, Ron's there. He's very good.'

'I'm sure they'll fade in time, it's early days.'

'Yes.' Vicky reflected how lucky she was to have Tony as a friend; they could talk about anything. He was a fascinating character. When you thought you understood him, he did something surprising. As for Tony, there weren't many people he felt totally at ease with, where he could relax and be himself. Vicky was one of the rare and privileged individuals he allowed to be close.

Vicky glanced at her watch, put down her cup and picked up her coat. 'I think I'll go and see if Ron's ready to leave yet.'

'I'll come down with you and say hi.'

They left the flat and walked down the stairs. On the way they passed a door. Vicky had been past the door a hundred times. She paused. 'What *is* in there?'

'It's the mezzanine floor, above the ceiling in the club and below the flat.'

'Do you use it?'

'Sometimes.' Tony said no more, and Vicky didn't want to appear nosy. They passed the door and exited behind the upstairs bar. Tony's expression grew solemn. It was the face he showed the world. He nodded curtly at the barman and lifted the counter for Vicky to leave. Tony walked slowly, standing tall with shoulders back. He projected an air of steady composure and confidence.

As they descended the Victorian metal staircase to the club below, they could see Shades and Ron. They were standing - Ron appeared happier - and shaking hands across the table. It seemed the conversation had proved fruitful.

Tony and Ron chatted briefly, Vicky noted that Ron looked a lot brighter. 'Shades has had a brilliant idea; it's spring-boarded all kinds of thoughts. I can't wait to get back to the flat and write it down.'

Vicky was delighted. She hugged the brothers and they departed. She noticed that Ron walked quickly and was uncharacteristically quiet. All good signs.

In the car, Vicky watched him. Ron had one hand on the ignition key but instead of turning it, he hesitated and stared blankly at the bonnet. Vicky knew scenes were playing out in his head, a very good sign. 'Ron.' Then louder, 'Ron!' Louder, short, sharp. 'RON!'

He jumped. 'Yes?'

'Are we going home?'

He became aware of the key in his hand and where he was. 'Yes, yes, home.'

Vicky wasn't convinced he was going to give his driving the attention it deserved, so, for both their sakes she felt compelled to ask. 'Do you want me to drive? So you can think?'

'No, no, I'm fine.'

'Shades had a good idea then?'

'Mm, yes, definitely got possibilities.' He started the engine then headed for home and Ron's big, white, lined, writing pad which now seemed a lot more friendly.

Vicky told Ron about the talk she'd had with Tony. It produced only a series of 'Oh's and 'Mm's. Eventually, Vicky was needled into asking rather sharply. 'Are you listening to me?'

'Yes.'

'I don't think you are, you're not concentrating on your driving either!'

'Yes I am, you're quite safe. I'm always focussed on my driving.'

'Really?'

'Yes.'

Vicky smiled to herself, like a card player about to throw down an unbeatable hand. 'If you're so focussed, why did we just drive past our flat?'

Ron glanced around, taking in his surroundings. 'Shit!' His eyes flicked to the mirror (clear) and his foot stamped on the brake. Vicky cried out and lifted her arms to save herself. The passenger seat had slid forward, violently plunging her into the dashboard. As the car came to a halt, Ron turned to her. 'Are you okay?' His worry was short-lived.

Vicky pushed hard with her arms and legs and slammed the seat back. It had frightened her in the moment but now she was angry. 'Bloody seat!'

Realising she was unhurt, Ron leaned over and examined the seat. 'Oh look, I think a weld has failed. Don't worry, I'm sure my friend Dave can fix it.'

Vicky glared at him. 'I'll bloody fix you! That frightened the life out of me, stupid car.' She smacked the car HARD on the dashboard. The engine died.

Ron frowned. 'Now look what you've done.'

Vicky responded hotly. 'I thought you'd fixed that loose wire.'

Ron knew he should have done, and a wise man would have said sorry. Unfortunately for *him*, he decided to calm her by saying, 'Well, I wasn't

164

expecting someone to give the dashboard a good slapping!'

Vicky didn't trust herself not to give Ron a good slapping so she leapt out, slammed the door, and walked off quickly toward the flat.

Over the following days, things settled down into a routine. Vicky worked happily on the shoot with Jane and Maggie. Ron worked equally happily on his story, muttering encouraging comments like, 'Yes, yes! That's good, mm,' punctuated by delighted little chuckles. The story layout dropped into place like a literary jigsaw puzzle and a finished picture formed in his mind.

At the house, a routine of sorts also developed. Salvatore took long walks or sat in the house, reading. Rifsky became quite the tourist and visited several London landmarks. Bruno also walked the streets or sat brooding in coffee shops. He didn't stray far from the house in the square as he found the Autumn weather unpleasant. He felt he could think better away from the house. He had formed a rough plan, of which the fine details were as yet unclear. One thing *was* certain, Anna needed to be brought to London.

PART ONE

CHAPTER 12
THE HOUSE IN THE SQUARE
MONDAY AFTERNOON

While Rifsky was wandering the miles of exhibits in the Victoria and Albert Museum, Bruno sat in the living room, thinking and smoking. He enjoyed a smoke; it held an added pleasure to smoke in the house, because it annoyed Salvatore. He could just hear the faint murmur from upstairs as Salvatore spoke to Anna on the bedroom phone.

Bruno finally had it. He knew how to rid himself of Salvatore and get away with it, then finally assume his rightful place as the man who ran Milan. It was a simple plan, that's why it was so beautiful. He smiled to himself contentedly and exhaled a lungful of smoke. *At last!*

Salvatore finished his call and came downstairs to the living room. A surprising and vaguely unsettling sight awaited him. Bruno was smiling. He was also humming and leafing through a magazine. He looked up as Salvatore entered. 'All okay?'

'Q still hasn't located Dr Linsky. Today is Monday, the beginning of our second week. Dr Linsky may have decided to make his trip a fortnight.'

'Mm, looks like Rifsky will get to see some more of London; I think he's wandering around a museum today.' Bruno shook his head, but didn't appear irritated. In fact, he seemed in a very good mood. Salvatore didn't know why, but he was sure he didn't like it. He sat down slowly, still watching Bruno and carefully picked up his book.

As the afternoon slipped into early evening, Salvatore glanced occasionally up at Bruno, whose good humour remained. He had finished with a pile of magazines and was now smiling at a book. Finally, he closed it, stretched and declared he would take a shower. That said, he left the living room. Salvatore put down his own book and stared thoughtfully at the closed door.

Moments later, he heard Rifsky's key in the front door. As he entered the room, Salvatore beckoned him over. They stood near the large doors which led to the garden. They were on the far side of the room from the living room door.

Rifsky was suddenly alert. 'What's wrong?'

Salvatore answered quietly. 'I'm not sure anything is wrong, but Bruno's in a very good mood.'

Rifsky looked at the ceiling and back at Salvatore, then answered cautiously, 'is he?'

'Look Rifsky, I'll be honest with you. I'm probably jumping at shadows, but I'm sensing something is going on. Something's amusing him and I can't think what. Since we arrived in England, he's done nothing but scowl and gripe. Suddenly, he's smiling, humming.'

'Humming?'

'Yes.'

Rifsky frowned and looked away, turning the problem over in his mind. Salvatore was his boss, and if he was concerned, it was Rifsky's job to get to the bottom of it. He smiled, 'What we need is a truth drug.'

Salvatore wasn't in the mood for jokes. 'You're not in Russia now, we don't have truth drugs.'

Rifsky remained in good humour as he looked across the room to the drinks table. 'We have vodka.'

When Bruno came downstairs sometime later, he found Rifsky sitting looking at yet more tourist pamphlets and Salvatore still reading.

'Oh, you're back. Enjoy the museum?' He smiled and sat down. Something was definitely going on.

'Very interesting. Small though, only eight miles of corridors. Compared to The Hermitage, it's a broom cupboard.' He grinned, pleased with his joke.

Bruno answered carelessly. 'If you miss Russia, why don't you go back?'

'Yes, I'm sure Russia would *like* me to go back, but I prefer Italy; although I miss Russian food sometimes.'

Bruno looked in the direction of the kitchen. 'Thinking of food, have we got any?'

Salvatore answered without looking up. 'Bread, cheese, wine... plenty.'

Bruno wrinkled his nose; like all the top people, he was accustomed to fine food. He found English food bland and the climate cold. He wanted something hot and with flavour.

169

Rifsky was aware of this and held up a glossy pamphlet. 'Look, Russian restaurant! I'll show you good food.' He stood up. 'Let's all go!'

Salvatore said the cheese was good enough for him. Rifsky looked at Bruno. Bruno didn't like Rifsky, but to be fair, Bruno didn't much like anyone. He hesitated. 'It's cold outside.'

'We can have hot, rich Stroganoff cooked beautifully, a couple of drinks, some amazing Russian dessert or... stay here, have bad imported wine and processed cheese with white bread.'

It was the thought of bad wine and processed cheesed that clinched it. Also, Bruno was in the mood to celebrate. Still no sign of the elusive Dr Linsky and Salvatore was clearly missing Anna. It shouldn't be a big problem to get her over. Salvatore listened to Rifsky. Perhaps while at dinner he could convince Rifsky to suggest Anna come. At the very least, he would get a decent meal.

The restaurant turned out to be rather opulent and Bruno was impressed. They were shown to a table. Rifsky had chatted to the waiter in Russian. Bruno lost interest, not understanding a word. He looked approvingly at his surroundings. A large chandelier hung in the centre of the room, illuminating snow white-tablecloths laid with glittering silver cutlery. Immaculate waiters glided around the room, serving drinks and food. Traditional Russian music drifted softly from concealed speakers, adding to the sophisticated ambience. This was more like it! Let

Salvatore stay home with his bread and cheese, ha! Bruno smiled at the grandeur and basked in the feeling that this was a setting more in keeping with his stature. He didn't notice Rifsky shake hands with the waiter, discretely transferring a fifty pound note. The waiter smiled at Bruno as he hurried away, his curiosity and questions dulled by the note in his pocket.

Without much interest, Bruno asked. 'What were you talking about?'

Rifsky answered smiling. 'It's good to talk Russian again. I ordered drinks and asked him the restaurant's speciality.'

The waiter soon returned with two vodkas. Rifsky smiled at Bruno. 'To Russia!' He threw his drink down in one. 'That's good vodka, another!'

They had drunk three by the time the food arrived. It was an excellent meal and the waiter was very attentive, their glasses never remaining empty for long. Rifsky chatted about London, comparing the city with Moscow. Bruno let him talk. He ate, he drank. He was just infantile enough to view the vodka shots as competitive so he kept up with Rifsky's energetic pace.

Much later, they stood up to leave and Bruno couldn't help noticing that he didn't appear to have normal control of his legs. This, he decided, was simply because the floor wasn't as stable as when he arrived. It seemed to lurch as if he were at sea. The glistening chandelier had also undergone an interesting transformation. There was a second one overlapping the first. No matter how much he stared at it, the thing refused to become one. He pulled back his shoulders and walked with dignity in a straight-ish line toward the exit. He was ridiculously pleased with himself to reach the door, his slack face grinned at Rifsky, who held it open for him. Outside, the fresh air was lying in wait and hit him like a cosh. 'Ooow.' He held onto the restaurant wall and waited for the street to settle down.

Rifsky threw a friendly arm around his shoulder and began to move slowly down the street. 'I think we get a little air before a cab.'

This seemed reasonable. Bruno wasn't in the mood for a moving vehicle, the street was swaying about quite enough.

Rifsky talked cheerfully. 'Salvatore, he's quite the man! Killed someone in the street with the press watching and finds a way out!' He laughed. 'You have to be impressed, he's got brains, hasn't he?'

Bruno gave a sarcastic laugh. 'Ahh! Brains? I'll tell you this… he's nothing! Big man, going to meetings, bits of paper… little bits of paper… he's made of paper. It's guts that count.' To emphasise the statement, Bruno slapped himself in the stomach and immediately wished he hadn't. He took a moment, then continued, 'Strength, that's what the organisation needs. People like me!' As he said *me*, Bruno poked himself in the chest with his thumb, thinking it would be a safer bet. He was wrong. The violent movement of his arm caused him to stagger again and bump into the wall.

For a few steps, Rifsky was silent, then gave Bruno another nudge. 'Don't suppose you'll get the chance to show what you can do. Salvatore isn't going anywhere.'

'Isn't he?' Bruno laughed. 'I got plans for Mr Paper Man.'

This was it, Rifsky kept his tone casual. 'Oh yes, what're you gonna do?'

Bruno turned to face him and still smiling, put a finger to his own lips. 'Shhhh, can't say... ish a secret.' With that, he turned and staggered on.

Rifsky didn't give up so easily.

It was very late when Salvatore heard the tapping and fumbling of Bruno's attempts to put a key into at least one of the two locks he could see. Finally, the front door opened and Salvatore could hear staggering footsteps in the hall. He lowered his book and waited for the living room door to open, which it did with force. Bruno lurched into the room. 'Good night, good bye!' He laughed and swayed back into the hall to attempt the stairs. Rifsky walked across the room and sat in a chair near Salvatore. The room was subtly lit by two lamps. Salvatore sat in a pool of light cast by his reading lamp. The curtains had been drawn to keep the cold night out of the warm, comfortable room.

Salvatore and Rifsky sat in silence and listened to Bruno floundering about upstairs, presumably attempting to take off his clothes. Finally, all was quiet.

Salvatore took his eyes from the ceiling and regarded Rifsky. 'I see you administered copious amounts of truth drug.'

Rifsky grinned. 'More than a bottle each I think.'

'You appear to be immune?'

Rifsky nodded. 'The waiter was very helpful, I had shots of water while Bruno enjoyed his vodka.'

'Did you find out anything?'

Rifsky grew serious. 'Not much. I'm sorry. He's an angry and jealous man, he believes your position should be his.'

None of this was news, as Salvatore was well aware that Bruno wanted his job. The big question was, did he intend to do anything about it?

'I can tell you this.' Rifsky hesitated. Was he being foolish telling Salvatore what he thought? Possibly, but he would do it anyway. 'I believe he may have a plan, he wouldn't say what. He kept putting his finger to his lips and saying he has a secret. He seems really pleased with himself. Of course, it may all be a fantasy, some scenario he's made up in his head and it's nothing but wishful thinking, but I believe if he gets an opportunity to do you harm he'll take it, for sure. I will watch him. You should also be vigilant, I believe his anger goes deep.'

Usually, Rifsky wasn't particularly loyal to anyone. He went with the flow, it was a way to survive. However, he *liked* Salvatore, he respected his brains and he didn't like Bruno. But he was mindful that if something went wrong, he could easily find himself working for Bruno. 'This stays between us?' Rifsky phrased it as a question.

Salvatore was equally cautious. Bruno was a favourite of Q's. Before he made open accusations, he needed to be certain, 'Uncle Q thinks a lot of Bruno.'

Rifsky nodded, understanding the gravity behind Salvatore's simple statement. Uncle Q wasn't a man to annoy; very *few* did it more than *once*.

They both looked solemn. Rifsky was many things, some not very pleasant, but he was an optimist. He tended to find things in life to be pleased about. As he stood up to go to bed, he smiled at Salvatore, 'You don't have to worry about him tonight. He's not in any condition to do much harm. In fact, I'd be surprised if he's able to do *anything* before tomorrow afternoon.'

Salvatore gave him a faint smile. 'Good night, Rifsky.'

The next day was Tuesday. Bruno opened his eyes and attempted to get out of bed. He got only as far as lifting his head, to find the room spun. He lay very still and raised a hand to touch his forehead, just to be certain he hadn't been attacked. He was slightly surprised not to find a meat cleaver embedded in his head, because it certainly felt like it. He licked his dry lips and replayed what he could remember of the night before. Good food, ugh, don't think of food. Vodka! Lots of vodka. He had shouted, what about? He'd made some kind of speech to Rifsky. Suddenly he was worried. *What* had he told Rifsky? He vaguely remembered walking in the street, but didn't remember getting home. *What had he said?*

An hour later, when he felt able to stand and make the stairs, a very pale face peered around the living room door. Salvatore glanced up; he had been sitting reading again and - judging by the empty sandwich plate and coffee cup beside him - for some time.

'I hear you and Rifsky had quite the party last night.' Salvatore was smiling.

Although Bruno felt ill, he relaxed a little. Salvatore seemed to be acting normally, which was encouraging. Bruno sagged into a seat. He wished he'd sat more carefully, as the room shifted and quivered slightly. He held his head very still until the room stabilised and the knife attack on his head abated. 'Where's Rifsky?'

'I think he can handle his vodka better than you, he's gone sightseeing.'

Bruno was slightly surprised that anyone who had drunk as much as they had was capable of wandering the streets of London. He doubted he was capable of wandering into the kitchen for a glass of water even though he badly wanted one.

Salvatore went back to his book. Bruno leaned his head into the soft leather of the chair and shut his eyes. He really wished he could remember exactly what he'd said last night. It was a deep worry.

Salvatore lowered his book slightly and regarded the wreckage that sat in the chair opposite. When Bruno had first entered the room he'd appeared not only ill but worried. The man still looked pale and sick but not so worried. Why?

As Rifsky predicted, Bruno wasn't fit enough to make much of the day. He said very little, sipped water and managed half a sandwich very late in the afternoon then took himself to bed early.

PART ONE

CHAPTER 13
FILM LOCATION, SOUTH EAST LONDON
WEDNESDAY MORNING

For Vicky, the day had begun well. She was up and out before first light, therefore spared the familiar spectacle of Ron's rise from the bed. She always imagined it must be similar to watching a sole survivor of some terrible catastrophe crawl from the wreckage. Though Vicky loved Ron dearly and spoke of him highly, even she could never claim - at least, not with a straight face - that Ron was a morning person.

Vicky had arrived on set by six. As she entered the make-up trailer, the familiar scent of hairspray and the faint odour of acetone greeted her; she loved it. Every day, her knowledge of this challenging and exciting world grew.

Maggie and Jane were already there, setting up. The call sheet was checked and the first of the actors brought in. The girls worked steadily until after eight, then filming began. Maggie told them both she could handle removing the make-up so they might as well head off. The shoot was scheduled to wrap before lunch. The director was in dialogue with the stunt team that afternoon so none of the make-up artists - or MUAs as they are known in the business - were needed for the rest of the day.

Since Vicky had finished working, dramatic things had happened to her. She sat at the wheel of the Chevvy and drove across London at speed, desperate to get home. Anyone able to view her closely would have been shocked that she was *able* to drive at all. She took her eyes from the road and moved her head slightly to view herself in the rearview mirror, then turned her attention back to the road and tried to concentrate on driving, her hands gripping the steering wheel tightly.

On arriving at the flat she swung the big car into the alley with practised accuracy, the parking space being part of the residency when Ron had purchased the flat. She locked the car and hurried up the steps.

Ron looked up from his desk in the living room as he heard the door open. Vicky walked slowly down the hall, entered the living room and leaned heavily on the doorframe for support. They stared at each other. Ron's stomach tightened momentarily. Her injuries were extensive and the attacker had clearly targeted her face. Her right eye was puffy and a dark bruise was beginning to form beneath it. She had a very angry looking gash on her forehead, blood from this had formed a dark, matted clump in her hair. There were multiple abrasions to her cheek. It seemed she had been in a violent collision with something hard and rough. Her small nose had a deep cut on the bridge and was swollen, possibly broken. The gash on her neck was worryingly deep and looked as if it would require careful stitching. Her knuckles were red and grazed, it seemed she had put up a fight. Her injuries were truly terrible. Neither said anything.

Vicky slowly smiled as Ron stood up from his desk. 'Would you like a cup of tea?' He asked mildly.

Vicky's grin melted. 'Is that all you can say?'

'Oh, I'm sorry, did you want a biscuit with it?'

She managed to convey plaintive disappointment with a touch of exasperation in her one word response. 'Ron!'

He laughed and hurried over. 'No, it's fantastic, you honestly had me scared for a moment, you really did. It's your best yet, it really is very good, even up close.'

'We had some time after the make-up was done early this morning so Maggie has given me some more tuition. I did it *all* though, under her instructions, in the mirror and that's *really* hard!'

When Vicky had first brought her work home to show him, in the form of small cuts and light bruising, it had been quite a shock. The phrase, "Bloody hell, Vicky, you're trying to kill me!" had been used, accompanied by a splayed hand across his chest to check that all was still ticking. At the time, Vicky's unrepentant response had been, "I thought you'd be pleased for me! I worked hard on this," indicating her face. Lately, the effects had gradually escalated as she learned her craft, culminating in this triumph of misery.

'You look really disturbing and pukey.'

She beamed. 'You're not just saying that?'

'No, you look truly terrible.'

'Do you really mean it?'

'Yes.'

'It's very important, do I *really* look stomach-churning?'

'I know your work is important to you and I honestly think you look horrible.'

'That's so sweet, thank you. I have to admit I am very pleased with the swelling, it's a lot more tricky than bruising.'

'Tell you what, if I didn't know you, I'd call an ambulance.'

Vicky was delighted but became a little shy. 'I don't know if it's good enough for an ambulance, I was hoping for a doctor.'

'No, definitely an ambulance. Look at the deep one on your neck, you could bleed out at any moment, it's marvellous.'

'Thanks Ron.' She kissed him.

'How on earth did you do the swelling and deep cuts?'

'They're called prosthetics; silicon moulds. Maggie makes her own, they're glued on and the thin edges melted out and blended with acetone then make-up paint. It's *really* tricky in the mirror. Maggie was ever so complimentary.' Vicky was obviously pleased with her accomplishments and Ron was deeply happy to see her so animated. Her eyes sparkled with energy and enthusiasm.

She asked eagerly, 'How's your creativity going?'

Ron glanced at the pile of scribbled paper on the desk. 'Great, I've written the complete storyline and one or two full scenes. Of course, the story is mostly only a skeleton outline with a list of events. I'm going to let Shades have a read, see what he thinks before I expand the scenes.'

'That's wonderful.'

'What with me getting the framework down and you managing to look truly mutilated, let's go to the club to celebrate. We can have a glass before lunch and I can drop this off. You'd better remove the make-up.'

'Aw, I wanted to show Shades and Tony.'

'I don't think we can walk into *The Blue Parrot* with you looking like that. Someone *will* phone for an ambulance or pass out.'

The lavish praise was making her feel self-conscious. 'Oh, shut up.'

'It's true.'

She kissed him again, but this time, as Ron kissed her cheek, Vicky pulled back quickly and sucked her teeth as if the kiss had hurt her bruised, swollen face. They both laughed and Vicky strode off to the bathroom in high spirits.

After thirty minutes of peeling, scrubbing and dabbing, they sat in the car. Ron glanced at the now normal face in the rearview mirror. Ron had been so wrapped up in the book he still hadn't phoned to ask his welder friend Dave to repair the front passenger seat.

'Vicky?'

'Ron?'

'You don't mind Shades reading it first, do you?'

'No, I know it's how you like to work.'

'I do want you to read it but not in this raw form. I'd like your opinion when it's closer to the final draft.'

'I don't mind. Stop worrying. By the way, you haven't forgotten you're doing that book signing and talk at the library?'

'No, I prepared all that before I got the story idea.'

'Good. Right, come on, let's go. I have to say, I rather like sitting in the back, I can pretend I've got a chauffeur.'

'Where to, m'Lady?'

'To *The Blue Parrot,* my good man.'

And off they went.

CHAPTER 14
THE BLUE PARROT
WEDNESDAY, 11.30AM

'Sorry, guys, he's out, said he wouldn't be long. Do you want a drink while you wait?'

Ron and Vicky sat at one of the downstairs bars in the club. The barman waited patiently for an answer. A few customers sat at nearby tables but the club wasn't busy.

Ron was cheerful, the writing had flowed as is sometimes the case and he had high hopes for his storyline. It was such a relief. 'Yes, two glasses of Champagne. Let's crack one of those half bottles.'

'Coming right up, Mr Moon.'

Vicky and Ron raised the bubbles high and touched glasses... *tink.* Vicky called the toast. 'Here's to another bestseller.'

'Well, it's a bit early for that but I am pleased with the storyline. Can't wait to show Shades.' They chatted happily for a while, then, 'Right, it's still early. Now, you could spend the morning sitting around here listening to Shades and me talking murder, plots, old films, great directors, camera angles and writing or...'

'Mm, or...?'

'Hop on a train to Charing Cross, get a taxi up West and celebrate in your own way with some shopping.'

'Mm, tricky one.'

There was a pause, a very brief pause. He grinned. 'See you later, have fun.'

'I will, I'll have a late lunch when I get there. You'll be okay?'

'I'll have a sandwich here, or at home, I don't know.'

'After you have your meeting with Shades, go home. I'll get a cab back.'

Ron kissed her goodbye and Vicky slid off the barstool, slipped on her coat and headed for the door.

As she was leaving, Bruno, Salvatore and Rifsky were coming in. They passed each other with hardly a glance. The men moved to their regular table in the far corner and Salvatore sat in his usual seat with his back to the room. Out of habit, Rifsky carefully scanned the huge room. The bar had a mix of customers: a few young couples deep in conversation, absorbed in each other's company; a sprinkling of office workers out for a light lunch and a glass of wine. There was also a group of older men playing cards. Rifsky's eye lingered for a moment on one of the group; big shoulders, a possible problem when he was young, but those days were obviously long gone. A loud group of very young men sat near the card players; kids! All mouth, no substance. Rifsky found nothing to worry him and offered to get the drinks.

Salvatore was growing restless. When Bruno and Rifsky had decided to have a lunchtime drink and a sandwich, he had decided to accompany them on impulse. Now he wasn't sure it had been a good idea. At first, Bruno hadn't seemed happy that he had joined him and Rifsky, but then, on the way to *The Blue Parrot,* unexpectedly, Bruno had begun talking about Anna.

Unsettled, Salvatore suddenly spoke. 'I don't know if I'll stay. I shouldn't really be away from the phone in case Q or Anna calls.'

Bruno answered quickly, 'As I said, I don't know why you don't get her over. She has a sister in London, hasn't she?'

Salvatore regarded Bruno with open suspicion knowing that Bruno didn't like Anna. Cautiously, he responded, 'Could be dangerous.' He looked to Rifsky for his opinion.

Rifsky shrugged. 'I could ensure she isn't tracked in Milan; the security team are all good men. I could also make some calls, have her picked up here in London. Again, make sure no-one's following her, have her driven here by our people. I would collect her from some public place, not too far. Then I *personally* would be happy she's not followed. The official story in Milan would be she's visiting her sister, seeking family support after your death.' He paused as he considered the idea. 'Yes, it would be logical for her to come. Don't believe it would raise suspicion.'

Salvatore trusted Rifsky's opinion a great deal more than Bruno's. What he didn't understand was what Bruno would have to gain by bringing Anna to London.

'I'll think about it.' What Salvatore meant was, *I'll think about what Bruno is up to.*

Bruno decided not to push. If Salvatore was thinking about bringing Anna over, it was progress. Now he needed to get him out of the club. 'So, what are you going to do today? Just wait by the phone?'

Salvatore sighed; this waiting was beginning to play on his nerves. As each day passed, he grew more frustrated. 'Same as yesterday and the day before, I'll take a short walk, get some food and go back to the house. What about you?'

Bruno didn't like roaming the chilly streets. 'I'll get a snack here and probably wander back.' After the night of vodka, he had little interest in drinking. A half glass of red was probably his limit, if he could find a decent one.

Salvatore turned his attention to Rifsky, who grinned and produced a pamphlet from his pocket like a conjuror. 'I'm going to see Trafalgar Square and then walk down The Mall.' Bruno grunted but Rifsky ignored him and added, 'Unless you need anything?'

Salvatore shook his head. 'No, you go. No point us all being bored. I'll let you know what I decide about Anna, see you both later.'

To Bruno's relief, he rose and walked to the door. As Bruno watched, Salvatore opened the door, but instead of walking through, he took a step back. Shades was coming in, carrying three boxes of crisps and two boxes of peanuts. Bruno's knuckles became white as he clenched his hands.   Rifsky noticed Bruno's stare and followed it.

Shades said, 'Thanks mate,' to the stranger who he couldn't see from behind the pile of boxes.

Salvatore answered. 'You're welcome.' He slipped out without a backward glance.

Bruno relaxed: that was too close. He *must* keep Salvatore out of the club. Suddenly, he became aware that Rifsky was watching him. 'What?'

'Is everything alright, Bruno?'

'Yeah, why shouldn't it be?'

Rifsky shrugged again. 'No reason.' He continued to regard Bruno. *He was lying.* Something was going on, perhaps he should stick around. 'I think I'll have a small vodka, before I head off.'

'Yes, it's freezing out there.' Bruno raised his shoulders and shivered.

Rifsky laughed. 'This is Summer! In Russia, we get minus forty, that's chilly.'

Bruno rarely travelled much outside Italy and the thought of minus forty degrees caused him to pull his heavy long coat more tightly around him. He shivered again, in spite of the warmth of the club. *The Blue Parrot* was comfortable and welcoming. Bruno's lack of tolerance to the cold amused Rifsky.

Shades just made it to the bar without dropping the boxes. He acknowledged Ron with a nod. 'Ron.'

'Hi, been shopping?'

'The delivery didn't turn up. I had to go to the wholesaler to get some for tonight. I'll put this lot away, hang up my coat and I'm with you, okay?'

'No problem.'

Ron barely glanced up, he was studying the rough outline of the story and chewing his pen thoughtfully.

From his table, Rifsky watched the exchange. He noticed that as Shades moved away, he laid a hand momentarily on Ron's shoulder. It was clear they were friends. Rifsky was wondering who Shades was and if Bruno's reaction was anything he should take an interest in, so he repeated his offer to get the drinks. 'Right, I'm getting a vodka, do you want one?'

Bruno was going to say yes, then remembered the last time and his terrible hangover. He thought about wine but it would be the house red. 'No.'

'Okay.' Rifsky turned and walked towards the bar. He wasn't offended by Bruno's sharp tone, in fact it made him laugh. He knew full well why Bruno wasn't drinking. After the hangover Bruno had just endured, Rifsky wouldn't have been surprised if he'd decided to become teetotal forever. He approached the bar close to where Ron was sitting, and asked the barman for a vodka.

Ron glanced up at the sound of Rifsky's voice. 'Excuse me, I'm sorry to trouble you, my name's Ronnie Moon. I'm a writer... I write thrillers. Couldn't help noticing your accent, it's not Russian by chance is it?' Rifsky's unblinking stare prompted Ron to elaborate; 'You see, I'm looking for a typical

Russian name for a fictitious character.' Ron tapped his writing pad with his pen indicating the problem paragraph.

Rifsky relaxed a little. In Russia, you were careful what you said to strangers. Old instincts to be cautious were strong. But he wanted information from Ron and he sensed the writer's story was true. He smiled faintly. 'Boris is a good solid Russian name, or Victor.'

Ron was pleased. 'Ah, Boris, Victor, mm... both good, thank you.'

'You are welcome. This is a nice bar.'

Ron glanced around the solid Victorian building, with its beautiful brickwork, the elegant, gunmetal grey iron girders and he smiled. 'I like it here, it's a marvellous old building.'

'You are a regular?'

Ron answered enthusiastically. 'Yes, the owners are friends of mine.'

Rifsky tipped his head towards Shades, who was busy at the other end of the bar, opening boxes and stacking the contents.

'He owns this place?'

'Yes, with his brother, Tony.'

'Who is he?'

'That's Shades, Shades Manning.'

Rifsky had never heard the name Shades before. He suspected there were lots of English names he wasn't familiar with. He didn't realise Shades was a nickname.

Ron confided in his new friend. 'As a writer, I'm always having to come up with names. Take this new story, there are lots of characters. I need an Italian name too for this shifty character. Shades is good at suggestions and he sometimes helps with names.'

Now Rifsky actually grinned. 'Bruno is a typical Italian name for your shifty character.'

'Is it?'

'Oh yes, I have travelled through Italy on business. Bruno is... I think the English phrase is... "common as muck".'

Ron was interested. 'Really?'

Rifsky was enjoying himself now. 'Yes, yes most ordinary like..., Smith. Somehow, I think it suits a shifty character.'

The barman put Rifsky's vodka in front of him, he paid for it and turned to go. 'Good luck with your book.'

'Thanks.'

Rifsky returned to his table. A burst of laughter from the young men caused him to look in their direction. The group of elderly card players were glaring at the young men and the broad-shouldered man was pointing a warning finger at one of the youths, who seemed to find it amusing. Children and old folks. Rifsky was still smiling at the thought of Bruno being cast as a shifty character in a book. He found the idea disproportionately amusing. He wouldn't forget Bruno's reaction to Shades, but at the moment, he couldn't see how a London bar owner was connected with Bruno or the organisation. Perhaps he reminded Bruno of someone.

Rifsky sat down. Now it was Bruno's turn to be suspicious. It was out of character for Rifsky to talk to strangers. Normally, he kept himself to himself and blended into the background: it was what he did best.

'Who's the guy sitting at the bar?'

Rifsky's smile widened. 'He's a writer... writes thrillers.'

'What's funny about that?'

'Nothing.' He took a sip of his vodka. 'I'm off to see the Queen.'

Bruno's frown deepened. Why was Rifsky so happy and what the hell was he talking about? 'The Queen?'

'Well... her house.' He slipped a small map from a pocket and pointed. 'At the end of The Mall, off Trafalgar Square. First, I'll see the Square, then the Queen.' He put away the map and added proudly, 'Trafalgar Square is a postage stamp compared with Red Square.'

Bruno tutted. He just wanted Rifsky to take his smiling face and go. Somehow, he had the impression Rifsky was laughing at him. He soon got his wish. Rifsky downed the vodka and stood up, 'I'm off.'

'Good.'

He knew he was annoying Bruno and loved it. It would suit him very well if Bruno lost control, giving him an opportunity to rough Bruno up a little. Rifsky was a very good judge of people and Bruno had too much power for someone of his character. He was aware Bruno was dangerous and he believed only he and Salvatore fully understood how dangerous. If he provoked a move on his own terms, he could take Bruno down a peg and as head of the organisation's security, he would be listened to. But the problem was, an opinion without evidence to back it up would be frowned upon by men like Uncle Q. It would be a very stupid man who upset Uncle Q without a damned good reason. Still smiling, Rifsky picked up his coat and left to see the sights.

The Blue Parrot had begun to provide light lunches for which they had taken on extra staff to help. Today, it was Kirsten Kysow. As the young waitress hurried past his table, Bruno beckoned her over. He ordered bread, cheese, a bowl of salad and, against his better judgement, a very small glass of red wine. He needed to check Rifsky's story so he pointed to Ron, still sitting at the bar. 'Is he a regular? I think I know him from somewhere but I could be wrong.'

Kirsten was very happy to talk about Ron. 'Yes, that's Ronnie Moon, the writer. He's quite famous, you know.' The young lady glowed with enthusiasm, seeming delighted to have what she obviously regarded as a celebrity, in the bar. When Bruno didn't react, she elaborated, 'You probably saw his picture on the back of a book, or on a poster, they're all over the borough. He's giving a talk on Thursday morning at the library.'

As Bruno didn't appear impressed, the waitress felt she hadn't been clear so she reiterated, 'Ronnie Moon, the thriller writer, that's why he looks familiar.'

Bruno nodded. 'Ah, that must be it.'

'I read a lot.'

'Do you?' Bruno was losing interest fast, but Kirsten was on a subject dear to her heart and didn't notice.

'Yes, Ronnie Moon writes great stories, real page turners. I love a good story. He's best friends with my boss, Shades; of course, *he* prefers films, not books. It's all stories though, isn't it?'

Bruno had been under the impression that Tony ran the club with his younger brother. He didn't recognise the name Shades. To keep the waitress talking he feigned new interest. 'Shades? That's a strange name.' Although out of practice, Bruno attempted what he believed to be a friendly smile. 'And he likes movies?'

Luckily for him, Kirsten didn't notice as she was searching through her pockets for the notepad, or it might have unnerved her. Finding it, she looked up and after writing down his choice, continued enthusiastically to tell him about her colourful boss. 'It's a passion, he has regular film nights after the club shuts, on the last Thursday of the month; he's got a private cinema under the club.' She stamped the floor with her foot, just in case there was any doubt where "under the club" was. 'They all go, Tony, his brother Shades, Ronnie Moon and Vicky, that's his girlfriend.'

So it appeared Tony's little brother had got himself a nickname, Shades. And he knew where to find him and his friend, Ronnie Moon, on the last Thursday of the month. This could be useful.

Kirsten shifted her chat to more philosophical grounds. 'Stories, books, it's all food for the soul, don't you think?'

Bruno decided it was time to cut the conversation short. He didn't want anyone looking over at him, and the waitress had stood by his table long enough. 'Mmm, true, but today I was hoping for food for the body.'

She coloured a little, suddenly realising enthusiasm for her hobby might have bored her audience. This was her first job since leaving school and with the determination only youth can muster, she was going to make it a success. 'Of course, it won't be long... sir.' Kirsten tacked on the sir to show she was a professional, flashed Bruno a quick smile and hurried off to fetch his food.

Bruno lost interest in Ron. It seemed that Rifsky was telling the truth, the man was only some local author. He had other more urgent matters to consider. It was imperative to his plan that he convince Salvatore to bring Anna over from Italy. Also, he must prevent Salvatore coming to *The Blue Parrot* anymore, until he was ready and somehow, he needed to get rid of Rifsky for the day when the time came to bring Salvatore face to face with Shades. What a ridiculous nickname; he probably thought it made him mysterious. Huh!

Bruno reflected darkly on Rifsky. He was beginning to rival Salvatore as somebody he would take real pleasure in disposing of. It would be joyous if he could get rid of him, not only for the day but permanently and wipe the smug smile from his stupid face for good. He was sure Rifsky enjoyed needling him. He was really asking for it.

'You're asking for it, boy!'

Bruno was surprised to hear his thought articulated at that instant. He looked in the direction of the raised voice. It was the broad-shouldered card player. He'd slammed his cards face down on the table and begun to rise to his feet. One of his friends rested a restraining hand on his shoulder. 'Leave it, Danny! 'S not worth it.'

Danny glared at the young men on the nearby table, slowly sat down and picked up his cards. Bruno watched with interest; he enjoyed a good fight but it seemed it was only talk. Shame. Watching someone get their nose smashed in would have relieved a little frustration and cheered him up. He really enjoyed violence. He and Rifsky had different approaches to most things, that's why they disliked each other. Rifsky had been violent in the past and was prepared to be in the future. He was very confident in a fight and had walked away leaving bigger opponents on the ground, covered in blood. Sometimes, it was part of his job but he had no feelings about it... none. It needed doing, so he did it and moved on. Bruno was different, he enjoyed it and liked to watch. If he had to pay a call with some muscle to sort out an enemy of the organisation, he relished seeing the fear. Regrettably, this seldom occurred these days. He really missed the old days.

It wasn't only Bruno who noticed the altercation. After Shades had stacked the snacks behind the bar he'd nipped upstairs to the flat, deposited his coat and collected a large briefcase. He set the case on the bar and was about to sit on the barstool next to Ron when he heard Danny shout at the youths. 'I'd better go over,' he said to Ron, still watching the two factions.

Ron glanced over his shoulder. 'Leave it, they're okay. Look, I've made real progress on the story.' He was so enthusiastic that Shades gave in and sat down. Suddenly Ron noticed the case. 'What's that for?'

Shades patted it. 'Some paperwork for the club. Me and Tony do have a bar to run, y'know. Can't spend all my time giving brilliant storylines to clapped-out writers.'

'Shut up, you only gave me a whisper of an idea. *I* brought it to life.'

Ron's indignation made Shades laugh. 'Okay then, genius, what have you come up with? Hang on a minute.' Shades fished about in his jacket pockets. 'Here!' He produced two packets of crisps, tossed one onto the bar for Ron, and began to open his own.

Ron examined his crisps. 'Beef and onion?' He nodded towards his glass. 'Champagne is white wine, show some class.'

Shades stopped trying to open his packet and looked up. 'Oh, I'm so very sorry, what was I thinking! Have my chicken flavour.'

'Thank you.'

They swapped packets, Ron held his high. 'Cheers.'

Shades lifted up his packet and the bags touched with a mild crunch. They both grinned childishly. Ron was so happy to finally have his story idea. After putting down his crisps, he rubbed his hands together excitedly and looked down affectionately at his paperwork. 'Right then, and so to business. This first page is a list of possible book titles…'

'Mm.'

'…Then a detailed scenario. I've just decided on some character names, then there's a rough sequence of events. Finally, some complete chapters I'm sure I want to include… well, pretty sure. I want you to read what I've got so far. See if you think I've missed anything or if there are any inconsistencies that don't make sense. Can you do it quickly?'

'Quickly?'

'Yes, I'm really excited about this story and I want to dive straight back in and begin to flesh it out.'

Shades pointed to his case. 'I must look over some of the accounts. Tony's been dropping hints I leave too much to him. When he talks about plans to improve this or that I can't contribute because I haven't kept up with the numbers.' The disappointment on Ron's face prompted him to add, 'This evening. Promise.'

Instantly, Ron cheered up. 'Okay, thank you and we can talk early next week?'

'Sure.'

It suddenly occurred to Ron he could gain some brownie points with Vicky if he asked gently about Jane. 'You're free then, early next week?'

'Yeah.'

'I thought you were seeing a lot of Jane lately.'

'Yeah.'

'She's nice.'

'Yeah.'

Ron squirmed a little, 'I think she's *really* nice.'

Shades knew Ron was fishing, 'You wanna go out with her?'

It was no secret that Ron loved Vicky deeply. Shades' sarcastic answer annoyed him sufficiently to drop the subtlety. For a man who used words for a living, Ron could have used some lessons from Vicky on tact. He dived in feet first and didn't hold back. 'Okay, Vicky's worried Jane might get hurt. Are you serious about her? Vicky says Jane's getting mixed messages. She doesn't know what to think. Vicky feels Jane's falling for you.' Ron poured it out in a rush to get it over with, he was far from certain Vicky would have approved of the direct approach. Perhaps he wouldn't tell her. As soon as this thought crossed his mind, he knew it was a lie. He told Vicky everything.

Shades turned away and stared at the optics behind the bar.

Ron began to worry that his unique version of diplomacy might have upset his friend. He added gently. 'It's none of our business, Shades. It's only that Jane's been really good to Vicky, helping her after all the trouble last year. They're close and she would hate to see Jane hurt.'

'I'm honestly not sure, Ron. She's great to be with… You mentioned the trouble you and Vicky had last year…'

'Yes?'

Shades looked at him steadily, wondering if he wanted to explain. Next to Tony, Ron and Vicky were his closest friends. He glanced around to check no one was close enough to hear and took the plunge. 'You and Vicky were in pretty deep.' Ron nodded and raised his eyebrows; there was no denying things had been dicey. 'I mean life and death. You got to know each other in ways only that kind of pressure can achieve. You faced things together and came through. You know you can rely on each other, whatever life throws at you.'

'Are you saying you don't trust Jane?'

Shades grimaced. 'I don't trust *my* judgement. There it is, I've said it.'

'Why?'

'I just don't, okay?'

Ron knew when to leave it and asked no further questions. He would talk it over with Vicky, who was often wise in matters of the heart. Who was he kidding? She was just plain clever about most things. There was a thoughtful pause, then Shades added, 'Since we're being straight with each other, is Vicky really okay?'

'She still has nightmares sometimes.' They were silent for a moment.

Shades wasn't surprised. 'It'll take time.'

'Mm.'

'She's got you, she'll be alright.'

'Yes.' Ron brightened. 'She's shopping in the West End at the moment, so I know she's alright today.'

Shades slapped a hand down on the case. 'The sooner I look at this paperwork, the sooner I can read your story outline.'

Ron was happy to leave Shades to it. 'Right, I'll be off. Phone me, okay?' He hopped down from the barstool, Shades stood up and they shook hands.

After Ron had left, Shades sat thinking for a moment. He didn't want to hurt Jane but he'd been wrong before, very wrong. 'I don't know, I don't know.' The words were spoken softly. With his back to the room, no one witnessed Shades' face become melancholy. He missed Jane when she wasn't around and looked forward to seeing her. Watching films together in his cinema had been a joy. All the signs were there, he was beginning to care for her. The decision couldn't be delayed much longer, he would have to either walk away or commit. This 'close friends but no more situation' wasn't good for either of them. But what if…? He shook his head. Tonight. Tonight he would take a drink up to the roof of the club. Up there it was quiet, he could look out over London and think. He would make a decision tonight. Vicky was right, he wasn't being fair. He eyed the case. The club was in very good shape, the money flowing in. But because of Jane, lately he had left it all to Tony. Quite rightly, Tony had remarked that Shades needed to be up to speed. Tony always seemed to know what was right, what needed to be done. The sod!

Shades carefully placed Ron's manuscript to one side and opened the case. When he worked on the club's records, he often sat at one of the bars. He liked to keep an eye on things and he didn't find those around him a distraction. Somehow, the apartment upstairs was too quiet. Tony didn't approve but Shades did it anyway. He spread out the papers and began to read. After a few minutes he pulled a pen from his jacket and made little notes in the margins for Tony.

Bruno had received his food and was chewing his salad: not enough olive oil! Glancing around, he couldn't see the waitress. He tutted, stood and started to walk towards the bar to request some. He was halfway there when it happened. Danny launched to his feet with surprising speed for an elderly man, his chair flew back and he knocked over the table. This resulted in the explosion of four pint glasses shattering as they hit the floor. The usual background murmur of conversation ceased and all eyes were on him. Danny shook with rage. 'I'll bloody kill you!' He slid into the familiar stance of a boxer and focussed sharp attention on the three youths at the adjacent table. Slowly, they rose and backed away a little.

Shades approached swiftly. 'What the hell's going on?'

Bruno didn't want to be caught up in trouble or be noticed, so he quickly slipped past Shades and moved to the bar where Shades had spread his paperwork.

Meanwhile, Shades positioned himself between Danny and the youths. 'Well?' He demanded.

No one spoke. Shades glanced at the grinning young men then at Danny's angry face. He assessed the situation fast and made a decision. 'You!' He pointed at the youths. 'You're barred, get out!'

One took half a step forward to show he was the leader. 'You can't bar us, we ain't done nothin'! It's 'Enry Cooper's[4] grandad 'ere, 'e started it.' The young man grinned and pointed at Danny, who moved forward as if about to take a swing. The young man took a step back and bumped into somebody standing behind him. He turned, expecting to see a face. No face, just a chest. He looked up at the huge man. The grin evaporated. Tony leaned down, putting his face very close and said quietly. 'Out.' It was an indication of the young man's stupidity that momentarily, he considered arguing. After all, his mates were watching. But there was something in Tony's unblinking expression that made him realise that arguing would be a *very* bad idea.

'I was about to leave anyway.'

Tony said no more, maintaining his cold stare. He was absolutely sure the young man would do nothing, the fear in his eyes was unmistakeable. Tony had made

---

[4] Henry Cooper was a famous English Boxer at the time.

no threats but the young man was in no doubt Tony was capable of knocking him down with minimal effort. That would be bad enough, but in front of his mates, unthinkable. He walked away, his friends followed. After he had put a safe distance between himself and Tony with a more than fair chance of bolting for the door, he felt bold enough to say loudly, 'Let's get out of this dump.' They left quietly and showing wisdom beyond their years, didn't look back.

Tony glanced at Shades, who appeared irritated. They moved to the bar and sat. 'I had it under control.'

Tony ignored the statement and pointed at the now closed briefcase. 'I don't like you leaving the club's business scattered about on the bar for the world to see. I put all the papers away for you.'

Shades was about to inform him that he wasn't some child who needed clearing up after, when the young waitress hurried past, heading for the mess Danny and his friends had begun to clear up. Shades stopped her. 'Don't help them, Kirsten, they can do it, they caused it. Throw them a mop and a pan then leave them to it.'

The young woman nodded and moved off to fetch one then went to clear the uneaten food from Bruno's table. She discovered some money under the edge of the plate. Perfectly good food! People were funny. She stacked the tray, wiped the table and disappeared into the kitchen.

Danny and his friends finished tidying and Danny walked a little sheepishly towards Tony and Shades.

They both turned at the sound of his voice. 'I… I came over to apologise, I'll pay for any damage.'

The only damage was four broken glasses, Shades shook his head. 'There's no need for that, don't worry.'

Danny wore a troubled expression as he stood before them, searching for the right words. It wasn't time in the ring which had dulled his mind; he had never been what could be called an intellectual but he was a good man and a proud man, with a strong sense of fairness. Anyone should be proud to call him a friend. He felt driven to explain, 'Those kids were talking to me like I was nothin', laughin' at me.'

Tony spoke slowly, emphasising his words. 'Nobody would dispute you deserve respect, Danny, you were a champion boxer.' He resumed normal speech as he added, 'Also, no doubt those punks deserved a lesson, but take it outside, okay? We don't want the law sniffing around the club if one of 'em complains, alright?'

'Yeah, I understand. Sorry, Tony.'

Tony reached out and put a huge hand on Danny's shoulder. 'No problem.'

'I still feel bad about the damage.' Danny's face cleared, the worry lifted. 'I'll help with the monthly delivery.'

Shades answered before Tony could. 'You don't have to, Danny, really.'

'*I do*.' Danny responded quietly but firmly.

Tony regarded him thoughtfully; there was self-respect involved here. 'Thank you, I appreciate it.'

Danny, content, returned to his friends, who were dealing a new hand.

Shades turned to face the bar as Tony watched Danny walk away. Shades glanced over his shoulder to make sure Danny was out of earshot. 'Poor old sod, still thinks he's nineteen.'

Tony continued to watch Danny as he sat down and picked up his cards. 'If he had connected with those kids, he would have knocked them into the middle of next week.'

Shades was dismissive. 'He's old now, lost all his power.'

Tony wasn't so sure. 'He still goes to the gym once a week.'

Shades laughed. 'Yeah and he's in here the rest of the time.'

Tony shrugged; he had voiced his opinion.

One of the things that always annoyed Shades was Tony's unwillingness to argue. He said what he believed and if challenged he usually said no more, letting the original statement stand, refusing to be drawn in. He would listen calmly but if he remained silent, which he usually did, it indicated that your argument had failed and he hadn't changed his mind. What was even more infuriating, he was usually right and his judgement was never wrong when assessing people.

Shades decided to leave the paperwork for the day, since he simply couldn't focus on it. He had tried to defer the decision but in truth Ron's comments had unsettled him, he knew he wasn't being fair and now, he couldn't get Jane out of his mind.

PART ONE

CHAPTER 15
A LONDON STREET
WEDNESDAY AFTERNOON

'Do you wanna kill yourself?' The red-faced driver of the black London taxi glared at Bruno, who had jumped smartly back to the safety of the pavement. The driver shook his head as he slid his cab back into the stream of fast-moving traffic, receiving only two blasts and one waved fist from the other drivers, a personal best. Bruno watched him disappear as the heavy traffic closed in around the vehicle. A steady flow thundered endlessly along the busy street.

Bruno had been walking quickly, not paying attention. He was trying to make sense of it all. He spotted a little park close by. This small oasis of green was a welcome sight, not for the rich beauty of the Autumn leaves; because Bruno never noticed things of that sort. He needed to think and walked through the gates to sit on one of the Victorian benches. He stared at the ground and tried to reason it out. What was Rifsky's plan? How would he gain from this? Bruno was confused and angry: Rifsky was definitely playing games.

One of the many reasons Bruno would rise no higher in the organisation was his temper. It hindered good judgement, at odds with the cold money-making machine that was the organisation. Strangely, it was this reactionary violent attitude that Uncle found appealing. Bruno reminded him of younger days and old-school ways.

The thought of Rifsky's smiling face brought Bruno to his feet, fists clenched as tightly as his teeth. Rifsky was laughing at him! Well, Rifsky wasn't so clever, he didn't know what Bruno had seen at the club. Bruno sat down again and pulled some papers from his coat. After several minutes' reading, he was still confused. What was the purpose? How would these documents help Rifsky or anyone else? He brooded on the problem. The organisation was vast and though Milan had some of the key players it was by no means all. Who could Rifsky be working for? Perhaps someone wanted the Milan slice of the pie. It was one of the key spots. Perhaps they didn't want to be obvious. The days when different factions eliminated each other to advance were largely a thing of the past. But someone out there could be aiming to cause trouble. Send out a message that could take down some of the senior members: such as himself Salvatore and Uncle. It seemed a strange, convoluted method, but Rifsky was *Russian* and had worked for the KGB, who played odd smoke-and-mirror power games and of course, there was the night at the restaurant. *The night of the vodka.* Bruno balled one of his fists and struck his thigh. *If only he could remember what he had told Rifsky!*

He would return to the house, check on Salvatore, see if his attitude towards him had changed. See if he knew anything.

Bruno left the park and hurried along the crowded pavement, crossed the busy road and walked into the calm of the elegant square with the small, gated park at its centre. He marched eagerly up the steps and put his key in the front door. On entering the hall he pocketed the key, shut the door and hesitated. What if Salvatore knew what he planned? He shook his head; stupid! He'd *done nothing*. People would think Salvatore mad if he said he didn't like what he, Bruno, was thinking. But then there was Rifsky. If he had told Rifsky when he was drunk he was planning to kill Salvatore, what would Rifsky do? Would he tell Salvatore or Uncle? You just can't tell with Russians. He walked into the living room and received a warm welcome.

Salvatore was brighter than he'd been for days. 'Bruno! Great news!'

'Oh yes?'

Salvatore seemed to be genuinely happy. 'I've just spoken to Uncle. They have made contact with Dr Linsky. He finally phoned his office to check his messages. They told him a patient had been trying desperately to contact him. He phoned Uncle immediately. I think Uncle gave him a rocket. He's arranging things as quickly as he can.'

Bruno nodded, this was good. Salvatore was acting normally, so he didn't *know* anything. 'That's great, Sal.'

Salvatore was obviously relieved. Bruno had sat on a sofa to listen, but Salvatore paced about as he talked, clearly excited. 'He has to arrange the theatre staff, nurses, anaesthetist. Even though it's a private clinic, operations are supposed to be logged. Of course, this one will be off the books. The staff will be told I'm a VIP, I don't want publicity and they will be paid a high fee not to ask questions or talk about it. He told Uncle he must assemble a small team. He has a few names, some will have prior commitments but he feels confident that two to three working days will be enough time. So, today is Wednesday, he has till Monday to put together his team, that means we leave here Tuesday morning next week.'

'Oh right.' He nodded and frowned in thought. This wasn't so good, since his own plans weren't ready and it appeared they never would be. But he cheered up considerably at Salvatore's second piece of news.

'Also, Anna is coming over.' Salvatore had seriously missed his wife and little girl. Lucia couldn't come but the thought of seeing Anna lit up Salvatore's face like the glow from birthday candles.

'Oh, that's fantastic!' Bruno's delight extinguished the candles and cast a shadow of concern in Salvatore's mind. *Why was he so pleased?*

Now Bruno also felt too excited to sit still. He stood and spoke enthusiastically. 'It's coming together. When she arrives, d'you want me to meet her?'

'No, I'll send Rifsky. I'll talk about the various security aspects with him. We have to be sure she's not tracked.'

Bruno nodded. 'Of course, yes, absolutely. Great news, really.'

Again, the worry in Salvatore's mind, *why* was Bruno so happy for him? He was in no doubt that Bruno was jealous.

Bruno patted his empty pocket. 'I need some more cigarettes. D'you want anything?'

'No, I'm fine.'

Bruno even managed a flash of a smile as he left the room, leaving Salvatore to ponder further on his uncharacteristically cheerful attitude.

Bruno left the square, crossed the busy road and walked quickly. Anna was coming! He couldn't believe his luck but the doctor had been found, which meant that he must act soon. He needed to plan how to bring it all together. There wasn't much time; they were leaving the house on Tuesday morning, so Monday night was the last night, the last opportunity. Bruno stopped abruptly in the street, annoying a young couple walking quickly behind him. They tutted and veered round him. Bruno was oblivious to his surroundings, ideas where dropping into place like the barrels of a fruit machine: click, click, click, Jackpot! He needed a phone box. A quick call to Directory Enquiries and he had the number for *The Blue Parrot*. 'Hello? I'd like to speak to the owner. It's very important.'

A few minutes later, Bruno walked from the phone box, very pleased with himself. The call had gone well.

After buying his cigarettes, he made his way back along the crowded pavements, hardly noticing all the people hurrying past him, their faces made pale by the cold, their hands driven deep into pockets. He paused; Bruno was standing across the road from the square where the house stood. He could just make it out, slightly obscured by the trees in the little park. He couldn't think in the house with Salvatore there and he still had the problem of Rifsky to deal with. Ahead, the main road swept to the right. He noticed a coffee shop. It was so damned cold in this stinking country, perhaps he would think better in the warmth. Bruno believed he was beginning to deeply hate England. The food was bland, the wine was crap, the weather was cold and damp. As he entered the coffee shop, he wondered if they could make coffee. Judging by the number of people squeezed in there, the locals thought so. On reaching the counter, he ordered his coffee. 'Cafe correcto.' He turned from the counter and cast about for a table. Speed was vital: his coffee would be no good after a minute. The crema layer would dissipate. Suddenly, a man who had been sitting on a high stool near the window, folded his newspaper and got to his feet. Bruno moved quickly, but not quickly enough, as an older man reached the stool first. Bruno stopped abruptly, now close to the man. The elderly man looked up at him. Bruno's mood was plain enough to see, the man let go of the stool and opted to go. Bruno snatched the stool and settled down. He faced the window with his back to the other customers. Resting his arms on the narrow shelf in front of him, he glared out at the street. He sipped his coffee, which resulted in him hating the country even more.

So… three things stood in his way, or rather, three people. If his plan worked he would come out of this the hero, the avenger. Uncle would be happy, Milan would be his. Uncle was old. One day *he*, Bruno, would be regarded and respected like Uncle. The ghost of a smile crossed his face and like a spectre it quickly vanished. Rifsky! Rifsky had figured out *too much,* and he was *dangerous*. He was trying to stir trouble and keep his name out of it. Devious smug shit.

The coffee shop, positioned as it was on the sweeping bend of the street, was also slightly elevated. So from his window seat, Bruno had a clear view along the road. Among the many strange faces that bobbed along the pavement, one was familiar.

Rifsky was strolling along, taking his time and occasionally pausing to look in a shop window. He was smiling as he considered London.

Bruno was frowning as he considered Rifsky.

Rifsky: *Trafalgar Square, ha! Red Square, now that was a Square!*

Bruno: *Look at him smiling, he's having a holiday.*

Rifsky: *British Museum, ha! The Hermitage,* that's *a museum!*

Bruno: *He's laughing at me!*

Rifsky: *Russia is a unique country, but the London shops are better, you had to admit that.* Rifsky stopped to look at a department store shop front, smiling at the prices. Rifsky often smiled, he was after all, contented with his life.

Bruno stood up: he had energy, he had heat. *I'd like to wipe that smile off his stupid, ugly face.*

Rifsky was philosophical. *I've come a long way from a poor village forty miles outside Moscow. Yes, I've done well.*

Bruno bulldozed his way out of the coffee shop and started along the street, hands deep in his pockets clenched into fists. *No one laughs at me!*

Rifsky: *I'm Head of Security, I'm well paid, and respected in the organisation. I could buy anything in these shops I want.* Rifsky walked on.

Bruno had lost sight of him, passers-by were shouldered out of the way as he cannoned along the pavement through the crowds. He had to do something! All this talk, sitting around, wasting time. He wasn't going to play second fiddle to paper-pushing office workers like Salvatore. The organisation had lost its way. It needed *strong* people, people like *him* and no scheming little Russian shit was going to stop him.

I wonder if the Crown Jewels are worth looking at? Rifsky had reached the point in the street where he needed to cross the road to the house. He turned and stood on the kerb, waiting for a gap in the traffic. *Or the London Dungeon could be interesting. Yes, tomorrow perhaps…*

Something didn't feel right: it might have been a reflection, a sudden movement, a half-glimpsed face or Rifsky's nose for trouble; but whatever it was, he sensed danger. He began to turn. A stream of sensations followed in such quick succession, they almost merged into one moment. A powerful force struck him, knocking him off the kerb. A noise, a mixture of screaming tyres and a human scream. A blur of cars, people and sky. The flash of a lorry hurtling at his face. There was an explosion of pain: the front of the lorry was like a huge metal fist that punched his whole body with colossal force. For a sliver of a moment he was weightless, floating above the road. Then the road smashed into his body, the world greying out quickly. Echoing sounds faded and light shrank to a pinprick before it winked out. All sensation ceased.

Bruno stared for a moment at the still body that lay on the road. Bright red blood trickled from the temple, creating ugly streaks across the bone-white face. Satisfied, he slid backward into the gathering crowd. No one noticed him, as all eyes were fixed on the body. More people closed in, craning to see the spectacle. Shouts went up, 'Ambulance, someone!', 'Get a blanket!', 'I'm a nurse!' People stepped into the road and knelt down. The driver of the lorry had climbed down from his cab. He had both hands on the top of his head and was talking very fast. 'Ran out, nothing I

217

could do, just ran out, I couldn't do anything, ran in front…'

As Bruno melted further away the cries merged into an excited babble of voices. The traffic on the busy road was at a standstill on both sides, the cars on the opposite side having slowed to a halt to see what was happening. The tailback soon stretched as far as could be seen in both directions.

Bruno crossed the road, weaving between the stationary cars and slipped unnoticed into the square. He paused and looked over his shoulder to be sure no one was watching. Hurrying up to the house, he unlocked the door and slipped in, shutting the door quietly.

PART ONE

CHAPTER 16
THE HOUSE IN THE SQUARE
WEDNESDAY, LATE AFTERNOON

'What the hell do you mean, dead?'

Bruno shrugged, 'What can I tell you, Sal? There was a big crowd in the street. I wondered what was going on and there he was, lying in the road.'

'Are you sure he's dead? Are you sure it was him?'

'Definitely him. Lots of blood, face white as a sheet.'

Salvatore sat down and tried to take it in. After a moment, he looked up. 'Do you think it was an accident or is there more to it?'

'Accident! I mean, only Uncle and Anna know we're here. No one we've been in contact with knows who you are. Anyway, why would anyone take out Rifsky?'

'Rifsky was security. With him out of the picture, I'm an easy target.'

'He wasn't exactly a bodyguard, he spent most his time sightseeing. As I said, who knows you're here? The plane, the boat, the limo, all told you were a VIP and you were on private business. Only Dr Linsky knows why you're here and even he doesn't know where you are. It's all handled through Q. Why would

Dr Linsky knock off Rifsky? He'll be well paid for the cosmetic surgery.'

'Did Rifsky have any ID?'

'No, you know he didn't. We only carry cash and we didn't bring passports. Nothing. Officially, we aren't even in the country.'

'Yes, yes. I still don't like it.'

'Sal, accidents sometimes happen.' A thought struck Bruno, a worrying thought. 'You're still going to let Anna come, aren't you?'

Salvatore looked sharply at him. 'Why are you so keen on Anna coming?'

Bruno shook his head and threw up his arms, 'I don't care. You seem agitated, I thought it would be good for you. Do what you like!'

Salvatore didn't trust him, but, he missed Anna and she was already making arrangements. Bruno could be right, accidents do happen. All the frustration of waiting, the flight from Italy, the stress of the last few days; he knew he wasn't himself. But the thought of Bruno unsupervised while he recovered after the operation didn't rest well. For the life of him he still couldn't see how Anna's presence could benefit Bruno. 'You'll have to collect her.'

'Fine.'

'You must ensure no one's following her.'

'I'm not a fool, Sal.'

Salvatore rested an elbow on the arm of the sofa and held his head. On a personal level, he'd liked Rifsky. He was aware Rifsky had a past, and suspected there were aspects of his character that would be shocking. But he was loyal, paid well and, treated with respect; he could be trusted. Whatever his history, Salvatore had grown to like the man. 'I think we should be sure Rifsky is dead.'

'He looked bloody dead. I can't turn up at the nearest hospital and start asking questions.'

'I don't want you to.'

'Well then.'

'I will.'

'You're mad. I thought you wanted to keep a low profile?'

'I do. I can be subtle about it.'

'And I can't?' Bruno was irritated, Salvatore was always putting him down.

'Okay, let's just say I can be *more* subtle.'

CHAPTER 17
RON AND VICKY'S FLAT
THURSDAY MORNING

Ron sipped his coffee, the wonderful aroma drifting up from his cup in tiny, glorious clouds of steam. He stood cradling the cup and peered at the steel-grey cloud cover through the window. 'Looks as if someone has put a sheet of tracing paper over the sky. Autumn weather, honestly! In one week we get all the seasons; mild heat and sunshine, rain, wind, a light dusting of frost and sometimes fog!' He turned to Vicky who sat on a sofa. She was checking her freshly applied lipstick in a compact mirror. Satisfied, she snapped it shut and glanced out of the window. 'Not raining today though, should be a good turnout.'

'Do you think there'll be lots of people?' He asked nervously.

'Hope so, don't you?'

He shuffled from foot to foot, wrinkled his nose and mumbled, 'I don't know really, I'm a bit worried there'll be loads of people.'

She tutted. 'You'd be more worried if there were no people.'

'True.'

Vicky stood up and crossed the room and put her arms around him. He leaned down to accept her kiss.

The scent of her perfume increased. She let go and looked up at him, 'You'll be fine, you're all prepared. You've got prompt cards and I'll be there.' As she spoke she wiped his cheek gently with a tissue to remove the lipstick smudge.

'Yes I know. I'm being silly.'

'Look, come and sit down, I've got a surprise for you.'

'Really?'

Vicky knew Ron would be nervous delivering his talk at the library and against her better judgement, had made him a treat. She hoped the distraction would help his nerves. She fetched a tin from the kitchen and presented it to him with a flourish. 'Da da! I baked!'

Ron opened the tin and looked inside. 'Ooow.'

'They're chocolate brownies.'

'Thank you *so* much.' He took a bite then shut his eyes. 'Mmm, mmm, mmm, they're magnificent!'

'You can thank my friend Sally, she invented the recipe years ago and taught me.'

'I *love* your friend Sally and I've never met her.'

'She lives in the country now. We'll visit one day, you really would like her.'

'I *know* I would!'

Vicky laughed, 'Come on, you don't want to be late for the ladies.'

Fortified in the way only a good brownie can, Ron rose to his feet with renewed determination and dusted his hands. 'Right, let's get it over with.'

PART ONE

CHAPTER 18
THE PUBLIC LIBRARY
THURSDAY, 10.15AM

The old lady's face was framed with snowy white-hair, her soft rosy cheeks criss-crossed with lines. She had dressed for the occasion: polished brown brogues, long pencil pleat skirt, old-fashioned but carefully ironed twinset complete with the obligatory pearls, the outfit topped off with a blue Alice band in her hair. The epitome of a sweet old lady. She had risen to her feet to ask the question, her pale blue eyes sparkling with excitement. Ron stood on the small stage, leaning on the lectern he had been given and waited patiently.

The old woman's voice was soft but clear, 'Could you tell us your favourite method? I know a lot of my friends enjoy poisoning.' Several heads in the packed room nodded. The lady continued, 'Or shooting, but it's not personal, is it? I like a bludgeoning or stabbing, close contact with the victim. What's your view?' Susie sat down, her eyes shining with anticipation.

Ron cleared his throat. 'Yes,' he said, nodding to his audience. 'I understand close contact killing is more horrific. A stabbing, a smash over the head with something heavy or...' As he paused to emphasise the drama, some of his audience leaned forward a little. 'A good, old-fashioned strangling.' Ron raised his hands and held outstretched fingers apart, bringing them together slowly around an imaginary neck. There was a general murmur of approval and several white or grey heads nodded enthusiastically.

Vicky looked on from the back of the room. She was delighted that Ron's talk was going so well. The audience fascinated her; they weren't the mix of people she'd expected. Ron's nerves had subsided and he was actually *enjoying* himself.

'So, to answer the original question, I think first of all, the murder must be *planned*. No accidental killing in the heat of the moment. A premeditated murder shows *true* evil.' Ron stretched out the last words with relish.

More nodding and some whispered muttering. 'Evil, yes.'

'It's so hard to choose a favourite, there are so many.' Then, to the delight of the audience who, for some potentially dark reason, were all elderly women, Ron tripped lightly through the alphabet for them, 'Asphyxiation, Bludgeoning, Cutting, Drowning, Electrocution, Falling, Garrotting, Hanging, Laceration,...' He murdered his way to Z. Ron's eyes glinted with mischief as he looked at the sea of expectant faces. 'And finally, we come to Z, *Zetekitoxin*.' There was a tense silence as the ladies waited with excitement, hoping for an explanation. They weren't disappointed. 'It's a rare poison, found in the almost extinct Panamanian Golden Frog, extremely deadly.' He tacked on for good measure, 'It causes a heart attack.' He was rewarded with a passionate burst of applause, the duration of which wouldn't have disappointed the cast of a West End play.

As Ron took his bows, Vicky shook her head and laughed: it wasn't what Ron had said, it was how the ladies reacted that amused her. Whilst Ron basked in the admiration and waited for them to settle down, Vicky pondered the mature ladies, who relished the murder thriller with an almost alarming zeal. She wondered if perhaps the choice of reading material provided a safe release from the tension of ill-mannered grandchildren or perhaps the accumulated irritations of long-term marital bliss. Whatever the reason, they loved him.

While Vicky's attention was focussed on Ron and his ladies, an un-noticed figure wandered the canyons of the tall shelves. Gradually, he worked his way closer.

The library was a fine Victorian example of all a library should be. Its thick stone walls defended the building admirably, easily defeating the noise of the city. The reading rooms situated off the main floor were islands of tranquility in the busy metropolis. Graceful brass handles, worn smooth by decades of use, adorned the heavy oak doors. Chandeliers of white opaline glass globes the size of footballs illuminated the vast central space. This area held ranks of beautiful, dark wood shelving. They had a deep lustre, achieved over the years by many books gliding across them.   The artisans who originally designed their cathedral to knowledge and entertainment had spared no expense.   Small panels of stained glass further enhanced the feel of the building.   On even the dullest of days, a rich kaleidoscope of colours glowed from them.   If the daylight was strong enough, the coloured panes cast their rainbow light on the objects and floor in wondrous clusters of jewels.   The library was old but well loved.   It had transported the local readers on many armchair adventures over its long history.   Unfortunately, of late, numbers had declined. Concerned that this downward trend would continue, the staff had been busy.   There had been many innovations, such as this *Meet the Author* event, which had been advertised as *Award-winning Author Ronny Moon Shares His Murderous Thoughts*.   The area in which Ron was conducting his talk was also used for story afternoons.   Both children and adults thoroughly enjoyed these regular events.

The enthusiasm of the library team had also found its way to the labelling of the genres.   In an attempt to bring more colour and new readers, the sections had been renamed.   In the *Young Readers* section, *Birds of Prey* became *Winged Killers, Cookery* named as *Edible Experiments*, *Science* was now *Secrets of the Universe Explained* and *History* enjoyed the exhilarating title of *Time-Travel Manuals*.   Even one or two of the shelves in the adults' area had been rebranded.

If Vicky had glanced to her right, she might have noticed Fate's not very subtle warning, for by chance, Bruno was pretending to read a book, concealing himself in the section formerly labelled *Horror/Thriller*, which hadn't escaped the reforms. Consequently, he stood listening to Ron directly beneath a downward-pointing arrow with a large printed label bearing the legend, *Maniacs, Murderers and Malevolent Evil.*

The next question from the ladies sharply drew Bruno's attention.

'Do you discuss possible plot lines with an editor or publisher, or do you simply present them with the finished book?'

'I believe I work in a unique way. I have a close friend with whom I discuss lines. He's not a writer and has nothing to do with publishing, he's actually a film buff. Once I have a story, I rough out the whole thing and show him first.' Ron smiled at Vicky, who was still standing at the back of the room. A few heads turned to look at her. 'I don't even show those closest to me, that comes later. I show my partner when it's ready to go to the publishing house. She usually has one or two suggestions, but it's almost fully formed by then. I suppose I'm a little secretive.'

Bruno closed and put down the book he'd been pretending to read, Agatha Christie's *Murder is Easy,* and un-noticed, slipped quietly out.

Soon after this question, Ron's talk concluded to another boisterous round of applause. Vicky had insisted they bring some of his author copies for the ladies and Ron was kept very busy signing them.

As he and Vicky left the building, a jubilant crowd accompanied them, chatting to him about books they had read, favourite characters and pleas for some of them to reappear in future stories.

Bruno watched from a doorway, his hands deep in his pockets. One hand wasn't empty. One hand gripped the smooth, cold shape of his Beretta pistol.

The ladies walked with Ron and Vicky right up to his Chevrolet *Bel Air,* which was admired by all. There was much shaking of hands and smiling. Waving to everyone, Ron and Vicky thanked the ladies over and over again as they climbed in.

Bruno had no chance; too many witnesses and no clear line of sight. He turned and headed off back to the house. It wasn't a complete waste of time, he now believed only Ron and Rifsky knew anything and now of course, *only* Ron. He also knew where Ron would be tonight as it was the last Thursday of the month. If the waitress at the club was right, tonight was Shades' film night. Till tonight, then.

Ron felt considerable relief and couldn't stop smiling. Vicky was pleased and turned towards him. 'That went well.'

Without taking his eyes from the road, he answered, 'They were lovely.' He shook his head. 'I never would have guessed, my main fanbase are all sweet old ladies with a passion for murder!'

'It's been a great week. You finished the rough outline and gave it to Shades, the talk went really well and tonight we are at the club for film night.'

'Yes, we haven't had one for ages. Is Jane coming?'

'Mm, I think she's looking forward to it, although she's been a little quiet lately.' Thinking about Jane and her problems made Vicky more conscious of how lucky she and Ron were but also a little sad for her friend.

PART ONE

CHAPTER 19
THE HOUSE IN THE SQUARE
THURSDAY, 12.15AM

Bruno arrived back at the house only twenty minutes before Salvatore. He was pouring himself a small brandy in the living room as Salvatore entered. Bruno waved his glass in the direction of the decanter. 'You want one?'

Salvatore shook his head and sat down heavily. 'It's too early for one.'

Bruno hunched his shoulders in a shiver. 'It's too cold not to. He seated himself opposite and gulped a mouthful. 'So, did you find out anything?'

Salvatore stared at Bruno long enough to make him feel uneasy, then sighed and answered flatly, 'Dead.'

Bruno wasn't surprised. 'Mm. How did you find out?'

Salvatore stretched. He'd lost interest in Bruno and it had been a tiring morning. 'I looked at one of Rifsky's street maps and went to the nearest hospital. I found the porters' room. I told one of the porters I was a newsman and I wanted information, gave him a handful of money, told him to keep it between us. Serious accident on Swing Gate Road, brief description of Rifsky and the promise of more money if he found out anything.'

'Wasn't he suspicious?'

'Probably, but he took the money and disappeared. I didn't have to wait long, he soon came back with the story. An ambulance crew picked up a body on Swing Gate Road on Wednesday afternoon. Dead on arrival. The porter won't talk to anyone; he took my money and gave out information about a patient. He'd be risking his job.'

'So that's that.'

'Yes.' Salvatore answered flatly. 'As you say, that's that.'

Bruno relaxed a little and took another drink. 'Accidents happen, Sal.'

Salvatore actually looked sad, Bruno was slightly surprised. After all, Rifsky wasn't a close friend, only the security chief. 'We, er, we should keep Uncle in the picture. He'll need to organise a replacement. Do you want me to call him?'

'No. I'll do it.' Salvatore sounded weary.

Bruno felt the energy of irritation surge briefly. *I'll do it.* He, Bruno should be talking to Uncle. He Bruno, should be consulted about a successor. Salvatore treated him like an office boy, excluded from decisions. No matter, he had plans of his own, things to do. He'd killed Rifsky, he'd taken the first bold step. He was now on the road that would lead him to a position of real power and respect. The old ways *were* the best; strong people like himself deserved to rise in the organisation, not paper-shufflers like Salvatore. Certainly Rifsky had complicated what, after all, was a simple plan but he'd been taken care of. Bruno still didn't understand exactly what Rifsky intended to gain from exposing him and Salvatore. Not for the first time Bruno wished he could remember exactly what he'd said the night Rifsky got him drunk. Never mind. The important thing was, as far as he could make out, only Rifsky and Ronnie Moon knew anything. Rifsky was gone and he knew where Ronnie Moon would be tonight. He needed only to deliver an envelope to *The Blue Parrot* and he was set.

'What's so funny?'

Bruno looked up, Salvatore was watching him. 'Funny?'

'Yes, why are you smiling?'

'Oh, I was just thinking, now Uncle has made contact with the doctor, your plan is working out. You really have got away with murder.'

Salvatore wasn't convinced: he couldn't believe Bruno capable of being pleased for him. Without returning the smile, he corrected the comment. 'I told you, it was an accident. I didn't set out to kill Renzo.'

'No, but still...' Salvatore's grim expression told Bruno it would be wise to change the subject, something safe, 'It's good Anna's coming.'

'Why?'

'Well... you know, you miss her, don't you?'

Salvatore didn't answer. He wasn't about to discuss his feelings for Anna with Bruno. 'What are your plans for tonight?'

Bruno shrugged, 'Not much. Might take another stroll, pick up some food. See if I can find any decent wine in this country.' Bruno was pleased with himself: he needed an excuse to go out again, to deliver the envelope. He would also need an excuse to go out again much later. Perhaps Salvatore would be in bed by then. If not, he'd think of something. 'And you?'

Salvatore settled back into the leather chair; he was *really* very tired. 'Read.'

PART ONE

CHAPTER 20
THE BLUE PARROT
THURSDAY EVENING, CLOSING TIME

It had been a normal Thursday evening, a small hardcore group of regulars had drunk and chatted. A handful of new drop-ins had discovered the club for the first time. Gradually the customers had drifted - in some cases staggered - off to their homes. The bar staff were occupied in wiping down tables and washing glasses, preparing to go home and leave the club to the three people who sat on stools at one of the downstairs bars.

Jane was studying a list of new film titles Shades had acquired. It was always wise not to enquire too closely where Shades obtained his growing library of 16mm, 35mm and tape film collection. The club attracted what could be politely described as characters, one of whom occasionally swelled Shades' film archive. This particular colourful character had, in fact, not very much colour at all. His name was Tim White but was known as Pasty White, on account of his complexion. No-one that pale had any business walking about or indeed, having a pulse, let alone selling films of questionable ownership to bar owners. Pasty operated with only two provisos: one, Shades paid in cash and two, asked no questions as to the origin of said films. On this occasion, the set of reels had been so cheap, Shades hadn't looked too closely, spying one or two titles worth the money, even if the rest turned out to be duds. It seemed Pasty was in a hurry and needed cash, so had forgone the usual haggle.

While Jane perused the titles, Tony revisited his recent complaint that Shades wasn't doing his fair share in running the club. Shades wasn't paying Tony much attention; he shook his watch and held it to his ear. 'I think the damn thing's stopped again!'

Tony was irritated, 'Are you listening to me?'

'Yeah, yeah, I got it, get up to speed with the club's accounts. Jane?'

'Mm?'

'What's the time? My stupid watch has stopped.'

Jane wasn't listening to Shades any more than Shades was listening to Tony.

'Time...?'

Still staring at the list of films, she answered vaguely, 'I think it was nine o'clock about two and a half hours ago, give or take.'

Shades watched her, but she didn't look up, instead she pushed her glasses back up her nose and leaned forward slightly. A film title had caught her eye. 'Oh, that's a great film!'

Shades turned to Tony. 'That's the sort of thing that drives me nuts! "About nine o'clock two and a half hours ago." What's that supposed to mean?'

Jane tapped Shades' arm several times. 'Look, *It's a Wonderful Life*, I love that film. Can we watch it tonight?'

'No. I've already loaded a thriller.'

'Aw.'

Shades turned back to Tony. 'You want to watch a thriller, don't you?'

Tony didn't react well to being ignored. He wanted to discuss running the club. So to get his own back and partly because it was true, Shades didn't get the answer he wanted, '*It's a Wonderful Life* is a very good film, I'm sure Vicky and Ron would enjoy it.' Tony certainly enjoyed watching Shades squirm.

Jane was happy. 'So that's decided then, tonight's film will be *It's a Wonderful Life*.'

'No, it's not decided at all.'

The squabble between the three continued in much the same way. The bar staff bid them goodnight. Tony said he'd lock the main doors after his late night guests had arrived.

He tried a different tack with his younger brother. 'I got a phone call today.'

Shades wasn't overly interested, but even he knew not to push his luck too far. Tony would never be violent but he was capable of withdrawing into a dark, moody silence, which could last for days, very depressing.

'Phone call?'

'Yes, someone wants to hire the club late night next Monday. It's for a reunion.'

'What did you say?'

'Well, Monday nights are usually quiet, so I quoted him a fair price and he agreed.' Tony had kept the best bit until last and was interested in Shades' reaction. He added casually, 'The guy said it was ten years since the release of a film they all worked on. Seems everyone got on really well and it's a surprise reunion for the director, who's retiring after a long career.' Tony, having lit the fuse, sat back to enjoy the fireworks. He now had Shades' full attention.

'No! Who's the director? What film was it? Will there be any famous actors?'

'Oh, so now you're interested.'

'I'll do the bar.'

'Thought you would. I don't know any more. The guy said he wanted to keep the reunion a secret, didn't want the press involved and asked if I would keep it on the QT.'

'They must be famous, if he said that.' After reflection, Shades asked suspiciously, 'It's not a wind-up, is it?'

'Don't think so, he said he would send a downpayment to the club, balance to be paid on the night.'

'Did he?'

Tony pulled a brown envelope from his inside jacket pocket, clearly addressed with his name. 'Someone handed it to the bar staff for me this afternoon.' Tony passed the envelope to Shades, who opened it, thumbed the wad of notes and read the short letter which

240

accompanied it. *Downpayment as agreed, balance to be paid on the night of Monday next. Please leave yard gates open for surprise guest. Hang a* Closed - Private Function *note on main doors.*

'Wow, this is gonna be great! Look at this, Jane.' Shades passed the note, to her.

'You could be right, wonder if I've worked with any of them?'

'Did you want to come?' Shades hadn't meant to hurt Jane, but he *did.* Tony compressed his lips and said nothing.

Jane answered quickly, 'What day was it?'

'Monday.'

'Oh dear, I think I've got something on,' she lied. There was an uncomfortable silence. Jane tried to sound bright. 'Well, I wonder where our VIP guests are tonight?'

The guests in question, having parked in the yard behind the club, were hurrying around to the front entrance. Ron and Vicky walked up the steps. Ron allowed Vicky to go through the doors first and was about to follow her in when he spotted a penny on the ground. Remembering a rhyme his mother had taught him, F*ind a penny, pick it up, and all that day you'll have good luck*, he recited it for Vicky. 'Find a penny and pick it… AAAAAAAAH! My back!'

'Ooo, whoops-a-daisy, don't tell me your back's gone? Poor old man!'

Ron stumbled through the doors behind her, still stooped. 'It really hurts!'

241

She put her arm around him and although still slightly bent over, Ron allowed himself to be slowly steered in the direction of the bar. The three turned to welcome them. Tony slid from his stool and walked past Ron and Vicky to lock the club's heavy doors.

'What's wrong, Ron?'

'I've hurt my back picking up a penny.'

Tony shook his head, continued to the front doors and locked and bolted them. As he returned, he didn't like what he saw.

Vicky believed Ron had simply pulled a muscle, so she let go of him to hug Jane and Shades hello, but stopped abruptly. Turning quickly, she held out her hand. 'Ron, there's blood on my hand!' Ron stared and swallowed: he didn't like blood, *particularly* his own. Shades and Jane got quickly to their feet. Now alarmed, Vicky made Ron turn around. The four of them stared at the blood on his back. Vicky lifted her hand towards her mouth. 'Ron, what on earth have you done?'

Ron became frightened. 'What is it? I can't see. What's happened?'

She carefully lifted his sweatshirt. There was an ugly red gash, not very deep but about six inches long, across Ron's back.

Jane mirrored Vicky and put her hand to her mouth. 'Oow, that looks sore.'

Shaded tried to be more logical. 'You must have cut yourself on something as you bent down.'

'Like what?'

242

'Well, I don't know, something sharp.'

'It's stinging a lot.'

Vicky was upset and glanced at Tony, who saw the look and took over. 'Come on, let's go up to the flat, we need to clean and dress it. There's a First Aid kit up there.' He walked to the metal stairs.

They all followed, Ron muttering, 'Really stings!' and Vicky making soothing, 'Sssh, I know.' comforting remarks.

Shades whispered to Jane, 'I got shot once. Can't talk about it, but I didn't make this much fuss.' Jane looked at him sharply, promising herself that she would get to the bottom of it later. Shades hadn't lowered his voice sufficiently to escape an over-the-shoulder frown from Vicky.

Once in the flat, Tony quickly fetched the club's First Aid bag from a kitchen cupboard and handed it to Shades. 'I'm going to check something.' Without pausing to explain, he hurried off.

Jane pulled a chair from under the dining table and turned it round. Vicky guided Ron to it. He sat down carefully, straddling the chair, resting his chest against the back and leaned forward slightly. Vicky gently lifted his sweatshirt and held it up around his shoulders. Shades had removed a bottle from the First Aid kit and poured some liquid onto a wad of cotton wool. 'This might sting a little.' Judging by Ron's reaction 'sting a little' may have been a slight understatement. As Shades applied the soaked pad,

Ron's reaction was surprisingly loud, given that it was through gritted teeth.

'Bloody hell, Shades!'

'Not the strong silent type, are we, Ron?'

Ron's clenched hands gripped the top of the chair back.

Jane covered one fist with her hand and muttered sympathetically, 'Ooo, tut, ooo, ahhh.'

Vicky watched and winced every time Shades dabbed. It smarted so much, Ron asked heatedly, 'What the hell's in it?'

'Only antiseptic.' After a worrying pause, Shades added, 'I think.'

'What do you mean, *think*?'

Shades stopped dabbing and regarded the bottle. 'Label's come off, it's been in the First Aid kit a while.'

Ron was outraged. 'It could be anything!'

'Oh shut up, it's in the First Aid Kit! It's not going to be poison, is it?'

Vicky snatched the bottle with her free hand and sniffed its contents gingerly.

'It's okay Ron, it is antiseptic.' She glanced reproachfully at Shades. 'Be a little more sensitive, it must sting like mad.'

'I'm doing my best Vicky, it *is* only a graze. I was *shot* last year, remember?'

Vicky turned to Jane, 'Hold up Ron's sweatshirt for me.' Jane did so and Vicky took the wad of cotton wool from Shades. 'That was only a *graze* on your arm if I remember rightly.'

'Still hurt!'

'Well then!' She said sternly, then turning her attention to Ron, spoke gently, 'sorry, just a couple more dabs and we'll dress it, okay?' Vicky grimaced as she gently applied the antiseptic; she hated hurting him but it had to be done.

Meanwhile, Shades had been rummaging in the kit. He found a large gauze plaster sealed in a pack, he placed it on the table, then, spotting a bottle of Aspirin, held it up to examine the date. They appeared to be equally ancient. Shades became philosophical, speaking to no one in particular, he mused, 'Funny about expiry dates, I wonder if poison is out of date, is it more poisonous or less poisonous?' He threw the bottle of aspirin back into the bag and looked up at them. 'It's funny what you think, isn't it?'

Ron wasn't impressed. 'I don't think you would find it funny if I told you what I was thinking.'

Vicky opened the gauze plaster and carefully applied it to Ron's back, holding it in place with long strips of tape. Jane gently lowered Ron's sweatshirt. Slowly, he rose to his feet, turned around and sat down, being careful not to lean back. The experience had made him feel a little wobbly.

At that moment, Tony returned. Looking at Ron he asked, 'You bent down because you saw a penny?'

'Yes, supposed to be good luck... didn't bring *me* much luck.'

'Wouldn't be too sure. They say you can't put a price on health, but I think yours cost a penny.' He

245

held out a huge fist and opened his hand. They all looked at the small, distorted lump of metal. No one knew what it meant. 'I dug it out of the door frame with my penknife… it's a bullet.'

There was a shocked silence. Ron was the first to speak. 'But… but, why? Why would someone try to shoot me? I haven't done anything.'

'Mistaken identity?' Shades offered. 'I mean, *The Blue Parrot* does attract all kinds of people.'

Tony agreed. 'We do get some odd characters through the doors.'

Ron was frightened and said anxiously, 'Perhaps they'll try again!'

Vicky stood close to him and put a protective arm around his shoulders. She was trying to take it in, someone had fired a shot at Ron. He might well have been killed! She could have lost him! She held him tighter and only slackened her grip when he looked up at her sharply. 'Oooo, Vicky, mind the back!'

She snatched her hand away. 'Sorry.'

Jane was angry. 'We should call the police!'

'They won't protect me! They're not going to watch me twenty four hours a day. I don't know what to do!'

All eyes drifted to Tony. 'Ron's right, it's not as if they'll assign a bodyguard or anything; we can't even point them at anyone. The police would come to the club and ask a lot of questions we don't know the answers to.'

Vicky wanted to get Ron home. 'Let's sleep on it' she suggested. Ron agreed as he was feeling a little sick and longed for the security of familiar surroundings. The graze was by no means serious but it had been a close thing. Today could so easily have been his last. It was a matter of luck.

Vicky was worried because he looked very pale and had become unusually quiet. 'Come on, Ron, I'll drive.' He nodded and slipped a very slightly shaking hand into hers.

Tony insisted they all wait in the flat while he went down and checked around the small yard. On arriving he found It deserted. Not content with that, he walked out of the gates and looked up and down the street. Again, nothing. To be thorough, he walked slowly around to the front of the club. A few cars drove past but didn't slow down and the road was empty of people. Tony considered the problem. Neither Ron nor Vicky had mentioned seeing anyone and looking at the street, there wasn't really anywhere to hide. The only possible exception was a small doorway set in a building on the opposite side of the road, a fire exit door. Tony crossed the road. There were four cigarette butts lying on the ground in the doorway. It seemed likely someone had waited there for some time. Ron and Vicky hadn't mentioned hearing a shot, so the gun must have been silenced, was that significant? Did it indicate a professional? Again, he looked about the street. Whoever it was, they'd gone now. Satisfied, Tony hurried back to report.

A few moments later, Ron and Vicky climbed into the Chevrolet. Ron sat across the rear seat. With Vicky behind the wheel, they gave the others a brief wave and headed for home.

Jane, Shades and Tony watched them safely drive away. Jane had travelled to the film night by cab, thinking she would enjoy a glass or two of wine and that Vicky or Shades would probably drive her home. She was hoping it would be Shades. The atmosphere was subdued: they were all distracted by the same question; who could possibly want Ron dead and why?

Shades pulled his keys from his pocket. 'I'll run you home.'

'Thank you.'

Tony said he'd lock up and head home. Both he and Shades had homes not far from the club. The upstairs flat was convenient if one or both worked very late, but it wasn't where they lived.

Shades drove in silence, which Jane found a little uncomfortable. 'What do you think it means?' She wasn't expecting him to know, she merely wanted him to talk to her.

Without looking at her, Shades raised his eyebrows and shook his head slightly. 'I've no idea, it doesn't make sense, unless it really is a case of mistaken identity or a random nut job.'

It was a short journey to her flat. 'I'll see you to your door.' At the front door there was an awkward moment. 'Sorry it wasn't fun tonight.'

'Don't worry.   I'm just pleased Ron's not badly hurt.'

Shades leaned forward and kissed her quickly on the cheek. 'I better get off.' It wasn't a passionate kiss, more like a child kissing an aunt goodbye. He turned to go then hesitated, snatched her hand and squeezed it tight. 'I'm glad *you're* okay.' Then he was gone.

Jane watched the car pull away.   This was the problem: first a friendly kiss without passion, then a glimpse of real care; *I'm glad* you're *okay.* He'd held her hand very tightly. Jane truly couldn't make him out. What did he want from the relationship?

After Ron and Vicky arrived home, she had made a great fuss of him offering both food and drink and arranging his cushions. He gratefully accepted the cushions but neither of them felt in the mood to eat. They talked for a while, trying to make sense of the attack and what was to be done.   Finally, Ron confessed. 'I think I just want to lie down, Vicky.' He looked like he needed it and she eagerly helped him get as comfortable as possible. Vicky didn't believe she would be able to sleep but fear and tension are exhausting companions and she fell asleep quickly.

Ron lay on his side, staring into the dark, thinking. He had no clue who could possibly want to kill him. The creative writer in him began to suggest some unlikely theories.   One worried him a great deal. Maybe no one *did* want him dead and *he* wasn't the target. Vicky had been a little ahead of him when it happened. It was possible that they waited for a clear shot. When he bent down they tried to shoot her only she had just entered the club, so they hit the doorframe instead.

Vicky had her back to him. He reached out in the dark and slid his arm around her, she shuffled closer but didn't wake up. Ron gently kissed the back of her head.

It wasn't only Ron who stared into the darkness during that long night. After delivering Jane safely to her door, Shades had driven home, showered and gone to bed. He had intended to give serious thought to his relationship with her. He always found the roof of the club a good place to think. High up over London among the rooftops somehow he gained perspective, but here in his own bed he couldn't think clearly. Other thoughts crowded his mind, like voices shouting for attention. What was the shooting all about? Who were the film people who wanted to hire the club? And of course, there was Jane, poor, sweet Jane. He liked her, but was it *only* like? No, it was *more,* a lot more, but he had no confidence. Here in the dark he could be honest, if not to Jane at least to himself. All the jokes, the bravado, the honest truth was; he was frightened, it was as simple as that. He *couldn't* go through it all again if it went wrong. So where did that leave him? Safer to be alone? He wasn't being fair to her. The disappointment on her face when he didn't include her on Monday! Perhaps she would be happier with someone who didn't have such a past, a past that haunted the here and now.   Shades felt angry with himself; why couldn't he be like his brother?   Tony made a decision and seemed never to question it. Perhaps he did, privately.   Tony was a good man, a very good brother.   It was possible Tony kept *his* doubts to himself, not out of bravado, no, he wasn't like that, but because... because he sensed those around him needed someone to be sure, someone to say, *We'll do this and it will be alright.*   Suddenly, Shades had a troubling thought; was Tony ever lonely? Everyone looked to him in times of trouble, but who could he turn to?

'I've got to do better for people I care about.' It was only a whisper in the dark but it was spoken from the heart, as was the next observation. 'This is going to be a long night!'

PART ONE

CHAPTER 21
RON AND VICKY'S FLAT
FRIDAY MORNING

Ron's chocolate biscuits gave him a slightly ridiculous amount of pleasure. So the sight of the empty biscuit tin produced an equally disproportionate amount of sadness. He pointed at the tin. 'Look at that, it's empty!'

'Don't look at me, you've pigged them all. I haven't had one!'

'You sure?'

'Positive.'

'Oh.'

Ron moved to the sofa with his second early morning coffee, bereft without his early morning chocolate biscuit. He sat down carefully. Vicky had checked under the dressing as soon as they woke up and was pleased the wound appeared less red.

She chewed her muesli thoughtfully. 'I think you should cut down on those biscuits for a while, you're eating far too many.'

'What? I'm not well, you know? I've had a shock.'

Vicky became serious. 'Do you think we *should* phone the police?'

'No, you're probably right, it was me who emptied the biscuit tin.'

Anxiety produced a hot response. 'Not about the missing biscuits… Oh.'

He was smiling at her. Vicky knew that beneath the surface, he was just as upset and worried as she was. In spite of this he was still trying to make her laugh. Her frown melted. 'Seriously Ron, what do you think?'

His smile faded. 'I'm honestly not sure; I doubt they can do anything and you know Tony and Shades won't want them around the club.'

'Mm, so what do we do?'

'What *can* we do? Carry on, I suppose, and be vigilant. It may not be personal, could be mistaken identity as Shades said. You know the club gets some very strange customers.'

Vicky took her empty bowl to the kitchen and after opening some cupboards, called, 'We aren't only out of biscuits, we need some shopping. I'm not working today, I'll go.'

Ron had moved to the kitchen door. 'I'll come too.'

'Isn't your back sore?'

'Not much.' It was, but Ron couldn't help worrying that Vicky might have been the intended target. He didn't want to frighten her and equally, didn't want her to go out alone.

Not far away, Salvatore sipped his early morning Cappuccino; the house had a fine coffee machine. He was unable to enjoy it, however, because of the noise coming from the kitchen. On most days, Bruno's volcanic temper smouldered ominously, today a minor eruption appeared to be taking place in the kitchen. The beautiful teak cabinetry was being thoroughly tested. Drawers were being slammed and there were rummaging noises, as if the kitchen was being ransacked, which is because it was. Suddenly, the noise ceased and Bruno's angry face appeared around the living room door. 'There's no coffee!'

'No, I had the last of it.'

Bruno glared at Salvatore and his cup.

'There was only enough for one and I was up first.'

Bruno had slept badly. His attempt to execute Ron had failed and he didn't know where he lived. Sure, the plan would still work but Ron had to be taken care of. The problem had robbed him of sleep.

Salvatore threw petrol on Bruno's hot temper with his next suggestion. 'Why don't you do a bit of shopping?'

'…'

'We're out of milk, bread, cheese, ham, pasta.' He glanced at the decanter. 'Brandy.'

Bruno spoke very quietly, with all the control he could muster. 'Why don't *you* go?'

'There's somewhere else I've got to go. Get a cab, there's plenty of money in the drawer.'

Bruno didn't trust himself to say anymore. He snatched some cash from the drawer and blazed out of the room like a comet, trailing an aura of anger in his wake. In the hall, he seized the phone to call a cab. He didn't exactly slam the front door but Salvatore heard it clearly from the living room and couldn't help smiling. It would do Bruno good to do something menial to remind him who was boss.

Usually, Bruno hated the cold. Today, he was pleased to be outside in the sharp air and it was very cold, the air cooled by the Thames drifted up from the river. As it did so, it gained the slight fragrance of damp earth. The wintery sun sat low in the chilly pastel sky, the shadows cast by nearby buildings stretched cold fingers of violet across the road. The central park with few exceptions, was populated by the skeletons of trees. Clumps of ferns, bent low by the heavy morning dew, glistened. Puddles here and there appeared bottomless as they perfectly mirrored the milky blue sky. On the step, Bruno turned up his collar and clutched his coat around his neck. The light itself was cold for the London sky lacked the warmth of Milan. He took a deep breath and tried to calm down. So now he was shopping! Salvatore would have him picking up washing next! He gritted his teeth; not long now. So what if this Ronny Moon was loose out there? It wouldn't stop him.

Bruno didn't know how long he stood on the step. By the time the cab arrived, he had cooled down both mentally and physically and his feet were freezing. He suspected it was longer than the ten minutes quoted. It's a strange quirk of London geography that all cab offices are - according to them - ten minutes from any address, irrespective of distance.

'Where to, mate?'

'Nearest supermarket and I'm not your mate.'

The cab slalomed its way through the London traffic and in less than fifteen minutes Bruno found himself standing in the huge, grey carpark of a supermarket.

He was about to snatch up a basket and go in, when he froze. Bruno's grim face melted into a smile and he carefully replaced the basket. Far away on the edge of the car park was a familiar shape. Still smiling, Bruno walked slowly over to the baby-blue Chevrolet *Bel Air*. It stood quietly by itself. He ran a hand over the wing as he walked around it. 'Hello, I'm pleased to see you.' There was no one about. Surrounding the car park was a thin ribbon of green consisting of some low bushes in which unseen sparrows squabbled. There was also a number of small evergreen trees that whispered as a breath of cold wind stirred their branches. Bruno moved towards them for cover and settled down to wait.

Owing to the size of Ron's Chevrolet and his fondness for its paintwork, they usually parked well away from other cars. Whilst the other customers' cars were clustered near the entrance, Ron and Vicky's occupied a relatively lonely spot.

Twenty minutes later, Ron rattled the wire trolley over to the car's cavernous boot. Wincing slightly, he hauled the shopping bags out of the trolley and placed them in the car. He glanced at Vicky who was frowning at the shopping list and slowly moving a finger down each line. Ron finished loading and slammed the lid shut.

'I can't believe we got all this stuff and not biscuits! You do remember I'm completely out?'

Without looking up, Vicky responded curtly. 'I told you, you're eating far too many chocolate biscuits! You've gone through a whole packet already this week.'

'Well, I've been under pressure!'

'"Under pressure", huh! I'm sure we've forgotten something, with you going on about biscuits.'

'Yes, we have... my biscuits!' With this parting shot, Ron slid gingerly behind the wheel, his back was still tender, but driving distracted him from the discomfort.

Vicky was standing on the passenger side. Ron waited for her reaction and she slowly lowered the shopping list to give him the full benefit of a hard glare. The message was clear: *you're pushing your luck*. He grinned at her through the window. In most men the naughty child isn't far below the surface. Slowly, she shook her head. Ron started the car and Vicky was about to get in when suddenly, a strong hand seized her wrist and spun her away from the car. From Vicky's perspective, the car and Ron disappeared, the world became a blur. The tarmac appeared to spiral up and strike her. Vicky's knee and hand hit the ground in a painful, swiping blow. She had been flung aside with such force, she rolled after landing. She barely had time to glimpse his disappearing back, as the stranger wrenched open the passenger door and climbed in fast.

For Ron, Vicky's small face was suddenly replaced by the hard features of a thickset, balding man who now filled the passenger seat. The stranger pulled a small object from his pocket and there was an almost simultaneous *click, swish* sound. Ron's eyes darted to the stranger's hand and saw a flick knife gripped in his thick fingers, its stiletto blade pointing at him. The hand moved quickly forward and for a terrifying second, Ron believed the stranger was about to stab him. He inhaled sharply and gripped the steering wheel, shocked into paralysis. However, the tip of the blade, after making contact with his side, stopped. The knife pressed hard but did not penetrate.

The man shouted, 'Drive! Now!'

Out of the panicky jumble of thoughts, one surfaced, *get the danger away from Vicky.* He selected *Drive* and the car began to move. He glanced in the mirror and was relieved to see the shrinking image of Vicky scrambling to her feet.

Helplessly, Vicky watched the Chevrolet power away across the carpark, bump out through the gate and swing left into traffic. She stood motionless, unsure what to do. The pain in her knee caused her to glance down. It was grazed and bleeding. She also became aware of a stinging in her hand, which was also bleeding. Vicky took a shaky step toward the supermarket and stopped. What would she say to them? What could they do? Phone the police? It was hard to think, her heart was beating fast. *The Blue Parrot* was probably less than two miles away. Vicky began to walk; her knee didn't feel any worse, she began to run.

'What's the plan?' Bruno dug the point of the knife even harder into Ron's side.

'Plan?'

'Yes, you and Rifsky?'

'I don't know any Rifsky, who the hell are you?'

Bruno became more angry. 'I'm not a fool, don't treat me like a fool. You wrote it all down, the whole thing. Why?' He pushed the knife so hard, for a moment Ron thought it would draw blood. He squirmed sideways to ease the pressure.

'Who's behind it?'

'….!'

'Tell me who he's working for! Rifsky wanted everyone to know Salvatore wasn't dead then he got me drunk, he found out I was going to kill Salvatore, didn't he?'

Ron was petrified, he was also trying to both drive and understand what this madman was raving about. Instinctively, he wanted to run, this urgency to flee translated into driving at speed. The traffic was thinning out, they were heading toward the out-of-town dealerships. The rows of houses were interrupted by car sales forecourts, DIY sheds and tile centres. There was still the odd cluster of houses but the pavements were largely empty. Ron began to panic. If someone were to commit murder in a London suburb, this was the place to do it.

Still the man next to him asked questions. 'You and Rifsky, anyone else? Does anyone else know?'

Ron shook his head, he had no clue what this maniac wanted him to say. Ron's hands were sweating as he gripped the steering wheel.

Bruno interpreted Ron's shaking head as defiance. He removed the blade from his side and placed it against his neck. 'Tell me what the plan was; how was it going to work with this book? There's no point pretending you don't know what I'm talking about. You mentioned my name, it's all there. *TELL ME*!' Bruno barked the questions savagely. Bruno's anger meant the urge to kill would soon overtake his need for answers.

This wasn't lost on Ron, who was sure that if he didn't come up with some answers fast, the man was going to lose control. Ron drove faster still. He swerved round another motorist ahead of them. He was driving dangerously, but his passenger appeared oblivious of the danger. '*TALK!*' The pressure of the blade on his neck increased.

The Chevrolet took some skill to drive at speed and the car was travelling very fast. He did his best to concentrate, but the point of the knife was being pushed so hard into his neck it was becoming painful. Thundering down the wide road, Ron crossed the centre line to overtake a car. Another was coming toward them, but before the collision he jerked the wheel. It was a very close thing, the Chevy barely making it through. *Where the hell were the police when you needed them?* A crossroads came up fast, the traffic lights changed and they streaked through on red. Ron hauled the wheel both left and right swerving across, narrowly missing the traffic that had begun to move from both directions. If his passenger didn't kill him, driving like this would! Ron was sure he didn't have much time. The lunatic beside him wanted answers he couldn't give. At any moment, he would use the knife. Ron's mind was racing, if only he had a weapon, what could he do to stop him? Stop… maybe that was the answer, there wasn't time for anything else. It might work. *Oh please, please, please, let it work!*

Coming up fast on the left he saw a dropped kerb and across the pavement a patch of grass with a low hedge surrounding it. He swerved the Chevy over hard, the violent swing to the left flung Bruno and his knife to the right away from him. The car was extremely well maintained so when Ron stamped on the brakes, all four wheels locked. The faulty passenger seat that had moved forward, frightening Vicky, let go. The seat slammed forward, smashing Bruno into the dashboard, pinning him there as the car decelerated. The Chevy left twin black tyre marks as it slid left, mounted the dropped kerb and buried itself in the low bushes. Seconds before the car finally stopped, Ron flung open the driver's door and dived out. He hit the ground hard, rolled, and like his car came to rest partly in the bushes. Frantic to get away, he scrambled to his feet fast and ran. All the pent-up fear poured power into his legs. He pounded along the pavement faster than anyone would believe him capable, including himself. Behind him, he heard the violent slam of a door, Bruno taking his anger out on the car. Looking over his shoulder, Ron saw the man with the knife running after him. Ron had reached a street of Victorian terraced houses. He ran into it, but after his burst of speed his legs felt that they were growing heavier. He couldn't keep up the same pace and his lungs hurt.

Back at the club, Tony struck a match on the wall outside, lit his cigar and scowled disapprovingly at the poster pasted to the wall of his club. That bloody theatre down the road were using the building to advertise their latest play and it wasn't the first time. *Visited by an Angel*, stupid title for a play. Tony stood puffing his cigar, hands on hips, glaring at the poster. Suddenly, he grinned and said under his breath, 'They'll be visited by *me* this afternoon.'

'Tony!' It was Vicky's voice, the cry breathless and desperate. Tony turned quickly.

Vicky was so relieved to see him, she almost cried. He'd know what to do. As he turned toward her his shoulders lined up with the wings of the angel in the poster behind him, momentarily creating the illusion that they were his. As she stumbled toward him, she let out a cry somewhere between a sob and a laugh.

Tony saw both the blood on her leg and the wild look on her face. As she fell against him he hugged her and looked over her head for Ron. Without knowing the situation, he said simply, 'It'll be alright.' Ridiculous as it was, Vicky believed him. 'Come in and tell me what's happened.'

Ron made a grab for some railings to steady himself and sucked in lungfuls of air. His hands shook and his skin was clammy. A young couple were walking towards him. 'I need help!' He gasped out the words. 'Someone's trying to kill me!' The man put his arm around his girlfriend and steered her away. They crossed the road quickly and hurried on, not looking back. Helplessly, Ron watched them go. As he looked back along the street, Bruno appeared at the other end and started forward. Ron let go of the railings and tried to run. His legs felt heavy and lacked power; he attempted to swallow but his mouth was too dry. In spite of the cold, a sticky hot sweat covered his body. He was conscious of his heart pounding, it pulsed in his ears, almost drowning out a worrying ringing sound which had begun. *Don't pass out, don't pass out, please don't let me pass out. If I black out and he catches up, I won't wake up, I must keep going!* Ron had the impression he was moving in slow motion. He was frustrated by his own body: *why* wouldn't it move any faster? His mind screamed *run, run* but muscle and bone had so little left to give. *If he catches me I'll die.*

Between the retail outlets there were little islands of houses. Ron and Bruno had been running along a set of streets, all old but now they were valuable as London continued to expand. A number of the houses were being renovated. Ron had reached the end of the road, both physically and actually. He turned a corner and managed to stagger a small distance along the next street. Having painfully won a small lead on Bruno, Ron stopped running and stretched out a sweaty, quivering hand to lean on a cold corrugated iron fence for support. The fence surrounded the front of a three-storey house being updated. The remaining tiny reserves of strength weren't holding him up, it was the primeval need to survive, to cling to life. But even this wasn't going to be enough. The world had become blurred and a grey mist was clouding the edges of his vision. If he tried to run one more step, he would black out. He was near collapse and he knew it.

With his arm around Vicky's shoulders, Tony had guided her up the steps into the club. From his barstool across the room, Shades had seen them enter. Tony pointed to Shades with his free hand and to himself, then to the ceiling. Shades hopped from the barstool; the signal was clear, '*you and me upstairs, now.*' Something was badly wrong.

Upstairs in the flat, Vicky poured out the story. Tony went to the phone and Shades sat with a comforting arm around Vicky's shaking shoulders. Tony began talking to someone, but Vicky and Shades heard only his side of the conversation. 'It's Tony, I need a favour and it's very important....'

Ron knew he couldn't run any further. Still leaning on the metal fence for support, he looked behind him. No sign of his pursuer, but he would round the end of the road at any moment.

Bruno was slightly fitter than Ron. On paper, he should have caught up, but Bruno wasn't running for his life and this made all the difference. Ron had gained a minute's lead, only now he was finished. Bruno would soon catch up, and this time he was done with questions.

The effect of being terrified and quite literally running for his life resulted in stripping away all but basic thoughts. *Hide! If you can't run, hide!* Ron cast around him, there were low walls in front of the identical terraced houses but nowhere offered much in the way of cover. The occasional car passed, and though Ron held up his arm in an attempt to stop one, they all drove past without even slowing. Again, he frantically scanned the long street, now panicking. A few feet away was a skip full of rubble. A high, boarded scaffold arched over the pavement. It appeared that so much was being stripped out of the three-storey house, the builders had decided it was worth going to some trouble. From one of the windows a very steep slope had been constructed from scaffolding poles and boards to convey rubble from the building to the skip. But there was no hope that he possessed enough strength to climb onto the skip or clamber up the scaffold to the window. Exhausted beyond belief, Ron let go of the fence, placed both hands on his knees for support and bent over, taking deep breaths. It was at this moment he saw the small bend in one of the corrugated sheets. The bottom corner was slightly bent out of shape and not fixed down. He fell to his knees and with both hands seized the metal and pulled. It gave a little. Lying flat on the pavement, Ron forced his shoulder against the metal. Straining and wriggling, he squeezed his head and shoulders through the gap. His belly became stuck. Half in and half out, he struggled to get through. Now he was completely wedged. With desperate, almost insane panic he thrashed about. He strained to reach forward; there, close to his hands was a scaffold pole. Stretching for it, he could touch it but not grip it. If he could grip the pole he might be able to pull himself through. At any moment, he expected the stab and slash of a blade being plunged into his legs, slicing a major artery. His life would spill out onto the pavement. He would be found wedged under a the corrugated fence. He saw Vicky's face, twisted in horror and grief. No! It wasn't going to be this way. One last all-or-nothing gigantic effort. Bone, muscle, sinew stretched to breaking point. 'Naaaaaahhr!' Even to his own ears, the guttural cry didn't sound like him. This was because in some respects it wasn't. It was the primeval thing that lives deep inside, which hopefully, we will never meet but it rises up and pushes through the civilised veneer when fighting for life. The fingers of one outstretched hand closed on the pole. He pulled.

Tearing both clothes and flesh, unbelievably, he was through! He pushed hard against the twisted metal to bend it flat. Lying on his back, unable to move, he looked up at the sky, his chest heaving. He didn't realise that his ability to judge time was vastly distorted. Life and death are unimaginably powerful forces. Confronting them changes a person's concept of reality. Ron's mind was speeding; from losing sight of Bruno as he entered the street, attempting to flag down a car and diving headfirst through the metal fence had taken just twenty nine seconds.

Bruno rounded the corner and saw *nobody*. He walked slowly down the empty street, scanning carefully from left to right. He knew Ron was still somewhere close, since he hadn't had much of a head start and Ron couldn't have run the length of the street and be out of sight; no, he *must* be hiding close by. Bruno stopped beside the corrugated iron fence. If he only knew, all that separated him from his quarry was two and a half millimetres of steel.

Ron heard the footsteps on the other side of the fence. With effort he tried to breathe quietly, still lying on his back, he listened intently.

Bruno focussed his attention on the skip. It was full, so nowhere to hide in there. He circled it just to be sure, then slowly ran his eye over the scaffolding and planks stretching high over the pavement. It didn't seem likely that Ron had managed the climb, the chute was too steep. Bruno looked up at the house behind the fence; it appeared lifeless. Slowly, he turned around, looking about carefully. He was suspicious about the house but there didn't appear to be any way in. The builders had secured the building. Bruno walked away from the skip back to the pavement. He began to move slowly along the street, his eyes darting about as he went, trying to examine everything.

Ron felt a surge of relief as he heard the footsteps receding. He continued to lay on the ground. He heard more traffic pass by on the road but no further footsteps.

However, Bruno wasn't far away. He had stopped walking, his eyes still searching the street. Convinced he had missed something, he spun and looked back the way he'd come. This didn't make sense, he was sure Ron couldn't have made it to the end of the street. He *must* be close by. Perhaps he had knocked at a door and was in one of the houses, watching him.

Ron rolled over onto his stomach. He drew up his knees and leaned on his forearms. He straightened one arm and drew one leg under him. Transferring a hand to his knee, he tensed his exhausted muscles and hauled himself upright. As he straightened, fatigue caused him to stagger slightly off balance. He stretched out a hand and leaned on a water barrel for support. The cramped space was littered with building supplies. The air was musty and smelled of cement dust and plaster. He stood very still. How long would he need to stay here? When would it be safe to leave? He decided there was no hurry and would find somewhere to sit and wait until dark. Vicky would be insane with worry but he couldn't take a chance of meeting that maniac with the knife.

Ron began to calm down a little. This was fine, he was very happy to sit quietly, very happy indeed. The site seemed to have been abandoned in a hurry. It occurred to him that the builders might come back. Unfortunately for Ron this wasn't to be, for by chance, the builders' usual Friday pub lunch had morphed into an early finish when one of the men received news that he was a father a full three weeks earlier than expected. Cheers went up and drinks went down. Ron would receive no rescue from that quarter unless he remained in hiding until Monday.

The scaffolding fronting the building lay behind him, an intricate construction of planks and poles. The corrugated fence in front of him was too high for anyone to climb over. Still, he stared at it, his eye slowly examined the fence. He found no gaps, which comforted him. He *really* was safe. Ron leaned back against some of the scaffolding. He had been so frantic to squeeze under the fence he had barely noticed his sore back but now as he leant upon the metal tubes, it stung. He flinched, the sudden movement resulting in his arm colliding with something. Suddenly, there was a noise, a low whirring sound. He spun round in time to see a small off-cut of scaffold pole rolling along the plank. It had dislodged when he flinched. Ron made a grab for it, but it was too late. The tube was gaining speed and rolled to the end of the plank where it fell off. It landed in a wheelbarrow with a clang. The additional weight caused the wheelbarrow to tip over. Spades propped up on the edge of the barrow fell. The resulting clatter was considerable. Ron stared in horror and held his breath, listening... silence.

Then footsteps, coming quickly, right up to the fence. Ron jumped visibly as someone kicked the metal fence from the other side. There followed a fierce barrage of blows aimed at the metal barrier. Suddenly, the corner Ron had bent back sprang up a little. Abruptly, the noise stopped. Ron stared at the small opening, for a surreal moment his mind struggling to believe what his eyes told him. He'd been safe, the nightmare had been over. It couldn't be beginning again but the horrible reality of his situation slammed back into focus. His eyes widened in terror as suddenly, thick fingers appeared at the edge of the metal. Bruno was *stronger* than Ron, the metal bent and the gap was growing *bigger.* Ron had seen enough. Frantically, he looked about for a means of escape. There was nowhere to run. Again, animal instinct saved him; *can't run, can't hide, climb!* The water barrel was only a quarter full. He knocked it over and upended it then ran to the fallen wheelbarrow, tipped out what remained in it and placed it near the barrel. Ron stepped up and into the wheelbarrow. From this slightly elevated position, he scrambled up onto the barrel and from the top of it pulled himself up onto the scaffolding. He was now level with a window opening. He glanced down at the fence, where an angry face glared up at him. Bruno's head and

271

shoulders were now visible. As Ron stared, Bruno squeezed his upper body through, the rest of him quickly followed. Sitting on the ground, he reached into his jacket and pulled out a gun.

Without waiting to see what was on the other side, Ron dived through the window aperture. The house was having new glazing installed and thankfully, the new windows hadn't yet been fitted. Tumbling clumsily into the dim room, he landed on a trestle table, which collapsed. The builders had evidently used the table for tea breaks. Ron fell to the floor along with dirty teacups, sandwich wrappers, rotting banana skins and a foul-smelling liquid that once might have been a milkshake. The thought of the gun pulled him to his feet fast. He leapt across the room and wrenched open the door. Perhaps he could get to the roof and maybe shout for help or gain access to the next house. The door had opened on to a landing, Ron knew going *down* the stairs wasn't an option, so he pivoted and raced up as fast as his exhausted legs would allow. He caught one of the stairs with his toe and stumbled forward, throwing out a hand to prevent falling on his face. Now on all fours, he clawed up the last few stairs to the top. Levering himself upright with the bannister in one hand and the other pressed against the wall for support, he stood, chest heaving for breath, in a dim passage. Opening a nearby door, he discovered a large bedroom. The old plaster had been removed and two walls were freshly plastered. New paint tins stood on an old, heavy sideboard along with pots and brushes. Apart from that, the room was bare. Diffused light was coming from a sizeable window. The frame had not yet been delivered so to keep to schedule as a temporary measure, thick opaque plastic sheeting had been taped across the opening. Ron was about to leave the room when he heard the heavy, thump, thump, thump of someone coming up the stairs. His pursuer had found a way in from ground level. Ron needed to barricade the door to keep out this knife-wielding, gun-toting maniac. He attempted to move the heavy old sideboard and though he pushed hard, it refused to budge. The footsteps grew louder. His desperate panic barely gave him the strength to shift the Victorian monster. Finally, it shuddered, moving a few inches, again he heaved, the scraping of its wooden legs on bare boards created considerable noise.

Bruno heard the sound and picked up pace. Ron could hear his fast approach. He had seconds before Bruno came through the door. Switching to a different tactic, Ron took two steps back and flung himself at the stubborn piece of furniture. Slamming into it, he repeated this again and again. Each time he managed to scrape it closer to the door. Finally, it sat hard across the door. At the same moment, there was a violent bang. It was Bruno attempting to break in. Ron leapt back. After trying the handle, Bruno had kicked the door. Now, he lunged at it, slamming against it with his shoulder. Each time, it moved a fraction and each time it didn't fly open, Bruno became more angry. Ron backed away. He was on the third floor, there was *no way out and nowhere to hide.*

Across town, Vicky was now calmer. Tony had completed his phone call and was sitting opposite her. Shades sat next to her, holding her hand. 'Who were you talking to?' She asked.

'You know I play poker once a month?'

'Mm.'

Tony explained. 'One of the guys owns a cab firm, he's spreading the word to look out for the Chevrolet. He's also going to ask some of the other mini-cab companies. They all know each other. Don't worry, we'll find the car and when we do we'll find Ron.'

Vicky's worried face prompted Shades to add, 'Look Vicky, Ron's no fool, he'll lose this guy. I'm *sure* he's safe.'

The sideboard moved a few inches and Ron jumped out of the window. He had torn off the heavy tape holding the plastic sheet to the frame, expecting to see a three storey drop. To his relief, what he saw was a very steep slope made of scaffold boards, ending with the skip full of rubble far below. It would still be a dangerous descent but compared with waiting for a madman with a gun and a blade to smash down the door, Ron was prepared to chance it.

The chute was constructed three boards wide, with sides two boards high. This wooden chute had conveyed all the rubble to the skip parked in the road hard against the kerb. Ron slid, tumbled, bumped and scraped his way down, collecting cuts, grazes, splinters, bruises and sprains, before finally slamming into the skip. The impact blew all the air from his lungs. He had come to rest on his back, head and shoulders in the skip, with bricks and rubble for a pillow. His legs and feet lay on the bottom of the wooden chute. He stared up at the window he had exited moments before. He could still hear a banging noise as Bruno vented his frustration on the door.

Ron laughed. Nothing was remotely funny, it was a mix of relief to get down and fear of what would happen next. Inexplicably, he thought of Shades and his love of films. If he were a hero in one of those movies, he would jump up and run. In truth he was frightened to move, everything hurt. In the few seconds all these thoughts crossed his mind, Ron had been breathing hard. After recovering his breath, he moved his fingers, then his toes. Upstairs, the noise ceased abruptly. A moment later Bruno's red face appeared at the window. He glared down at Ron and in a fast, angry movement, he reached into his jacket. Ron knew he was going for the gun. If Ron had written this scene, the hero would spring to his feet, jump off the skip and hide behind it but life is very different to fiction. He simply stared up at Bruno, petrified. Bruno hesitated, his hand still in his jacket, his hatred clear to see. He had no problem with shooting Ron but he considered himself a professional and he didn't feel comfortable leaning out of a window in plain view and shooting someone. It should be quick, clean and he should have an equally quick and clean escape route. A three storey house and a hole in a metal fence to squeeze through was not the ideal escape, after an execution. There was no way he was going to follow Ron out of the window and down that rubbish chute. The way the man lay looking up at him, there was a good chance he'd broken bones. This happy thought went some way to cool his anger. He took his hand from his jacket, spun round quickly and headed for the stairs.

When Bruno vanished from view it was as if a hypnotist had snapped their fingers. Ron breathed deeply. His forehead felt cold, he raised a trembling hand and touched it. He stared at his fingers, which were wet with blood. He *had* to move but *could* he? Ron rolled onto his side, then onto his stomach, pulling his arms under his shoulders. He drew up his knees and hunched in this crouched position leaned forward, his forehead touching his clenched fists. He struck out with his left arm and straightened it, repeating the action with the right. Now squatting on all fours, he pulled up his right leg, then left leg. With his feet now relatively level on the rubble and one arm remaining outstretched with his palm flat on the broken bricks and concrete, he finally hauled himself upright. He had pain in his back and stomach but nothing appeared broken. He stood and swayed slightly, gaining his balance. Suddenly there was an explosion of noise behind him, a metallic hammering and banging. Bruno was kicking and wrenching at the fence. Ron looked quickly up and down the road, desperate for help. A car was coming towards him from his left and a double decker car transporter from the right. As the car drew nearer Ron waved. The driver, a woman, caught the movement, smiled and gave a quick wave back, then focussed her attention on the advancing lorry. The road was narrow because of the skip. She was sure the lorry would cross the centre line to manoeuvre around the skip, but she wasn't sure if she had time to nip past the skip before the transporter reached it. She slowed down. The lorry driver had assumed he would have to stop as the obstruction was on his side and had also slowed. The lady driver saw this, waved to acknowledge the other driver and accelerated quickly, passing both the skip and the lorry and drove away happily. The lorry driver had been concentrating on the oncoming car and hadn't noticed Ron. Now he looked in his right hand mirror to check it was safe to swing the big machine out over the centre line. He shifted gears as the transporter had almost come to a standstill. There was a growl from the engine and a metallic clunk from the gearbox as the driver selected a low gear. The engine speed increased as he accelerated. From behind him, Ron heard another sound, the rattle of the metal fence as Bruno wriggled through the hole and began to struggle to his feet. The transporter was passing the skip and gathering speed. Ron looked down at the gap between the edge of the skip and the transporter. He judged it to be about two and a half feet. It was a jump he would have thought possible but he was tired and his legs were shaky. The transporter had a double deck and there were two ladders, the one at the front behind the cab had already passed. The rear ladder would pass him in a moment so he had *one* chance. If he missed, he could go under the wheels or land in the road.

Ron flashed a look behind him. Bruno was raising outstretched arms, both hands gripping his gun. He tilted his head to take aim. Ron jumped with all his strength, seizing the rear metal ladder as it whipped past. He missed the rungs but caught the vertical box metal with both hands. The accelerating vehicle almost tore the ladder from his grip, but he managed to cling on, clamping his fingers to the metal in white-knuckle desperation. The forward motion resulted in Ron pivoting on his clenched hands and sweeping round in a tight arc before slamming hard into the heavy steel post that supported the upper deck of the transporter. As he came to rest, above the noise of the engine, he heard a sharp metallic ping and felt a tremor in the ladder. Bruno had let loose a shot. If Ron hadn't been swung violently by the movement of the transporter, the bullet would have certainly struck him. Quickly he clambered around the ladder and dropped to the metal deck. He scurried on hands and knees between two of the cars. There was just enough room to squeeze under the engine bay of the four wheel drive vehicle as it was higher than conventional cars. The metal deck of the transporter lurched and rocked under him. Ron made a grab for one of the taut webbing ratchet straps which secured the car to the transporter and held on tight. He could no longer see Bruno, houses, people, cars flicked past in a blur. It wasn't only the speed of the transporter that blurred Ron's vision, he was crying. Badly shaken, he clung on and was carried away from danger by the speeding lorry. The deck of the transporter, tilted at a sharp angle and consisted of a pattern of slots and holes, through which he could see the road streaking past. There was a smell of exhaust fumes, hot rubber and an oily metallic scent. The brakes on the machine worked extremely hard stopping the huge mass of the fully-loaded transporter and were hot as the vehicle laboured its way through the London traffic. The engine noise and whir of the twin set of wheels closest to him filled his ears, and though with every second that passed, the danger became more distant, Ron still maintained his fierce grip on the ratchet strap with both hands.

Shades felt Vicky squeeze his hand as the phone rang. Tony reacted quickly and snatched it up. 'Hello... mm, mm, mmm, mm, okay, we'll have it collected. I owe you one, John.' Tony hung up and tore a page from the pad he'd scribbled on. 'They've found the Chevrolet, no sign of Ron. It's parked, key in the ignition, doors unlocked.' Tony addressed his brother. 'You'd better go and collect it. Get one of the staff to drive you over in his car and you drive Ron's back here. Put it in the yard.'

'Okay.' Shades let go of Vicky's hand and stood up.

Vicky rose uncertainly to her feet. 'Do you think I should go too?'

'No, you stay here.'

'I feel I should be doing *something*, Ron's out there somewhere with a lunatic after him and shouldn't we leave the car, he may come back to it?'

Tony didn't want to increase her worry by explaining that the Chevy was half on the pavement and half in a bush, evidently hastily abandoned. 'The key's in the ignition, someone might steal it and it's not parked well, it may get towed. One of the cab drivers is going to wait with it till we pick it up.'

'Okay.' She desperately wanted to do something, *anything,* but it was hard to know what.

Shades felt for her. 'Try not to worry, Ron may be here when I get back.' He picked up his coat and hurried out.

Vicky turned to Tony. 'Do you think he would come here? Perhaps I should go to the flat and wait?'

'I think if he's in trouble he'll come to me and Shades. The Chevrolet is parked closer to the club than your flat. If he's on foot he'll come here first. It's safe here, we have a phone. He can phone the flat to see if you're home and if not, he knows we will drive him about to look for you.'

It all made sense so Vicky sat down. She loved Ron so much, it was hard to think clearly. Tony amazing, he and Shades were both wonderful but it was Tony who was always able to think logically under pressure.   Vicky tried to make sense of it all: she wanted to reason it out, to be like Tony but she didn't even have the beginning of an idea.   'I just don't understand! Who would be out to hurt him? It doesn't make sense!'

Tony rubbed his finger slowly on his lower lip and stared thoughtfully at the carpet before admitting, 'No, I can't see it myself.' Neither of them had answers, it simply didn't fit. Ron wasn't mixed up in anything that would warrant this. He was a successful thriller writer, a thoroughly decent and likeable man who had a passion for fifties music, fifties cars, classic films and chocolate biscuits. Who would want him dead?

The car transporter slowed down and Ron heard the driver shift down through the gears. Finally, it came to a halt. Ron tried to let go of the webbing he had been gripping but his hands didn't seem to want to move. With surprising difficulty, he opened his clenched fists. Quickly he rubbed his hands together to regain some normal movement, then crawled to the edge of the transporter and peered ahead to see why they had stopped. A line of cars was trailing back from a set of traffic lights. He swung his legs over the side and dropped the short distance to the kerb. No one saw him do it. He walked unsteadily across the pavement and leaned for a moment against a brick wall. The lights changed, the line of cars along with the transporter moved off, the driver, unaware that the stranger who leaned on the wall watching him would dearly have loved to shake his hand.

Ron was getting some curious side glances from passers by. His clothes were dusty and grubby from the trip down the rubbish chute and black grease from the transporter deck. Also, he had a cut on his forehead. He looked around, getting his bearings. Yes, he knew where he was. *The Blue Parrot* was about three or four miles from there, the flat was further. No sign of a phone box anywhere. He began to walk.

Bruno was a good deal cleaner than Ron, however, after crawling through the fence and running after him, his dishevelled appearance wouldn't go unnoticed. He needed to return to the house and clean up. He was anxious to avoid questions from Salvatore. After asking directions, he hurried along the street, glancing over his shoulder now and then in the hope of seeing a black cab. Even though he was tired, it was good to walk. He was very agitated and needed to burn off some of that irritation. He couldn't believe how this Ronny Moon had twice escaped him. He wondered if he was losing his edge. He had killed before but it was some years ago now. As he had risen in the organisation, he wasn't often involved in what could be politely described as the hands-on side of the work. Had it been too long? No, no, this Ronny Moon was merely lucky. The next time, his bloody luck would run out and there *would* be a next time, he'd make sure of it. Bruno glanced behind him again; a steady stream of traffic, no sign of a cab. He had no idea if he would get back before Salvatore, he didn't even know where he had gone. Salvatore hadn't told him. Why? Didn't he trust him or was he only excluding him from some organisation business? The sooner he could take care of him, the better, then he, Bruno, would be at all the meetings and when Uncle stepped down, which surely would be soon, he would control a very lucrative and large slice of Italy. He would be one of the very top players and would be treated with the respect fitting his position.

Ron walked slowly. He too was thinking. He hoped Vicky wasn't hurt when she hit the tarmac, he wondered if his car was okay and hoped he may see a cab and not have to walk all the way back.

PART ONE

CHAPTER 22
THE LONG ROAD HOME
FRIDAY AFTERNOON

The house where Bruno and Salvatore were staying and *The Blue Parrot* were only a few minutes' walk apart. Neither Ron nor Bruno was aware they were walking along the same street, their destinations so close to each other, this main thoroughfare being the most direct route to both.

The car transporter had given Ron a huge head start but he was plodding very slowly. Little by little, Bruno was gaining on him.

At the flat high above *The Blue Parrot*, Vicky had bathed her scrapes and grazes in the bathroom. Now she sat nervously, hugging a coffee Tony had made for her. She stood up quickly as Shades came through the balcony door. The fire escape outside led both up to the flat roof and down to the yard behind the club. Shades saw the expectant look; she was desperate for news. 'The car's fine, no sign of Ron, I'm afraid.' Disappointed, Vicky sat down slowly. Shades took off his coat and hung it up. He seated himself next to her and handed her the car keys. 'Funny thing though…'.

'What?' She looked up sharply.

'Well, the passenger seat was rammed forward. You said the man who forced his way in was stocky.'

'Yes, he was.' She was silent for a moment, then added thoughtfully, 'The seat is broken. If you brake hard, it moves forward. Do you think Ron remembered that? Maybe he stamped on the brakes and jumped out before the man could?'

Shades and Tony were enthusiastic, happy to give Vicky some hope. Tony spoke for both of them. 'Yes, yes, that makes sense. If the man was in the passenger seat and if he was a big man, he wouldn't move it forward on purpose, it would make it hard to get out. I bet that's what happened and Ron made a run for it.'

Shades added happily, 'I said he was resourceful, I'm sure he's on his way.'

Vicky was by no means convinced Ron was safe but she clung to this possible version of events.

She was right, Ron was by no means safe. While they had been talking, Bruno had some good luck. After looking behind him for what seemed the hundredth time, he spotted a black cab. He stepped off the kerb and practically stood in front of it. This was the first piece of good luck in this whole stinking day. Bruno gave the driver the house address and told him to stop at the first shop on the way. He needed some damned shopping or Salvatore would wonder what he'd been doing all day. Besides, he really did need to pick up some brandy, he could seriously handle a stiff drink.

The cab moved as fast as the traffic would allow. Ron's lead on Bruno diminished quickly. The cab closed in until finally it was so close that if Ron had turned at that moment he would have seen it. Bruno suddenly shouted at the driver, '*There!* Quickly, pull over!'

Ron's head hurt and his legs were so tired. Even so, he had begun to try and remember everything the man had said. It didn't make sense. The man was a complete stranger. Ron stopped and leaned on a lamppost for support; he really didn't want to think, all he wanted to do was sit down or preferably, lie down.

Bruno had spotted a small convenience store. He gave the driver instructions to wait after assuring him that yes, he would pay waiting time. He hurried across the pavement. Luckily for Ron, he didn't look right or left as he walked briskly into the shop.

Ron continued to lean on his lamppost: this was no good. He was probably only half a mile from the club, better push on. He glanced behind him once more; if only there was a cab. And there was, the first bit of good luck in this whole stinking day. He began to walk stiffly towards it but before he'd taken two steps, shock paralysed him. Bruno came hurrying out of the shop opposite the cab and crossed the pavement. All Ron's tiredness vanished: he was alive with energy. He turned and almost threw himself into a shop doorway. He flung open the door with so much force he gave the ladies in the wool shop quite a start. He dived behind a display of brightly coloured hanks of wool and stared at the door; had the man seen him? Wide-eyed, he clenched both fists and tensed. If the stranger came in he would need to fight, for what choice was there? *Please don't come in, please don't come in.* His heart beat fast and he breathed quickly. Unbelievably, through the shop window, Ron saw the cab pass with his pursuer sitting in the rear seat. He raised a shaking hand and held it over his heart for a moment to compose himself. With the other he gripped the display stand tightly to steady himself, then took a moment to compose his thoughts. He ran his tongue over his dry lips.

All at once, he became aware of being watched, the two sales assistants and three customers were all staring at him in alarm. He was, after all, very dirty and bleeding from his head. He felt compelled to say something before someone phoned the police. He tried to smile reassuringly but because he was so frightened it appeared creepy and unsettling to the ladies.

'Oh wool! It's very nice, but I'm looking for... biscuits!' It was the first thing he could think of.

One of the sales assistants answered uncertainly, 'Erm, wrong shop... Sorry.'

'Ah, yes, yes, well, good bye.' He moved swiftly to the door, conscious of eyes following him.

Outside, he hurried along the pavement. *That was too bloody close.* After losing the man, he'd come very near to leaping into a cab next to him. Ron's nerves had had about as much as he could handle for one day. He pushed himself on, his only thought being to get to

The Blue Parrot, friends and safety. The sudden scare generated enough adrenalin for a final effort. He began to… to say run would be an exaggeration, he could only manage a slow, lolloping, disjointed stagger.

Finally, he could see the club; it was so beautiful the relief was immense. Gasping for breath, he passed thankfully through the yard gates, having the presence of mind to bolt them once inside. It felt good to lock the heavy gates. As he plodded across the yard he saw his car! How did it get here? He couldn't even begin to understand how that was possible. Ron's quivering hand gripped the rail of the fire escape as he propelled himself up the metal steps, as much by his arms as his legs. It was as if gravity was somehow stronger than normal. Each step was a monstrous effort, each stair like conquering a mini-mountain. Every time he straightened his leg without it buckling was a triumph, a minor miracle. Finally, he reached the summit. Ponderously, he thumped three times on the door with his balled fist then let his tired arm fall to his side. If no one answered, he would simply lie down here on the balcony.

Vicky, Tony and Shades all turned to stare at the balcony door. There was no shadow on the glass. After knocking, Ron had swung round and was leaning his sore back against the brickwork for support, gulping down lungfuls of air and staring glassy-eyed at the silver grey sky.

As one, they got to their feet. Vicky began to move to the door but Shades swiftly stopped her by gently catching her upper arm. 'Hold on, let's see who it is first.'

Tony crossed smartly to the door and opened it. At the sound, Ron lurched away from the wall and swung into view, feeling a surge of relief to look up at Tony's face. Unable to speak, he reached out a shaking hand and touched Tony's massive shoulder, then with Tony's support he almost fell through the door.

Vicky tore away from Shades and rushed to him. 'Ron!' He was now doubled over and gripped both knees with his hands as he sucked air in long breaths. As yet, speech was beyond him. They grouped around him, Vicky held his shoulder with one hand and bent to bring her face level with his. She saw the blood on his forehead. 'You're bleeding! Are you alright? Ron!'

Still unable to answer, he let go of one knee and raised a hand, fingers widespread. Vicky took it to mean, *I'm alright, give me a moment.* When he was sure he wouldn't pass out, he managed to nod a couple of times. After several more gasps, he felt able to take a few shaking steps towards the sofa. Upon reaching it, he failed to sit down in the conventional controlled manner. His legs simply folded beneath him and the sofa saved the carpet from a sudden impact. He had the appearance of a life-size puppet with its strings cut. He lacked the strength to sit upright. Ignoring the pain in his back, his head lolled back and he stared unseeingly at the ceiling.

Vicky sat down next to him, snatched up a limp hand and held on tight. He squeezed her hand to reassure her. 'I'm… I'm… alright.' He swallowed. 'Just… need… to… get… my breath… back.'

It was a pleasure to hear his voice. 'Take your time, deep breaths.' In a ridiculous effort to help him she inhaled and exhaled slow, deep breaths as if to demonstrate the technique. He mirrored this slow breathing and nodded. Tony and Shades stood looking down at him. They had never seen him look this distressed. They were desperate to know what had happened but it was certain they would have to wait. Vicky asked anxiously, 'Can we get you some water?' He nodded and Shades went to fetch a glass.

After a few minutes, Ron was able to speak clearly. 'I'm so glad to see you all.' He gulped some more water. 'So glad! Are *you* alright?' The question was aimed at Vicky.

'I'm alright *now*, it's *you* we're worried about! How did you get the cut on your head? Do you feel alright? You don't feel dizzy, do you?'

'No, I'm okay. It happened when I jumped out of the window.'

Shocked, Vicky echoed his words faintly. 'When you jumped out of the window?' She stared at him incredulously.

Shades was unable to contain his curiosity, 'So, come on, Ron, what happened to you?'

Ron gave a hollow laugh, 'Nothing, but it damn nearly did!'

With Vicky still holding his hand and the brothers sitting together on the opposite sofa, Ron told his story.

As he finished, Tony got up and poured Ron a large brandy. While he was occupied, Ron spoke earnestly to Vicky. 'He was faster than me, he was fitter than me. I'll tell you Vicky, I need to lose some weight, watch what I eat, watch what I drink…'

'Here.' Tony handed Ron the brandy.

'Oh! Thanks Tony, I need this.' Passing his glass of water to Vicky he took a mighty gulp. The amber liquid slid down and hit his stomach with a comforting soft explosion of warmth. 'Ooo, that's better.'

Vicky gave an involuntary short laugh. She was so relieved to see him safe, she didn't have the heart to point out that Ron's new fitness campaign hadn't had the most encouraging start.

Ron clung to his glass with one hand and Vicky with the other. After two further gulps, his shoulders dropped. Taking a deep breath through his nose and exhaling brandy fumes through his mouth he began finally to relax. After one more sip, he noticed the calming effect on his trembling fingers and was able to set down the glass with only the faintest of clumsy taps. Holding Vicky's hand and feeling safe in the company of Tony and Shades was an immense relief. There had been moments when he had wondered if he would ever see them again. He stared into middle space, his mind slowing. The jumble of thoughts began to shuffle into some semblance of order. 'What does it all mean?' He was asking himself as much as those around him. 'When the man had me at knifepoint in the car, he kept asking questions.'

Tony leaned forward. 'You said he was raving then you stamped on the brakes and jumped out?'

'Yes.'

'Can you remember exactly what he asked?'

'Er… What's my plan? And em… he mentioned someone called Rifsky. He seemed to think I was working with him. I told him I didn't know anyone called Rifsky. He said I was lying. He said I wrote it all down. I wanted everyone to know Sal… Sal? Salveretty, Salveretty wasn't dead. I think that was the name. And oh yes, I wanted everyone to think this guy with the knife was going to kill him, this Salveretty.'

Everyone tried to make sense of the bizarre conversation. After another sip of his brandy, Ron added, 'He asked, "How was it going to work with this book?" What book was he talking about? I haven't published any new books for months. Do you think he was talking about my books?'

Tony answered slowly. 'You *are* working on a new book though, aren't you?'

'Well, yes but it can't be that one, only Shades has seen it. I haven't even discussed it with Vicky.'

Shades turned to Tony. 'Even I haven't seen it yet, it's still in my case. I certainly haven't discussed or shown it to anyone.'

Tony regarded Shades' silver briefcase on the table. 'That case containing some of the club's paperwork?'

'Yes.'

'You left it on the bar when you got involved with Danny and those punks.'

Shades was concerned that Tony was about to begin complaining about him leaving paperwork on the bar. He didn't want Tony to give him another lecture in front of the others. He answered hotly, 'Yes, yes and you tidied it up! Stop going on about it.'

Tony was silent, thinking it through. Shades was irritated. 'What?'

Tony didn't understand, so he answered carefully. 'There wasn't any manuscript with the papers you left on the bar.'

Shades fetched the case and opened it. As the others watched, he rifled through the contents. 'It's gone!'

PART ONE

CHAPTER 23
THE HOUSE IN THE SQUARE
FRIDAY AFTERNOON

A well-dressed woman climbed out of a cab, paid the driver and wheeled a case to the steps of the house where Bruno and Salvatore were staying. She waited on the step but no-one answered her knock. She hunched her shoulders against the cold and looked around her. As the cab had driven her to the house, she had seen the club with its blue neon sign, *The Blue Parrot*. Salvatore had mentioned on the phone that he, Bruno and Rifsky had had a drink and a sandwich at this club. It was too cold to stand on the doorstep so Anna decided to try the club. She lifted the case back down the steps, turned up the collar of her light cashmere coat and hurried off in the direction of the club.

At almost the same instant Anna left the square, Bruno's cab turned into it from the opposite direction. It stopped outside the house and Bruno struggled out with two shopping bags. He was in better shape than Ron but even so he had begun to stiffen up. The first shop had only cheap brandy and Bruno couldn't bring himself to suffer it so he'd insisted they find a better-stocked supplier. The organisation paid very well and Bruno, like Salvatore and Uncle, was accustomed to enjoying the best that money could buy. The cab driver was well compensated for tolerating the frequent stops and his ungrateful, miserable passenger. He stared at the handful of notes and called out to Bruno's disappearing back. 'Do you want your change, mate?'

Without a backward glance, Bruno put down a bag to look for his key. 'Keep it.' He opened the front door, picked up the bag, entered and slammed it shut.

The cab driver spoke to the closed front door, 'Cheers mate,' smiled to himself and drove off.

Over at *The Blue Parrot*, Vicky had insisted she attend to Ron's cuts and scratches. The questionable First Aid pack had been fetched and she and Ron disappeared into the bathroom. After Ron had washed, she carefully examined the cut on his head which didn't appear serious. She applied a new dressing to the one on his back, then they returned to the living room and between them attempted to understand how Ron's missing rough draft could explain a murder attempt and a virtual kidnapping.

Vicky began. 'I don't understand, what's this new book about? Could it be relevant?' She looked to Ron, then at Tony and Shades.

Shades shrugged. 'Don't look at me. As I said, I haven't even read it. I only gave Ron an idea. I don't know what he did with it.'

They turned their attention to Ron. 'It's about a Mafia boss who's been caught killing someone, so he fakes his own death. He comes to London to have plastic surgery to change his appearance to that of someone else. But while he's recovering, one of his own colleagues kills him to take over. I was toying with some love interest and involving the dead guy's wife.'

There was a thoughtful pause as everyone continued looking at him.

Shades laughed. 'No! No, no, no, this can't be right! You couldn't have written something that happens to be real? And the guy who forced his way into the car is actually a character you made up? It's too far-fetched.'

Tony wasn't as sure as his brother. 'Where exactly did you get the idea from, Ron?'

'Shades told me he heard a story, about a man who had come to London to have surgery so he could pass as his dead cousin, because he was on the run and needed a new identity.'

Suddenly, Shades felt uneasy, a worrying thought crossed his mind that perhaps this was somehow *his* fault. He spoke fast. 'Yes, hang on a minute. I never mentioned Mafia or anyone on the run because they killed someone.'

'No. Vicky pointed out that my book *The Italian Way* was very successful. It outsold nearly all the others. People seem to love Mafia stories so I combined Shades' idea and turned it into a Mafia boss on the run. Then to add further twists, I used the idea of a power struggle within the organisation; that was Vicky's suggestion.' Ron spoke carefully, reasoning it out as he went. 'You don't think this man who tried to kill me was … was Mafia, do you?'

Tony focussed his attention on Shades. 'Where did you get the idea you gave Ron?'

Shades liked to be thought of as cool, but he didn't like where this was going. In an attempt to sound a little more cool than he felt, he answered with, 'A little bird told me.' No-one smiled and Shades was forced to add, 'Actually, it was a big bird.' Still no-one smiled. There was the slightest hint of pleading in his next statement. 'It really was a big bird, it was *The Blue Parrot* itself.' He knew he wasn't making sense. 'You know I haven't been able to use my home cinema in the basement?' Vicky and Ron nodded. Tony watched him coolly, wanting to get to the end of the story without flowery references to birds. Shades wasn't impervious to Tony's stony stare, brother or not. 'After adding more equipment down there, like ice cream fridges, popcorn machines, lights, sound systems, three different options of projection…' He could see his audience was losing patience and got to the point. 'To cut a long story short, it got too hot! I hired a ventilation team and they ran new ducting down there. Some of it connects with the ducting already in the club. On disco nights, we can have a thousand people in here.' Shades slowed down, relishing the interesting part of his story. 'The work has created an unforeseen characteristic.' He paused for dramatic effect as long as he dared. 'Anyone sitting on table thirty-two over in the far corner of the club, can be clearly heard in the projection room down in the basement cinema! It came as a bit of a shock. I knew I was alone down there; then suddenly, out of the shadows there came a voice, as clear as day.'

Vicky interrupted. 'And that is where you got the idea?'

'Yes. Three guys were talking, one was explaining to the others why they were in London. Some dead cousin looked like him and with a few cosmetic tweaks, he could pass for him. So he'd staged his own death and hushed up a real death.'

Ron took up the story. 'It seemed logical that if a major player was dead, someone would move up and take his place. So I wrote that one of his close colleagues might get the idea to make his fake death real and murder him.'

Vicky chose her words carefully: the whole thing seemed too fantastic to be true. 'Shades heard something that *is* true. You invented a story based around what Shades said. You wove in some of my suggestions about a power struggle. You were inspired by your Mafia bestseller *The Italian Way,* and by chance you've come up with what is *really* going on?'

Tony added the last piece. 'It all fits, the story outline was with the club papers in Shades' briefcase. It was open because he was going to work on them but a fight broke out between one of our regulars, Danny Taylor, and some punks. Shades went to deal with it, leaving the case. When I came on the scene, I tidied away the papers but I don't remember seeing any manuscript. It had already been swiped.'

Vicky conjectured, 'So maybe one of the men Shades heard a few days earlier was in the club and he saw the scenario, recognised the situation and took the papers.'

When Ron spoke it was in a slightly dazed tone; this was turning into a bad dream. 'And then he tried to shoot me! He must have calmed down and decided first he wanted answers; What was it all about? Who was I working for? He thinks I'm trying to blow his cover and tell the world, and they *are M*afia.' Ron paused, trying to take it all in. He stared across the room, frowning hard. The others sensed he was trying to remember something. Ron spoke slowly. 'Hold on, hold on, the man in the car said something else.' Ron had the impression a detail that hid in the shadowy jumble of events was on the brink of revealing itself. His exhausted mind struggled to bring it into focus. 'Something important…' Suddenly, there it was and Ron's mind pounced on it. 'Yes! He said there was no point pretending I didn't understand because I mentioned his name.' Ron looked at the others. 'What name did I mention…? I'm so tired I just can't think.'

Tony decided brandies all round would be appropriate but the bottle was empty. He rose to his feet. 'This is going to take some thinking about. I'm going to get some more brandy from the bar. It's not every day you find out the Mafia has decided to kill you.'

Ron turned to Shades. 'Hey, did you get any names? Did you get a look at them?'

'No, no, the DJ was doing a sound check.'

Tony paused with his hand on the doorknob. He waited to hear if Shades had any more detail.

'I missed chunks of the conversation because of the DJ and when I came up the table was empty.'

Tony slipped out, walked down the stairs and emerged through the door behind the upstairs bar. The barman had bad news. 'Sorry Tony, the last bottle is in the optic, I was going to bring more up.'

'No worries, I'll go downstairs.' Tony walked down the metal staircase to the cavernous lower floor. The two bars on the ground floor would be well stocked.

Meanwhile, upstairs Ron had more questions for Shades. 'How did my car get here?'

'Tony phoned one of his poker mates who owns a cab company. They put the word out and found it. I went and collected it.'

'Thanks, and how did *you* get here?' The question was directed at Vicky.

'I walked.'

He held her hand. 'I was so worried when he knocked you to the ground but I saw you stand up in the mirror.' Suddenly, he noticed the graze on her leg. 'Are you sure you're okay?'

She squeezed his hand. 'I'm okay now! Now you're safe.'

Downstairs, Tony turned from the bar with a full bottle of brandy in each hand and was thinking of having sandwiches sent up from the kitchen when he stopped abruptly. Anna had entered the club, and was standing at the top of the three wide entrance steps, one hand resting on the handle of her wheelie case. She looked around the room as if searching for someone. Immaculately dressed in understated style, she seemed out of place. Even given the size of the club, Tony wasn't an easy man to miss, standing at six feet four and a half inches and looking directly at her. They stared at each other across the room. 'Shit! That's not a coincidence!' Tony spoke so quietly under his breath, no-one heard. He moved towards her.

Upstairs, the three of them were talking it over. Vicky and Ron couldn't help noticing Shades appeared more upbeat than he should be, given the dangerous situation but then Shades had always enjoyed excitement and danger. It occurred to Ron that he may not feel quite so perky if *he* had been chased across London by a knife-wielding maniac with a gun.

Vicky still had questions. 'I wonder if the man who chased you was the man who is going to have surgery or if he is the man who is going to kill the man who is having surgery, assuming we've got that bit right.'

'I think he is the man who is going to kill the man who will have the surgery. He said Rifsky wanted everyone to know Salveretty wasn't dead. I don't know who this Rifsky is.'

Shades shook his head in disbelief and rubbed his hands together excitedly. 'It's like a Clifford Johnson thriller novel.'

Ron stared at the carpet with a blank expression. He honestly couldn't believe this was happening. Suddenly, Shades' comment filtered through. He looked up sharply at him, offended by the comparison. 'Oh please! I think my storylines are far better than *his*!'

Shades shrugged. 'Well, I like his books; you never know what will happen next but it's always a *surprise*.'

At that moment the door opened and Tony entered, looking grim, even for him. There was something in the way he looked steadily at Shades. Feeling concerned, Shades got to his feet. 'What? What's the matter?'

Tony hesitated, then in a deep tone loaded with lead he said simply, 'We have a guest.' He stepped aside and Shades stared at the last person on earth he expected to see. All the colour and animation dropped from his face. Although his mouth opened, no words escaped.

'...'

Ron and Vicky looked at the woman who stood so still, framed by the doorway. They turned to Shades then back to the woman. She was strikingly beautiful and elegant. It seemed as if all the clocks in the world had stopped, their pendulums suspended in mid-swing. No-one moved, no-one spoke. The mysterious visitor had cast a spell on the room; charging the atmosphere, which crackled with human emotion.

Ron and Vicky didn't understand what was happening but somehow knew with absolute certainty they should remain silent. Tony, intently watching his brother, stood motionless, two brandy bottles still in his hands.

Finally, the woman spoke, her voice soft, well spoken with a slight but unmistakable Italian accent, adding to her considerable presence. 'Hello, Matty.'

Somehow, the spell which stretched time during those first moments was broken.

Shades shut his mouth and swallowed. For Shades and the woman the others didn't exist. Still staring at her, he answered, his own voice equally quiet. 'Hello, Anna.' His usual confident bravado was notably absent. It was as if this simple exchange re-animated the room. Tony crossed to the drinks cabinet and poured another brandy for Ron and one for Shades. He glanced at his brother and added some more to his glass. He handed it to Shades and the second glass to Ron.

'Ladies?'

Fascinated by the tension between Anna and Shades, Vicky briefly tore her eyes away. 'Please.'

'Anna?'

'No, thank you.' She answered without looking at him, her attention still fixed on Shades.

Tony watched her for a moment then poured himself and Vicky a generous one.'Let's sit down.' He moved to a sofa and sat, Anna slowly joined him. The others sat on the sofa opposite. The atmosphere felt awkward. Tony did the introductions. 'This is Anna, she's... an old friend Shades and I knew in Italy.'

For the first time Anna took her eyes from Shades. 'Shades?'

Tony gestured toward Shades with his glass. 'A nickname he picked up.' Anna nodded slowly but didn't comment. Tony waved his glass at the others. 'This is Vicky and Ron, very close friends. They've had a rough time lately.'

Anna didn't quite know how to respond. 'I'm sorry,' she answered politely.

Tony decided to test a theory, hoping he was wrong. 'Yes, tell Anna about the man. In fact, tell her the whole story.'

Ron didn't know this woman. Surely, they needed to keep this thing quiet until they decided what to do? Tony nodded at him, knowing what Ron was thinking.

Tony usually knew what people were thinking; it wasn't telepathy, although sometimes it seemed that way to others. Tony's mind was uncommonly fluent in body language.

Ron was exhausted. He really wanted to go home but sensed Tony must have his reasons so he took a deep breath and began. 'I'm a writer. I was having a hard time thinking of a story idea...'

While Ron talked, Tony watched Anna's face. As Ron explained details of the conversation Shades overheard in the basement, Anna actually touched her lips. Ron read it as merely surprise, Tony *knew* differently. When Ron described the man who had forced his way into the car, it was plain she *recognised* the description. She was obviously upset.

The tension in the room was too much for Shades. Abruptly getting to his feet, he quickly crossed to the balcony door and exited, closing it quietly, behind him, no-one commented.

Turning to Tony, Anna said quietly, 'I didn't know you were both here.'

'I know.'

'Do you think I should talk to him?'

'He needs a moment, but it's time he was told the truth.'

Speaking more to herself than Tony, she whispered. 'This makes it complicated. I don't know what to do.'

'Can you stay while I talk to Shades?'

'Yes. I'm not expected here until tomorrow, I caught an earlier flight.'

'When I come back we have things to discuss.' Tony phrased it as a statement of fact. Anna neither acknowledged nor denied it, but was grateful to have time to think. Tony also left via the balcony door, taking two coats as he went.

Anna sank back on the sofa and stared at the ceiling. She hadn't expected to ever see Matty again. Ron and Vicky exchanged looks, neither knowing what to say to this woman.

Tony plodded up the metal fire escape to the vast roof terrace. This was a conversation he had hoped would never happen. For all his perception, Tony was not at all sure how his brother would cope with the situation. He wasn't even sure Shades *could* cope. He reached the top of the fire escape and stepped onto the roof. A low wall surrounded the roof a little over waist high. He saw his brother leaning on the wall, looking out at the London skyline. He walked over and without speaking, tapped Shades on the shoulder and held out his coat. Shades took it, slipped it on and turned back to the view. Tony pulled a cigar from his coat pocket, removed the cellophane, which he pocketed, bit off the end and put the cigar in his mouth. He pulled out a lighter, then, cupping his huge hands around the flame, puffed the cigar into life. After slipping the lighter back into his coat he leaned on the wall, allowing his strong hands to hang relaxed over the edge.

The low sun had decided to put in a late appearance and between the clouds the sky glowed golden. The temperature had begun to drop and a breath of cold air played on Tony's hands. He was transported back to a faraway time and place. As children in Italy, they had played in a rowing boat on a lazy river. Sometimes, on hot days, Tony had dipped his hand over the side into the cool water. He smiled at the recollection and made a sound somewhere between a laugh and a grunt.

Shades looked at him sharply. 'What's funny?'

'I just remembered when we were kids.'

'Kids?'

'You 'n' me, messing about on the river in the…, in the …?'

Shades finished the sentence. 'In the *Invincible*, our rowing boat.'

'Yeah, that was it.' Tony smiled at the image in his mind, his strong features softened and he appeared younger. 'It wasn't only a rowing boat though, was it?' He didn't wait for an answer. 'It was a battleship, a pirate ship.'

Shades turned to his brother. 'What made you think of that now?'

Tony shrugged. 'I don't know, simpler times… it'd be nice to go back… sometimes.'

'Yeah.'

Tony took a puff from his cigar and let the smoke drift out of his mouth. Another memory surfaced and he frowned slightly. 'We capsized it having a fight.'

Shades snorted a laugh. 'I mutinied.'

Tony smiled again. 'Mmm, that's right.'

'It was your fault, you kept bossing me about.'

Tony was unrepentant. 'Course I did, I was the captain.' He was silent for a moment, then remembered the unfortunate consequences. 'Us both getting soaked resulted in a court martial.'

Unexpectedly, Shades laughed. 'Yes, I remember, a land-based authority in the shape of Mamma; she banned us from going to sea for a fortnight that summer.'

Tony nodded and added wistfully. 'It was a good summer too.'

They fell silent for several minutes. Tony smoked his cigar and the smiles fell from both their faces; that summer was long ago and this was now. The moment couldn't be postponed any longer. Shades needed to know the truth. '*Anna didn't walk out on you*, not in the way you think.'

'*What!* What are you talking about? She broke off the engagement and married Salvatore Conelli, bloody Mafia boss... *Salvatore?* Ron said the guy who forced his way into the car was asking about Salveretty. Do you think he got it wrong and it's Salvatore who's pretending to be dead?'

'Yes. I told Ron to tell his story and I was watching Anna while he was talking. She recognised the name Rifsky and when Ron mentioned the part about the conversation you overheard in the projection room, she almost passed out.'

'I didn't notice her reaction.'

'Well, you were distracted, seeing her after all these years. What is it? Five, six?'

'Six. What do you mean, she didn't walk out on me? What do you know?

Tony took a moment, Shades *really* wasn't going to like the next revelation. He drew on his cigar and exhaled slowly before continuing. 'You remember Q?'

'Q? Oh Cupid! Uncle Q, course, everyone knew him back then. What's he got to do with it?'

'Salvatore Conelli took a liking to Anna. She gently made it clear she wasn't interested. He became really depressed, he'd fallen in love with her. Salvatore is a real favourite with Uncle Q. He... he had a talk with Anna.'

Shades stared at Tony. 'Talk?'

'He told Anna that Salvatore was a fine young man and any girl should be honoured. Anna knew who and what Uncle Q was, she was frightened. She told him

Salvatore was a lovely man and he would make some girl very happy. It was then that the conversation got dark. Uncle Q told Anna Salvatore wants *you*. Anna explained she was engaged to you. He said if you were the only problem it was *easily* fixed.'

'What are you saying?'

'She left you because Uncle Q would have had you killed and she knew it.'

'How do you know this?'

'Because she came to me, told me all about it and asked me not to let you try and come after her and to look after you.'

Shades was both shocked and angry in equal measure. 'And you never told me? You let me think she walked out, that she didn't love me.'

'Oh, she loved you.'

'You should have told me! I wouldn't have let her do it!'

'Exactly.'

'What's that supposed to mean?'

'That is exactly why we couldn't tell you. Why *I* couldn't tell you. You would have gone after her and Q would have taken it as defiance. These people have to have fear and respect to operate. If Q tells someone to do something and they ignore him, he has to act or he loses all his power. He wouldn't have let you get away with it, you'd be dead.' Before Shades could argue, Tony turned as a sudden movement caught his eye. Shades also turned to see what he was looking at. Anna had climbed the fire escape and appeared on the rooftop.   She remained still, uncertain whether to approach.   Tony touched Shades' shoulder.   He was aware that this was very hard for him.   Tony also believed the worst was by no means over, Shades and Anna should be alone.   Tony left his brother and moved toward her.   'I've told him.'   She gave a curt nod.   Tony left them and returned to the flat to join Ron and Vicky.

Anna walked across the roof and stood near Shades. He stared at her: it still didn't seem possible she was here.   He'd thought about her so much in the years since he and Tony had left Italy.   'Anna, what have you done?'

She reached out and touched Shades' cheek. 'Matteo, Matty.   I did what I had to... Uncle Q didn't leave me a lot of choice.'

'We could have left Italy together.   You should have told me.'

Anna sounded tired.   'No, no, Matty.   Running wouldn't have helped.   The organisation is vast, nowhere would have been safe.   They have long, long memories.'

'But you ruined your life.'

'No.   Salvatore is a good man.'

'How can you say that?'

'He is.   He didn't know what Uncle had done. Uncle made it clear I was never to tell him.   For a long time I could only think of you.   Gradually, I got to know Salvatore.   He's clever, he runs the property side of the organisation.   You know, a lot of it is legitimate.

Slowly, I made a life. We have a child. He's a very good father.'

Shades blinked. He hadn't considered a child.

Anna continued her story. 'Lucia, she's five.'

As Anna said it, Shades saw the happiness and pride in her eyes. At that moment, his anger flared. How *could* she love this man? 'He's the one having surgery, he's the one on the run, isn't he? What did he do, kill someone?'

'Yes.' She said it quietly and looked down.

Shades was rendered speechless by a combination of shock and exasperation. When he did speak, it was harsh. 'And this good chap, this lovely man, tried to kill my friend Ron because he found out he was alive.'

'No, no, Sal wouldn't do that. Apart from some close family, he doesn't think anyone but myself and Uncle knows he's alive and in London. From your friend Ron's description, it's a man named Bruno who's trying to kill him.'

Shades suddenly felt tired... very, very tired. 'Anna, what's going to happen now?'

'I don't know.'

PART TWO

CHAPTER 24
THE FLAT AT *THE BLUE PARROT*
FRIDAY, LATE AFTERNOON

Some time later, Anna walked slowly back into the flat. Shades followed. Tony noted that Shades sat on the sofa next to Ron and Vicky. Anna joined him on the sofa opposite. Tony was aware that everyone was watching him, but wasn't surprised. Vicky and Ron didn't understand the full story; Ron was exhausted, Vicky worried. Shades and Anna were hardly in the frame of mind for rational thought and clear thinking was needed now. The situation was dangerous and required careful handling.

'Okay, let's put our cards on the table. It's clear your presence here is no coincidence and the way you reacted when Ron told his story, you know the man who forced his way into the car; it's not your husband, because Ron said the man was short and stocky and Salvatore is tall.'

Ron interrupted. 'Er, how do you know?'

'Where we grew up in Italy, everyone knew Salvatore Conelli.'

Anna spoke softly and turned to Ron and Vicky. 'I told Matty it sounds like a man called Bruno.'

Ron's eyes widened: the name was familiar. 'Yes, that's it! That's the name I used for the villain in my story outline.'

This raised questions in Tony's mind but he would let it pass for the present.

Tony felt Anna's admission was encouraging. It seemed she was prepared to admit that Salvatore's colleague was responsible for Ron's attack and abduction. Tony took control. 'Right, good choice for a villain. Bruno was a nasty piece of work, I remember him from before we left Italy. The problem is, he remembers *us*, me and Shades.' Tony's agile mind was slotting the pieces together and he didn't like the picture that was forming. 'If Bruno found Ron's story lying on the bar, he would have definitely seen Shades. Now, I don't think Bruno was trying to kill Ron because he thought Ron was going to expose Salvatore's secret. It was what Ron wrote about someone in the organisation taking the opportunity to move up the ladder by killing the top man and taking his place and you actually used his name! No wonder he tried to kill you, he thinks you're trying to tell the world what he's doing. How did you come to use the name Bruno?'

'Em, well, while Shades was busy, I got into conversation with this Russian businessman I met here at the bar. I was looking for names to slot into the story outline. He said he had conducted a lot of business in Italy and Bruno was a very common name. I remember he laughed and said it would suit a shifty

314

character. Oh Tony, I'm having trouble hanging on to all this! Who the hell is the Russian?'

To answer Ron's question, Tony looked to Anna and because he was, so did everyone else.

Anna lowered her eyes and answered very slowly, she was sure that her husband wouldn't approve of her discussing the organisation. 'I was worried about Salvatore. Q told me not to because a security man came over with him and Bruno, he's Russian.'

Tony sighed, 'Look, I'll admit I'm not completely sure but I believe we know enough to make some confident guesses. Perhaps the Russian was amusing himself, telling Ron his colleague's name, when Ron told him he needed a good name for a villain.' Tony turned his attention to Ron. 'And this villain of yours planned to murder his way to the top.'

Ron's voice had the tiniest suspicion of pleading. 'I didn't *know*. I invented that part. The second in command bumps off his boss and hangs the blame on someone else.'

For Tony, it was all becoming frighteningly clear, now his brown eyes focussed on Shades. 'And who better than an old flame of Anna's. A man who was actually engaged to her years ago.'

Everyone now turned their attention to Shades, who avoided their eyes. For confirmation of his theory, Tony addressed Anna. 'Why are you here in London?'

She was unsettled, also a little frightened. 'Salvatore asked me to come, to support him.'

'Are you sure it was his idea?'

Anna answered thoughtfully. 'I believe it was Bruno who first suggested it. I was surprised, I didn't think he liked me.'

Tony made everyone jump by slapping his thigh with his great hand. '*I knew it!*' Then very quietly, more to himself than the room, he added, 'How was he going to get Shades and Salvatore together?'

'We are leaving London on Tuesday morning. It only leaves this weekend and Monday.'

'Mm, the club's shut Monday night for a private... Oh, oh, how could I be so stupid? *He's gonna do it Monday night*!'

Everyone stared and waited for Tony to explain. 'Shades, remember I said someone was booking the club for a private function?'

'Yes?'

Tony explained for the benefit of the others. 'I got a phone call, someone wanted to hire the club on Monday night. He said it was all on the QT, it was a surprise for a big film director and the cast of a successful film who were getting together for a reunion. He sent a hefty deposit to secure the date. A fat envelope with instructions was left at the bar for me. All hush-hush because there were some big well-known celebrities invited. The note stipulated we needed to leave the fire door to the club unlocked for a surprise entrance and to hang a sign on the main door *Closed for a Private Function.* It's public knowledge Shades is a film buff. There was no way he would miss being here if he had the opportunity to meet some

Hollywood actors. The guy on the phone even laughed when he said it was a reunion. A reunion all right. You,' he pointed at Anna, 'and you,' the finger aimed at Shades, 'in the same room.   He shoots Salvatore, maybe both of you and tells the organisation Shades shot Salvatore. And he, Bruno, shot Shades. Or he doesn't even bother and tells Uncle Q Shades shot Salvatore then sits back to let the organisation take care of both of you.' Tony looked from Anna to Shades.

Tony's theory was greeted with stunned silence. They all thought and the more they thought, the more it seemed possible.

Vicky asked a question. 'Who exactly is this Uncle Q?'

Anna answered. 'Uncle Cupid, it's a nickname he acquired when he was young. He's over seventy now.' She trailed off, not wanting to explain or think about the details.

Ron was desperately trying to cling to something good, *anything.*   'Uncle Cupid, sounds like a nice character, perhaps he can help us somehow.' He said it hopefully, but the way Tony stared at him made him turn to Shades for comfort.

Shades sighed heavily, propped one elbow on the arm the sofa and held his forehead in the palm of his hand.   'When Tony and I were growing up in Italy, everyone knew who and what Uncle Q was, he got the nickname because, like Cupid, he always went for the heart.'   To kill any hope Ron might be clinging to,

Shades lifted his right arm and squeezed an imaginary trigger.

Ron stared at Shades for a moment, then fumbled for Vicky's hand, which he held tightly. This was a *very* bad day.

'Anna?' Somehow, at that moment, there was something comforting in Tony's steady, deep baritone and everyone listened carefully. 'Do you think you could get Salvatore here tonight? Would he trust you enough to come alone, without Bruno?'

'Yes.' She didn't sound sure. 'Yes.' She said it again with more conviction.

Tony saw the lack of confidence; it couldn't be helped. He *must* talk to Salvatore. Tony's reasoning was simple. Running wasn't an option, fighting the Mafia was suicide, negotiating was all that remained. 'Look, Anna, we *must* talk to him, *I* must talk to him. If Bruno's plan works, Salvatore will die and if Bruno doesn't kill Shades, the organisation will. As for Ron, Bruno's got it into his head Ron's playing some strange game and trying to expose both Salvatore's existence and his plan. Maybe he thinks Ron's working for someone. You must get Salvatore here tonight, we don't have much time.'

'If I do persuade him to come here, what are you going to do? Bruno is very highly thought of, Q has always praised him. I think he sees Bruno as his younger self, the way the organisation used to be. Bruno is aware of this and emulates Q, he carries a blade as Q did and...' She lowered her voice to no more than a whisper. 'He has killed like Q, he aims straight for the heart. They think I don't know but I do! Some of the wives and girlfriends of others in the organisation told me... They seemed to find it amusing.' As Anna spoke she looked sick, disgusted. She glanced down and nervously rubbed her cold hands.

With his free hand, Ron absentmindedly rubbed the spot on his chest over his heart and ran his tongue over his dry lips. No-one spoke, then with reluctance, Tony answered Anna's original question.

'Honestly, Anna, I'm not exactly sure what I'm going to say. Perhaps we can somehow get Bruno to reveal his true colours. Just get Salvatore here.' Tony checked his watch. 'It's four forty. Can you try and come back at say, nine? Come up the fire escape to this flat. I'll leave the gate open down in the yard.'

'What about my case?'

'Shades will fetch it for you now.' Tony looked to his brother and added, 'It's behind the bar downstairs, the one stage right.'

Shades nodded.

Anna rose to her feet, Shades quickly followed. 'I'll see you down and I'll get your case.'

Anna gave Tony a weak smile, she glanced at Ron and Vicky, the phrase *nice to have met you* crossed her mind but didn't seem appropriate. She attempted a friendly smile, which failed. Clearly very anxious and without another word, she exited via the balcony door, closely followed by Shades. Outside, she stopped and rested a steadying hand on the balcony rail and turned to him. 'I'm sorry to bring all this trouble to your door.'

'None of it is your fault, though we do need to talk to Salvatore. Do you *really* think he'll come?'

'He trusts me, so yes but I don't know how it will help. I wish I knew what to do.'

'Look, try not to worry. Believe it or not, this isn't the first time the four of us have faced a dangerous situation together. We're resourceful people, we'll come up with something, promise.' Shades spoke a good deal more confidently than he felt. 'Anna, this is possibly the last time we'll be alone together. I hope you *are* happy with your life in Italy with your little girl and...' He couldn't bring himself to say husband. 'And him.'

'Salvatore is good to me. I wish he didn't work for... them. But I am happy Matty, I really am. And *you're* safe... well, you will be.' In her heart, she wasn't sure anyone was safe. Anna leaned forward and they kissed.

Shades was thinking how she had given him up to save him, how much courage it had taken to do that and start a new life. Anna truly loved Salvatore but Shades had been her first love and the path untrodden was still sad. The kiss was the goodbye they were denied six years ago. They both knew it was the very last and final embrace, truly the end. They held each other for a long moment and when Shades let go, he knew he was letting go forever.

From her parked car, Jane sat paralysed, one hand on the door handle, the other on the steering wheel. She'd been about to get out. The yard gate was bolted from the inside and she hadn't been able to park behind the club as usual. From across the road however, she *did* have a clear view of the fire escape. She felt as if she had been physically punched in the stomach; her cheeks prickled, she felt hot and there was an odd feeling of unreality. Letting go of the door, she fumbled blindly with the key, started the engine and the car jerked away from the kerb. She had to get away, had to... Home! She wanted to be home.

Unaware they'd been seen, Shades walked Anna down the fire escape. She waited in the yard near the fire exit while Shades went in to fetch her wheelie case. He soon returned with it. As she reached to take the handle, their hands touched momentarily, they paused and stared at each other. There was so much unsaid and so little time in which to say it.

Finally, Anna spoke, her voice soft and a little sad. 'I *have* to go.'

'I know you do.'

She reached up and gently touched his cheek. 'Goodbye Matty.'

Shades slowly stooped, pulled the bolts on the heavy gates and swung one open. Anna turned and walked away. Shades watched her for a few moments then remaining in the yard, shut the gate. Lost in thoughts of what might have been, he turned and leaned heavily on the closed gate. Lifting his hand, he touched his cheek, then let it fall to his side. Taking a long, deep breath, he exhaled slowly and gazed into middle space. He didn't know what he felt; this would take some thinking about. He pushed himself away from the gate and climbed wearily back up the fire escape.

The group was subdued, though perhaps stunned was a better description. Shades dropped heavily into his seat. Vicky was almost certain she understood the situation but it was so fantastic she felt the need to run over the facts as she saw them, just to be sure she'd got it right. 'So… This man Bruno wants to kill Ron because he thinks somehow Ron is trying to expose his plan to kill this other man, Salvatore and they're both Mafia. Salvatore has killed someone in Italy and is pretending be to be dead but the four of us know he isn't.' No one spoke. Vicky continued to articulate the next logical and worrying sequence. 'He won't be too happy that we know.'

The three heads turned towards her slowly shook.

'So he may come after us, or if not, this Uncle Q may come after us.'

The three heads slowly nodded.

'To add to the problem, Salvatore is married to your ex.' Vicky turned to Shades; all the light had left his face, and she'd never seen him look so sombre, so serious.

They fell silent, after a few moments, predictably, all eyes drifted towards Tony.

Ron asked what they all wanted to know. 'What are we going to do?'

PART TWO

CHAPTER 25
THE HOUSE IN THE SQUARE
FRIDAY, EARLY EVENING

Anna walked up the steps with her case and paused with her hand on the door knocker. Bruno was in there too. Could she look him in the eye and pretend everything was normal? She took a moment to compose herself then rapped smartly on the door and waited. Finally, it opened slowly then it was flung wide, arms stretched out and seized her.

'Anna!'

'Sal!'

'I wasn't expecting you til tomorrow, come in, come in.'

It was a shock to see her husband without his beard, he appeared younger. She was pleased to see him and with his new appearance. Anna stretched out a hand and stroked the smooth cheek. 'I think I prefer you without the beard.' She checked herself: this could wait; her talk could not, she *must* speak to him and fast. 'Is Bruno here?'

'Bruno, yes. He's in his room.' Salvatore shook his head dismissively. 'Never mind Bruno, are you okay? Is Lucia alright?'

'Don't worry, Lucia's fine and now I've seen you, I'm fine too.' Anna leaned towards him and whispered. 'Where's Bruno's room?'

Salvatore pointed up the stairs.

She looked about her. 'And the security man, the Russian?'

Now worried, Salvatore whispered back. 'He's not here; how did you know about Rifsky?'

'I happened to mention to Q that I was worried about you and he said I had nothing to worry about, with Rifsky, the organisation's Russian head of security along for the trip.' Anna felt uncomfortable talking in the hall, so in a loud voice she said, 'This is lovely. Show me around.'

Salvatore was puzzled; Anna seemed, odd, tense. 'Sure. This is our living room.' He gestured to the open door leading off the hall where they were standing.

Anna feigned enthusiasm. 'Let me see.'

'Okay.'

As they entered, Anna closed the door quickly and beckoned Salvatore across the room away from the door. 'I came here looking for you, but when I couldn't find you I tried *The Blue Parrot*. You mentioned on the phone you went there for a drink sometimes.'

Salvatore was still confused why Anna seemed in a hurry to tell him something out of Bruno's hearing. She was talking very fast and in a whisper close to his ear.

'Tony and Matteo Manning own the club. There's been trouble. They believe Bruno has been trying to kill a friend of theirs. Tony wants to meet with you tonight at nine.'

'They know I'm here? I'm alive?'

'Yes. It's not safe to talk in front of Bruno. Will you go tonight? I really think you should. Please, just listen to Tony.'

'You were engaged to Matteo Manning, weren't you Anna?'

'Yes.' Anna's frightened eyes stared at Salvatore. She wasn't frightened *of* him, she was frightened *for* him. 'But I'm married to *you*. Tony thinks you're in danger.'

'What does he care?'

'He cares because if anything happens to you, he thinks the blame will be laid at his door. You know he knows who you work for.'

Salvatore trusted Anna, and also had his own reasons *not* to trust Bruno. 'Okay, I'll go.'

'Can we go?' Ron was speaking to Vicky, his voice barely more than a whisper. They had talked over the grim probabilities but he was unable to think clearly. Ron looked over at Tony. 'I'm sorry Tony, I can't concentrate. I ran halfway across London, being chased by a Mafia hitman, I'm done in. This is too much to get my head around.'

Tony understood. 'Go home, get some rest. I'll phone if I have news.'

Ron struggled stiffly to his feet. He and Vicky left via the fire escape and Tony followed them out.

Ron half sat, half lay on the rear seat of the Chevy, Vicky drove. Tony saw them safely out of the yard, shut the gate but left it unbolted.

Vicky drove carefully, trying to give Ron a smooth ride. Occasionally, she glanced in the mirror to check on him. He was very quiet and pale. She desperately wanted to get him home.

Ron wasn't alone in his troubles. Not far away, another unfortunate soul was experiencing one of the worst days of her life. Jane's vision was blurred with tears but somehow, she had made it home and was relieved to shut her front door on the world. Jane dropped her bag, kicked off her shoes and flung her coat on the sofa. Moving quickly to the bedroom, she threw herself on the bed. The dam burst in a flood of tears. She lay face down and sobbed.

Emotions were also running high in the flat over *The Blue Parrot*. Tony looked anxiously at Shades, who sat opposite.

'Are you okay?'

'No… Yes… I don't know. It's been a lot to take in.' Unable to remain still, he stood and moved about the room, touching objects. Suddenly, he became conscious Tony was still watching him. Shades knew his brother wanted to know how he was handling the revelations about Anna. But he couldn't be sure what he felt himself.   To avoid any further questions he changed the subject.   'What are you going to say to Salvatore?'

Tony rolled his bottom lip.   His elbow rested on the arm of the sofa and he stroked an eyebrow with his finger, thinking; it was a good question.   When he finally responded, he avoided it altogether. 'I think I'll have a bath.'

Shades knew his brother well. Tony wasn't having a bath because he was dirty, it was because he didn't have an answer.   Soaking and relaxing in the quiet of the bathroom, he would be hoping to find one.

'What about you?'

'I think I'll wander down to the cinema.'

Tony knew *his* brother well and Shades wasn't going to the cinema to watch a film.   Deep below the club in the quiet sanctuary of the cinema, he might be able to find some answers to the questions that chased one another across his mind.   They went their separate ways.

Vicky and Ron had arrived safely at their flat.   She wouldn't allow him to help with the shopping bags, which were still strewn about in the boot of the car. Vicky found them to be much like Ron; battered and a little the worse for wear, but basically in one piece… barring the eggs.

Once upstairs, Ron had showered, Vicky had applied fresh plasters from their own less-adventurous First Aid kit and he'd eaten a sandwich she'd given him. After eating, Ron had promptly fallen asleep on the sofa. He was exhausted, both physically and mentally. Vicky sat opposite stroking Finbar, and watched Ron sleep. She was also tired but the events of the day troubled her mind and kept her very much awake. She hoped to goodness Tony or Shades came up with something.

Big Tony was an interesting man: with many facets to his character. The stony mask he adopted while in the club gave nothing away. At well over six feet tall, with broad shoulders, strong, dark features and powerful hands, he appeared formidable, even slightly intimidating to those who didn't know him. He had interests and passions for subjects that wouldn't readily spring to mind, given his appearance. He enjoyed playing poker with friends, and even though money was involved, it was very modest amounts. He shared his brother's interest in films and enthusiastically attended Shades' film nights in *The Roxy* with the others. The secret dove coop in a corner of the roof only Shades, Vicky and Ron knew about. His boat, *The Grey Lady*, moored on the Thames, also gave him a lot of pleasure. He loved books and like Shades, enjoyed opera, a passion learned from their Italian mother. One of Tony's more eccentric secret pleasures was long, candlelit baths. He relished the peace and private thinking time and Tony *did* have an awful lot to think about. Hopefully, Salvatore would come to the

330

club tonight with Anna, and Tony needed to know how to handle the meeting.

While Shades wandered down to *The Roxy*, Tony ran hot water into his oversized bathtub, lit five candles and one cigar, switched off the light and let his robe fall to the floor. Then with the cigar in his mouth, slipped into the bubbles. Leaning back, he lay watching the cigar smoke mingle with the gently rising steam. He soaked for some minutes, quietly enjoying his smoke. The aroma of cigar, hot wax and bath fragrance wasn't everyone's idea of the perfect blend, but Tony loved it. Occasionally, he dropped ash into the ashtray which sat within easy reach on the wide ledge that encircled Tony's monster-sized bathtub. It accommodated his candles, ashtray and on occasion, a brandy glass.

He tried not to think about the problem. In the past, he'd found that solutions to tricky situations revealed themselves better if he didn't approach them head-on. He was confident that, with slow careful reasoning, there *was* an answer but it couldn't be forced.

Tony turned his mind to other subjects. He revisited his concerns regarding Shades. Beneath the wisecracks and confident persona, Tony was aware that Shades still thought about Anna, and he hadn't been in a serious relationship since. Perhaps now he knew the truth, Shades may have closure. Anna seemed content with her marriage, and when she'd mentioned her little girl, the joy was clear to see. Shades was a good man, he loved Anna, he would be pleased she had found happiness. Also she had saved his life. Tony was in no doubt Uncle Q would have executed Shades without hesitation. Hopefully, he would be able to move on and find some happiness himself with Jane. Tony smiled as he thought of Jane. Yes, if the relationship deepened, it would be good for both of them. Shades was lucky to have found her: she was funny, clever, good-hearted, very good at her job... 'Mmm, Jane's job'. There was something there, the beginning of an idea. He pushed it away; it was too vague, not ready. Jane had been kind to Vicky. It would be wonderful if Shades and Jane could be as close as Ron and Vicky. Vicky was happy in her work, too. Tony remembered his recent conversation with her. She was so enthusiastic, chatting about how much she was learning from Jane and Maggie... 'Mmm, Maggie.' Vicky had told him that Maggie, aka Magic, was a special effects genius. They could do with some magic to sort out this mess. Maggie had a high regard for Vicky, who was obviously grateful for her help. Clearly, it was a two way thing... Two way? '*It works both ways!*' A slow grin spread across his face. 'Mmm.'

The vague idea slipped into focus. If it was possible to hear table thirty two from the projection room, it would work both ways. 'No, no, no. Wouldn't work, couldn't work... *Could it?*' Tony often talked to himself when alone. The dialogue was a blend of thoughts and spoken words. Too many bloody films, he'd watched too many films with Shades. 'Ridiculous.' The cigar glowed brightly as Tony drew a mouthful of smoke and gently let it drift out and up with the steamy heat of the water. He flicked some ash and got down to business. Okay, let's phrase the problems properly. It comes down to people; Salvatore, Bruno and Q. Perhaps, if the meeting went well, he could convince Salvatore they were no threat to him, that they had discovered his plan for a new identity accidentally and would say nothing. Frankly, they didn't want to be involved.

The next problem was Bruno and Q. If Bruno killed Salvatore and pointed the finger at Shades, Q would act. What if one problem could solve the other? The ridiculous idea drifted back. 'No, too many variables... or are there?' The thing to do was list them and figure out what the odds were for it to work. To begin with, would everyone agree to attempt it? Shades would love it because it was daring, theatrical and dangerous. Vicky and Ron would hate it for the same reasons but if he, Tony, told them it was the only way, yes, they would all be in.

Would Maggie Moorcroft help? Vicky had mentioned that Maggie treated her like a daughter, so there was a fair chance Maggie *would* help. How much did they need to explain? It would be better for Maggie if she didn't know the full story; they could explain just enough to get her on board. He could go with Vicky to meet her. Still, it was asking a lot. If she agreed, it left only Salvatore. Tony needed his help the most, also they had to *trust him*. 'Mm, that's the key.' If Salvatore didn't believe Bruno was a threat, it could all go very badly wrong. In the worst-case scenario, Salvatore would pretend to go along with his plan then murder, or arrange for the organisation to murder, all of them. It was possible. He didn't really know the man, he knew of him, had seen him, but didn't *know* him. He would need to use all his powers of observation and intuition at this meeting. He must be sure or as sure as he could be. One thing was sure, Vicky was right, Salvatore wouldn't be too happy that they all knew he was alive. Unhappy enough to get rough? Tony stubbed out his cigar and sat considering the meeting. 'Tricky.'

Bending his knees, Tony slid beneath the water. For a moment, he held his breath and enjoyed the comforting heat on his face and shoulders, then pushed with his feet, straightened his legs and surfaced slowly, his dark hair clinging to his head. He sat very still, his mind working hard. Rivulets of water ran down his face and dripped from his chin. Even if he could convince Salvatore that Bruno was a danger, would he act? Anna had mentioned that Uncle Q liked, even admired Bruno, so would that make Salvatore hesitate? And time was a problem. 'Time!' If this stood any chance, he must act quickly and in the right sequence. 'First, phone Vicky, see if she can set up a meeting with Maggie.' Tony felt a surge of excitement. Yes, it was dangerous, but oh, if it worked! 'It *would* be sweet,' he whispered, and smiled.

Far below, Shades sat in one of the sumptuous viewing seats in his private cinema deep beneath *The*

Blue Parrot. The house lights were very low, set at viewing level. He stared up at the big, shadowy silver screen. The scenes he viewed weren't stored on any roll of film, they were projected by his mind.

It was years ago. He wasn't Shades then, he was Matteo Manning. *Matteo* means gift from God, his mother never tired of telling him the story. As a baby, he'd nearly died and against the odds, clung to life, hence the name.

When Anna had entered his life, he'd been the happiest man alive. Their love was strong and deep, everyone was happy for them. The engagement was short; why wait? The wedding date was arranged, but then her mood changed, literally overnight. She broke off the engagement, returned the ring and told him it would be a mistake they both would regret. She simply walked away.

He had spiralled into deep depression; the family had been gravely concerned and feared he may do something terrible. He would never speak of it, but the family had been right to worry. Sometimes, when the sadness smothered him, it was too much to bear. He thought of those troubled nights, the four o'clock in the morning surreal moments when he felt he was the only person on earth awake, staring into the darkness. Hopeless; it's a word often used but few understand the true horror of it. To feel so unimaginably sad and to be without *hope*, is a lethal combination. For without hope, there is no belief in ever feeling happiness. The misery will go on without end and if you believe that,

335

really believe it, what's the point? What *is* the point of living? Being dead wouldn't make him happy but the pain would stop. Sometimes, after long nights of little or no sleep, Shades had sat alone outside in the small hours, his red-rimmed eyes looking up at the black sky. It was then, once or twice during those still and silent nights, he had believed oblivion was preferable to existence. In those fleeting moments, if the means to end his life had been at hand, he would have used them. He had made it through the tunnel but it had been so terrifyingly close.

Shades actually flinched as suddenly, he became aware of his surroundings, safe in his beloved cinema. The memory was so powerful that just for a moment, he was reliving it and the intensity he'd felt. He rubbed his hands; his grip on the arms of the seat had been so fierce he'd squeezed the blood from his fingers and he'd been *wrong*! She hadn't left him because she didn't love him. She'd left him because she'd loved him so *much*! Now she had a child, Anna had managed to build a new life. Was she *really* happy? Or was she pretending, to spare his feelings, still protecting him? The way she had defended Salvatore, *"He's a good man"*. Perhaps she *was* happy.

What now? Anna was in too deep. Married with a child, she would never be free of the organisation. If this all worked out, she would return to Italy and continue the life she had made. How did he truly feel? He wasn't the same man he was six years ago; come to think of it, he wasn't the same man today he was yesterday.

For a long time now, deep, deep down, he'd worried that he couldn't read people the way Tony could. He thought he'd been so wrong about Anna, he hadn't felt able to allow Jane to get close. Jane, poor Jane; he'd pushed her away, he'd probably hurt her. She didn't deserve that. Of all people, he should know what it felt like.

He'd make it up to her and see where it took them, but not until this mess was sorted out. Should he tell her what was going on? No! They weren't even sure what would happen to them, now they knew Salvatore's secret and no-one could predict how Q would react. Seventy-something or not, he was psychopathic, not the kind of guy to mellow with age. If anything, he was potentially more unpredictable.

No, it wouldn't be fair to put Jane in danger. He needed some excuse to keep her away, but gently, he must do it gently. He took a deep breath and exhaled in a long sigh. Even with so much still to worry him, Shades felt a little better. He looked about the cinema, the details of the room lost in the darkness. How he loved it down here. Thinking about it, his love of films had begun not long after he lost Anna. He realised suddenly it had been a form of escape: where other desperate souls might turn to drugs or alcohol, for him it had been classic movies. If he was lucky for two blissful hours, his mind would give him some peace, taking refuge in a good story. Even when he hadn't needed this distraction quite so much, the fascination with films had remained. He smiled at himself. 'Can't believe I never noticed the connection.'

'Shades?' It was Tony's voice.

'I'm here.'

Tony moved to the row of seats and sat next to him in the almost dark room. 'Good film?' He asked, looking at the blank screen.

'I was thinking…'

Tony didn't answer, he wanted to draw Shades out to see if he *was* okay, if he could handle a stressful, dangerous plan.

'…Thinking about Anna… she really did love me.'

'She did.'

'Do you think she's happy, Tony?'

'I think her little girl gives her happiness.'

'What about her husband?'

'What do *you* think?'

'I think he does.'

'Are you pleased for her?'

'I told her I was, outside on the fire escape. She said she was happy and I said I was glad.'

'Are you?' Tony asked gently.

There was silence. Tony felt an unaccustomed rise in tension.

Shades finally answered quietly. 'I know now Anna gave up her future happiness to save me. At the time, she couldn't know she would find love again or ever be happy but she did it anyway. If it's impossible for us to be together, I wish her happiness Tony, I really do. She

did it for me, she married Salvatore to protect me. I...
I think I'd feel worse if she wasn't happy with him.'

Tony had some idea what that took and he was
proud of his little brother, pleased that he may be able
to move on and finally make peace with his past.

'I've been thinking about Jane.' Shades said
thoughtfully.

Emotions of those around him were easy for Tony to
read and Shades was riding a rollercoaster. 'She loves
you.'

'Yes and I...' Shades was shocked to find the word
love lurking at the end of the sentence and quickly
amended it. '...Think a lot of her too. But I think I'd
better keep her away until we've sorted this out. I
don't think we should tell her what's going on. We
don't know how they'll react when Anna tells them we
know their plans.'

'I agree.'

'You've got an idea, haven't you?'

'What makes you so sure I've thought of
something?'

'For one thing, you've cut short one of your usually
epic baths and you seem a hell of a lot more upbeat
than you did half an hour ago.'

'...'

'Also, you're grinning!'

'It's dark! How can you know that?'

'Because I'm your brother. Come on Tony, he'll be
here soon. Tell me!'

Tony spoke seriously. 'It's very dangerous and it may not work. I need to check some facts. Also I need some help. I've got to make a call, then hopefully, a quick visit. After that, I'll tell you all about it, okay?'

'You'll be back before Salvatore and Anna get here?'

'Yes and I think it would be better if you're not here when I talk to him.'

Shades wasn't convinced. 'We'll see about that.'

Tony didn't have time to argue so he let it go for the moment.

Vicky snatched up the phone. She wanted Ron to get more sleep. Speaking in a whisper, she answered. 'Hello? Tony, look, hold on a moment. I'll take it in the bedroom. Ron's asleep on the sofa in here.' Leaving the living room phone off its cradle, Vicky hurried into the bedroom, shut the door and picked up the extension. 'Hello.'

'Vicky, exactly how close are you to Maggie?'

She was puzzled. 'Er, very. Why?'

'Would she help you, if you told her it was important?'

'I believe so. What's this about?'

'Do you trust me?'

Vicky didn't hesitate. 'You *know* I do.'

'Let Ron sleep. Try phoning Maggie and if you reach her, tell her you have a problem. Ask if you can come over immediately to talk to her and is it okay to bring a friend?'

'Yes, I can do that but I can't guarantee what she'll say. She may not even be home.'

'We haven't much time, I'll set off to you now. If it's all okay, leave Ron a note and meet me outside your flat.'

'I'll try her now.'

Tony hung up but held the phone in his hand and paused. Was this madness? Probably. He let go, stood up, swiped his car keys from the table, then exited the flat and moved quickly down the fire escape to his car. It was only a short drive to Ron and Vicky's flat and on arriving, he was relieved to see her standing on the pavement outside. He swung the car over to the kerb and wound down the window. 'She said okay?'

'Yes.'

'Get in, we'll talk on the way.'

Vicky hurried around the car and slipped into the passenger seat. She gave Tony some directions and he moved off smartly.

'What did you tell her?'

'I said Ron and I were in trouble. A close friend of ours was trying to help and he wanted to talk to her.'

Tony was driving fast but with precision and confidence. 'Fine. That's fine.'

'So how can Maggie help?'

All at once, Tony's usually grim expression adopted what looked suspiciously like a grin. Vicky felt a worrying tingle: Tony and his brother enjoyed action and drama on the silver screen but unfortunately, they also enjoyed action and drama in real life. It occurred to her that he may have concocted a solution which involved copious amounts of both.

'Tony, what are you planning?' It was said sharply, with more than a little concern.

Tony ignored her tone. 'At this moment, I'm not sure. It all depends if Maggie will help and how my meeting with Salvatore goes tonight.' He changed the subject to avoid more questions. 'How's Ron?'

'Still asleep. I left a note on the coffee table *"Back soon, gone to see Maggie."*' Vicky didn't waste her breath asking any further questions. Tony would explain when he was ready.

PART TWO

CHAPTER 26
JANE'S FLAT
FRIDAY EVENING

The image in the mirror was merely a blur. Jane felt around in the pocket of her bathrobe for glasses, they were large, with thin red frames. She put them on and poked the bridge with her finger, sliding them further up her nose. As she surveyed the unhappy view in the bathroom mirror, two thoughts struck her: firstly, she looked better without them, as a blobby blur, and secondly, her eyes now matched the red frames.

She had cried most of the afternoon, then taken a shower. She removed the glasses, picked up a tissue box and headed back to the living room. Sitting down heavily in her reading chair, she leaned back and stared vacantly at the ceiling. She felt hurt, angry, foolish and heartbroken but what if it was all a mistake? Her mind replayed the image of Shades standing with the woman at the top of the fire escape. He'd leaned forward and kissed her on the mouth. You *don't* do that to a sister, cousin or friend. The woman *must* be a lover. It explained why she had never been able to get really close to him. She'd told herself it was because he was shy or maybe he wanted to take things slowly. Perhaps he'd been hurt before. But now, she had the answer, he was seeing someone else. Maybe he had wanted to tell her but didn't want to hurt her feelings. He must have known how she felt. No, she was only making excuses for him. It could be he was simply a rat! A lying rat. Jane punched a cushion then snatched it up in her arms and hugged it. She shut her eyes tightly, causing fresh tears to run down her cheeks. She leaned forward and buried her hot face in the soft material, her shoulders shook as she cried, her sobs muffled by the cushion. She cried because she truly loved Shades: she cried because he'd made a fool of her; lied to her; she cried because behind the cheerful face she showed the world, Jane was lonely. She was tired of being lonely, she wanted desperately to love and be loved. For a while, she'd believed Shades was the one, but her hopeful future had been snatched away in the time it took for a kiss.

It was a cheerful flat; the only sad thing in it was Jane herself. Indeed she believed herself a forlorn little scrap of neglected humanity.

A home generally reflects its occupant and Jane's was no exception. It was clean and tidy, with her knowledge of colour evident in the cheerful pastel hues she'd chosen for the walls. Large canvasses, mainly depicting wild flowers, graced the flat. They were Jane's own creations, for she enjoyed painting and when she painted, her choice was usually flowers. The subject suited her character; the paint was applied fast, giving the pictures energy and vibrancy however, there was nothing vibrant in their creator's attitude today.

There were no harsh overhead lights, instead the room was lit by lamps. The huge wooden bookshelves near her reading chair were festooned with small, colourful fairy lights. Silk cushions were scattered about on the furniture. A brown teddy bear Jane had owned for as long as she could remember looked on as she drew up her legs and curled into a ball. The huge, comfortable reading chair was her favourite spot, a place where she usually found peace and comfort. Today, she felt neither of these things: this was it, the end. She couldn't be hurt like this, she would finish the relationship. Jane would show him she was strong and honest, even if he *wasn't!* Yes, if there was no future, she would finish it properly, face-to-face and she'd have the courage to look him in the eye. She would tell him not to phone or talk to her, they were done. 'Yes, I won't be upset, I won't! If he doesn't want me, I'll find someone who does!' Saying it aloud, she felt somehow made it true.

The phone rang, making her jump and she sat up quickly. Automatically, she reached out to answer it, but her hand stopped short. What if it was him? While Jane tried to make up her mind what to do, the answerphone clicked in and the tape snapped on. *"You've reached the home of Jane Flutter. I can't get to the phone right now, so please leave a message after the tone, thank you.* Beep."

'Jane, it's me, Shades.' Jane stared at the machine. 'Look, we've got some problems here at the club, you know we get all sorts of people here. Thing is, it's

345

probably best if you don't come over for a couple of days, till me and Tony sort it out, okay? Don't worry, we'll talk soon, I'll call when it's safe okay? Bye.' The incoming message tape beeped and cut him off.

At the other end of the line Shades still held the phone. The long tone sounded in his ear, indicating he had been disconnected. 'I'll miss you,' he whispered into the phone, knowing no-one could hear him. Shades felt lighter, freer. He felt he could be on the brink of a kind of peace he hadn't experienced for years. If a person carries a trouble for long enough, it's only noticeable by its sudden absence. He still couldn't quite take it in. He had been right. Anna *had* loved him and *would* have married him. Shades sensed that reconciling with his past would help his future. He *could* trust his judgement.

For some time now, he'd felt a closeness to Jane, a connection, but had doubted himself and through some sense of self preservation, held back. Jane was very different to Anna, not only in looks but character. He sensed that this was a good thing: if he had feelings for Jane only because some aspect of her reminded him of Anna, then that wasn't healthy or fair to Jane; he liked Jane for who she was. Shades wanted very much to see Jane. He wondered again if he should tell her everything. Would he be putting her in danger if she knew about Salvatore? Perhaps if they managed somehow to work it all out and Salvatore and Anna returned to Italy, it would be safe but at the moment, the next couple of days were, at best, unpredictable. With so much in play it was better if Jane stayed away, stayed safe.

At the same moment Shades finally made his decision about Jane's involvement, Tony and Vicky drew to a halt outside a gated drive. Tony was impressed. 'This is where she lives?'

'Maggie's the very best at what she does; make up and SFX. They don't call her "Magic" for nothing.'

Through the gates in the gathering gloom, Tony could make out the low, modern, single-storey house at the end of the drive, slightly obscured by trees. The drive swept round in a gentle curve but he could see enough of the house to realise it was very modern and very expensive. 'She's a clever woman, isn't she?'

Vicky answered firmly, 'Very.'

Tony didn't get out of the car immediately. He seemed to be thinking. Vicky watched him and waited in silence. Finally, he turned to her. 'I didn't want to tell her everything, but I think I'll have to. There's no way she'll help unless she knows what it's all about. Even then… She may not want to get involved.'

They sat for a moment, considering the problem. Tony made up his mind. 'I'll tell her everything but we don't tell her his name, okay?'

'Right.'

Tony climbed out of the car, Vicky followed. She pressed the gate intercom. 'Hello? It's Vicky.'

A tinny voice answered brightly, 'It's open, come on up.' There was a click and the electric gates began to move.

They got back into the car, Tony drove slowly through the gates and advanced on the house. Maggie was waiting at the open front door. Vicky saw the wary look in Maggie's eyes as she introduced Tony. To Vicky, Tony was a kind-hearted man she trusted and felt completely at ease with; she loved him and Shades like brothers. To Maggie, this huge, serious man who looked down grimly at her was slightly frightening. Tony recognised her reaction: this was going to be an uphill battle. He had to gain her trust, then ask a big favour and there wasn't much time. The day was vanishing fast, he needed answers from Maggie before his meeting at nine with Salvatore.

Vicky continued the introduction. 'Tony and his brother are my and Ron's closest friends. We're in trouble and Tony is trying to help us. He thinks your special skills may solve our problem and he wants to talk to you but it's a long story.'

Tony spoke quietly; Vicky was accustomed to the deep rich timbre of his voice but to Maggie, it was a new and charming experience. 'Thank you for seeing us at such short notice. If you're not able to help, we totally understand.'

Maggie looked steadily at Tony then turned to Vicky. 'A long story, you say?'

Vicky gave a quiet sigh and nodded.

'Well, you'd better come in and tell me all about it.' Maggie stepped back and held the door wide. Tony and Vicky walked into a spacious hallway, immaculately clean. The smooth, dark-tiled floor was shiny enough for Tony to offer to remove his shoes. 'If you'll be more comfortable,' was Maggie's subtle way of saying yes.

Leaving coats and shoes in the hall, they were shown into the living room. Although the building was single storey, it was built on a slope and the living room was four steps down from the hall. One wall was constructed of floor-to-ceiling glass panels through which could be seen a well-manicured garden sloping away from the house. This was possible owing to the outside lights beautifully illuminating the evergreens. The room had a wall of books and several large artworks in the form of paintings and sculptures. Unlike Jane's library of stories, Maggie's consisted mainly of tech manuals encompassing a wide range of subjects, including pyrotechnics, lighting effects, ballistics, make-up SFX, guns, metallurgy and tool catalogues, to name but a few. If Vicky hadn't been so preoccupied, she may have noticed that two were written by Maggie herself. Vicky was drawn to another wall of shelves as the silver, gold and glass sparkle was hard to miss. As she gazed at the rows of glittering objects, her voice was full of wonder. 'Maggie, *look* at all your awards!' She read aloud some of the labels, on the shields and trophies. 'Special Effects Invitation, Service to the Industry for make-up of Exceptional

Calibre.' The list went on. Vicky shook her head in disbelief; she knew Maggie was good, but the trophy wall was impressive by anyones standards

Tony glanced at them and was pleased: this lady could certainly help. The question was, *would she*?

They were offered coffee but as time was short, declined. Maggie sat on the sofa, Tony and Vicky in armchairs facing her. 'You'd better tell me what this is about.'

Vicky looked to Tony who took a deep breath and began. 'It all started when Ron was trying to come up with a new plot for a book...' Maggie listened patiently, her face reflecting the drama of their story. She was in turn surprised, shocked and concerned for Vicky. Tony left nothing out.

After thirty minutes, Maggie was up-to-date with events. She looked with sympathy at Vicky. 'You've had a bit of a time of it, haven't you, love? The film we're working on isn't as frightening as this.'

With alarm, Vicky remembered the film. 'We aren't holding you up, are we Maggie? Are you on set tonight or working on anything?'

'Not today, love, they're reshooting three interior scenes tomorrow morning, Jane's handling that. Tomorrow afternoon, the director is viewing and editing so I'm not needed for a few days. What do you think I can do to help?'

Vicky wasn't certain how Maggie fitted in, as Tony hadn't discussed his plan with anyone. He began to explain. 'I had an idea: tell me if it's possible...'

A few minutes later, Tony sat back and waited for Maggie's verdict. She took her time. Vicky couldn't be sure she would be pleased if Maggie agreed or pleased if she didn't. Now Tony had explained what he was thinking, it sounded dangerous. They both sat quietly.

Maggie spoke thoughtfully. 'Well... what you're asking is certainly technically possible. Whether it's a good idea to do it, I'm not too sure. I suppose you've thought of the police?'

'Yes. If we tell the police everything, we expose the fake death and their attempts to create a new identity for one of their key players. He'll go on trial and we would have made enemies of a vast, powerful organisation no police force would be able to protect us from. I told you I'm meeting this man tonight. He may not go along with my idea but if he does, we don't have much time. I don't believe you're in danger or I wouldn't have asked. If you feel uncomfortable getting involved, we understand.'

Vicky added quickly, 'Yes, please don't worry, Maggie, you've done so much for me already and this is asking a lot. I don't think it was fair of us to come.' The more Vicky thought about it, the less she liked it. She was more than half-hoping that Maggie *wouldn't* help.

'Okay, I'll help. It'll make an interesting chapter when I write my memoirs.'

Tony was sharp. 'That's the thing. If you help, you can't tell anyone, it's not safe.'

'I realise that, don't worry.'

Vicky felt her stomach tighten; *Maggie was actually going to do it.*

Tony got down to practicalities. 'Time is very short. We...,' he glanced at Vicky, 'haven't even spoken to Ron or my brother. We're going to do that now. If they agree, I'll phone you straight away. Then after my meeting, if he also agrees, I'll phone with the calibre. Do you have a selection?'

Maggie smiled, 'There's a rather large, fully-fitted workshop here in the grounds. I like to tinker with a few gadgets; I think I can accommodate most models.'

Vicky knew that Maggie was being extremely modest, downplaying her incredible innovations with her description of tinkering in her workshop. She was surprised to find herself feeling disappointed as Maggie continued her conversation with Tony; Maggie was clearly warming to the project.

'I definitely have the rest of the FX, it's fairly standard. Vicky is familiar with that.'

'Right.' Tony stood up to leave. 'Expect my call. Thank you, Maggie.'

Maggie held up her hand. 'Hold on, not so fast. My help comes with conditions.'

Tony sat down and waited.

'This man is dangerous.'

Tony nodded.

'I don't want Vicky going near him.'

Tony and Vicky exchanged a look, Tony answered slowly. 'You could show me how to rig the gear and I could do it.'

Maggie shook her head. 'I could but it's vital for everyone it's done right.'

'I'm not a fool.'

Maggie wasn't to be deterred. She was a woman of decision and once she had decided on a course of action, there was little that could change her mind. 'I'll do it or I don't help.'

Tony perceived that arguing was useless. Maggie's deep concern for Vicky's safety was something he hadn't factored in. A shadow of concern passed across his mind. What *else* had he missed? He pushed the thought away, rose to his feet again and held out his hand. Vicky also got to her feet, but a handshake didn't seem enough, so she hugged Maggie, tightly. Tony caught the sad look in Maggie's eyes as she leaned her head against Vicky's. 'Hope it all works out, love. Who needs movies?'

It was true! Vicky reflected that if they all came out of this alive, it may be some time before she wanted to watch another of Shades' thrillers or read one. Life was quite enough drama. As Maggie let go, Vicky reached out and took her hand, her words tumbling out in a rush. 'Maggie, I don't like this, I don't want you to do it. Look, we only came here for advice and to borrow some props, it's our problem. If anything happened, I…'

Maggie squeezed Vicky's hand. 'I'm doing it and there's no more to be said.' She managed to speak both in a friendly but determined way that would stand no argument. Vicky caught a glimpse of the tough, strong character that carried Maggie through her personal tragedy and enabled her with hard work, brains and grit, to rise to the top of her chosen field.

Vicky suddenly felt very young; Maggie seemed so sure, so confident, she was inspirational. 'Oh, Maggie.' It was because Maggie cared for her so much, she would do this. Vicky had tears in her eyes. She had faced her own tragedy when merely a child, losing her own parents on New Year's night in a London bomb attack at the height of the Northern Ireland Troubles. Her parents weren't political, just in the wrong place at the wrong time. She thought about them sometimes, especially her mother. This was one of those times.

It was plain to Tony these women had a close relationship. Suddenly, he had an uneasy feeling. Usually, he weighed up the chances, the risk involved, the possible reward, then made a decision and took each step logically. These were all very good people; Maggie, Vicky, Ron... everyone. Was there too many variables? What if something went wrong? On the spot, he decided to cancel the whole plan if, after his meeting with Salvatore, he had any doubts. 'I'm sorry, we have to go, there isn't much time.' He glanced at his watch, which showed a couple of minutes past seven. 'Thank you so much.'

In the car both were silent, Tony thinking about Maggie and Vicky worrying about the uncertain, dangerous aspects of Tony's plan.

Tony broke the silence. 'Maggie really cares about you.'

'Yes, I'm not certain it was fair to involve her.'

Tony shared her concern but kept it to himself. 'Vicky, we *have* to do something, Ron and Shades are in real danger, so are Anna and Salvatore himself. Like you, I don't much care what happens to Salvatore Conelli, but it's all connected.'

'Mmm. Where are we going?'

'To pick up Shades then over to your place to talk to Ron. If my meeting with Salvatore goes well, we have to be ready to act quickly. Do you think Ron will agree to it?'

'You know he will, if you tell him it's the only way.'

Tony's lips tightened; she was right. Both Shades and Ron would go along with it if he told them to. He brooded silently on the problem: Salvatore, Uncle Q, Bruno, all unpredictable; this *was* risky. He really hoped he would feel more confident after the meeting. He needed to look Salvatore in the eye and *know* he could trust him. He didn't let on to Vicky that he was worried and would cancel everything if the meeting didn't go well. The problem was, he had no Plan B.

They lost no time collecting Shades from the club, then headed for the flat to talk to Ron. *En route*, Shades was full of questions but Tony refused to be drawn. 'I'm not explaining it all twice, wait till I talk to Ron.'

Shades wouldn't have to wait long, since it was a short drive to the flat.

A few minutes later, Vicky put her key in the front door. As she walked in she called, 'Ron! It's only me and the guys.'

'I'm in here.'

Vicky found him sitting on the sofa and as he looked up at her she saw he was bleary eyed. 'Are you okay? You still look tired.'

'Yes, I'm alright. I woke up just before you came home.' He smiled. 'I'm turning into an old man, sleeping during the day.'

Sitting next to him, Vicky took his hand. 'You've had a shock, you needed some rest. Did you get my note?'

'Yes, I saw it. You've been to see Maggie; I wondered why?'

The brothers sat down and Tony leaned forward. 'That's what I want to talk to you about.'

'Oh?'

'I've come up with an idea and want to talk it over with you and Shades. Vicky's heard it.'

Ron glanced at Vicky's face to gauge her feelings about Tony's idea. She appeared tense, which wasn't encouraging. Sensing trouble, Ron became fully awake. With a feeling of foreboding, he asked carefully. 'What's the idea?'

Vicky's anxiety drove her to her feet. 'I'll make some coffee.'

Tony noted Ron's worried face. Was he up to it? It was probably better if he laid it on the line and didn't try sugaring it, so Ron knew what to expect from the start.

'How do you feel about being the bait?'

'Not happy.'

'Shot at?'

'Not getting any happier!'

By the time Vicky returned with a tray, Tony had almost finished explaining his plan. Vicky noticed the excitement on Shades' face. Ron's expression was best described as horrified. Finally, Tony finished outlining his idea. 'So, there it is. If all goes well, it will be over by Monday night but I have to admit, it's dangerous. A lot could go wrong, the timing has to be spot on and the characters involved are unpredictable.' The look on Ron's face caused Tony to add, 'I'm sorry, Ron.'

Before Ron could comment, Shades echoed Tony's words. 'Yes, it's going to be dangerous.' If Shades had said *delightful* in place of dangerous, his tone would have better suited the word.

Vicky decided he would benefit from a sharp reality check. 'Yes, it *is* going to be dangerous! Meaning, if anything goes wrong, someone may get hurt, possibly *killed.* This is serious business.' She hammered home the point by looking Shades in the eye and projecting an uncharacteristically cool expression.

Shades reflected offence with a dash of sulk. 'I know that! I do realise! Didn't I just say it's going to be dangerous?'

She responded with a short, unconvinced, 'Humph.'

Tony would be lying if he'd said he didn't feel exhilarated by the risk but he was a little older than Shades. His excitement was tempered by the sobering thought that this was *his* scheme and if any harm came to them, the blame would fall on *his* shoulders. He was pleased that Vicky had cooled Shades' enthusiasm. Poor Ron didn't need anyone to remind *him* the plan was hazardous, or cool his enthusiasm, because he didn't have any! His colour was on a par with a page from one of his books. Tony wasn't blind to Ron's evident worry. 'How do you *really* feel about this, Ron?'

'Well...,' he coughed, his mouth was dry and his voice sounded like a feeble croak. He tried again. 'Well... I mean... *Mafia!* It's hard to take in. Obviously, we need to do something. This guy Bruno is going to frame Shades and come after me. But, er... can we trust everyone to play their part? I don't know any of these people. You and Shades knew them years ago. Will Salvatore believe us? What's stopping him killing Bruno himself, then us for knowing he's alive?'

Tony considered, before answering. 'Salvatore is more business-based than rough stuff.'

Ron interrupted. 'He *is* trying to assume a new identity because he killed someone!'

'Yes, I know, but Anna says it was an accident.'

Strangely, this didn't make Ron feel any better. He grumbled his reply. 'Hope he's not accident-prone then, for our sakes.'

Shades was more enthusiastic. 'It would be a neat solution though, wouldn't it? If it works?'

Ron had to admit it would. 'Yes... if it works.'

Tony turned to Vicky. 'Vicky?'

'I wish we could think of something.' She shrugged. 'A bit less theatrical and a lot more controllable. But yes, if it works, it will be a very neat solution.'

'Vote?'

Predictably, Shades said, 'Let's go for it.'

Vicky looked at Ron, who hesitated then gave a curt nod. It needed to be fast in case he changed his mind. Vicky gave a resigned, slow nod.

Wasting no time, Tony moved to the phone. He glanced at the card Maggie had given him and dialled. 'Maggie, we're on. I'll call tonight after the meeting to confirm the detail of calibre. Yes... goodbye... oh, and Maggie... thanks again.'

PART TWO

CHAPTER 27
THE FLAT AT *THE BLUE PARROT*
FRIDAY, 8.30PM

'I can't believe this, I'm not a kid!' Shades was irritated. Tony calmly watched him pace the room. 'Basically, you want to send me to the pictures!'

Tony refused to rise to Shades' anger and spoke in his normal patient manner. 'Because of your history with Anna, it's best you aren't here. I want Salvatore's full attention. I want him relaxed. I don't want him feeling he has to show off in front of her. I don't want two to one, making him feel intimidated. Go down to the Roxy and polish your lenses or whatever it is you do down there. Look, you're gonna be in the final scene, the important bit, the *dangerous* bit.'

'Yeah, yeah, yeah. You made your point. You come straight down when *he's* gone, won't you?'

'Yes, course, I'll tell you all about it. Look, it's half past eight. In case he comes early you better... er.'

'Yeah, I know, get lost.'

'Shades.'

'What?'

'Look, everything I just said is true, also I don't think it's good for you to see him with Anna.'

Shades dropped the brotherly half-joking, half-serious banter. Tony was watching out for him; he was *always* watching out for him. 'I'm okay. It's been a lot to deal with, but I really think I'm okay. In some ways, I feel better than I have for a long time.'

'I'm pleased.'

'Look, Tony, be careful up here with Salvatore, won't you? We don't *really* know his character, do we? Just because he shows Anna a good husband, good father side, we don't know exactly what he gets up to at work. Remember, as Ron said, he's only here because he killed someone.'

'Mm. I'll know a lot more after I meet him and don't worry, I'm not taking any chances. See the second ice bucket?'

Shades looked across the room at the drinks cabinet. 'Yes?'

'I've put the gun in there.'

One night when the police had searched some of the club's customers, the gun had been dumped in one of the big plant tubs, that housed the giant metal palms. Tony had found it and kept it. The fact he had hidden it in the ice bucket was worrying. Clearly, he had reservations about the meeting, which unsettled Shades. 'You *sure* you want to do this?'

'Yes, now get lost.'

Shades smiled and repeated his warning. 'Just be careful.'

Tony nodded and Shades left reluctantly through the front door. He walked down the narrow staircase and exited the door marked *Private* behind the upstairs bar.

PART TWO

CHAPTER 28
THE HOUSE IN THE SQUARE
FRIDAY NIGHT

At the same time Tony was talking with Shades, Salvatore was having trouble with Bruno.

'A restaurant?' Bruno was surprised. 'I thought you were trying to keep a low profile.'

'I want to spend some private time with my wife. I'm talking about an obscure little local restaurant, not *The Ritz*. Only you, some key family and Uncle know I'm alive. I'm not widely known in London. I'll be fine.'

Bruno shrugged. What did he care? If Salvatore was spotted it would be fine with him and if Salvatore was comfortable being seen out with Anna, this could be the opportunity he was looking for. 'I was thinking, Monday night is our last night here, before we go to the clinic, right?'

'Right.'

Bruno tried to sound casual. 'Well, the club is probably busy at the weekend but on Monday, perhaps we should celebrate, you know, the three of us.'

Salvatore was doubtful. 'It's a bit early for celebrating.'

'Nothing much, maybe just raise a glass in *The Blue Parrot*.'

'We'll see.' With that, he moved to the hall, Anna followed. They collected their coats and stepped out into the street.

A light drizzle had begun to fall. From the steps of the house, they could hear the swish of car tyres on the wet road beyond the square. The air was cold and smelt of rain and damp earth. The private park in the centre of the square was dark but they could hear the sound of the water as it pattered on the evergreens and dripped from leaf to leaf. They turned up their collars and walked out to the main street, Anna slipping her hand into Salvatore's.

Anna spoke first and with feeling. 'I'm so relieved to be out of there. Being near Bruno is unsettling, you know I've never liked him or trusted him. He's so tense, I always feel he's like a sort of brooding storm, ready to lash out with a bolt of anger.' She shuddered. 'I wasn't comfortable with you over here with only Bruno for company. I didn't mention Bruno but I told Q that I was worried about you. He smiled and said nothing could happen to you with Rifsky on the job. I asked who Rifsky was and Q said he was a security expert, acting as your minder and not to worry. I felt a little better at the time; but *where is he*?'

Salvatore was experiencing the familiar tension, he hated keeping things from Anna but knowledge could be dangerous. He always strived to keep the organisation's business and his home life apart, if it could be done. 'Rifsky isn't here and he's not coming back. Anna, please don't ask and never mind Bruno.

Do you want to tell me what exactly happened at *The Blue Parrot*?'

Anna understood Salvatore's reluctance to discuss company affairs and his desire to keep her out of them. She hoped the missing Russian was nothing to worry about. Salvatore looked very stressed. She changed the subject. 'Look Sal, I didn't mean to add to your problems but when I went to *The Blue Parrot* to look for you, I came face to face with Tony. He recognised me, of course. There had been some trouble, a friend of Tony's was very frightened. Someone had chased him through the streets and tried to kill him. From the description, it sounds like Bruno. I was there when they pieced it all together. I'll admit I confirmed what they thought but I didn't tell them. It's better if Tony explains everything himself. You will listen, won't you, Sal?'

'I'll have to, I need to know what they know. How they found out and what they intend to do.' Salvatore frowned. 'Why would Bruno try to kill a friend of the brothers? Are you sure it was Bruno?'

'Yes. It's a long story. Please, just listen to Tony. I'm worried about you.'

'Me?'

'It's a wild story but if they've got it right, you're not safe and neither am I.'

Salvatore looked hard at Anna's pale face. He trusted her but he didn't trust Tony. He wished, not for the first time, she was safe in Milan and not trudging through the freezing streets. Briefly, he wondered if

365

this meeting was dangerous and if he should ask her to go back to the house. He noticed Anna shivering. 'Are you cold?'

'I'm freezing Sal, I didn't realise London would be this cold. It's only autumn.'

It was indeed a miserable night, misty and wet. It wasn't raining hard but the damp air collected in Anna's hair, creating small pearls of water that sparkled in the light from the street lamps. The grey pavements and roads glistened and reflected the coloured lights which spilled out from shops and cafes. Cars swished past. Anna and Salvatore hurried along the street. It was a short but depressing walk to *The Blue Parrot*. The blue neon sign above the entrance glowed and reflected in the puddles on the pavement and danced on the edges of the steps.

Salvatore's arm was around Anna's shivering shoulders as he made for the front door. Anna stopped, catching his hand, as she explained quickly, 'Tony said to come to the flat. It's high up above the club. He said to come in the back way. It's around behind the club and up the fire escape. I'll show you.' She led him past the entrance doors and around the corner to the yard. Behind the club the bulkhead lights above the emergency exits were illuminated. Items in the yard cast deep shadows. Two cars were parked there but the yard was silent and appeared to be deserted. Salvatore looked carefully into the shadowy recesses behind the cars and the lock-up. He was suspicious of the small lock-up garage but the door appeared to be secured and as far as he could see they were alone.

Slowly, they climbed the fire escape. Anna noticed Salvatore was on full alert, looking about warily. Touching the metal handrail was actually painful with bare hands as it was so cold. The sound of their feet on the metal treads reverberated and appeared louder in the quiet stillness. Finally, they reached the platform and the balcony door. More steps disappeared into the darkness above, leading to the roof.

A light inside glowed through the curtain covering the door. Salvatore spoke sharply, 'Let me go in first.' He tapped on the door, seconds later the curtain was drawn back and Tony opened the door. He looked at them, then past them, relieved to see they were alone. He stepped back. 'Please, come in.'

They entered, the warmth a welcome relief. The flat was bigger and more grand than Salvatore had been expecting, it smelled slightly of cigar smoke and bath oil. He looked quickly around the room. Although still on his guard, Salvatore felt reassured: it was just the three of them.

'Please, take a seat. Can I get you a drink?' Tony was behaving as if they were old friends who had dropped in to be social.

Salvatore wanted answers, not drinks. 'No, thank you.'

Tony glanced at Anna. 'You look cold. Scotch, Brandy?'

Anna looked to Salvatore to see if he minded. He wasn't looking at her, all his attention was focussed on Tony. She had the impression he was trying to decide if Tony could be trusted. She *was* cold, it *had* been a long day. 'Yes, brandy please.'

Tony turned his back on them and went to the drinks cabinet. He was conscious he had his back to Salvatore and hoped he was demonstrating a measure of trust, which frankly, he didn't feel. He was careful to watch their reflection in the ice bucket. As he reached the cabinet he was able to pick up the glasses and brandy bottle without watching what he was doing, their positions being familiar. Now as he stood close to the cabinet, he could no longer see their reflection in the shiny ice bucket, but enjoyed a multi-facetted view of them in the crystal decanter stopper. Fifteen tiny images had slowly seated themselves on the sofa. No sudden movements, no guns. So far, so good. He poured Anna a double and himself a small one. Slowly, he turned and walked over, handed Anna her drink and sat down facing them.

Salvatore decided to get to it. 'Anna tells me you know why I'm here. I want to know how and I want to know what you meant by telling Anna that Bruno is dangerous.'

Tony sipped his drink and put it down carefully. 'Yes, it's quite a story. Are you sure you don't want a drink?'

'Sure.' Salvatore said it with considerable conviction. Clearly, he wanted answers and fast.

'It all began because a friend of ours called Ronny Moon was looking for a story idea for his next book. He's a very successful thriller writer. Sometimes, he has brainstorming sessions with my brother…' Tony told the complete story, leaving out nothing. Some of Salvatore's body language wasn't encouraging. The slight frown at certain points indicated a reluctance to accept the facts. As he related it, the story seemed incredible even to Tony. But before he could discuss a possible way out, he needed Salvatore to believe him. When the tale was told there was a worrying silence. Tony watched Salvatore's apparently emotionless face. He was plainly a measured, thoughtful character. Tony had the impression he was carefully weighing all that he had been told, probably looking for a hidden agenda, possible traps, also trying to decide how much he believed and trusted him.

Tony decided a nudge may be in order but needed to be careful. This wasn't a man to be hurried. Tony hoped, by laying his cards on the table, Salvatore would recognise the honesty. 'Look, I'm not a fool. The people you work for are going to a great deal of trouble and expense to give you a new identity. I don't suppose you or they are happy that me, my brother, Ron and Vicky know you're alive. I realise it's dangerous that we *do* know but once we figured it out we couldn't have remained silent. Your friend Bruno…'

'He's *not* my friend.' Salvatore didn't hesitate, the statement was clipped.

Tony was pleased to hear that. He continued quickly. 'Your colleague Bruno intends to kill you and I believe he'll try to frame Shades for it, because...' He glanced at Anna.

She finished Tony's sentence. 'Because Shades and I were engaged years ago and it gives him a motive.' Anna wanted to demonstrate that she was completely open about her history and that it *was* history.

'Exactly. Bruno has tried to kill Ron twice. Not because he knows you're here but because he knows what he, Bruno, is planning. If it was just because Ron had discovered you're here, Bruno would have told you all about it.'

Salvatore didn't trust Tony entirely because he didn't know him. And he didn't trust Bruno because he *did* know him. 'So why am I here? Are you warning me because you believe the organisation will come after you if I'm killed?'

'Partly that, also I've had an idea. Something that could help all of us.' This was it. Tony enjoyed gambling but he wouldn't bet money on Salvatore agreeing to his plan. The man wasn't giving much away. Tony was concentrating very hard but he simply couldn't be sure what Salvatore believed. 'Look, this Bruno is pretty high up in the organisation, isn't he?'

Salvatore didn't like to talk to outsiders about the organisation and Tony already knew too much. He gave a reluctant nod.

Tony wasn't surprised but he needed it confirmed. 'I assumed he was. You wouldn't bring just anybody here with you. I remember Bruno was ambitious even back then when I was younger. I assumed by now he would have risen in the company, not an easy guy to get rid of. I suppose he is quite highly thought of.' Tony paused, he would phrase the next comment with confidence he didn't possess. 'Uncle Q thinks a lot of him.' He said it as a statement, not a question.

'Yes.'

Tony caught the disdain in the response. This was good, this was *very* good. 'So, Bruno is a problem for both of us and I may have the solution. This is a unique situation and I think you'll agree, the solution needs to be unorthodox.'

'You believe you have a solution, then?'

'Yes, but I'm gonna need your help.'

Salvatore smiled. It worried Tony because despite all his powers of perception, he couldn't read what the smile signified.

'Tell me.'

Tony regarded Salvatore for several seconds before deciding to proceed. 'This is what I propose…'

PART TWO

CHAPTER 29
FRIDAY, 10.30PM

The shops were now empty and closed, the pubs and clubs now open and full. The streets were cold and lonely. Salvatore and Anna hurried along the now-deserted pavements towards the house in the square. His silence prompted Anna to ask. 'What do you think? You told Tony you would go along with his plan but I know you, Sal. You're not totally convinced, are you?'

He smiled. There could never be any real secrets from Anna, she *could* read him. 'I believe he's telling the truth, at least as he sees it. I'm not sure he's got it right, but he is right about one thing, Bruno is a favourite of Uncle Q's. If I'm going to accuse him of murder plots, I'd better be damned sure of my facts. I may be his boss but Bruno is well regarded, not only by Uncle but also by a few powerful men in the organisation. Men who miss the old blood-and-thunder way of operating. I need to be careful.'

'I'm sure the organisation will support you and listen. You make them a lot of money.'

'I wouldn't take anything for granted. I've killed a man in broad daylight and had it splashed across the papers. I've caused a lot of trouble and expense to the organisation. As for Bruno, I'll know a lot more at eight-thirty tomorrow.'

Anna didn't understand and Salvatore seemed to have no intention of explaining further. Since Lucia had been born, he'd tried even harder to keep the two worlds separate. He felt uncomfortable Anna being so close to Tony's plan to deal with Bruno. Seeing her while he had his surgery was one thing, but this situation was something else entirely. He changed the subject. 'Look, we're nearly back at the house. Let's tell Bruno we had supper in that restaurant.' He pointed at a pleasant-looking restaurant across the street. 'Let's take a look at the menu so we won't be caught out if he asks.'

They read the the illuminated menu card in the entrance, discussing briefly what each would order. Anna knew Salvatore was under considerable pressure, so in an attempt to lighten the mood, she made a joke out of it. 'Since I'm not going to eat it I suppose I can be a glutton.' She ran through her starter and main but lingered over the dessert. 'I think I'll have hot apple pie with a double scoop of dairy ice cream and double cream poured over all of it, followed by coffee and brandy.' She smiled at him.

Salvatore snatched her toward him and held her tight. It was unexpected; usually, he was very controlled. As he held her, he whispered, 'Anna, I'm so sorry, so sorry, to bring all this worry. I wish we were normal, you and me and our little girl. I wish I could get out, get away, away from the organisation, from Bruno, from the whole business.'

She drew back a little so she could see his face. He needed her support and she was pleased to give it. A great many women have inner strength, an unbelievable resilience that lies beneath the surface of the most gentle of souls. In times of great stress, this strength reveals itself. Salvatore was surprised at the veracity of Anna's words. 'Now listen to me. It's going to be alright. We'll get through this together. Whatever it takes. *I wish* you didn't work for them, but you *do*. It's not like you can resign. So since we're stuck with them, let's use them, let's *use* Q.'

Tony was sitting, thinking, when Shades cautiously entered the room. He'd listened at the door, had heard nothing so decided to chance it. 'I couldn't wait any longer.' His eyes darted around the room. 'They're gone, then?'

Tony nodded slowly. He was distracted, still deciding what conclusions he was able to draw from the meeting.

Shades was impatient for news. 'Well?'

Tony looked up. 'Well what?'

Shades was so full of nervous energy, he almost hopped from foot to foot. He answered with exasperation, 'Well, how did it go?'

When Tony answered, his voice was flat. 'Yes, they're going for it.'

'You don't sound pleased, what's the matter?'

Tony regarded Shades for several seconds. He *was* his brother and deserved to know the truth. 'I'm not sure I trust him.'

Shades was surprised. Tony's talent for reading people and situations was a given. This was very concerning, if not frightening. 'Why exactly don't you trust him?'

Tony grimaced. 'I don't know, really. There's something else, something he's not telling me. I'll tell you what I *do* know, I know he doesn't like Bruno. He said he'll go along with the plan. I think... he will, but he's nervous about Q, I could feel that. Even if his life may be in danger, he's reluctant to point the finger at Bruno. He also doesn't completely trust me.'

Shades considered what Tony had said. He shrugged. 'He doesn't know you and you don't trust him either. But what I don't understand Tony, is why is *he* nervous of Q?'

'It seems Bruno is a favourite with Q, reminds him of his younger self, the son he never had, sort of thing. I can understand Salvatore being cautious. After all, he *has* caused the organisation a lot of trouble. He's probably not in Q's good books.'

'We need Q.' Shades said it sharply with concern.

'We do.' Tony agreed.

'Well, what do you think? Do we still go ahead?'

That was the question Tony had been trying to decide. Do they? This was new territory for him. For the first time in his life, he wasn't *sure*. If it were only *his* life on the line, it would be different, but they would *all* be in the room together and with Q. Uncle Cupid, who'd earned his nickname because in a fight he blew the heart out of an opponent's chest with a single shot.

Shades enjoyed edgy situations spiced with a little danger, but he read the indecision on Tony's face. At that moment, Shades too, entered uncharted waters. He felt fear. If Tony had no plan and Salvatore *was* killed, he would most likely have a contract out on him. Slowly, he sat down. They were both silent for a time.

Shades almost jumped when, abruptly, Tony spoke. 'We do it.'

Shades was relieved. 'You've decided you can trust him?' But his relief was short lived.

'No, I don't trust him. But it's better to try a risky plan than face certain death.'

Of course it was logical but it wasn't exactly comforting. However, Shades roused himself. This was no way to behave, he was Shades Manning. 'It's a good plan, if it works it really will be a neat solution.'

Tony wished he felt more certain but he had made a decision. Without another word, he reached for the phone and dialled. 'Hello Maggie, have you got a pen? I have the details you need, the time, address and gun calibre…'

PART TWO

CHAPTER 30
THE HOUSE IN THE SQUARE
FRIDAY NIGHT, LATE

Anna was lying propped up on the bed, having showered and slipped into a bathrobe. She watched her husband who was sitting very still in a chair near a small desk. Salvatore's eyes were fixed on the skirting board, all the while his mind painting possible future scenarios. He had the same problem as Tony: the palette of characters involved was hard to predict. He had somewhere to go the following morning. Hopefully, this visit would clarify matters, but again, like Tony, he was aware that time was a big factor.

'Sal?'

Salvatore was so deep in thought, he'd almost forgotten Anna was in the room, her voice making him start. He smiled at her and himself. 'I'm sorry Anna, I'm not ignoring you.'

'I know, don't be sorry. This situation needs plenty of thought. I was wondering about something myself.'

'Yes?'

'Well, I believe Bruno capable of everything the brothers say and if he saw his plans written down, I can understand why he would try to kill Ronny Moon. But how does he think Ronny found out his plans? I mean, attempting to murder you, it's all in his head, Bruno wouldn't have told anyone, would he?'

Salvatore had considered this aspect himself and had a theory. 'I believe it's possible that Bruno believes he *did* tell somebody. Look, Ronny Moon the writer, makes up the part of the story where I am to be killed but Bruno doesn't know that and believes Ronny *knows* it's his plan.'

Anna waited for Salvatore to explain.

'Our security man, Rifsky, got Bruno very drunk a few days ago: he was trying to find out what Bruno was up to; Bruno didn't tell him anything, but I don't think Bruno remembers what he said. Bruno was certainly very nervous when he first saw me the next day. I greeted him normally and pretended I didn't notice, but I could see the relief on his face. It made me wonder at the time. I can't pretend to understand all Bruno's reasoning, I doubt reason has much to do with it anymore.'

Anna frowned. 'What do you mean?'

'I believe his craving for more power, his hatred and bitterness towards me, has warped him; he sees plots and hidden agendas everywhere. We must be very careful. I'm sorry Anna, but it's best you know. I firmly believe that Bruno is both dangerous and unstable.'

It wasn't a new idea for Anna, she'd always believed Bruno was dangerous but to hear Salvatore voice the same opinion was still unnerving. Her jaw tightened, she got to her feet, walked across the room and squeezed his hand.

Salvatore held on and read the deep concern on Anna's face. He gave her a brief smile and made a decision. Releasing her hand, he stood up, walked to the bedroom door, carefully opened it a crack and peered out. No one was about. He could hear the muffled sound from the television downstairs in the living room, Bruno was watching something. Salvatore quietly shut the door, moved to the phone beside the bed and dialled a familiar number. Anna watched and listened as Salvatore spoke quietly. 'Q, I think we have a situation, how fast can you get over here?' He gripped the phone hard and pressed it close to his ear. 'Mm, mm. You'd better bring two useful people with you.' *Useful people* was the term used in the organisation to mean muscle, men who were reliable, tough and free to act without obstacles like a conscience to get in the way. Salvatore evidently expected things to get rough.

PART TWO

CHAPTER 31
THE WEEKEND

The weekend was like no other for the little group. Relaxation was out of the question for anyone.

In Italy, Uncle Q made arrangements for his unexpected trip to England.

In London, Bruno was also busy. He visited the library where Ron had delivered his talk and attempted to learn Ron's address. When that failed, he tried the club. He chatted to Kirsten, the other waitresses and the bar staff, but this proved equally fruitless.

While Bruno was occupied, Salvatore took the opportunity to slip out. Anna offered to accompany him but he wanted to go alone. Anna was both surprised and worried. However, he soon came back but on his return seemed preoccupied and spoke very little. Finally, Anna asked if he was alright. He assured her he was and not to worry. But Anna was worried, she was *very* worried. Uncle Q was coming over and he was capable of *anything*. She was frightened, not only for Shades but for Salvatore and herself.

Too nervous to go out, Vicky and Ron tried to read or listen to music. No matter what they did, Tony's plan cast an ominous shadow over them. Vicky didn't even have the distraction of work to occupy her. Jane was on set on Saturday morning for a reshoot of an interior scene but as only two actors were involved, neither Vicky nor Maggie was required. In the afternoon, the director was editing so had declared a full weekend off. Monday morning, a shooting needed re-filming as the director wasn't happy after viewing the scene in sequence with the next. Again on Monday, only one make-up artist was needed. Jane was keen to keep busy as she found working helped to calm her troubled mind, so she volunteered. She made quick, breathless calls to Maggie and Vicky explaining the situation. Both asked if she was sure she would be alright but having distractions of their own, didn't press. Luckily for Jane, these preoccupations prevented either Vicky or Maggie noticing Jane's odd behaviour, for Jane loved company and her apparent desire to work alone was very much out of character.

Ron was unable to work, his enthusiasm for the new book was a good deal more than merely dampened. Worrying circumstances had rained heavily on his project. He was depressed, also feeling guilty. On more than one occasion over that long weekend, he apologised to Vicky. She refused to listen and told him again and again it wasn't his fault.

Over at *The Blue Parrot,* Shades was uncharacteristically quiet. He had a good deal to think about, reframing his view of the past and what his new perspective would mean for the future.

Tony worried. Normally, Tony never worried. He would think on a situation, make decisions and follow

384

a course of action with confidence. Yes, he had given it all a lot of thought, and yes, he'd made decisions and on Monday they would follow a course of action. But the usual confidence was lacking. He had failed to get the measure of Salvatore and Q had always been unpredictable. Had he made a terrible mistake?

Jane was unaware of the drama and anxiety of her friends: she had plenty of her own to deal with. She was very pleased to be busy on set Saturday morning. Uncharacteristically, Jane was also happy to be the only make-up artist on set: hiding her feelings from the crew was one thing, from her friends was something else entirely. Sadly, everything at the shoot went well and she was home before lunch. The remainder of the weekend gave her the unwelcome chance to reflect, having decided to tell Shades it was over to his face. She needed to decide when. Jane's weekend was a mixture of busy activity punctuated by bouts of sitting motionless and brooding. She had cleaned the already spotless flat, rearranged her tidy books and baked cakes she had no appetite to eat. The problem was, when she visualised herself telling Shades it was over, she cried. When she confronted him, she didn't want him to see her cry. She *wouldn't cry!* It was stupid, he was seeing this other woman behind her back. *Why* was she so upset to lose this... this liar? When he'd phoned, he said he didn't want to see her, some excuse about trouble at the club. She would take this time to compose herself, to plan what she would say. She would walk away with pride, with dignity. But not this weekend. Soon, but not today. Her busy mind would give her no rest over the cursed weekend. It ran endlessly through fantasy conversations. If she said this and he responded with that, she would say this. Jane dreaded the confrontation but also wanted to have it over with.

PART TWO

CHAPTER 32
THE HOUSE IN THE SQUARE
MONDAY, 7.35AM

No matter how desperately we would wish to hold back time, to avoid some dreaded event, the world cares little for the souls who cling to it, and spins on, regardless.

Monday arrived.

The early-morning dew was so heavy it shrouded the city in a silvery cloak, but soon, the fresh, clear air drifting over its many streets began to dissolve it, and a gossamer mist drifted up in the cold morning light.

Inside the warm house on the square, Anna, Salvatore and Bruno had eaten breakfast together. Salvatore was finishing his toast as Bruno felt in his jacket for his cigarettes. 'Bruno please, I'm still eating.'

With an irritated grunt, Bruno tossed the pack onto the table.

Salvatore turned to Anna. 'Our last full day in London. Did you have any plans?'

'If you don't need me, I thought I might visit the West End, have a wander around Knightsbridge. Don't know when I'll next get the chance to compare London shopping to Milan.'

Salvatore smiled. 'That's a good idea, it's been very stressful lately, you deserve to treat yourself. There's plenty of money in the drawer over there, take what you want.'

'Thank you.' All at once a shadow of doubt eclipsed her bright mood. After a moment's thought she shared her misgivings. 'To be honest, I'm nervous about the London Underground and I don't really know my way around. My sister always takes charge when I've visited before. Perhaps I'd better not go.'

Salvatore was insistent. 'You must, you may not get another opportunity for some time. I have some business to do, but Bruno will keep you company.'

They turned to Bruno for his reaction. First, he was surprised, then looked more annoyed than before. 'I'm not a personal shopper,' he growled irritably.

Salvatore answered smoothly, 'Tell you what, Bruno, help Anna today and we'll all go out as you suggested for a last drink at *The Blue Parrot* tonight, before we head off for Devon tomorrow.'

Bruno couldn't believe his luck, perfect! He didn't think he was going to manage it. Salvatore hadn't been keen, but it looked as if he was going to get him, Shades and Anna in the same room together after all. He found it hard to hide his delight. 'Yes, that would be good, raise a glass. But I'm still not sure about shopping.'

'Listen, Anna will be carrying a lot of cash. I'd feel better if she wasn't wandering around an unfamiliar city alone. Think of it more as a security job. You will help, won't you?'

It was phrased as a question, not an order and the prize for going along would be to get his way. Get Salvatore together with Shades and kill the pair of them. The thought of killing Salvatore was a powerful motive. 'Okay Sal, I'll look after Anna.' Mentally, he tacked on *and I'll take care of you too.* He managed to dredge up a smile aimed at Anna, who did well not to shudder. Salvatore finished his breakfast in peace. Bruno pondered on his proposed shopping trip. Suddenly, he was suspicious. 'Why can't you go? What business stops you going?'

Salvatore appeared bored with the question. 'It involves some of the properties I'm handling in Milan. Q has someone standing in for me and I'm supposed to advise them. Q wants me near the phone after lunch today. I wouldn't be back in time.'

'Hmp.' Bruno was unimpressed by Salvatore with his meetings and business calls. There was a time not too long ago that men ran the organisation, not paper-shuffling office workers. Part of him was grateful he would be spared the sight of Salvatore holding court with his oh-so-important conference call. 'I'll order a cab.'

'No, you're much better travelling in by train.'

Bruno frowned. 'What's wrong with a cab?'

'I did some property work for the organisation in Chelsea and Greenwich a few years ago and had to travel between the two. Take it from me, you don't want to be driving through The Elephant and Castle and along the Old Kent Road during rush hour, it will take you forever in a cab. Take the train, then once you're there, use a cab.' Salvatore was being honest, he also didn't want them to be late back.

Bruno shrugged. 'Right. Train then.'

Thirty minutes later, Anna and Salvatore stood in the hall. Anna was wearing her coat, ready to go. They stood very close, their conversation conducted in whispers. Salvatore was concerned. 'Sure you'll be okay?'

'Spending the day with Bruno isn't my first choice but it needs to be done.'

He took her hands, lifted them to his chest and squeezed them. 'Thank you, Anna.' He let go then raised his voice so it would carry upstairs to Bruno's bedroom. 'Bruno, are you ready?'

The answer sailed back, slightly muffled by distance and fine oak doors. 'I'm coming, I'm coming.' He didn't sound enthusiastic. Salvatore smiled at Anna and whispered. 'Your personal shopper doesn't sound keen.'

Finally, Bruno appeared at the top of the stairs, wearing a smart suit. He descended and joined them in the hall. His heavy overcoat hung there and as he reached up to unhook it, he dropped one of his gloves. He bent to retrieve it but as he did so, his suit jacket fell open and Salvatore glimpsed the shoulder holster. 'Bruno!'

'What?'

'You can't wander around Knightsbridge carrying a gun.'

Bruno stared at him. 'Why not?'

'Because someone may see it!'

'I always carry a gun. Anyway, security, remember?'

'We're not in Milan. The local police turn a blind eye because they know who you are. It's different here. If anyone sees it and reports you to the police, it would cause a whole heap of trouble we don't need.'

'No one's gonna see it.'

'I saw it. I want you to leave it here.'

Bruno glared at him. It occurred to Salvatore that he might refuse to hand it over. The atmosphere grew very tense, but Salvatore maintained a steady stare. Bruno hesitated, the temptation to execute Salvatore then and there was strong. No, no, he was smarter than that. Tonight, if he had the chance, he'd take it. Bruno hated being told what to do. He shook his head in annoyance. Angrily, he removed his jacket, slipped off the holster and flung it on the table. Putting the jacket back on, he fumbled in the pocket for the silencer, which he slammed down, denting the surface of a beautiful console table, which until that moment, had survived unblemished for over a hundred years. 'Satisfied?'

Salvatore didn't rise to Bruno's anger and remained silent.

Bruno snatched his overcoat from the hanger and turned a red face to Anna. 'Are you ready?'

'Yes, let's go.' She kissed Salvatore, and as she did so, squeezed his arm. For a terrible moment, she felt Bruno may have been on the brink of violence. The moment had passed but Anna sensed Bruno's deep, burning anger; it was an ugly, unsettling thing.

Salvatore saw them out with a smile and a brief wave. As Bruno turned and moved away from the step, their parting smiles dropped; Anna and Salvatore exchanged sober expressions. She didn't want to leave him and he didn't want her to. He was more than a little uneasy leaving Anna with Bruno all day.

Reluctantly, he closed the front door, then picked up Bruno's gun and silencer and carried them into the living room. The gun was a Beretta 92F 9mm. Typical Bruno, he thought too much of himself to choose a standard model. The gun was fully chromed with an intricately carved gold pattern on the custom blue grip, which also featured a stylised B in its centre. Salvatore placed the gun and silencer on the table, eyeing the weapon thoughtfully. Bruno wasn't unusual; nearly all the men in the organisation carried guns and a good many of those were custom-made. Bruno had been right when he'd argued that no-one would know he was armed. Detection was unlikely as Bruno, like others in the organisation, had his suits specially tailored in such a way as to conceal a gun. Salvatore's eye drifted to the silencer. No-one outside Hollywood referred to them as silencers. The correct term was suppressor. A gun cannot be completely silenced, however the suppressor Bruno owned was almost worthy of the

392

term silencer. It was highly prized and in the organisation, considered something of a badge of honour to possess one. The organisation had obtained a small number of these Russian-made devices uniquely engineered for the KGB and one or two other shadowy departments. They were top secret and significantly quieter than a standard suppressor.

Salvatore looked away. He felt revolted by the gun, the silencer, Bruno, the organisation, everything! Suddenly, he felt very tired. He stared down at his hands which rested in his lap. They had killed a man. It had been an accident, but he'd done it all the same. How could he hold his little girl with these hands? He'd never liked Renzo but he'd never intended to kill the man!

Five to seven years to become a doctor, years of study to be a lawyer or teacher and thirty seconds to become a murderer! That was all it had taken for him to transform from a normal human being to a murderer. Was he through? Is a murderer someone who sets out to kill? Or is it merely the act of taking a life? He had lost control and in those moments, he'd changed not only himself but the lives of people he cared for. And what now?

He allowed his body to lean back into the leather chair, closed his eyes and exhaled slowly. Why, oh why, had he ever become involved in this world? When he was young, it had seemed exciting and glamorous. Those who were *connected* wore the best clothes, lived in magnificent homes, and drove beautiful cars, but beneath the veneer of gloss and beauty was rot and ugliness. He would trade the beautiful house and all that went with it if only he could live peacefully with Anna and Lucia. Lucia was growing fast, changing every day. Time was slipping by, time he would never get back. If only...! He lifted an arm and let a balled fist fall to the arm of the chair. No point wishing, this was his life and if he wanted a long one, he needed to stop feeling sorry for himself and concentrate.

With something approaching determination, he fetched another coffee and returning to the chair, sat cradling the cup. He was sure that the next twenty four hours were going to be very dangerous. It was vital he make the right choices. This wasn't going to be easy. He didn't trust Tony or his brother. He certainly didn't trust Bruno. It wasn't as if he could even rely on Uncle, because the man was unpredictable, at least for him. The problem was, Uncle could be capable of things so far outside Salvatore's sphere of comprehension, it made it impossible for him to guess with any certainty, what he might do. It wasn't completely out of the question he would lose patience with the complicated situation and think it simpler to murder everyone. Salvatore dearly wished this thought hadn't occurred to him because it could so easily be true. Phoning him might have been a very big mistake. Should he have tried some other solution? But what? Well, what did it matter now? He had phoned him and he was coming.

For a little respite, he thought of Anna. Anna was the one person he trusted completely. In the swirling blur of this whole mess, Anna was the only certainty. However, even here, he was conflicted. He was pleased to have her close but at the same time, he wished her to be safely in Italy and not wandering around the West End of London with Bruno.

Time passed without notice and Salvatore mulled over the situation and the various individuals in it. A knock at the door brought him back to the present.

Maggie Moorcroft waited patiently on the doorstep. As usual, she was dressed stylishly, sporting a wide-brimmed hat, richly coloured heavy wool coat and brown leather and fur boots, which easily defeated the chilly morning. In one gloved hand, she held a silver flight case. The door opened and Salvatore smiled politely, 'Maggie, I presume?'

'I am she.'

'Please, come in.' He held the door wide and Maggie stepped inside.

Two identical silver flight cases sat on Ron and Vicky's kitchen table. Ron scowled at them as he walked stiffly past with his second coffee of the day. He joined Vicky in the living room. The act of sitting down prompted odd noises. 'Arrrr, mmmmp.'

'Alright, Ron?'

'It's just my neck, shoulders, back, hands, stomach, knees, ankles and feet. Apart from that, I'm fine.'

'Ah, good.' Vicky may have been more sympathetic if Ron had been a little less frequent in his health bulletins. The reports of aches and pains were approaching double figures for the morning alone.

'I think I've got rigour mortis.'

'You can't, you're not dead.'

'Well, I'm seizing up then.'

'You take no exercise, the last time you worked up a sweat was eating a curry, you drink too much and live mainly on chocolate biscuits. Then you run for your life across London: it's no wonder you feel rough.'

They sat in silence, Ron sipping his coffee. He reflected on the situation and Tony's solution. Gradually, his mood darkened. 'You know, I'm not sure about this, Vicky. I know we have to do *something*, but this seems very elaborate and...' He shrugged and shifted uneasily in his seat. 'I don't know. The timing has to be perfect and it will happen very fast. Look, if Shades and I do it, I don't think I want you there... What?'

Vicky had adopted what Ron always described as '*The Look*'. There were, in fact, two versions. One was reserved for communicating the message, *You are pushing your luck, I'm going to lose my temper;* the other being, *I'm doing this my way or we can discuss it at great length, then I'm doing this my way.* Ron was withering slightly under the glare of the latter version.

'I'm not sitting about this flat, waiting for Tony or you to phone and tell me how it went. I'm going to be right there, no argument. Anyway, I'm the one Maggie has been training how to use the props. I've got to be there to explain it to Shades.'

Ron sighed but made no comment. In the early days of their relationship, he had attempted to talk her round. These days, when Vicky's mind was made up, he knew better.

Vicky changed the subject. 'I hope Maggie will be alright with Salvatore, she should be there by now.'

Ron became even more worried. 'Yes.' He glanced at his watch. 'She left here twenty minutes ago, she's probably running him through it now.'

'Mmm, I asked her to phone and let us know how she got on. Then, I'm to ring Tony.'

Maggie closed and secured the silver flight case. She looked up at Salvatore, who sat across the dining table, watching her. 'Any questions?' Maggie hoped not, she wanted to leave.

'Not about this. Thank you for explaining.'

'Right then, leave the SFX props at the club and I'll collect them when Tony phones me.'

'Hold on, I'd like to know how exactly you know Tony and what you've been told? For example, do you know who I am?'

'No and I don't know Tony.'

Salvatore raised his eyebrows and waited. Evidently, a full explanation was required.

'I work closely with Vicky, she's… she's important to me. She and her friend Tony came to see me. They explained that she and Ron were in trouble. They needed my knowledge of SFX and equipment to get them out of it and would I help?'

'If Vicky works in SFX, why involve you?'

'Vicky is learning the business; she doesn't have all the knowledge and equipment I have. For example, you can't simply put ordinary blanks into a Beretta, it would only fire one shot, it wouldn't cycle. You need special military-issue blanks. I have all that kind of hardware, it's what I do. Vicky and Tony didn't want me to come at all. They only wanted to borrow the props, but I wouldn't help unless I came here.'

'Why?'

'Because I had the impression that coming here was dangerous and I didn't want Vicky doing it.'

Salvatore searched Maggie's eyes for signs of a lie. She returned his gaze unblinkingly.

'So you stepped in to help, you didn't ask questions?'

'All they said was the situation was delicately balanced and dangerous. Vicky said to tell me more would place me in danger.'

'So, here you are, even though you don't know what's going on and you think it's dangerous.'

'Yes.'

Salvatore thought he believed her but to feel comfortable, he decided a warning would be prudent. 'Vicky is right, this is a delicately balanced situation and it *is* dangerous. But for you, the only danger is discussing it with anyone. You won't, will you Maggie?'

'No, I won't.' Maggie didn't like being threatened by this charming, polite man in his charming, polite house. As an act of defiance, she added, 'Because Vicky asked me not to.'

They stared at each other, Maggie tilted her head slightly, challenging him to try more threats. Salvatore however, was satisfied. With little knowledge of the situation, she was willing to help her friend without reservation. Initially, he had been suspicious of Maggie's story. The sad thought crossed his mind that, outside the organisation, not everyone had a motive, a scheme. There were friendships and good people sometimes helped each other, simply because they were good people.

Vicky replaced the receiver. Ron was watching her, unsure of what he wanted to hear. Part of him would be happy if, for some reason, Tony's plan couldn't be attempted. 'Is she okay?'

Vicky allowed her shoulders to sink into the sofa as some of the tension left her body. It was a huge relief that Maggie was out. 'She said it all went well, he understands and there's no problem, she's going home. It's only Jane working today.'

'That's good, I'm glad she's safe.' Ron was pleased for Maggie but he wasn't totally happy that the preparations for Tony's scheme seemed to be gathering pace.

Vicky could plainly see he was worried. She spoke quickly, 'Look Ron, you don't have to do this, you could tell Tony you've changed your mind.'

'No, I'm fine, it'll be alright.'

It occurred to Vicky that although he was a good writer he made a poor actor. She leaned forward and spoke with a hint of alarm in her voice. 'If you think this is too risky, for goodness sake, tell Tony.'

'Really, I'll be alright.' He licked his dry lips. His restless hands stroked Finbar who was dozing next to him on the sofa. Should he back out? What would they do if he did? No, what choice was there? Tony's idea might be wild but if it worked, he had to admit it really would be a very good solution. 'Phone Tony, tell him Maggie has delivered and she's out, safe and sound.' He said it with conviction, but Vicky remained sceptical. She shared Ron's reservations, but what else could they do? Still watching him, in case he suddenly changed his mind, she slowly lifted the receiver and dialled.

'Hello Tony, it's me. Maggie has delivered the SFX equipment and she's now on her way home. Yes, it all went well. Ron and I will be over at seven as arranged to run through it all with Shades.'

PART TWO

CHAPTER 33
LONDON
MONDAY, 5.30PM

All over the great city lights began to blink on. The chilly day grew colder still, pavements and streets glistened, freezing and damp, the lights of London reflecting on the glossy surfaces. Soon, the sky was a moonless, inky blue. Shops blazed with orange light. Commuter trains jammed with people rocked and screeched as the metal wheels trundled across the many points. The usual mass exodus had begun.

Two additional people, unable to find a vacant seat, clung to a handrail as the five-thirty out of Charing Cross station laboured on its journey to the south-east London suburbs. Outside, the air temperature nosedived, but in the packed carriage it was hot and stuffy.

Bruno reflected grimly that it was probably just as well he wasn't carrying his gun or he might have been seriously tempted to plug the irritating fool who was jammed next to him. The young man, wearing the ill-fitting suite two sizes too large for him, was evidently enjoying the honeymoon phase of his relationship and appeared eager to share his conversation with the whole carriage. His fellow-travellers were united in their silent relief that the communication appeared to be on the verge of termination.

'You hang up, no, you first.' He laughed. 'No, you, no, you, one, two, three... you didn't hang up. Okay, we do it together, one, two, three.' Luckily for the young man, his new girlfriend actually hung up, just as Bruno remembered he had his stiletto flick knife in his pocket. He probably wouldn't have done anything but he *definitely* wanted to. He fingered the knife with his free hand. Salvatore had made him leave the gun behind but at least he had his knife; he would have felt lost without it. Bruno had acquired it years earlier after learning that Q carried one. It was something of a tradition, the stiletto was invented in Italy, first as a tool, then as a weapon, its thin blade able to utilise gaps in armour and occasionally, even penetrate chainmail. Bruno loved the knife, of course, it was very expensive and precision-made. Like Q, Bruno had used his knife on several occasions while building his reputation and moving up in the organisation. He'd done well; not as well as he believed he deserved, but of course, that was all about to change.

Anna also had time to reflect. She held tightly to her small clutch of shopping bags in one hand and one of the train's hand grips with the other. All the passengers swayed in unison to the rock of the train as it trundled agonisingly slowly towards Greenwich and all the depressing, grubby little stations in between. She was exhausted. It wasn't only the noise and bustle of the West End, but pretending to express interest and enthusiasm for shopping.

After arriving at Charing Cross station, they'd taken a cab to Knightsbridge. Later, they'd travelled across to the end of Oxford Street, lunched, then walked along Regents Street, stopping at Hamleys toy store to pick up a small teddy bear for Lucia. Bruno had refused point blank to enter the store, preferring to stand in the street, smoking and glaring at passing tourists. Finally, footsore and tired, they'd caught a cab back to Charing Cross station. All Anna had really wanted all day was to go back to the house but she'd promised Salvatore she'd keep Bruno out of the way. He was tiring company, he rarely spoke and she was thoroughly sick of his miserable face. She'd given up the pretence altogether of them having a fun day and neither had spoken for forty minutes.

To avoid looking at Bruno's sour face, she scanned the faces of her fellow-commuters. Unfortunately, she found little consolation. The train was crammed with the usual mixture of office workers and shop assistants. For them, this was merely another commute, a succession of journeys which for many, stretched back years and in all likelihood would go on for many more; the almost endless treadmill of commute, work, commute, home. How they managed this day after day, was unimaginable. With all her problems and worries, she wouldn't swap her complicated life for theirs. The hopeless expressions were so sad.

Someone laughed. It was unexpected and at odds with the mood. She searched for the source. Three young women stood squeezed together near a door, all holding bags of shopping. Like her, they were visitors to London, there for the shopping. A girls' day out. Anna could picture it: trying on clothes, lunch, a glass of wine, laughing together, sharing secrets over coffee and cake; probably making cheeky jokes or being downright rude. Suddenly, Anna felt her eyes prickle with tears and a wave of sadness swept over her. She had no girlfriends to share a shopping trip, to lunch with, laugh with. In the early days, she had tried to make friends with other women in her circle but they were the wives or girlfriends of men who, like Salvatore, worked for the organisation. It was always in the background. She seldom went shopping, even in Milan. The staff in cafes, restaurants, bars and shops were always polite and respectful to her and the other women. But beneath the smiles lurked fear. The fear spoilt the mood. The other women didn't seem to notice, or if they did, chose not to care. But Anna cared. She had gradually let the acquaintances slip away. She focussed her time on Lucia. Anna truly loved Salvatore but sometimes she felt lonely. The three young women whispered and giggled over some shared joke. They were so happy, so normal. Anna deeply wanted to be home. She yearned for the warmth of Milan and her little girl's smile. She desperately wanted to hold her little girl. It took all her willpower not to cry where she stood in that packed train, surrounded by strangers.

Anna wasn't the only troubled soul. A few miles down the line, Vicky was having some equally dark thoughts. The living room curtains were open and she could still see the world outside. What little light remained was fading fast, the scene losing colour and definition. Everything was taking on shades of blue-black and detail was quickly vanishing. The warm living room lights meant the window was transforming itself into a mirror, the room being reflected in the darkening glass.

Ron had been wandering restlessly about the room. He didn't like the uncertain aspects of the plan, he was also worried that Vicky had insisted she would be there. He stopped and gazed out of the window as he sipped his coffee. Although he had his back to her, Vicky could see his face in the reflection from the window, but it wasn't a solid image. She could see through him to the world outside. The ghostly effect gave her a tingling feeling on the back of her head. She sprang from the sofa and quickly crossed the room, the movement making him turn. He barely had time to put down his drink before Vicky seized him and held on tight.

'What's the matter?' He hugged her back.

Silently, she clung to him. As she finally let go, she brushed a tear away quickly. 'Nothing. I'm alright. Just… just… felt like giving you a hug, that's all.'

He knew she was worried. Ron's fear crossed the line to anger. He hated to see Vicky upset. 'Bloody Tony and his stupid ideas! Bloody Mafia! This is madness. Why can't they leave us alone?'

Vicky had a logical, sensible nature. She was angry with herself, allowing her mind to suggest ridiculous premonitions. It was probably Jane's dream about Shades covered in blood at her feet. She was being very silly. *There was no such thing as premonitions.* It was merely the subconscious worry manifesting itself in wild scenarios. She must be sensible and strong for Ron. 'No, you're not being fair to Tony. I know it's risky but he's trying to help you and Shades. If it all works the way Tony plans, we'll be free from worry.'

'I know, I know. Sorry, I'll be relieved when this is over.'

She sighed, 'Me too.' She checked the clock on the mantlepiece with her watch. 'I suppose I'd better show you how Maggie's box of tricks works.' She walked into the kitchen to retrieve one of the silver flight cases.

PART TWO

CHAPTER 34
THE BLUE PARROT
MONDAY, 6.40PM

Tony stood alone in the yard leaning against one of the fire doors, smoking a cigar. The harsh light from the bulkhead lamp above his head accentuated his strong features and if possible, made him appear even more grim than usual. He welcomed the quiet interlude before the action to come. Q would arrive any time now.

High above in the flat, Shades sat quietly on a sofa, his mood as serious and contemplative as his brother's. He'd always believed the past was fixed, events that happened could not be changed. Of course, he realised, as he grew older, his interpretation of the past may change a little, because he himself was different. This process happened to everyone but in his own case, the new information had turned his view completely on its head. If it hadn't been for Uncle Q threatening Anna, their lives would have been completely different. This one man had altered the course of his life by threatening to take it. Shades' anger began to rise. Q decided who married who, who lived, who died and when. The earth was his universe and he'd cast himself as God.

Downstairs, a large luxury car slid into view as it entered the gates. Tony took a last draw on his cigar and tossed it to one side. He had mixed feelings, gratified this part of his plan was becoming real but also aware of the potential *danger*.

Not far away, Ron and Vicky walked slowly to the Chevrolet and climbed in. They sat quietly for a few moments. Ron didn't want to go and neither did she. Somehow, starting the engine heralded a beginning, committing to something. It was with trepidation that Ron finally turned the key, the familiar deep burble of the cars engine broke the silence. Ron laid his hands on the steering wheel but sat motionless, thinking. Vicky reached across and squeezed his hand. He gave her a weak smile and selected "Drive". The engine note rose and the car moved off.

In the yard at *The Blue Parrot*, Tony watched the car, the occupants made mysterious by virtue of its tinted windows. Abruptly, the doors clicked open and two very big men climbed out. They looked coolly at Tony, surveyed the yard, then opened the rear car door for its occupant. Q climbed out. He was compact, with broad shoulders, immaculately dressed in a light suit and heavy overcoat. He was bald with closely clipped white hair on the sides of his head, yet he moved like a man half his age. His quick eyes took in the surroundings before settling on Tony.

Moments later, in the flat above, the balcony door opened. Shades looked up. Two powerful men entered and looked suspiciously about the room. Shades slowly got to his feet; the men seemed not to regard him as a problem. One of them returned to the balcony and nodded to someone unseen who waited outside. Q walked calmly into the room, followed closely by Tony.

Tony knew Shades' first encounter with Q wouldn't be easy or pleasant but neither was prepared for how *dangerous* it would be. After all the years, Shades was face-to-face with the man who had single-handedly brought so much misery into his life. *What gave him the right?* Shades experienced a powerful wave of hatred and anger.

Few people on earth could read body language like Tony, and Shades' made for terrifying reading. It wasn't merely the clenched fists and tight jaw, he had *never* seen his brother so angry. The pupils in Shades' dark brown eyes shrank to sharp black points. If he lost control and attacked Q, the result would be catastrophic. Tony knew for certain Shades would never reach Q, the two armed protectors would kill him first. Tony strode hastily across the room. With his back to Q and his men, he rested a firm, steadying hand on his brother's shoulder. In those few, terrifying seconds, Tony simply didn't know what Shades may do next. To his huge relief, Shades gave an almost imperceptible nod as reason overtook hatred and fortunately for them all, won the race. Tony was sure

Shades had control. He let go, turned his attention to Q and so the discussion began.

Ron and Vicky had parked the Chevrolet two streets away as Tony had asked, explaining he didn't want Bruno made aware of Ron's presence until the last moment. They made their way along the pavements towards *The Blue Parrot*, Ron carrying the second of Maggie's silver flight cases in one hand and holding Vicky's hand with the other. Neither spoke. Finally, they turned a corner, the familiar and usually comforting image of the club lay before them.

It had been several hours since the pale sun had given up trying to cheer or warm the grey streets. London was given over to the night and the cold, and it *was* very, very cold. Vicky gripped the collar of her puffa coat and drew it tight around her throat in an attempt to keep out the freezing night. Upon reaching the front door, they stood and looked up at the huge building, which loomed over them. Somehow, tonight, it didn't feel friendly. All the good times they had spent within its walls: the banter with Tony and Shades, film nights in Shades' subterranean cinema *The Roxy,* drinks with Jane, the fabulous New Year's Eve party; it all seemed long ago and far away. The club was ominously quiet, normally, when this close, muffled sounds of music and voices could be heard through the massive doors. But tonight, it was silent, as if it was somehow waiting.

Vicky shivered and it wasn't only the cold, damp air. While staring up at the club, she whispered, 'I don't want to go in.'

Ron swallowed and whispered back, 'Neither do I. Tell you what, let's run back to the car, drive down the A2/M2 to Dover, hop over to France, motor to the South of France and have a nice holiday.'

Vicky smiled. 'Yes, let's. Tony will have it all sorted out by the time we get back.'

They turned to look at each other, their bright smiles dimmed.

Ron knew the answer but asked anyway. 'You could still take the car back home and pick me up later.'

'We've been through all that. Come on.'

They walked on past the front door. A sign had been hung on the handles, *Closed for Private Function, Sorry for the Inconvenience. T & S, Management.* They trudged without enthusiasm along the pavement, around the corner and into the yard behind the club. The bulkhead lights above the fire exits threw a hard, white light. Obstacles such as cars and the small lock-up interrupted the light, casting sharp, black shadows. Like the normally friendly club, the yard felt somehow sinister, as if danger lurked in the shadows, *which it did.* Tony's car was in the yard, as was Shades'. Parked in the shadow cast by the lock-up was another car which Vicky and Ron didn't recognise. They couldn't be sure but someone could have been sitting in the driver seat, watching them. They walked over to the left-hand fire exit, the right-hand one being blocked by several barrels and some crates of bottled beer. Ron eyed the delivery; it wasn't like the brothers to leave stock outside. In fact it wasn't sensible to leave *anything* of value outside in South East London.

Ron placed his hand on the door handle, but before he opened it, he looked at Vicky. She was naturally pale but in the glare of the light, looked positively ghostly. He didn't have to say anything, she knew what he was thinking. 'I'm *sure*.' Ron gave the handle a downward wrench. Nervously, they entered the club.

After the bright light above the door outside, the club appeared relatively dim. In the tubs the lights beneath the giant metal palms were lit. The lights over the bars were also burning. There were no customers or bar staff and the club felt eerily quiet. Suddenly someone called down to them from the upstairs bar. 'Okay?' It was Shades, he'd left Tony with their guests and come down from the flat to meet them, his voice echoing slightly in the empty club.

They looked up, Ron answering. 'Yes, is everything alright here?'

'So far, so good. Come up.' In an effort to spare them worry, Shades was painting the situation a good deal more rosy than the reality.

Vicky and Ron quickly climbed the metal steps that led to the upstairs bar. Their footfalls seemed unusually loud in the uncanny silence.

Shades didn't look his normal, cheeky self. If Ron were pressed to give it a label, he would have said, 'upset.' It made him feel even more anxious. 'Are you sure everything is alright?'

Shades' demeanour was a direct result of his first encounter with Q. Shades was fully aware that he was far from alright but was determined to see the thing through, to play his part. 'Don't worry, everything is fine.' His mouth tried to smile but his eyes spoilt the attempt. 'Our visitor is here, Tony's with him, they've already gone up.'

Vicky commented. 'We saw the strange car, parked behind the lock-up.'

Ron added, 'I think someone's sitting in it.'

Shades' reply was sharp and the smile vanished. 'There *is*, don't go near it, will you?'

Ron and Vicky shook their heads. The way Shades had spoken was *so* serious, they felt they didn't want to know anything further about the dark car which sat so quietly in the shadows or its mysterious occupant.

Vicky changed the subject. 'Did you know your delivery is out in the yard?'

Shades dismissed it. 'No staff to bring it in, no time. Don't worry about it, it's serving a purpose anyway. Our next guests will use the other fire door, so we only need to watch one.'

Ron held up the silver case. 'Vicky had better run through this with you, I'm set.' He touched his chest very gently. 'Do we come up to the flat?'

'Yes. Tony says to come up, but listen guys, don't talk to our guests.' Vicky and Ron stared at him, clearly expecting him to explain. 'Things are a bit tense, they don't trust us.'

Vicky and Ron exchanged a worried glance. At that moment, the joke about running for the door, the car, Dover and France seemed very appealing. As they followed Shades through the door behind the bar Vicky just caught Ron murmur. *'Merde.'*

Across London at the shoot, the day had finally ended for Jane. It was an unexpectedly late finish as the Director had decided he wanted to capture some key scenes before they wrapped. Some of the crew called 'goodbye' to Jane as she walked to her car. With keys in one hand, she stopped to wave with the other. 'Bye, lovelies.' The other cars swept past, two blowing their horns as they went. Jane was very popular with the crew. Her natural way with people and her character which almost fizzed with warmth and energy was easy to like. Wanting to keep busy, she had maintained her normal, cheerful attitude all day, smiling and chatting, not even stopping for lunch, but now, she was exhausted in a way that was unfamiliar. It was so tiring, putting on a show, pretending she was her usual, happy self. She opened the car door and sank wearily into the driver's seat. Alone! Finally alone. She closed her eyes which stung with tiredness and let out a long sigh.

All day, she had planned to go to *The Blue Parrot*, to tell Shades it was over; to tell him to leave her alone, to finish it. But now the time had come, she felt less sure, less brave. What she wanted to do more than anything, was go home. The idea of a long bath, some food, opening a bottle of wine and losing herself in a book was a hell of a lot more appealing than an unpleasant scene at *The Blue Parrot.*

Jane glanced down at her clothes. Her pale green jumpsuit was comfortable and with its many pockets, practical for work, but not what she would choose to wear to the club. She felt angry with herself for even thinking about her clothes. So what! This wasn't a date. Who cared what she was wearing? But the truth was she *did* care. Part of her wanted to look her best. To make Shades regret losing her. What if *she* was there, the woman on the fire escape? Again, Jane glanced down at her work clothes. She raised her eyes and tilted her head to glimpse her reflection in the rearview mirror. She looked tired, there was a faint darkness under her eyes, the result of a bad night and a long day. If she could have it over with today, would she feel better? Probably not in the short term but ultimately? If she did go to the club, she mustn't cry, not in front of Shades and definitely not in the presence of this other woman, if she was there. Jane wasn't certain what she could or should do.

She started the engine. The decision would need to be made when she reached the end of the car park. Right to go home, left for *The Blue Parrot.* If it was to the club, it would take a while to weave through the busy London streets and it really had been a very long day.

Anna's day had felt equally long, Salvatore joined her in the bedroom. He found her lying on the bed, fully clothed, one arm across her eyes. He sat carefully on the edge of the bed. She felt the bed tilt and lifted her arm to look at him; she also appeared tired.

'Was it bad?'

'Mm, I've a slight headache.' They were both speaking in whispers.

'I'm sorry Anna. Look, you don't need to be there tonight. Stay here, rest.'

'I *need* to be there, I'd go mad sitting here waiting. Did everything go well today?'

'Yes. Maggie came and ran through it with me. My little visit this morning went better than I expected. Also, I received a call this afternoon to say Uncle was en route.' He glanced at his watch, 'By now, the brothers should have guests.' He tried to sound bright. 'So far, so good. I must say we had some luck getting the gun away from Bruno this morning.'

The memory of Salvatore's encounter with Bruno in the hall stirred fresh concern in Anna. 'I didn't think he was going to give it up, he looked so angry. Please be careful, Sal.'

'Don't worry. I made him leave it here, that's all that counts.'

'It isn't only Bruno I'm worried about. Q will be here, he terrifies me. You know what he can be like. He's capable of executing three people, then arriving at

Lucia's Birthday party fifteen minutes later, all smiles and presents.'

They both knew he hadn't actually done this but equally, they both knew it was *possible*.

Salvatore didn't insult her intelligence, he made no attempt to play down the danger answering slowly and gravely with a thoughtful, 'Yes.'

They were silent for a moment, then Anna asked, 'What's the time?'

He checked his watch. 'Almost seven thirty.'

'I'd better freshen up, we'll be off soon. I wish tonight was over.'

'Soon, it will be.' He kissed her aching forehead.

She sat up and swung her legs to the floor. They sat together on the edge of the bed. Anna took his hand and repeated. 'Please be careful, Sal.'

Over at *The Blue Parrot*, the mood was equally tense. In the kitchen, Vicky was explaining to Shades how Maggie's FX worked, while in the living room Ron sat on the sofa with Tony next to him. The sofa opposite was, shall we say, fully loaded. Q sat in the centre, each side of him sat one of his useful people. No-one looked happy to be there. Ron found the tense silence almost unbearable. Q was openly staring at him and Ron was trying hard to pretend he didn't notice. Q was over seventy, however, in spite of his advancing years, was able to project a formidable aura of menace. He wasn't tall but shared Bruno's compact build. He had a surprisingly small amount of wrinkles, his skin seeming to be stretched tight over his face. His small eyes were sharp and quick.

Ron was relieved when Shades and Vicky emerged from the kitchen. 'All okay?'

Shades answered. 'Yes, all set. It's simple, Vicky explained everything. We're ready to go.' He looked almost happy. Now that the crucial moment was almost upon them, the danger and risk excited him, it was simply part of his nature. He had also decided to force Q from his mind: for everyone's sake he couldn't afford to be distracted.

Ron could feel Q still staring at him. He didn't want to look in his direction, the man seriously unnerved him, however, he had little choice when Q spoke to him directly.

'So, *you* are Ronny Moon.' Q's voice was soft and pitched low; he had long ago realised he didn't need to trouble himself to speak at a normal volume for when Uncle Cupid spoke to you, you listened. It was rumoured that if the correct level of attention and respect wasn't given, his voice might well be the last you ever heard.

Sounding slightly apologetic, Ron owned up with a meek, 'Yes'. Looking directly at Q caused his stomach to tighten. He knew little of the man's past, except general warnings from Tony that he was high ranking and dangerous. Ron didn't know any details and sensed he didn't want to. The way Shades and Tony behaved in his presence was a worrying clue. The writer in Ron was simultaneously fascinated and

418

repelled. How could someone say and do so little and still emanate a tangible aura of fear? All his senses screamed *be careful what you say and do, the danger is real*.

Q regarded Ron with open cold hostility. 'You have made accusations which have caused a great deal of trouble.'

Ron didn't know what to say: he was relieved when Tony answered for him. 'We've gone over that with you. A few comments overheard by chance and Ron's imagination combined to come up with a scenario which happened to be real. If we are right, you will have proof one of your own people is a threat.'

Q slowly looked at them all. 'I don't trust any of you.' He leaned forward.

Tony had the impression he was about to leave, this would blow the whole plan. Tony raised his hands, spread his fingers and gently patted the air in a gesture of calm. 'Why don't we just see how this plays out? Listen, watch and judge for yourself.'

Q didn't like being told to do anything, even if it could be to his advantage. But, he conceded to himself, if Bruno *was* a traitor, he needed to know. What he would do with these people after, he hadn't decided.

Tony felt they should get in position. It was ahead of schedule but he thought activity would go some way to break the tension. 'Why don't we get ready, in case they're early? Shades, you and Ron go downstairs to the bar.' He was careful not to tell Q what to do, but

419

asked, 'Perhaps, I could get you gentlemen a drink and a table in the upstairs bar while we wait.'

There was no response from Q. Ron was pleased to be out of there and made for the door, Shades followed. Q rose slowly to his feet, so did his two useful men. They all filed out behind Tony and Vicky. Tony could feel Q watching him.

They emerged through the door behind the upstairs bar. Vicky hugged Ron. 'Please be safe.' She turned a worried face to Shades. 'Both of you.' She reached out and squeezed Shades' hand.

He answered brightly. 'Don't worry, it'll be fine.' The waiting had been difficult but now it was actually happening, he felt exhilarated and alive.

Ron felt sick; he echoed the last part of Shades' comment with far less conviction. 'It'll be fine.' The two friends walked down the metal stairs and crossed to one of the bars opposite the fire doors.

Tony pulled extra chairs from under other tables and arranged them around one for his guests. The table was situated near the metal steps but back from the edge so it wasn't visible from ground level. He hurried to the bar and returned with two bottles and five glasses on a tray. Q watched him, his men standing close by. Finally, he sat down, his men sitting either side. Tony unloaded his tray and set the drinks on the table. Vicky sat nervously with them. Q unscrewed the scotch and poured himself a small drink.

Tony nodded to the two men. 'Help yourselves.'

They stared coldly back at Tony, one answering for both. 'This isn't a social visit, we're working.'

Tony chose to ignore the hostility and kept his tone cordial, 'Well, it's there if you change your minds. Vicky?' She shook her head but by the worry on her face, Tony felt she could use one.

Downstairs, Ron and Shades stood with their backs to the bar and watched the fire door. Ron glanced up at the upstairs bar; Tony was looking down at them and Ron could just see his face. Tony was standing back from the edge, holding the safety rail at arm's length. He was ready to step quickly out of sight, as soon as the fire exit door sprang open. Ron knew that Q, his men and Vicky were also up there, listening, waiting. He whispered to Shades. 'I feel like cheese.'

Shades was surprised and took his eyes from the exit door to stare at him. 'Really? Well, if you're peckish, there's some cheese and onion crisps behind the bar, but I don't think we really have time for snacks.'

'…!' Ron stared back, his anxiety made him sharp. 'I'm not hungry, you stupid sod! I mean, I feel like cheese in a trap!'

It made more sense. 'Oh, right, got you.' Shades grinned. 'It's exhilarating though, isn't it? You really feel you're alive.'

Ron didn't share Shades' enthusiasm. 'I'm just hoping I'm going to feel alive in an hour from now.'

Shades dismissed Ron's nerves. 'Don't you think it's exciting?'

'No, it's bloody frightening. Aren't you scared?'

Shades was, but unlike Ron, found it thrilling. 'No, excited, they'll be here any minute.'

Ron's answer was a tense, hissed whisper. 'Yes, I know. That's *why* I'm frightened. If the people coming through that door don't get us, that psychopath upstairs or his gorillas will.'

Shades' eyes sparkled with excitement, he relished the danger with as much passion as Ron hated it. 'It'll be alright, Tony knows what he's doing.' Bravado generated Shades' next observation. 'Anyway, just because something is unwise, dangerous and possibly, insane, doesn't mean it won't be fun.'

Ron shook his head slightly. 'There's something *wrong* with you.' Although they were very close friends, it crossed Ron's mind, stupid statements like that brought home just how different they were in some ways. Ron had huge respect for Tony, but was painfully aware Tony shared Shades' love of films. The brothers relished edgy situations where they could live out action and drama in reality, like their heroes on the silver screen. It wasn't the first time the brothers had attempted to write their very own blockbuster and dragged their friends in to the scenario as extras. This time however, Ron was wrong: Tony was *not* enjoying the situation and was experiencing serious misgivings. It was as well that Ron had no clue how worried Tony was.

The tension mounted. Ron had to admit, he understood, or partly understood, what Shades meant about feeling alive. While standing perfectly still, his

422

heart was beating fast, he had energy, the world around him felt somehow sharp, as if all his senses were in overdrive, giving the impression that reality itself was in perfect clarity. He was aware of what was happening; it was the raging conflict generating these sensations. He wanted more than anything in the world to run, to get away, to be safe. The problem was, to be truly safe, he needed to see it through, which meant he had to stand there, in full view, and wait. Wait for that fire door to open and two unpredictable senior Mafia bosses to enter, both armed. This *was madness*!

Suddenly, Ron began to panic. The adrenaline pumping through his body diluted rationality. *To hell with logic,* he couldn't go through with it! He risked taking his eyes from the door and looked at the upstairs bar. He could still see Tony's face looking down, all his attention focussed on the fire door. Tony believed these people were predictable: he had weighed up the possibilities and decided this was the right thing to do, but it wasn't *him* standing down here! Ron couldn't get his breath, he felt faint, the panic was beginning to spiral out of control. In his mind he told himself *hold on, breath slowly. Count!* That was the thing to do. In slowly, *1.. 2.. 3.. hold, 5.. 6.. out, 1.. 2.. 3..* He repeated the counting and regained a little control. *Think about this logically.* Shades was standing right next to him; and he *knew* that Tony wouldn't risk his brother. If he was honest, Ron knew Tony wouldn't risk *his* life either, unless he was *sure* this was the right thing to do.

Ron chanced a look at his watch which seemed to be running very slowly. 'Do you make it two minutes to?'

Shades quickly glanced down at his wrist, then back to the door. 'Yup, any second now.'

Ron tried to swallow but his mouth was completely dry. They stared at the fire doors. They had almost ceased to be doors at all. In Ron's mind, they were less like doors and more like a macabre jack-in-the-box. They would spring open any moment and something unpleasant and dangerous would appear.

High overhead, Tony wasn't feeling much better than Ron. He remained close to the thick brass safety rail and stared down, his attention also focussed on the doors. He gripped the rail with considerably more force than was necessary. This situation was entirely of his own creation and he had doubts, *serious doubts*. Ron and Vicky were his closest friends. Behind him, Vicky was sitting at a table with Q. Tony shared Ron's view that Q was a psychopath, who would kill all of them without a second thought if it suited him. Ron and his own brother were, effectively, bait. He would gladly swap places with them in an instant but the men coming through the door would only react in the way he wanted if suddenly confronted with Shades and Ron. The logic of the situation gave Tony no comfort. If this went wrong, all the people Tony cared about were in one room with a bunch of murderers and he, Tony, had arranged it.

Outside, Salvatore spoke to Bruno with suspicion. 'I thought you wanted a drink at *The Blue Parrot*?

'I do.'

Salvatore and Anna walked side by side, slightly behind Bruno, as they hurried along the bitterly cold street. Bruno had turned left and not continued along the pavement which would bring them to the front door of the club. 'But the club isn't this way.' Salvatore protested.

Bruno stopped and turned. 'I heard some regulars talking, a lot of customers use the back door. This is the way to the yard behind the club, better for us to slip in quietly.'

Salvatore nodded, but he didn't believe him.

Bruno smiled to himself as he turned away and continued to lead on, his hand sliding up into his jacket to check on the gun. Yes, it nestled in its usual place.

Behind his back, Salvatore and Anna exchanged tense glances and reluctantly followed.

The real reason Bruno didn't want to approach the club from the front was because when he hired it for the evening he had specified that a private function sign be placed on the front doors and he didn't want Salvatore to see it. If he had the opportunity he hoped for, he didn't want too many witnesses.

As Jane drove past the club on her way to the yard at the rear, she slowed to read the large sign on the doors *Closed for a Private Function.* Her anxiety had risen considerably during her long drive across town, and she desperately wanted to have the confrontation done with. If she didn't finish with Shades right this moment and say her piece, her courage may fail. She didn't want to lose him but she wouldn't be lied to, wouldn't be treated this way, it was too much, it was too painful. She drove on and took the corner fast. Three people were crossing the road, seemingly heading for the yard, probably guests for this private function. As Jane reached the yard gates, she saw it was full. Three cars and it appeared the brewery had delivered not only the weekly top-up but the large monthly order. She could have squeezed her car in but it was tight and she wasn't in the right frame of mind for careful manoeuvring. In irritation, she drove on past and searched for a nearby space with no parking restrictions.

Ron's eyes hurt: he was trying not to blink, but wasn't sure he could stand there much longer. The slow breathing wasn't helping anymore, he was sweating and beginning to feel faint.

The club was silent, its thick walls absorbing the sounds of the city outside. Tables, normally full of people, were empty. The huge metal palms which soared toward the cavernous ceiling, glinted metallic blue and silver, lit as they were by the powerful lights set in the enormous tubs that housed them. The usually busy bars were entirely bereft of customers. Ron had the fanciful impression that the ancient building, which had witnessed so much in its long existence, was holding its breath, waiting for the next drama to play out and be added to its rich history. *The Massacre at The Blue Parrot.* Ron could see the headline. *No! No! Don't think that!* A fine imagination was a wonderful thing but it didn't come without a price. He felt a dizzy nauseating surge of panic. *It's no use, I can't do this! I..*

The door handle moved.

Ron and Shades knew it would but when it did, it was still shocking. They couldn't run now, it was too late, they were committed, past the point of no return. Ron felt a queasy sinking sensation in his stomach as if he'd stepped from the safety of the plane and had begun to plummet. He prayed the safety measures worked as planned and it wasn't a suicide leap.

The door opened. Two men and a well-dressed woman entered. After the bright glare from the bulkhead lights outside, Salvatore, Bruno and Anna took a second for their eyes to adjust to the low lights inside. They began to move, very slowly. The moment was just that, a moment in time. But when so much fear, emotion and energy are compressed into a fraction of a second, time itself is also compressed for those experiencing it.

Ron was terrified, the sudden realisation that although he would need to move very quickly, he wasn't sure he could. Would his legs work or would raw terror freeze him to the spot?

Salvatore halted abruptly and stared at Shades, then he shouted so close to Bruno's ear it made him jump.

427

'That's Matteo Manning! He knows who I am!' He pulled a gun from his shoulder holster and knocked Bruno aside as he plunged forward, quickly closing the gap on Shades.

Bruno hadn't expected either to see Ron, or Salvatore to be carrying a gun. For a second, he hesitated, then drawing his own gun, dived after Salvatore. Anna was left standing at the door.

The moment Salvatore shouted, Shades begun to move. He had sprung between the counter hatch and flung himself through the door which led down to his cinema. Ron's worry about his ability to run proved unfounded: he was so close he almost knocked Shades down the stairs.

Bruno and Salvatore ran to the bar.

Tony had pulled back from the rail as the door opened. After Salvatore's shout, he had peered down, knowing that both men would be focussed on Ron and Shades and unlikely to look up. He whispered curtly, 'Let's go.'

As Tony and the rest began to descend the metal steps, the door behind the bar swung shut behind Bruno.

Deep beneath the club, Ron and Shades burst into the cinema, Shades veering into the projection room. The lights in the cinema had been left on intentionally but the projection room was in darkness. The idea was to gain vital seconds to allow Tony and his party to reach table thirty-two upstairs.

Bruno and Salvatore arrived at the cinema door with guns drawn. They paused: knowing the two men were trapped, they could afford to be cautious. Bruno whispered, 'I didn't know you had a gun.'

'I can be old school too.' It was a lie, the gun having been supplied by Maggie when she visited. Salvatore spoke quickly in whispers. 'I recognised this guy, he was once engaged to Anna and he sure as hell recognised me. I can't have him know I'm alive, we take care of both of them and get out of London tonight.'

Bruno had, of course, recognised Ron, and Salvatore's plan to get rid of this witness as well was perfect. He glanced over his shoulder; no Anna, she was waiting upstairs. Perhaps he wouldn't need to kill her. When he walked out and told the story of how her ex had shot Salvatore in a struggle, who could argue? He, Bruno would be the hero. He would shoot the man who killed Salvatore. This was fantastic! But first, they had to find them. Bruno slowly pushed open the door, whispering to Salvatore, 'You wait here by the door.' Salvatore nodded and Bruno crept in carefully and began to search the room. It didn't take long to realise it was empty. As Salvatore watched him, Bruno shook his head and nodded in the direction of the darkened projection room. Together, they edged towards to the door.

At the same moment upstairs, Anna joined Tony and the others at table thirty-two; she appeared pale and

429

strained, she acknowledged Q with a brief nod and sat down slowly. They were all listening intently for sounds of life or death coming from the air-conditioning duct near the table.

Suddenly, the fire door was wrenched open and Jane entered the club, her face a mixture of trepidation and determination. She had been expecting a room full of people and stood for a moment, looking about the empty club.

Tony got quickly to his feet and moved with surprising speed across the floor. The two security men became alert and also got to their feet but stayed close to Q, who remained seated.

Tony reached Jane and put his strong hands on her shoulders. 'Jane, you have to leave now, we've got a situation here. It's not safe, you can't stay.'

'What's going on Tony? I've come to talk to Shades.'

'Look, I'll get him to phone you. You must leave and *please* keep your voice down. There's no time to explain. Go!'

The light in the projection room came on, Salvatore's hand dropped from the switch. He and Bruno stared at the two wide-eyed, frightened men, who stood on the opposite side of the room. Bruno's face cracked into a slow grin. Shades held up his hands to show he had no weapon. 'You don't have to shoot anyone, we never saw you. Just go, we don't want any trouble or to get involved.'

Salvatore spoke without emotion. 'But you *are* involved.'

Vicky jumped at the sound of a gunshot. Tony turned slightly to look at the group seated at the table. Jane was shocked into silence. Then, Bruno's voice clearly came from the duct and carried across the silent club. 'No witnesses.' There was a second gunshot.

Vicky, unable to keep still, sprang to her feet.

Ron joined Shades on the cold floor. Both men shot in the heart, both covered in blood.

Salvatore slipped the gun into the shoulder holster under his jacket. 'Let's go.'

Bruno remained where he was, standing just inside the door, effectively blocking it.

Jane whispered, 'Shades!' Pulling violently away from Tony, she took a step back. 'Where is he?' Thankfully, shock resulted in her whispering the question.

Tony cursed himself the very moment he did it, but the involuntary glance at the door behind the bar was all it took. Jane hurled herself towards it: she was going to ruin everything! 'Jane, no!' Tony's voice was a tense, quiet plea.

Bruno's voice however, could be heard loud and clear. 'Not just yet.' The gun which had shot Ron was levelled at Salvatore's chest.

'What the hell are you doing, Bruno? Put away the gun, we must leave.'

'I'm leaving, you're not!' He fired as Jane burst into the the projection room she was just in time to see Salvatore fall to the floor. As she looked down, she screamed at the horrifying sight of Ron and Shades' blood-stained bodies.

Bruno wasn't expecting anyone to burst in but before he had time to react, Jane turned and fled. Bruno raced after her.

The door behind the bar slammed open and Jane careered through it, she turned slightly, fearing the killer was gaining on her. Suddenly there was an explosion of noise. Bruno had let loose another shot aimed at her. Jane fully cleared the door and bar then crumpled as her legs gave out and plunged face down, landing hard, her glasses skidding across the floor. She rolled onto her side, her jumpsuit drenched in blood.

Vicky, shocked and terrified, ran forward screaming, 'Tony! Something's gone wrong! *Jane!* Oh my god, *Ron*!' Before Vicky could get to Jane's body, Bruno stepped out from the doorway and into the club. Vicky was now nearer to Bruno than the group behind her: he aimed at her and fired.

From his position, Tony could see only Vicky's back. She stopped dead at the sound of the gunshot. Tony's stomach lurched as he waited for her to fall. Her body was rigid, if the gun had one live bullet, it might have more. Tony had taken a sharp breath as the gun fired, now he quite literally held it, shocked into paralysis as he stared at her back.

Vicky didn't know what it felt like to be shot, but surely, she should feel something? Mechanically, she looked down at her body, expecting to see blood. There was none.

Salvatore however, was covered with it as he appeared in the doorway. Bruno saw movement from the corner of his eye and took his attention from Vicky. He was stunned to see Salvatore standing there, looking at him. Bruno took two or three staggering steps sideways, then Shades appeared behind Salvatore. Pushing past Salvatore and ignoring Bruno he fell to his knees beside Jane. How *could* Jane be dead? The gun *must* have had a live bullet still loaded. Jane wasn't part of the plan, she *wasn't* wearing a blood pack, her blood was *real*. Oblivious to those around him, he reached out a trembling hand and gently touched her shoulder. 'Jane!' He whispered.

Uncle Q and his two useful men had moved quietly forward.

Vicky, rooted to the spot, was staring at the door, willing Ron to appear. She drew the same conclusion as Tony and Shades; if Jane had been shot, perhaps Ron *was* too. Maybe there was more than one live bullet left in either of the guns. She whispered, 'Ron, Please! Please! Please! Be safe!'

At that moment, Ron's frightened face slid into view as he peered nervously around the door.

Bruno put it together fast: there had been four shootings and three of the victims were still standing. As soon as Salvatore spoke to Q about what had happened in the basement cinema, he, Bruno, was done for, the organisation didn't tolerate its top people executing one another. This was a setup! He needed to get out of there, fast.

Vicky was so relieved to see Ron's face, she rushed towards him, but before she had taken four steps, Bruno dropped the useless gun and lunged at her. He grabbed her arm with one hand and spun her towards him. She came to rest with her back against his chest. His clothes smelt of stale cigarette smoke. She was about to fight him off when his free hand came up around her shoulder. There was a short *hiss-click* sound and something shiny flashed as it moved past her face, it was Bruno's stiletto flick-knife. It felt cold and hard against her throat, she dared not move.

The tense silence was suddenly broken. Q said calmly, 'Forget the girl, get him.'

His men began to move forward.

'WAIT!' Tony said it with enough force, authority and volume to cause the men to hesitate.

Q was angry to be contradicted, Tony held Q's arm gently and said quietly, 'If you just wait a moment.'

Q angrily shook him off.

Ron's tense, high pitched voice came out in a long, pleading, whisper, 'Tooooneeeey!'

Tony raised his voice, which remained steady. This was all *his* fault and he *must* save the situation, he mustn't allow anyone else to die. 'Nobody move. Vicky, it's going to be alright, Bruno just wants to escape. Don't struggle, let him back up to the exit, he's going for the exit, that's all.'

Indeed, that is exactly what he was doing, while watching everyone intently in case they rushed him, Bruno was slowly backing up towards the fire exit, dragging Vicky with him, his eyes darting from one to the other in an attempt to watch everyone simultaneously.

They were all watching him; Shades from the floor, Ron and Salvatore standing together near the bar. Anna, who always kept her distance from Q if she was able, looked on, still standing by table thirty-four. Tony, Q and his men were grouped together, facing the slowly retreating figure of Bruno.

Tony had no doubt that Bruno was capable of cutting Vicky's throat as a diversionary tactic before diving through the door. 'You're doing great, you're a real champion, a knock-out. You can do it.'

Vicky was confused. What the hell was Tony talking about? This psycho was going to cut her throat and escape. She didn't understand.

But Danny did. Danny, the long-retired boxer, still light on his feet, had slipped in unnoticed through the fire exit. He had remembered that Monday was delivery day and being a man of his word, had come to help move stock to atone for the damage he had caused during the confrontation with the young men earlier in the week. He was shocked to find a stocky man reversing towards him, holding a young woman at knife point.

You can do it, you're a knock-out. Tony's instruction was clear. But *could* he? Danny never spoke about getting old, he tried hard not to think about it. To see his power seep away slowly as the years passed was hard to accept. What should he do? What was he *capable* of doing? If he got this wrong, he wouldn't only lose a fight, the young woman would lose her life. If he wasn't up to it, he *must* be honest. The price of failure was too great. He hesitated, the man was now very close. If he caught sight of him what would he do? The tension and indecision were powerful forces. Danny felt some of the old strength flow back, but was it enough?

The stress Danny was under, although significant, failed to compare with what Ron was feeling, he was close to insanity. His fists were clenched so tightly, his knuckles showed white and his nails dug crescents into the palms of his hands. Ron saw plainly the look of fear and indecision on Danny's face. He wasn't going to do anything: Bruno would see him at any moment. How would he react? Would he panic? Would he lash out? Ron began to move forward slowly. He didn't decide to move and he had no plan, he was drawn forward, it was impossible not to move towards Vicky. Bruno caught the movement and pushed the blade harder into Vicky's neck, Ron could see the skin depressed beneath its edge.

'No closer!' Bruno looked like a cornered beast desperate for escape.

Ron stopped moving, quivering with raw anger and frustration. Life or death was only a matter of a few millimetres of skin between the blade's edge and an artery.

When it happened, it happened quickly and without warning. A blur of violent energy and it was over.

Behind Bruno, there was a movement. Still gripping Vicky with one hand around her wrist and the other holding the blade to her throat, Bruno turned his head very slightly.

The sensations were separated by such small fragments of time they felt as if they occurred simultaneously, but there was a sequence. First, a blur of movement, then an explosion of pulsating noise, at the same instant, a flash of orange with mauve edges and the metallic taste of blood. The ground seemed to lurch, the floor slid forward with Bruno's feet still connected and reared up to become the wall. A curious falling sensation, too small to measure, ceased abruptly. A bone-jarring force slammed into the back of his head. The orange and mauve transformed into grey-black, just before the darkness enveloped him.

Danny looked down at the body at his feet. Bruno didn't move. Danny relaxed his fighting pose and unclenched his fists.

For a moment, no-one moved, then Ron rushed forward. He clamped his arms around Vicky's small frame, squeezing the breath out of her. She could feel him shaking, for both of them the relief was beyond words. When they finally drew apart, each had tears streaming down their faces.

Tony walked forward unsteadily and picked up the dropped knife. Q lifted both arms and pointed with each hand at Bruno. 'Help Bruno to the car and keep him company.' His men lurched forward, seized an arm each and hauled the unconscious man to his feet, before dragging him out through the fire door.

Tony was focussed on his brother, who sat very still on the floor next to Jane's body.

Q addressed him twice before Tony realised he was speaking to him. He dragged his attention away from his brother and looked blankly at Q. 'Tony, keep everyone here, lock the fire door. I'm going upstairs to talk to Salvatore and Anna.'

Tony nodded.

'Come.' Q pointed at Salvatore, then turned and began to walk up the steps to the upstairs bar. Salvatore and Anna obediently followed.

Tony heard the door close behind the upstairs bar. He stood motionless. What had he done with his clever plan? Jane was dead: this was *his* fault. Tony's hand was far from steady as he raised it slowly and held his forehead. In misery and shocked disbelief, he finally found the strength to move forward to join Ron and Vicky, who stood looking down at the heartbreaking scene at their feet. Shades was still kneeling by Jane's body: he had covered his eyes with one hand, the other resting gently on Jane's small shoulders. In his mind, Shades could see Jane's face, alive, chatty, full of energy, making little jokes. Dear, sweet, big-hearted Jane whom he'd hurt and pushed away when he should have held her close. All because he was frightened of being hurt himself. He was a coward. He'd had a second chance of happiness with Jane and he hadn't taken it. We pay a price for everything we say and do in this world and Shades was paying dearly. Now it was too late. He would never see her laugh or hear her voice again, only in memory. He simply couldn't bear to look at her still face; better to keep his eyes shut tight, the crushing sadness was beyond endurance. Jane had traded the cares of today for the peace of eternity and at that moment, Shades would have gladly joined her. He wept softly as the others looked on.

Danny moved forward and the little group stood silently: no-one could find the right words because they simply didn't exist.

Shades felt a small hand on his arm. Without taking his hand from his face, in a muffled voice he begged. 'Please, please, Vicky, leave me alone.' The choking words sounded almost childlike, all his cool persona stripped away by intense sorrow and regret.

'It's not Vicky, it's me, Jane. Are you okay?'

Shades tore his hand from his eyes and found himself staring at Jane's worried face.

'Are you alright?' She repeated.

Vicky, Ron and Tony dropped to the ground. It was more the case of their legs giving way than a conscious decision to kneel down. They gathered close.

Shades couldn't speak, he gaped and blinked, frightened to look away in case he was hallucinating and Jane disappeared.

Tony pulled himself together and took charge. 'Jane, don't move.'

'Why not?'

'You're hurt.'

'Am I?'

Vicky leaned forward to examine Jane. 'Are you?' She asked shakily.

'I don't think so, I think I fainted. I haven't eaten much lately…'

Shades pointed a quivering finger and managed to whisper, 'Blood!'

'Mmm, I bet it won't come out.' She glanced down at the huge red patch on her jumpsuit, which capillary action was trying hard to spread as wide as possible. 'Look, never mind about me, are *you* alright?'

Still in a state of shock, Shades pointed to his own chest. 'Blood pack, detonated by squeezing an elbow… Maggie's.'

'Oh! What a relief! You too?' She looked at Ron, who nodded slowly. He didn't think he could handle much more but managed to ask the question everyone wanted answered.

'But… Jane, you weren't part of the plan.   You *weren't* wearing a detonator and blood pack.   We thought… we thought…' He trailed off.

'I've come here straight from work.   Re-shooting… a shooting.' She chuckled at her own joke, so relieved that Shades and Ron were unharmed.   Also, the deep concern on Shades' tear-stained face warmed her.   'I keep all sorts in the pockets of this jumpsuit when I'm working.   I was so desperate to get over here, I forgot to empty my pockets as I usually do.   I've got a spare blood pack in the pocket.' She looked down again at the red stain on her chest and added, 'Or I did have, it seems to have burst when I hit the floor.' She tried to stand. 'I do feel wobbly and a bit sick.'

Shades helped her up and placed his arm around her waist for support.   Vicky retrieved her glasses which, luckily, were unbroken.   The others scrambled to their feet and moved to a table.

Tony headed for the bar. 'Drinks. Vicky?'

'Yes, a big one.'

'Ron?'

'Same.'

'Shades?'

'Very big one.'

'Danny?'

'Half a Guinness… make it a pint.'

'And Jane?'

'Could I have a cup of tea please? Very sweet.'

Tony's strong, serious face softened and bloomed into the most surprising smile, Jane was unhurt and the relief was immense. 'You can have anything you want, you wonderful girl.'

'Alright. I'll have tea, a biscuit and an explanation. What on earth is going on?'

Danny had similar thoughts, not including the tea and biscuits.

Tony nodded. 'Of course, I'll get the drinks and explain everything to you and Danny. We wanted to keep you out of this but now you're involved, you must understand what's happening. We're not out of the woods yet.'

While he was talking, he poured Ron and Vicky's drinks. They took a gulp and, unable to remain still, stood up and wandered away from the seated group. Ron put his glass on the bar. Vicky noticed a slight tremor in his hand. She placed her glass next to his and they embraced again. Vicky whispered in his ear. 'All safe.'

They both knew that wasn't entirely true but he appreciated her trying to make him feel better. Her voice was unsteady: in the last few minutes she had feared for Ron's life and her own, also witnessed what she believed was her best friend's murder and the day was still far from over. They picked up their drinks, turned their backs to the bar and leaned against it. Vicky and Ron had a good view of the group seated at the table. In spite of the very worrying presence of Q upstairs, they couldn't help feeling happy for Shades and Jane.

Shades couldn't take his eyes from her. One hand held hers, the other was about her shoulder holding her close.

Tony was pouring more drinks at the table. 'Guinness and tea for one, coming up.'

'Don't forget the biscuits.'

Upstairs in the flat, Salvatore sat with Anna on the sofa and Q sat opposite. Even Salvatore felt nervous. He was fully aware that although they inhabited the same world, they were very different characters.

Q fixed his attention on Salvatore but remained silent. Anna felt her anxiety rising: you could never predict what Q was thinking or what he might do. The stories about his exploits in his younger days were disturbing, and if only half of them were true, horrifying would be a better description.

'I think we need to make some changes.'

Salvatore didn't know what this statement meant.

Q explained. 'You haven't handled this situation well, it's cost a lot of time and money.' He raised a hand before Salvatore could protest. 'I know you have made a lot of money for the organisation, buying and renting property. You've done well, but...' He shook his head. 'Keeping an eye on Renzo, handling the string of nightclubs... not good, not good.'

Now Salvatore was frightened, not only for himself, but for Anna and Lucia. He spoke quickly, 'Look Q, I told you Renzo was an accident. I never meant to...'

Q cut him off abruptly and with some heat. 'Renzo was a shit! If you hadn't taken care of him, we would, but not on the street, not in full view of a journalist. A journalist holding a camera!' He shook his head again. 'No, no. Renzo shouldn't have got away with taking *any* money. You should have been keeping a closer eye on him.'

'Yes, you're right. I gave him too much latitude, it was a mistake.

Q was slightly appeased. 'Yes, that's why I've decided to make some changes.'

This was it. Both Anna and Salvatore braced themselves.

'I'll still support your plan. First, a little cosmetic surgery, then back to Milan. Getting out of this country is easier than getting in. Money buys you a ticket on a fishing boat, then transfer to *The Leonardo*. We'll work something out, it's not a problem. You are now the cousin up from the country, come to Milan to help Anna. You take on some of Salvatore's work in the property market. No clubs, no String, just property. You take a step back and leave that side to people more suited.'

'A demotion?'

Q rolled his bottom lip. 'Let's say, less responsibilities, so you focus all your attention on what you're good at.'

Q sat back to gauge his reaction. Salvatore glanced at Anna and saw in her eyes the relief and happiness. The truth of the matter was, one did not leave the organisation, it never happens. Once in, it was for life. However, if the organisation decided to take a step back from you, that was different. As Q said, Salvatore had the opportunity to do what he was good at; buying and leasing property around Milan and nothing else. It was as close to legitimate employment as it was possible to get. Tax was even paid on the profits. Probably not as much as it should be, but what large, successful business did?

'I enjoy working on the property side and if I have no other responsibilities, I can spend more time with the family. Thank you.'

Q was satisfied. 'It's settled then.'

'Yes. What about Bruno?'

'Bruno is having his own reunion about now.'

Outside in the shadowy yard behind the club, something strange was happening. For most people upon waking, the nightmare ends. For Bruno, it was about to begin. There was darkness, there was an echoing pulse of voices which seemed to vibrate faster, then a feeling of coming up from the deep and breaking the surface into consciousness. Bruno sucked a lungful of air; he was sweating and felt nauseous. Abruptly, reality hurtled into focus as he stared into the face of a dead man.

It wasn't merely the fact the man was dead that made Bruno pull away, the dead man was smiling at him.

445

'Hel-lo Bru-no.' The greeting was spoken in a happy singsong manner, not unlike that of a child. The cheerful rhythm of speech took on a deeply sinister and horrifying twist for Bruno.

Rifsky enjoyed the look of terror on Bruno's sweating face. Bruno tried to get away but escape wasn't possible. He found he was sitting on the back seat of Q's car with very large and solid men each side. Rifsky was sitting in the driver's seat and had twisted round to face him. Apart from some bruising on his right temple and some minor cuts, he appeared terrifyingly healthy. Thoughtfully, Rifsky lifted a tour guide so Bruno could see it. He projected a comradely air. 'Did you know Karl Marx is buried in Highgate Cemetery?' He paused, acting disappointed. 'Aw, it's probably shut this time of night.' Then his voice changed and grew hard with deep suppressed, *burning anger*. 'But, we go to a grave all the same. *YOURS.*'

In panic, Bruno struggled to escape but powerful arms held him.

Above the club in light and comfortable surroundings, neither Salvatore nor Anna wanted to know any details about Q's plans for Bruno. You didn't get caught trying to take out a senior member of the organisation without consequences. On the surface, the procedure for dealing with a bad employee was similar to that of any other big company, they got rid of them. In the organisation's case, the procedure was more literal and carried out in such a way as to deter other employees from similar indiscretions. It would be brutal and in all likelihood, not quick.

Conscious of Anna's presence, Salvatore swiftly changed the subject. 'What do you think we should do about Rifsky? He's still in hospital. The last time I visited, the pressure in his head was down and they had just brought him out of the induced coma.'

Q smiled. 'He's not in hospital, he's in my car outside keeping Bruno company.'

'How?'

'On the way here, I visited the hospital to see for myself. Rifsky told me he saw Bruno in the crowd before he was hit. He's *sure* Bruno pushed him into the road. He was shaky and weak but...' Q appeared amused, remembering the scene. 'He's a tough Russian; he demanded his clothes. The nurses fetched them and a neurologist.' Q actually *laughed*. 'She tried to be very stern, lots of warnings. "Give it a few days, the police want to interview you." Rifsky stripped off the hospital gown in front of her, put on his clothes and said, "Thank you, goodbye." A nurse wanted him to sign some papers and we were gone.' Q became serious. 'He's obviously not back to full strength, that's why I told him to wait in the car, but he's angry, and *insisted* on being here tonight. I told him about this plan of yours; he thought it had a good chance and if Bruno made an attempt on your life and we witnessed it, he *wanted* to be outside, waiting.'

'This part is Tony Manning's plan, not mine.'

Q nodded, his smile now completely gone as his demeanour became almost flint-like. 'Will they keep their mouths shut? There's a lot of people involved now.'

Anna cut in quickly. 'Yes, I'm sure all they want is to go back to their lives.'

'You think so?'

Anna didn't feel comfortable the way Q was staring at her. She had the distinct impression he was weighing where her loyalties lay.

Salvatore had regained some of his smooth composure. He backed Anna's statement. 'I don't think any of them wants more trouble. They have nothing to gain and a lot to lose. I'm certain you can explain it to them.'

Q's expression remained hard and thoughtful. 'There's only six of them down there and one is already dead. If there's the slightest chance of them causing trouble, they don't have to leave the building.'

Anna gave an involuntary gasp and before she could stop herself, blurted, 'You *can't*!'

The muscles in Salvatore's jaw tensed, Anna couldn't have said a worse thing.

Q's answer came back fiercely. 'I certainly *can* and if I choose to, it's done!'

Accidentally killing Renzo had begun all this trouble, and Salvatore didn't want it to end with multiple murder. Even though he wouldn't carry out the act, he would, nevertheless, be ultimately responsible. Q wasn't an easy man to control; he didn't react well to being told what to do. Salvatore was aware he would need to employ considerable tact and choose his words with care, or more than fake blood would be spilt. 'Of course, it's your decision but I don't think you need to, Q. I'm confident they are already frightened. They're in over their heads, they never intended to get mixed up in our world. Also, there's the other woman to consider. She brought the blanks, my gun and this special effects device. We'd have to find and deal with her too. From what I gather, she's high profile, well-regarded in TV and film. It would be messy, there would certainly be a big investigation, seven people killed, who all knew each other.' Salvatore finished his little speech with as much confidence in the conclusion as he could muster. 'They won't talk, I'm sure of it.' He looked steadily at Q.

Anna watched Q with unmasked anxiety.

He was silent. Finally, he spoke. 'Alright, I'll explain the situation to them and we'll see how it goes. But if I am not convinced, I'll send you out with a real gun to wait with Rifsky and keep an eye on Bruno. You tell my men to come back in here with me. I want no arguments.'

Salvatore nodded and glanced at Anna, who looked both terrified and pale. If Q wasn't satisfied there would be little she or Salvatore would be able to do. To openly challenge him could easily place them both, quite literally, in the firing line. Q rose to his feet and moved to the door.

449

Downstairs, the mood was much improved. Although alcohol isn't the answer to life's problems and worries, it cannot be denied that in the short term it does dilute them nicely. The group was feeling less fractious and looking a more healthy colour - with the exception of Jane, whose complexion had been restored to a more normal and healthy hue by tea and biscuits.

Without taking his eyes from Jane, Ron nudged Vicky and whispered, 'Look how Jane's colour's come back. That's biscuits, that is.'

Vicky turned to stare at him, unsure if he were joking or honestly believed that biscuits had health-giving properties. Deciding he was pulling her leg, she turned her attention back to the group.

As Vicky and Ron looked on, Shades still sat very close to Jane.

Danny sat to the right of Jane and Tony was leaning towards all three of them from the opposite side of the table. He was talking in a low voice, speaking quickly.

Jane and Danny had been brought-up-to speed with the situation. Tony had emphasised how dangerous Q was and that they must all be extremely careful what they said. Nobody was safe until Q and his men were out of the club and preferably, out of the country.

In spite of the very real danger, Jane and Shades were in good spirits. She was trying hard not to look too happy, in case Tony thought she wasn't paying attention to his warnings. But the revelation about Shades and Anna had explained Shades' previous hesitation to enter a close relationship and his farewell kiss on the fire escape was now understandable. As she sat close to him with his arm firmly around her shoulders, Jane felt she was basking in sunshine. To show she was following and partly because she was interested on a professional level in the mechanics of the shoot out, she asked some questions.

'So, how did you *know* this man Bruno would shoot for the heart? How did you know where to place the blood packs? And why did Salvatore bother to fall to the ground and pretend to be dead after Bruno shot him? He'd already shown his intent to kill him.'

Tony was pleased she'd asked questions as it gave him the opportunity to underline how dangerous Q was. 'Because, when I talked the plan through with Salvatore during our meeting, it came out that Bruno emulates how Q behaved in his youth. He's a kind of role model: Q aka Uncle Cupid, always killed people with one clean shot to the heart. Also, like Q, Bruno carries a stiletto-bladed flick knife. So, by pretending to be dead, Salvatore was in no danger from the knife and Bruno could run upstairs into the arms of Q and his heavies. That's assuming of course, that he shot Salvatore last. We had no guarantee in what order Bruno would shoot, we only knew he wanted to kill three people if he had the chance, so everyone needed to wear a blood pack and detonator.'

Jane lost a little of the colour she had regained and acknowledged with a softly spoken 'Oh.'

Having finished the story, Tony glanced over his shoulder at Ron and Vicky. Vicky was unsettled to see how worried he looked; she knew Q was dangerous, they both did, but to see Tony looking so worried was disturbing.

Tony didn't like being told to wait. What were they waiting for? He'd tried to push away the thought that Q might decide to kill them all, he was easily capable of it. If that was so, it was madness to sit waiting for him to return. But where would they hide? The organisation had very, very long arms, long enough to reach any part of the world. So what was the sense in running?

Vicky and Ron had been under a great deal of stress. Tony had given them a little time together, but now he gestured for them to move closer. They came over, pulled up chairs and sat at the table with the others.

Tony looked around the table, he had their full attention. 'He'll be back any minute. When he talks to us, don't say anything unless he asks a direct question and when you answer, don't give him anything to worry about. He and Salvatore were never here, we know nothing, we won't talk about it, even to each other or anyone else. We only want to get on with our lives. All agreed?'

Everyone nodded.

Tony lowered his voice and they all leaned forward to catch his words. 'Remember, don't let the white hair fool you. We…,' he glanced at Shades, 'grew up in Italy. Everyone knew Uncle Q, he's vicious. He may

452

be old but his word is law and he's capable of things you couldn't imagine in your worst nightmares, so I'm begging you, be careful.'

Everyone looked suitably worried and Tony was content. He didn't enjoy frightening his friends but they had to understand, as long as Q was still around, no-one was safe.

The sound of a door opening made everyone look up at the metal steps, the anticipation mounting. Suddenly, the man himself appeared, Q was aware they were all watching him, it was expected. After all, he was very important. Salvatore and Anna followed at a respectful distance. On reaching the ground floor, Q made his way over to where they were sitting. He took his time; the world moved at a pace *he* set. As he passed a table he picked up a chair and placed it in front of them. The chair was positioned facing the wrong way, Q swung one leg over the seat and sat down in a smooth, fluid movement, surprising for a man of his years. He folded his arms, which he rested on the chair back and cast a disapproving eye over those seated before him.

Anna and Salvatore stood close to him, looking decidedly uncomfortable. Neither Salvatore nor Anna could be sure what Q intended to do. Tony read the concern on their faces and it worried him, it worried him a *great deal*. A horrifying idea crossed his mind: Q had told them what he intended to do and it wasn't going to be pleasant.

Q's eyes settled on Jane. He glanced at the large bloodstain, then focussed on her face. She wasn't sure what she should do or say so she smiled at him politely in her open, friendly manner.

He hadn't expected the reaction and wasn't sure he liked it; people were usually frightened. 'So, you're not dead. More special effects?'

'Oh, no, not really, I've come straight from work, I work in SFX and make-up. I had a blood pack we use in the industry still in my pocket, I forgot it was there and when I fainted, it...' Q's cold expression caused Jane's verbal canter to slow to a walk. 'split open when I landed on it.' Jane finished with a lot less enthusiasm than when she began. She looked away from Q and met Tony's gaze. He tilted his head down slightly and raised his eyebrows. Jane's natural empathy read the message *What did I just say? He is dangerous, be careful.* She'd chatted to him as if he were a new friend, not a powerful Mafia boss with psychopathic tendencies and the power of life and death at his command. She felt Shades' arm tighten on her shoulders and glanced at him. He had lost his smile and was watching Q intently, waiting for his reaction.

Much to their relief and Ron's horror, he turned his attention to Ron. 'You're the writer.'

Determined not to follow Jane's example, Ron answered with a clipped, nervous, 'Yes'.

Q stared at him thoughtfully: this was more like it, real fear. He addressed everyone. 'They say I'm a hard man, a man with no empathy, a man who doesn't understand people. They are wrong. I do understand people, people are simple. To make them do what you want, you need to know what they're frightened of. People are frightened of dying, of pain, of being alone.' He paused. No-one spoke, everyone was focussed on him. He regarded the group for a moment before continuing. When he did speak it wasn't only what he said that was shocking but the emotionless way he said it. 'Outside in my car is a man I've worked with, known for some years, liked. He has not behaved well, he has broken the rules, *my* rules. Tonight, he is alone, he has no friends. Tonight, he will feel pain. Tomorrow, when the sun rises, he won't exist to see it.'

The stunned silence lengthened as the full impact of his words sank in. This man cared *nothing* and felt *nothing* about taking a life. His former friend was now viewed as a problem, so would be eradicated. Q looked into their eyes, one by one and saw *real fear.* In that single moment, they were safe, because he was satisfied. He knew they would remain silent about what they had seen, what they knew. Still, he pushed the point deep. 'You never speak of this, I have never been here.' He gestured towards Salvatore and Anna. '*We* have never been here. And you.' He pointed at Ron, who flinched and drew back a little. 'You find something new to write about, no more Mafia.'

Ron shook his head quickly, 'No.' He whispered.

Q continued. 'Good, old-fashioned murder. But *no* Mafia, okay?'

Ron nodded.

'I'm told you're well-known, something of a celebrity?'

Ron stared back, he didn't know how to answer.

Vicky spoke without thinking: she was normally the sensible one, but her pride in Ron eclipsed her good judgement. 'Ron's very famous, he's written lots of best-sellers.'

Everyone was surprised at Q's reaction; he seemed pleased. 'Best-sellers?'

Already regretting her outburst, Vicky nodded. 'Mmm.'

'So, Mr Ronnie Moon is very famous?'

'Yes.' Vicky, although nervous, smiled a little because Q was smiling at her.

Then Q dropped the hammer blow. 'Famous, well known, that's good.' His warm smile cooled and Vicky suddenly found herself looking at a face that made her stomach tighten. 'An easy man to find if I wanted to.'

Unnerved, Ron and Vicky stared at him. As the words soaked in, their expressions escalated to terror. Q was delighted. 'Tony.'

'Q?'

'You have found a traitor in our little family, I'm grateful.'

Tony remained silent.

'I don't like owing favours, is there anything you want?'

Tony spoke without hesitation. 'Yes.'

Q was slightly surprised and vaguely amused. 'What can I do for you?'

'Perhaps when we say goodbye, we *mean* goodbye?' It was a bold question and Tony wasn't sure if he'd gone too far. Under normal conditions, he knew how to handle most people, but Q wasn't most people and this situation was far from normal.

'You don't want to see me again? You don't like me, is that what you're saying?'

Tony was aware Q was amusing himself as a cat plays with a mouse. In the same way, things could quickly turn ugly and bloody if he said the wrong thing. Tony had an objective and to reach it safely, he knew, meant demonstrating the correct level of respect. He was *extremely* careful how he phrased his answer. 'It's not a matter of liking or not liking. Shades and I, in fact all of us, we watch films; wonderful stories, action, drama. We are the audience. You... well, you *are* the action, the drama. They are different worlds. I hope you understand.'

'So, for your help, you ask nothing.'

'I ask a great deal. For you to allow us to continue our lives because, as you said, none of this ever happened.'

Tony and Q looked at each other. Tony and Shades truly did love films and drama but this was the real thing. Exhilarating as it was, it could have gone badly wrong. For a while, Tony believed it *had*, their friends were *too* precious. Tony wanted distance and assurance that "goodbye" meant just that. He was also concerned that if Q lingered, the club's success may be of interest. It was extremely profitable, the brothers had a considerable income and it was growing steadily. If the organisation decided to become partners, they would never be free of it. Behind Tony's cool expression, he waited anxiously for Q's reaction.

Abruptly, Q appeared to make up his mind. 'Good bye.' He turned to Salvatore and Anna. 'Let's go.' He walked to the exit, Salvatore followed. Anna glanced at Shades who still had his arm around Jane's shoulders. She smiled at him.

Shades mouthed, 'Thank you.'

Anna turned and followed her husband. Shades knew they would never meet again.

Outside in the yard, Q stopped. 'You walk back to the house, I'll take the car. I'll see you in Milan after the surgery.' Salvatore shook his hand. He and Anna walked briskly through the gates, being very careful not to look at Q's car. Turning left, they walked hastily along the street. Behind them, they heard the big car leave the yard, its powerful engine surging as it turned and drove off in the opposite direction, its taillights fading into the darkness.

Anna had her arm linked through Salvatore's: they both felt happy and free. The huge weight of worry had been lifted, their uncertain future had crystallised and the image was clear.

Tony stood by the fire exit, peering through the crack of the slightly open door. Everyone waited,

458

anxiously watching him. Q's warning had struck hard and the fact he had calmly walked out of the club to execute someone was shocking. His considerable aura of menace hung heavily even though the man himself was out of sight.

Tony closed the door and turned to face them. 'They've gone.' It was too fantastic to be true. He added, 'We did it, we're in the clear. It's over.'

Everyone became animated. Shades threw both arms around Jane and hugged her tightly, Ron hugged Vicky, Tony shook hands and slapped Danny's shoulder. There was much laughter, albeit a release of nervous stress rather than genuine humour. More drinks were poured and glasses raised.

Vicky wandered over to Jane, the two women hugged and chatted, relieved each was safe. As she stood with Jane and Shades, Vicky glanced over at Ron, who stood very still with a blank expression on his face. Vicky stopped talking and watched him, slightly concerned. Jane and Shades saw the worry on her face and followed her gaze to see what she was frowning at. Tony and Danny, noticing the sudden lull in conversation, also turned to look at Ron, who stood statue-like, apparently deep in thought. As they all looked on, his serious expression melted into a slow grin; he looked about, suddenly aware everyone was watching him. 'Do you know what?' Everyone waited. 'I told Vicky I seldom get great ideas for stories, sitting in front of a keyboard or holding a pen and pad. They come when I'm in the shower, driving, trying to sleep etc. Well, I can add a new one to the strange places I get inspiration.' He made them wait to build the drama, then added happily, 'While chatting to a Mafia boss who's threatening to kill me. Q had a great idea when he suggested an "old-fashioned murder". That's what I'm going to call my next book, *An Old-fashioned Murder*. I've got a rough plot line already.' He beamed at them. Everyone was happy for him and began to smile, then Ron spoilt it. 'Do you think I should send him a copy when it's done?' A sort of thank you?'

Five voices joined together in a loud, clear answer, 'NO!'

PART TWO

CHAPTER 35
THE BLUE PARROT
SPECIAL CELEBRATION AT *THE ROXY*
A FEW DAYS LATER, MIDNIGHT

The Blue Parrot stood silent in the deserted street, its neon sign darkened. A thin drizzle of rain fell softly. The great entrance doors were closed and locked but a faint glow showed through them. Inside, the lights in the huge bar area were set low, the giant metal palms rose up and disappeared into the gloom of the ceiling high above. All the customers were in their homes, the bar staff long gone, all the doors were secured to keep out the world. The normally busy bars were deserted and almost silent, but for a murmur of voices, then a faint tune. The soft sound was coming from an air duct close to table thirty-four. It was the opening score of *It's a Wonderful Life*, directed by the great Frank Capra, starring the arguably even greater James Stewart.

Deep below the club, Shades' cinema, *The Roxy,* was neither silent nor deserted, for this particular night it hosted one of Shades' celebrated film nights which he referred to affectionately as 'Late Night at the Roxy.'

After their recent experience, none of the group was in the mood for a thriller. Jane's request for *It's a Wonderful Life* had been warmly received. For Shades,

461

it was especially poignant, since the parallels of hard lessons learnt and *treasuring* what you have if given a second chance, certainly had resonance for him. Six happy faces flickered with reflected light as Jane's choice opened on the big screen.

Vicky nudged Ron and he turned in his seat to see what she wanted. She tilted her head to her right, indicating he should look in that direction. He leaned forward to gain a better view. Jane sat contentedly between Maggie and Shades, her head rested on Shades' shoulder, her arm linked through his. Tony, who sat at the far end of the row next to Maggie, caught Ron looking and glanced to his left to see what he was smiling at. His little brother had finally found contentment. Tony turned back to the screen and grinned.

They all settled back to watch the film, each basking in the joyous thought that they were *safe and together.* Vicky held Ron's hand and snuggled close.

PART TWO

CHAPTER 36
A NEW CHAPTER

Q, his men and Rifsky (on a false passport) returned to Milan. Anna followed a week later, after spending some time with her sister. Bruno stayed in England in a lonely spot where he is unlikely to be disturbed, and remains to this day.

Salvatore returned to Italy some weeks later after successful cosmetic surgery. In time, he joined Anna in the city to help with Salvatore's workload and support Anna as planned, in the guise of a visiting cousin from the country. Lucia wasn't fooled and hugged him home, delighted he had lost the prickly beard. Anna spread the story that she hadn't the heart to tell her little girl that Salvatore was dead and allowed her to think the cousin from the country was indeed, him. Uncle Q made it known he didn't want Lucia upset and not to challenge her belief or discuss it. No-one asked too many questions.

Salvatore and Anna spent more time together. As Salvatore's legitimate business dealings expanded, Anna met a new circle and eventually had a close group of ladies she could call friends.

Shades was finally able to let go of the past. Anna had made a new life and seemed content and he was determined to do the same. During the minutes he believed Jane dead he'd wished a great many things. He had been granted something no money or power on Earth could buy; a second chance, a chance to revisit opportunities lost. His relationship with Jane blossomed. It made Vicky so happy to see Jane smiling and chatting, her love for Shades now mirrored.

The friendship between Vicky and Maggie deepened, both aware it would be one for life.

Even Danny was changed by the experience at The Blue Parrot. He remained a welcome and frequent visitor. However, he spent more time at the gym helping teenagers learn the art than he did at the club.

Ron did write his next book, *An Old-fashioned Murder,* and although it broke his previous records, delighting both the publishing house and Ron, no copy was ever sent to Italy.

Even with everyone's help, Jane's quest to find the lost chocolate from her youth still continues.

THE END
(Or, to be more accurate for Shades and Jane: The Beginning.)

Dear Reader,

I hope you enjoyed *Grip.* If you did and have time, I would very much appreciate it if you would be kind enough to leave a review and/or tell others about my book.

If you have enjoyed meeting Vicky, Ron and their friends, read how they all met in: *Bolt from the Blue.*

Clifford Johnson

Printed in Dunstable, United Kingdom

68485641R00268